ellen c. maze

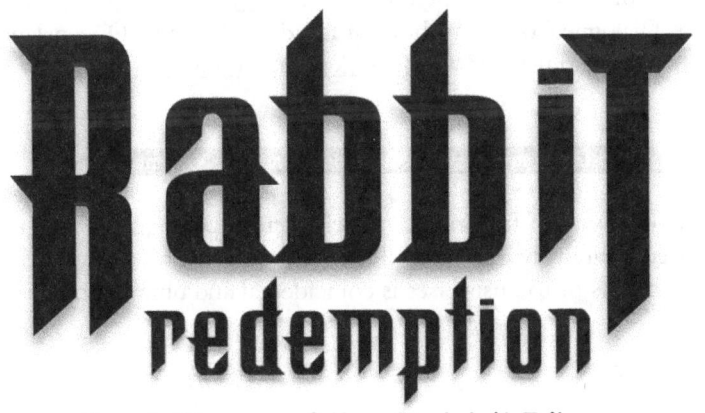

Book Three of the Rabbit Trilogy

Rabbit Redemption
By Ellen C. Maze Sallas
First Edition
©2018 by Ellen C. Maze Sallas

ISBN-13: 978-0692050408
Also available in eBook

Little Roni Publishers
Byhalia, MS
www.littleronipublishers.com
v.03062019
Cover Art & Design: Hyliian Graphics, http://hyliian.deviantart.com
Cover Art Blood Drop Element © www.123rf.com/profile_mizina
Australian Dialogue Coach: Author Stu Loudon, Brisbane, Queensland,
Australia. www.facebook.com/loudonstu

Mild Language, Sexual Situations, Vampire Violence

The following is a work of fiction. Names, characters, places, and incidents are
fictitious or used fictitiously. Any resemblance to real persons, living or dead, to
factual events or to businesses is coincidental and unintentional.

PUBLISHED IN THE UNITED STATES OF AMERICA

Rakum (RAH'-kum) – a.k.a **Wraith**, from Heb. *raca*; "vain thing." Def: From Semitic mythology; a race of vampire-like beings thought to be descended from fallen angels.

Main Characters
In Order of Association
Novel Time 2017

Canaan – b.1652, apparent age ~30; Rakum Elder, mate of **Marcy Haddle** (human, age 56) since 1971, currently serving Isaac under duress

Isaac – b.1965, apparent age 13; Rakum Father, assumed control after Elder Rufus, currently resides in Jackson, MS, a.k.a. *Yitzhak Akaron, The Last*

Boris – b.1720, apparent age ~35; Isaac's "favorite," Rakum grunt, served under Rufus, now serves and resides with Isaac

Beryl – b.1901, apparent age ~19; Rakum captain, of the infamous Rakum twins, currently serving Isaac under duress, residing with him in Jackson, MS

Javier – b.1877, apparent age ~35; *former Rakum grunt*, now human, resides with David in Tuscaloosa, AL

Simon – 27, human, *former Cow to Javier*, Athens, GA

Roman – b.1633, apparent age ~50; *former Rakum Elder*, now human, currently resides in Los Angeles, CA

David Walker – b.1935, apparent age ~21; *former Rakum grunt*, now human, resides with Javier in Tuscaloosa, AL

Chloe Mina Bushman – 20, human, student at the University of Alabama, dating David, currently resides in Tuscaloosa, AL

Damien – b.12AD, apparent age ~70; *former Rakum Father*, has been human one week

Theophilus – b.0AD, apparent age ~75, Last living Rakum Father, captive of Ta'avah, Yazoo City, MS

Ta'avah – ageless, a spirit/demon that had inhabited Father Abroghia in Book One, then Meryl in Book Two

Kilmeade – b.1633, apparent age ~40, Rakum Elder, Roman's fraternal twin, San Francisco, CA

Rafael – b.1772, apparent age ~30, Rakum grunt, resides in Larkspur, CA with **Santiago** (Cow/human, age 50).

Catch up with the Rabbit...

Rabbit: Chasing Beth Rider / **Book One**

1 The decimation of the Rakum began with Beth Rider seven years back at what became known as "Last Assembly," when a woman marked as a Rabbit brought down their leaders with an amazing power the Rakum knew nothing about. After that night, the 100,000-strong Rakum population had been reduced to half.

Rabbit Legacy / **Book Two**

2 Over the next few years, Elder Rufus—insane and bloodthirsty—rose up to lead them, destroying thousands upon thousands of the Brethren who refused to bend the knee to his psychotic agenda. By the time Isaac The Last showed up with Canaan to destroy Rufus, a mere twenty thousand brethren remained.

Now the time has come for...

Book Three of the Rabbit Trilogy

"And everyone who calls on the name of the Lord
will be saved."

~ Prophet Joel

"Hell is a cold place. A ruthlessly cold place.
And you will keep me warm."

~ Elder Rufus

"The best laid schemes o' mice an' men, gang aft a-gley."

~ Robert Burns

PROLOGUE

Year 1885

First Ritual is hell.

Compelling a pre-pubescent Rakum to scorch his flesh in the sun, depriving him of sleep for weeks on end, expecting him to endure joyfully the breaking of his bones night after night... All this and more did Elder Roman have fantastic propensity for and the Fathers lauded him for his success with proselytes. Tonight, they sent him Javier d'Millier.

It was midnight when eight-year-old Javier arrived at Roman's secluded log cabin in the wild forests outside Montreal. All legs and arms, Javier stumbled through the front door accompanied by a Rakum senior student who had escorted him from their burned-out group-lair fifty miles south. The youngster took in the room with huge green eyes, his lips parted in a comical "O". His black hair was buzzed short and his hand-me-down clothes two sizes too big. Roman regarded the wafer-thin pup with an amused grin and shooed off his chaperone leaving the two of them alone.

At a new eight, Javier smelled more human than not and Roman breathed through his mouth more than once in disdain. He was not accustomed to such young ones, but soon enough, he'd begin to transform the boy properly. Purge the weak, beggarly elements and replace them with immeasurable, unstoppable Rakum gifts. Born to a mortal woman by a Rakum Father, Javier would grow much like a human boy until he reached thirteen. At that point, his metabolism would slow gradually until he aged only days as the years passed him by. As his appointed guardian and Elder, Roman was expected to prepare him for an eternity of life at the top of the food chain.

Little Javier stopped in the middle of the room, took in the four walls slowly, and then faced his superior. When Roman didn't acknowledge him for several long seconds, he shifted his weight to one foot and bent his knee, throwing his balance to one side. He looked like a tiny gymnast, double-jointed and loose-limbed, perhaps able to contort himself into any number of odd shapes. Roman pondered all this as he watched the kid bear up under the scrutiny. He wanted to know what kind of pup they'd sent him. This would be the youngest Rakum Roman had ever discipled, yet he was up to the challenge. The Fathers requested him specifically and that had to count for something.

Roman softened his gaze and attempted to send the boy a telepathic directive. *"Come close."*

Roman watched the kid's face, but gauged no reaction. His eyes were wide and intelligent, taking in every detail, yet he heard nothing telepathically. It was not unusual; most Rakum developed the more mystical skills as they approached puberty.

"Come close, Javier," Roman said, his voice low, and the boy stepped up without hesitation. "What stage did you complete before your group-lair was destroyed?"

"Stage five, Master," Javier responded in English with a thick French accent.

"Parlez-vous du français?" Roman asked and the boy nodded shyly. *"Quelles langues parlez-vous?"* If the kid spoke more than two languages, it would suggest a higher-than-average IQ. Roman spoke fifty mortal languages and was prepared to test the boy in each one if he showed a propensity for linguistics.

"English, German, Spanish, French, Aramaic, and Hungarian," Javier answered in English, no doubt in an attempt to dazzle his new Elder with his accomplishments. Roman nodded with approval.

"We'll get along fine, young man." Roman allowed a small smile and Javier's eyes sparkled. Roman grimaced. The kid was a romantic. From that point forward, Roman made an effort to disguise his affection.

Very rarely, a Rakum was born with an over-developed sense of joviality, and now he understood why the Fathers chose him. They wanted to test him. Roman had never missed with a proselyte and the Fathers were capricious. Presumably, they sought to trip him up, or at least see if they could.

Roman cleared his throat and laid a heavy hand on the youth's shoulder. Javier was at stage five: drawing blood from humans. At first, the boys would learn to draw from a *Cow*, a mortal with a supernatural and visceral desire to give blood to his people. But as the proselyte grew adept, he would take blood forcibly from a mortal male resister. Even an eight-year-old Rakum was expected to procure his own food and now Roman knew where to begin.

"Stage five, then. How efficient are you?"

"Top of my class, sir," Javier responded, puffing out his chest.

"Are you ready for stage six, then?" Roman removed his hand from Javier's shoulder and pushed up his sleeve. Stage six was initiated by an Elder's blood. The immature Rakum would experience extreme pleasure at ingestion, but crippling pain as the Elder's time-enriched blood seeped

2

into his system. Plus, the leeching effect of stage six lasted several nights. Despite knowing all of this, Javier's green eyes widened and he nodded his head eager to experience and enjoy what was essentially his birthright.

Five years passed, the pup reached thirteen, and Roman did what was necessary. Only vicious and violent instruction would propel the sensitive youth through First Ritual. Why didn't they send him a brute? A wild-child that no one else could control? Roman looked up at the ceiling as memories of other Rakum he'd discipled over the years filtered down to him. There had been dozens. But somehow this one connected with him on a deeper level. Roman closed his eyes.

The Ritual began at birth, but by the time a Rakum reached his thirteenth year, he was expected to accelerate his training and hasten his development so that he could be released into the brotherhood a fully functioning member. Ideally, a proselyte would progress from First Ritual onset to a fully graduated Rakum in four years. By the looks of Javier's first seven days, he was going to need a lot more time.

At the moment, Javier was lying on his bed writhing in pain, enduring silently, but just barely. The first tests of the Ritual were physical ones, tests of stamina and fortitude. Various bones were broken, in a specific order, over a period of weeks. The bones would heal slowly at first, but as the weeks progressed, the young Rakum's body would heal faster and faster until a broken bone meant no more than a sting from a mosquito. It took enormous audacity to submit to the tests, but tremendous courage to return the next evening for the next treatment. Thirteen-year-old Javier was on his seventh day of *The Broken Bones*.

Roman glanced at the axe handle he'd used tonight. The first few nights, he fractured Javier's pointer fingers with his bare hands. But tonight, he was to snap the youth's forearms with anything of wrought iron. Roman disregarded tradition and opted for the wooden handle hoping to lessen the discomfort, but Javier nearly fainted during the lesson. He didn't cry out, but the pain in his eyes caused even Roman to wince. He watched Javier from across the small room, twisting in agony, cradling his left arm. Roman was supposed to break them both, but he had refrained. It was only day seven and he was altering the kid's training. Yet, he knew best. Isn't that why the Fathers chose him? Because he never missed?

"Oh." A small sound came from Javier's direction and Roman rose to his feet. Crossing the room quietly, he reached the side of the bed and looked upon the pitiful youth crying silent and waterless tears, bearing up under tremendous torture. Against his will, Roman's heart went out to him

and he whispered the boy's name. Javier opened his eyes and clenched his jaw.

"Yes, Master?" he asked, his voice raspy and nearly inaudible.

"Javie, put out your arm." The nickname was born a few years earlier. Roman used it sparingly and usually unintentionally. Javier carefully put out his slowly healing arm and watched with trusting eyes. Roman wrapped his own hands around the fracture and commanded the injury to repair. He had an extraordinary gift for healing and it did not go to waste this night. As the bones knit together, the pain subsided and Javier took in a deep and careful breath.

Finished, Roman stood to his full height and managed a miniscule grin. Javier blinked several times in succession and gratefulness filled his eyes. Roman held up his hand to prevent the boy from thanking him, but Javier's gaze said it all. He motioned brusquely for the youth to sit up, and Javier did so at once.

"Yes, Master?" His voice full of reverence, the youth clasped his hands in his lap and grinned ear-to-ear.

"We'll revisit *The Broken Bones* later. *The Stinging Sun* is your next test. When was the last time you endured the day?" Roman took a seat next to him on the edge of the small bed. The youth came up to his shoulder, already. He would be tall and he was filling out; no longer the bean-like character that arrived on his doorstep five years ago.

"Not since Group Lair, Master," Javier said. To Roman's approval, his accent was fading. "I didn't like it," the boy finished with a frown.

Roman chuckled and pushed up his sleeve. "I guess not."

Javier eyed his bare arm and swallowed. Part of his current stage was bi-weekly ingestion of a mature Rakum's blood. With Roman being the only adult within a hundred miles, he put himself to the task of strengthening the boy in this way. The blood no longer pained the youth. In fact, now that his digestive system had matured, Javier desired Roman's blood nearly as much as the occasional human that Roman brought near for feeding.

"Where's your knife, Javie?"

Javier felt in both pockets and then hopped up to look around the bed linens. After several moments he found the small blade hidden in a leather holster. He popped the knife free and waited for the invitation. Roman thrust forward his arm and nodded his head. Javier was an excellent disciple. Loyal and respectful. It was good

1

Something was not quite right and Canaan blinked his eyes several times to clear his vision. Below him, lying on the carpeted floor, undergoing a violent rejuvenation treatment administered by The Last, Isaac Akaron, was *his* body, pale, limp, and apparently deceased. Yet, Canaan wasn't dead. On the contrary, he watched the scene as if suspended from the ceiling. The last thing he recalled was Elder Rufus invisibly lasering his spine with skill Canaan never expected. If he'd only been more cautious. Yet who would have ever imagined an Elder insane with the Dying Buzz could remain potent enough to incapacitate an Elder as powerful as Canaan?

Standing in a semi-circle around his still form, he recognized his brethren watching the show with keen interest. Dimple, a sturdy Rakum grunt from New Orleans; Boris, six-foot-six and black as night, hailed from Rufus's pack before the Elder went bananas; and Hoss, a muscular grunt known for being slow-witted and obedient. From his insane ethereal position, Canaan counted one more, just outside their group, sitting against the wall and leaning over his knees. No matter how familiar, without his flesh, Canaan had no extrasensory abilities to discern this one's identity.

"YAH-HAH!" Isaac yelped with apparent joy below him, both palms against Canaan's head. "RETURN!" he bellowed and flashed his face toward the ceiling where Canaan hovered. Canaan blinked with surprise and when he reopened his eyes, he was looking into Isaac's face from the floor.

"I am amazing!" the boy said and removed his hands. He rolled onto his rear, crossed his legs Indian-style, and put one hand to Canaan's blond curls. "Hey, there, buddy," the kid said, a victorious smile in place.

"Hey," Canaan said and nodded, trying to appear as unaffected as possible. He was the only Elder present and as such, must maintain superiority—at least among the grunts; Isaac's top-level position remained a brand new revelation.

"How do you feel? Rufus cooked you a little," Isaac said, still awaiting a report. He swirled his fingers a few more times in the wisps of hair on Canaan's forehead and then smoothed his long sideburns with one forefinger.

Canaan did not reject The Last's affections, the previous hours clear in his mind. This blond and perfect, seemingly thirteen-year-old boy was High Father Abroghia's last laugh, the most powerful Rakum ever born. Now, the kid would be in charge of their race, what was left of them. Canaan kept his thoughts positive—the kid was more telepathic than them all.

"I don't mind if you ponder my amazingness, Elder Canaan," Isaac said then, his voice soft.

"Thank you for bringing me back."

"Of course I'd bring you back, silly," Isaac said and hopped to his feet with athletic agility. "I'm not sure it's completely *fair...*" he stressed and turned toward the thick red-headed Rakum nearest him. "Dimple shot Rufus just when it was getting really interesting."

"Shot him?" Canaan said, not really asking. He had heard several explosions before he lost consciousness and now had his explanation.

"Don't get me wrong, Canaan. I want you with me. I *need* you, actually, but..." the kid shrugged, "a gun?" He looked at Dimple again and the guy winced as if he'd been struck. Isaac returned his attention to Canaan, still lying flat on the carpet. "Um, buddy...naptime's over."

"Of course," Canaan agreed and commanded his body to stand. His limbs responded sluggishly, but all-in-all, he probably looked pretty sturdy to those watching on. He had no pain, and only a vague tickle remained along his spine from Elder Rufus's attack to his nervous system. The Last truly was amazing.

An unexpected thought popped into Canaan's mind and he knew Isaac would read it and respond: *Did Roman and the rest get away safely?*

"I let them go, they're gone," Isaac said, ending the discussion. "But that's not all..." Isaac grasped Canaan's hand. "I healed Beryl, too. He had burnt to a crisp running to the house at dawn." Isaac laughed out loud and shook his head.

Canaan was familiar with the twins, Beryl and Meryl, in many ways. Most recently when they served Rufus. A mere week ago, Meryl and Beryl were dispatched by the insane Elder to kidnap Canaan's lover, Marcy, to lure him to Jackson. Meryl had actually buzzed off her before Canaan could intervene. This breach cost the youngster dearly—Canaan broke his neck and left him to die. In addition, Canaan shot Beryl in the gut before the guy healed from the slug Marcy put in him minutes earlier. So... they had survived. Deep down in a place he wouldn't peek into, Canaan was glad they had.

Isaac caught Canaan's eye and winked. "You can be dangerous, can't you," he giggled, not truly asking a question. "Don't worry, Canaan, Beryl's all fixed up," Isaac said, still giggling at the man's misfortune. "It *was* hilarious, though. He was oozing puss. Completely black and red when *Officer Dimple* yanked him inside." Isaac tugged Canaan to where the Rakum sat with his head over his knees.

Canaan had seen Rakum burnt by the sun, and if they were allowed to crisp up even a few minutes, they would expire. Yet, Beryl had no apparent burns. Canaan looked at The Last in wonder; healing consumed tremendous energy and Isaac had healed two Rakum in one night. Isaac squeezed his hand.

"All of you..." He took a moment to catch the eye of every Rakum standing. "You guys are going to help me set things right."

"Ta'Avah..." Beryl whispered from their feet.

"Pffft," Isaac responded, spitting. He caught Canaan's eye. "Just so you know, while you were passed out..."

His eyes actually shined with humor then, reminding Canaan of their new leader's ruthless nature. Sure, he was the youngest of them all, but there would be no limit to his power or his ambitions.

Reading his run-on thoughts, Isaac smiled as he completed his statement. "...our maker stole Father Theophilus from the basement."

Canaan had questions, but Isaac beat him to it.

"From now on, we will know him as Ta'avah, but he embodied High Father Abroghia in a previous incarnation. All of you," Isaac said to each, "must understand our maker is a spirit, and for the moment, he inhabits this Rakum's dead twin." The kid gestured to the kneeling man.

Canaan sighed; he had his answer regarding Meryl's condition. It was a damn shame. Before he attacked Marcy, Meryl had been his favorite between the two brothers, their personalities more alike. Beryl had always seemed *less than*, and Canaan hadn't been the only Elder that thought so. Without his twin to balance his periodic fragility, Beryl's un-Rakum-like tendencies would only increase.

"Yes, he's a moron, Elder Canaan, we all agree." Isaac interrupted his thoughts. "You're the only one not paying attention. Focus on me. Got it?" Canaan nodded. "I will get Father Theophilus back and he will serve me," Isaac continued easily, "and I will vanquish Ta'avah. It is my birthright to rule our people."

"I'm with you, Boss, one hundred percent," the lumbering black Rakum to Isaac's left said in a low baritone.

"I know you are, Boris," Isaac said touching his arm. "The rest of you—are you with me? Will you stand with me as your Father, against anyone—man or Rakum—who dares challenge me?"

"I will," Hoss said without hesitation, and then Dimple agreed in a low voice. Canaan nodded, which Isaac acknowledged with a wink.

The Rakum on the floor still hadn't moved or looked up. Canaan leaned forward to help him rise, but Isaac booted Beryl with his tennis shoe.

"Beryl, are you with me?" Isaac said and waited. A low "yes" was his response. Isaac paused another second and kicked Beryl in the shoulder harder than before. "We're fresh out of pacifiers, Beryl," Isaac said. "This is no house for babies. Is that what you are?" Isaac looked to Boris and stroked Beryl's soft, brown hair. "You can eat this if it's a baby, Boris. You're my favorite."

"No, Master, I am a Rakum," Beryl said and rolled to his knees, then to his feet. "I will serve you."

The Rakum's gaze remained downcast, but Canaan's eyes grew at the sight. In the history of their race, never had there been born more perfect and beautiful Rakum than the identical twins, Meryl and Beryl. Since their youths, both found it to be child's play to manipulate anyone—man or Rakum—with their looks and charm. Canaan now understood Beryl's depressed demeanor. Isaac had only healed half of the Rakum's face. The other half puckered with red, yellow, and black oozing flesh, trying to heal and being prevented by a consistent and opposing force.

Isaac laughed then and turned away from the circle. *"I do what I want,"* he sent telepathically to Canaan alone. *"Now, come feed me,"* he said silently and crawled into what used to be Rufus's throne. "Come now," he said aloud, although all present understood whom the kid wanted. Canaan crossed the room and rolled up his sleeve.

2

Memphis, TN
November 7th, 7 p.m.

Javier dialed the number from long memory. Once a year, since he'd been mortal, he called Ruth Miller's house to check on her nephew Simon. The kid was picked by a Major League team before finishing college and had made quite a name through the years. Javier never spoke with him, never identified himself to the aunt, he only pretended to be a sports writer, collected the bare facts, and hung up. He had to know the boy was safe and doing well. Tonight, as he dialed Aunt Ruth's number, he would ask her how to contact her nephew. He needed help and since he was not ready to call Roman, his former Elder, his former Cow remained the only option.

The phone rang across three states as Javier waited, preparing the script in his mind. On the third ring, panic rose in his throat. What if the call forwarded to the answering machine? Then what? He had nowhere to go, no money, no shelter, and nothing to eat. He couldn't call anyone from his past life—they'd despise him for what he'd done in the darkness of the Stone's basement. Why did he do it? And the question that plagued him the most since he emerged from the hospital boiler room at sundown: what exactly had he done?

He was no longer human—he could feel it. His body was too strong and his senses too sharp. Unpleasant and alien sensations plagued his musculature and violent thoughts crept into his mind unbidden. But he also was not a Rakum. He had no interest in blood, and more importantly, the sun did not blind him or burn his skin. He had tested it before sunset by creeping up the boiler room stairs and slowly allowing the sunlight to fall across his body. Nothing happened. He had stepped into the waning light, the sun inches from falling below the Tennessee mountains, and he experienced only a touch of nausea. Javier's reaction to the daylight was

9

uncomfortable, but not dangerous. So he wasn't a Rakum and he wasn't a man. That left, what?

The landline rang a fourth time and was snatched up with a loud clack.

"Yeah?" a strong male voice barked. "What is it?"

Javier swallowed, his mouth suddenly dry.

"Who's there?"

"Simon?" Javier asked, cupping the handset in both palms. "Simon Miller?" There was a three-second pause that seemed much longer and then what sounded like a hand muffling the receiver for muted shouting. A few more seconds elapsed as Javier glanced around his phone booth. He spoke into the phone again. "Simon?"

"Javier? Is it really you?" a quiet voice asked, more like that of a child than the grown man Simon had certainly become.

Javier smiled and nodded to no one in the old-fashioned phone booth. "Hey, Simon. It's good to hear your voice."

"Ohmygod! I can't believe it!" Simon gushed, dispensing with the irritated adult voice he had used to answer the phone. He shouted at someone on his end and apologized to Javier. "Aunt Ruth was buried last night. It's a madhouse. Where are you? Are you in Athens?"

Javier's face fell, Simon would not be able to drive to Memphis and pick him up.

"Are you coming here?"

"I'm in Memphis, Simon, and I don't have transportation," Javier admitted, sorry that he sounded so helpless. "I was calling to see if you could help me out."

"Of course, I can, Javier! Hang on." Simon was gone a few seconds and hopped back on the line. "Can you fly? Take a plane? I mean, last I heard—well, uh, you were mortal."

Javier smiled despite his anxious state of mind. So much water had passed under the bridge since they parted ways. He hadn't seen the guy since Last Assembly and Simon had been a teenager then. Seven years ago and newly-human, Javier parted ways with Simon over the phone fearing it would be too weird to face a man to whom he had once been quite addicted. The kid had returned to his classes and Javier departed with Beth Rider to find a life among mankind in Alabama. Simon knew nothing about Rufus and his attempted coup in Jackson. He knew nothing about Javier's break from Roman. And of course, he knew nothing of Javier's biggest secret, the transgression that kept him separate from Rakum and friends alike.

"Javier, you okay? Can you get to the airport? Have any money?"

"Simon, a lot has happened. I don't have anything. I don't know why I even called."

"Because we're friends, Javier! Look," Simon shouted away from the phone and was back, "I'm wiring you some money. Get to the closest Western Union and claim it. It'll be under my name with the password *motorcycle* and no ID requirement. Can you do that?"

"Motorcycle," Javier said with a sad smile. He had met Simon because the kid crashed his bike the same night Javier and Roman were out for a joyride. Before the memories washed back fully, Javier shut them out. His days of being a Rakum were over and he needed to work *with* God to keep it that way. "Okay, Simon, that'll work."

"Good. Get here as soon as you can. They're sitting Shiva,[1] but you come on. Nobody's keeping my best buddy out."

"Okay," Javier said and listened as Simon gave wiring instructions to the side.

"I'm sending plenty so pick up a disposable cell. I want you to call me when you have your schedule. I'll have Pink pick you up at the airport. That work for you?"

"Yes, okay, thank you." Javier was not embarrassed that he needed help, but now that it would soon come to pass, seeing Simon again might be awkward; Simon literally worshiped him as a Rakum. How would the guy see him now?

"Javier," Simon said then, "Pink just sent the money. Hurry. We'll work it out, whatever's going on."

"Thanks again, Simon," Javier mumbled, pulled the phone from his ear, and stared into the receiver. What else could he say? How would Simon perceive him? Their initial attraction had been a supernatural one, brought on by his connection with High Father Abroghia. Now he was connected to the Boy-Father, Isaac, in the worst way. Javier gulped and hung up the phone.

He would find a Western Union. He'd get the money and a phone and call for an Uber to the airport. With any luck, he would be at Simon's before sunup. Javier left the phone booth and jogged toward the lights of the drugstore ahead, now racing the sun for altogether different reasons.

---

[1] At-home Jewish tradition designed to honor the deceased.

3

Yazoo City, MS
November 7th, 8 p.m.

Father Theophilus shrank further into the shadows beneath the staircase as Ta'avah finished off the family whose home they invaded. The past forty-eight hours had been a nightmare, but hadn't the past seven years been nearly as bad? The immense and nearly limitless power a Rakum Father possessed had filtered away as his apathy expanded nightly. Theophilus inhaled deeply, held the air in his weary lungs, and then deliberately exhaled slow and careful. His body ached from lack of sustenance, his spirit ached from woe over his people, and his soul languished in a battle between God and Satan.

Yes, Satan; the Devil of Old—ha-satan in Hebrew, the Adversary in English, and Ta'avah today—fifteen feet away, sucking the blood out of the father of two boys who had already been beheaded by the monster. It was no accident that brought the old Father here; Theophilus made his choice eons ago.

He wasn't born a Rakum. Rather, two thousand years ago he was born to a normal Jewish couple in a small Grecian town. His dream was to be a tailor like his papa, making ordinary tents for the am *ha'aretz*[2] and extraordinary *tallit*[3] for the *chasadim*[4]. But on a fated pilgrimage to Jerusalem, his plans detoured when he met not only the amazing new Rabbi from Nazareth, but also the miscreant who he today knew as Ta'avah.

Theophilus frowned at the sound of the demon finishing off his victim off with vicious gusto. Ta'avah dropped the man's corpse to the ground and headed upstairs. The wife had been gagged and tethered to the bedpost, and since his belly was full, Ta'avah would no doubt abuse the

---

[2] Ordinary folk, literally, "people of the land."
[3] A Jewish prayer shawl worn about the shoulders during prayer. Means "little tent."
[4] Hebrew for "holy ones," or religious people.

woman in other ways. Oh, how Theophilus longed to ask the God of the mortals for help. But how could he?

Yeshua[5] of Nazareth had given him a choice and when put to the question, Theophilus chose the father of the Rakum, a race of monsters spawned by a demon cast from heaven when the world was new.

A scream sounded from the second floor and then hushed just as quickly. Ta'avah would not show mercy because there was none in him. Being privy and complicit for millennia, Theophilus knew the creature's entire history. Ta'avah was one-hundred-percent spirit. Six thousand years ago, when Ta'avah was first cast to earth by Elohim[6], he took the form of a man and called himself Abroghia. Using his abilities to procreate, he spawned a new race combining his seed and the wombs of mortal women. Each male child born was imbued with his blood and evil nature. By the time Theophilus's path crossed his at that long ago Festival, Abroghia had raised over a hundred of these "sons" and was ready to enlist the aid of specially-chosen men to help him increase their numbers.

"Theophilus, come. I need you."

The words Abroghia had whispered to him came to his long memory, so vivid and substantial that it was hard to believe two thousand years had passed. Theophilus had just left Yeshua's side, convinced beyond a shadow of a doubt that the Rabbi was more than a man, but the Son of God—the Messiah they'd all been awaiting. Yet, when Abroghia called him, Theophilus listened...

It was what became known as 32 AD, in a scrubby valley in Galilee, and Theophilus lay on the sand, flat on his back, overwhelmed by the simple touch of the Healer of Nazareth.

"Theophilus, come. I need you."

At the sound of the commanding whisper, Theophilus opened his eyes. In the clear moonlight, he recognized the man he'd met the night before as Abroghia, not a Jew, but a curious sort. A man who knew much about the ways of the Hebrew people as well as all of the local gossip concerning Yeshua of Nazareth.

"I need you to rule beside me," Abroghia continued with an excited urgency in his deep voice. "Teach these younglings what you know. Help me grow a great nation of men who live to serve their leaders."

"Why me, honorable Abroghia? I am a tailor, not a leader. I've never married, nor owned land. I have seen the Son of God and I want to follow Him." Still lying flat on his back, Theophilus met Abroghia's gaze and

---

[5] (Hebrew) "Jesus"; *yod-shin-vav-ayin*, ישוע - Pronounced *Yeshua*; literally, "Salvation"
[6] (Hebrew) "God," specifically the God of Israel.

13

ignored two other men who stood nearby. They were younger, one Roman and the other possibly a native of Galilee. Theophilus touched his tingling cheeks still glowing as a result of meeting the Messiah face-to-face.

"You have been chosen, Theophilus. My sons will need a Father. You are the first I have called and there will be eight others. You will sire thousands of Rakum directly from your loins. Through your seed you will do a great service to the world."

Abroghia had hit a nerve, for Theophilus harbored secret dreams of grandeur, fantasies of bringing the nation of Israel out of bondage by his own power.

"Come. Say not a word until I show you what I am capable of. Rise up, and come."

One of the youngsters lifted Theophilus off the ground. When he found his feet, the Rakum youth steered him across the now-deserted field directly behind Abroghia. Within minutes, they reached the trees and Abroghia pulled a full-sized sword from a sheath at the other young man's side.

"Markus," Abroghia said gesturing to the teenager who supported Theophilus on his thickly-muscled shoulder. "Ionious," Abroghia said, this time pointing to the dark blond man on his right. "My best sons. Theophilus, you and I will create a legion; you, and the other Fathers I will choose, will raise up a nation of a hundred thousand Rakum, all of which will worship you as their god and Father."

Theophilus's mind spun. How could this be? Abroghia answered his questions without him voicing them aloud.

"You will serve a master who can never die." Abroghia held out the sword, hilt first. "Thrust this blade through and through, Theophilus."

Shaking his head, Theophilus's eyes grew wide. He voiced his doubts with vehemence until Abroghia grew weary of his complaints and handed the weapon to the thick-armed Markus. The teen thrust it through his master's middle without hesitation and Theophilus rushed to his aid.

"Abroghia! What is the meaning of this?" Theophilus gasped, but the man was miraculously uninjured.

Smiling, Abroghia turned side-to-side twice, displaying how the blade entered just below his sternum and exited out the back. Blood oozed from both wounds and to Theophilus's horror, Abroghia put his hand to the hilt and drew it slowly out. After tossing the bloodied item to Ionious, Abroghia ripped the already torn tunic wide. As Theophilus watched, the wound in the man's torso closed before his eyes.

"Impossible!" Theophilus gasped, his heart hammering in his chest.

Abroghia laughed.

"With man, perhaps, but not with me. I cannot die, Theophilus. I am a powerful god and I need you to help me with these young ones." He gestured to the boys who stood obediently by awaiting command. "We will populate the earth with men who are stronger, smarter, and longer-lived than the earth has ever seen."

"Who do you follow, Abroghia?" Theophilus had to know. Yeshua ben Elohim[7], or another? How was he to follow anyone other than the God of Israel?

"I have walked this earth in different forms for four thousand years. I have power beyond your imagination and if you join me, I will lend that power to you. You could never imagine what you will be capable of once you devote your life to my purposes."

Theophilus considered his words. Power to make a change in the world, power to decrease the suffering of his people, power to please his Creator—these are things Theophilus wanted. Could the man before him do what he said? His immortality had been confirmed, had it not? Theophilus looked at the two young men on his either side, and then back to Abroghia.

"What of the Elohim of Israel?" he asked, his voice cracking.

"Who do you think gave me this power?" Abroghia asked. "Will you come? I will prove myself to you a million times over." Abroghia stepped close and placed a heavy hand on Theophilus's shoulder.

Energy transferred between them and Theophilus could not deny the desire that welled in him at the contact, a lust for supremacy accompanied by a possibility of fulfillment.

"But," Abroghia said, lowering his chin and holding eye contact, "you must consent. You must submit to my authority. I will reward you for thousands of years and you will never be without fine food, luxury, all the pleasures of life. And you will *rule*." Abroghia fell quiet and silence filled the night sky.

Theophilus's heart yearned for all the man promised. Pushing all thoughts of Jesus from his mind, he placed his hand on Abroghia's opposite shoulder. "If you can do all you say, then yes, I will follow you."

"Good." Abroghia smiled and in a quick movement grasped him by both shoulders. "You will never regret it, my son," Abroghia whispered as Markus and Ionious stepped closer. "Answer me this: The life is in the blood, correct?"

Alarmed at how firmly he was being held, Theophilus squirmed, but

---

[7] (Hebrew) "Jesus, Son of God"

15

Abroghia asked his question again, this time deep in his mind.

"The life is in the blood, correct?"

The man's ability to speak without words further convinced Theophilus and he nodded his head. "Er, yes. So says Elohim."

Aloud, Abroghia said, "Then it stands to reason if I pour my life into you, you will take on my attributes. Yes?"

Theophilus tilted his head with wonder, nodding slowly.

"Tonight we begin the process of making you over into a god." Abroghia produced a small bone knife from his sash and sliced deep his wrist. He thrust the wound toward Theophilus's face. "Take my life into you, Theophilus. Then you will know power like you've never imagined. Do it now."

Perhaps in shock, perhaps frightened, but utterly enthralled, Theophilus did not pull back when the man's blood rushed into his mouth, spilling over his lips and down his beard. Markus stabilized him with a palm to his neck and Ionious stood by with a hand on Theophilus's chest. He wondered why they held him so tightly, but within moments, he knew. The stranger's blood burned his gut, causing him to thrash in excruciating pain. Before long, his gagging turned to heaving, which then evened out into panting, the pain a distant memory. In his body, a sensation of immeasurable strength permeated from his core outward. He was different, he had become a new man—a Rakum, a spawn of the demigod, Abroghia.

"From this moment on," Abroghia announced to the night, "you are Father Theophilus, a force to be reckoned with. And these men are your servants. Greet your Father, pups."

Markus turned to face him and dropped to both knees, his face to the sand.

"Kazak, Abba,[8]" he said in Hebrew. Mimicking the prostrate gesture, Ionious repeated the phrase in Greek.

"Welcome, brother," Abroghia smiled, his eyes far away. "In the months to come, I will further transform you into my image through ceremony and deed until you shed your humanity to the utmost. You will claim your deity alongside the Fathers of the Rakum race and we will rule our world, taking apart anything and anyone who does not serve our purposes."

Theophilus took a deep breath, for the first time sensing a multitude of new smells, sights, and sensations as the stars in the sky seemed to give him praise. He was a god and he owed it all to a spirit manifest in the flesh

[8] (Hebrew) "Be strong, Father."

named Ta'avah Rakha[9] Abroghia, his god and king.

A choice he now regretted. Back to the present, Theophilus rubbed his face wishing he could muster tears as the mortals so easily did. He couldn't weep, he couldn't mourn, and he couldn't pray. For an instant, he looked up in the dark vestibule and parted his lips, so close to speaking to Elohim. Then he stopped himself. An unclean monster, a killer, a filthy abomination for two thousand years—the God of Israel wouldn't, *shouldn't,* hear him. Theophilus slumped to the carpet and closed his eyes. If only he could die.

"Please, I want to die," his heart cried, thinking that he spoke only to himself. A lightness moved in his middle and he held his breath. Another spirit had entered the space and it wasn't Ta'avah's kind.

"Please, let me die," he begged, silently as before, but this time he willfully addressed the Creator of the universe.

"I love you," the Entity under the stairs said in his mind.

Theophilus exhaled, mouth ajar, eyes wide, and screamed.

Contact.

[9] (Hebrew) "Vain Lust"

4

Larkspur, CA
November 7th, 8 p.m.

A low noise escaped his throat as Rafael leaned over his lap, waiting for the buzz to pass. Santiago's blood tickled his system as deeply as when the kid was thirteen. He peeked at his friend with one eye and smiled. Santiago caught him looking, groaned, and slumped to the carpet despite the expensive cashmere sweater vest he wore. He kicked off his Berlutis and rolled onto his back, covering his eyes with one hand. Since the kid came under his care, Rafael had been dressing him like a Macy's mannequin; if he minded, he never let on.

"You could leave off the creepy moans, Rafa," Santiago joked and covered his first hand with the other, enveloping his wrinkle-free forehead, his thick black hair only just beginning to salt. The signs of age were apparent only regarding the soft middle that replaced the rock-hard physique of his youth and crow's feet encircled eyes that laughed often.

"Shhh," Rafael whispered.

Santiago chuckled and then winced, increasing the pressure of his fingers over his eyes. "You're killing me, amigo."

"*Cállate*,"[10] Rafael hissed without venom, his smile in place. "I'm buzzing here."

"Whoop-dee-do," the man replied, managing a grin despite his discomfort.

Rafael fell silent as did his partner. His pain would be tended to when the buzz passed; it was the way of things between them.

Santiago was his oldest mortal friend; he'd known him since the guy was knee high. Was *friend* the right word? Santiago's father, Martin Rivera, and his father before him, Luis, were voluntary blood donors to Rafael, making the current Rivera what the Rakum referred to as a Legacy Cow.

---

[10] (Spanish) "Be quiet!"

18

What was uncommon in their relationship was that through a series of complicated happenstances, Rafael became Santiago Rivera's legal guardian when the child was five.

Rafael's grin fell and he leaned back in the soft chair. It was extremely un-Rakum-like, but the man complaining histrionically on the carpet at his feet was his virtual son, his only friend, *and* his Cow. When the Fathers held the throne, they threatened to destroy the man more than once if Rafael didn't adjust his attitude. Now, the Fathers were gone and Rafael stayed as far away from their new leader, Elder Rufus, as possible. Telepathic communication had all but disappeared between Rafael and his brethren, but he had gleaned along the grapevine that Elder Rufus was drinking strictly from the dying and had gone insane. Rafael forced down a vague warning in his subconscious that something big had happened to their deranged leader in the last few hours. Rafa didn't care. The only thing that interested him these days was spending time with Santiago, and of course, enjoying the man's blood on occasion.

"Rafa," Santiago said and uncovered his face, rolling onto his stomach. "My head hurts worse than before."

Rafael considered Santiago's sincerity. The man had turned fifty a month earlier and his doctor warned him that he was in danger of becoming anemic. They'd both brushed off the diagnosis, neither willing to admit that the sculptor was getting old.

"*¿En serio?*" Rafael asked and his friend responded with a low noise. Rushing the lingering effects of his meal, Rafael slumped out of the chair and joined Santiago on the floor. Sitting cross-legged beside him, he laid his hand between the man's shoulder blades. "Really bad, eh?"

"*Sí,* I'm sorry," Santiago whispered and brought his fingers to his temples to rub in a circular motion.

Rafael remained still, his hand on Santiago's back, wishing he could heal with his touch. He had talents, but restoring health wasn't one of them. He must have sighed because his friend rolled onto his back and looked him in the eye, forcing a smile through a fog of pain.

"This is not your fault, Rafa. I'm fifty years old. Next year I'll be fifty-one, the next year, fifty-two, and on and on. We knew this was coming." Santiago stopped rubbing his temples and touched Rafael's knee. "Go and find another companion; it's foolish to hang with a used-up *paria*."[11]

"*Cállate,* Iago." Rafael leaned forward to cover his friend's clammy forehead with his palm. "I'm going to take you to see the Elder. It's time we stopped this, this—"

---

[11] (Spanish) Unwanted person

"This slow death?" Santiago asked, eyebrows arched under the edge of Rafael's cool hand. "Diabetes and prostate cancer—that's what your man is going to heal? Why would he? Your people are divided and angry, dangerous and schizophrenic. You told me that monster in Jackson has the Rakum slaughtering each other like animals." Santiago sat up carefully. "No, if it were safe, you would've taken me there already. Don't go making plans to visit this spooky Elder when you don't know if he's *amigo* or *enemigo*."

Rafael rubbed his face until his eyes throbbed and then got to his feet. He loved Santiago's blood and his friend loved donating it to him, but he was pretty sure their extended Rakum-Cow relationship was what made him so sick at a relatively young age. The Elder he referred to was a healer; Rafael had met him on several occasions before the Last Assembly. They enjoyed an amicable relationship in those days and if he was still alive and still a Rakum, he'd probably lay hands on Santiago to heal him. He might also be a lunatic; that was his reputation, anyway.

"No, we keep on like we are until I give out. I don't want to risk whatever time we have left on a *loco* Rakum Elder. It's not worth it." Santiago put out his hand and Rafael pulled him to his feet. His friend wavered and fell into him heavily.

Rafael held him up under his armpits and spoke into his ear. "Let me carry you to bed. It's the least I can do."

Santiago grunted his consent and Rafael picked him up as if he were a child and carried him to his room. Elder Kilmeade reportedly lived fifty miles south, in San Francisco. Out of options, Rafael determined his next course.

5

Jackson, MS
November 7th, 8 p.m.

Canaan paced the tiled foyer wringing his hands very much like a mortal in the throes of worry. He had plenty to be concerned about; any minute, his human lover, Marcy Haddle, would arrive, and the Rakum headquarters was no place for a Rabbit. He duly regretted marking her and as soon as she arrived, he'd regret it even more. Isaac laughed then and Canaan realized he was being read.

"Is that her car?" Isaac asked from the next room lounging on a cream-colored sofa that faced the front windows.

"Yes," Canaan replied. Marcy was at the broken security gate picking her way down the drive, no doubt concerned only with seeing him again and completely oblivious of the danger that awaited her in the house.

"She didn't waste any time! Bring her upstairs to meet everyone," Isaac said, hopping to his feet. He bolted up the stairs looking every bit a teenager in his tattered jeans and Lady Gaga T-shirt.

Literally trapped, Canaan's throat constricted. If he didn't turn her over, Isaac would fry his brain and take her anyway. If he did, Marcy would hate him forever. Canaan reached for the front door and swallowed hard. His life was in the crapper and Marcy was guaranteed to make things worse with her volatile personality and short temper.

"Oh, God! Canaan!" Marcy screamed as she jogged up the porch steps and clambered into his arms. "I could kill you for making me worry! You didn't call me at all—don't tell me you ain't got reception, 'cause I know better!"

Canaan held her without speaking so she filled the dead air with complaints.

"I had to rent a damn car; I shouldn't be expected to wait for Michael

Stone to get back when my husband needs me now!" Marcy squeezed him tighter for a few seconds then broke off, leaned out of his arms and met his eye. "You shoulda warned me about making me a Rabbit. That was real sly, Canaan! I said no, didn't I? Have you no care what I think? Are you so much smarter than me?"

Canaan put his hand to her hair and whispered placations in her ear. He had marked her only hours before she ended up being sought and attacked by the twins. If he hadn't marked her, Meryl and Beryl wouldn't have found it as easy to track and find her that night. *How could I have known our whole world was about to go to shit?* He didn't possess precognitive ability and he hoped Marcy would forgive him in time.

If they only had more time. Even now, he sensed Isaac growing impatient with Marcy's histrionics. And she was still going.

"…Beth tried to help me understand, but dammit! I want to be with you! After all I've been through, that's not too much to ask!" Marcy leaned back and looked into his face. "Isaac told them you needed me. But you look fantastic, honey. Everybody at Beth's house is so melodramatic."

Canaan said nothing; Marcy couldn't see how weak Isaac's blood demands made him. The Last had been in charge all of forty-eight hours and had taken Canaan's blood three times. *That* is why Isaac told Michael Stone and his crew to send Marcy to Jackson. Isaac hoped that with a Rabbit in the house, Canaan would have all the blood he wanted, evidencing that their new leader had a lot to learn. *Elders do not chase Rabbits,* an age-old Rakum tenet Canaan had no intention of altering. It made a lot more sense before Beth Rider arrived and changed their world forever.

"Canaan!" Marcy grabbed his biceps and shook him forcefully, although because of his size he wasn't fazed. "Snap out of it! What's the matter?"

"Shhh, Cee," he said and lifted his palms to her face, his heart bursting. At fifty-six, Marcy remained fit and lithe, her rose-colored hair shimmering in the light of the moon. To Canaan, she hadn't changed since the night they met—she sixteen and as plucky as an old mule, and he a Rakum Elder in his prime, king of the world.

"What's going on?" she asked in a low voice, finally catching wind of Canaan's somber mood.

"I love you, Cee. You know that, right?"

Marcy's eyes narrowed. "What's going on? Is it that kid? It has something to do with the kid, Isaac, right?"

"I'm sorry," he whispered. Upstairs, now perched in his throne-like chair, Isaac grumbled for him to hurry up.

Marcy touched Canaan's cheek, a tear welling in her eye. "Please, tell me, hon."

Canaan swallowed and kissed her forehead as if for the last time. Then, he straightened and put his left hand to the back of her neck.

"I'm taking you upstairs to meet everyone," Canaan said as she fell in beside him, dwarfed by his height and weight. So fragile, yet full of spunk, Marcy would fight Isaac's goons. Since she was a Rabbit, when they struck back, she'd heal instantly. Over, and over, and over. Canaan's wife was about to become a plaything of the entire house of Rakum.

At the first stair, he whispered over her head. "Cee, Isaac is in charge. You must do whatever he says. Without question."

Marcy stiffened and stopped her forward movement. "The hell I will!"

"Marcy!" Canaan growled, turning to look her in the face. He'd known her forty years and never had he raised his voice nor hand to her. Tonight, he felt he might have to do both if only for her own good. "Submit to Isaac or he will make a sure hell out of your time here. Understand?"

"Why are you cowing to that little creep? Why don't you—"

"Listen!" Canaan hissed, his hand firm around the back of her neck. Marcy's eyes widened. "You're marked, Cee! There are Rakum grunts here that will suck you dry every night if they want. Go along and maybe they won't hurt you. I'm hoping some measure of respect for me and the Old Way might prevent them from raping you. See what I'm up against? I can't protect you. I'm nothing here, Cee. Get it?"

"Canaan—" Marcy mewled, paler than before. Powerless to do anything else, Canaan averted his gaze.

"Come on," he urged none too gently and headed up the grand staircase. Marcy struggled, mumbling his name, trying to get him to stop and listen, but Canaan had shut down and blocked out her voice. When he reached Isaac's room, he pushed the partly-open door and met the eyes of his demonic new family.

Dimple and Hoss stood on the right of Isaac's big chair and Beryl and Boris on his left. The kid wonder sat cross-legged with his hands balled in his lap. All four of the inferior Rakum twitched in their skin, having detected the Rabbit's scent in the air pretty much as soon as she crossed the county line. Now that they'd been forced to wait for her to arrive, all four salivated, anticipating their turn at her blood. His skin crawling with fury at the thought, Canaan entered the room fully. He literally dragged his beloved across the threshold as she kicked and bit at his arm. If only she weren't so high-spirited…

Isaac had met Marcy before the Rabbit debacle, so he trained his gaze to the inferior Rakum. "Brothers," Canaan said, his voice low, "this is Marcy Haddle."

"Boris goes first!" Isaac chirped. "He loves me best."

Boris met Canaan's eye momentarily before stepping forward. In their former days, before the Fathers were defeated by Beth Rider's God, Canaan would have squashed the guy with a focused thought, but he had no such authority now. Isaac held the cards and in his childish demon's mind, he dealt them as he saw fit.

Still, Canaan didn't have to like it.

His free hand clenched into a fist and he aggressively forced it to remain at his side. The tall black Rakum came within six feet and reached out for Marcy's upper arm. Canaan growled deep in his throat, unable to stop himself. Four decades he'd protected the woman, held her close, never allowing harm to come to her, and now? He was completely impotent in every way that mattered.

"Canaan," Isaac sang sweetly as a searing pain tickled and then scorched Canaan's spinal cord. Reflexively, he released Marcy and Boris took custody. "Good boy," Isaac said smiling.

Marcy put all of her effort into escape, throwing punches in Boris's face and kicking with both feet. After dodging a few blows, he spun her around, grabbed her around the chest, and lifted her off the ground. Canaan could see, but barely, the pain in his neck and back too severe. He slumped to the cold floor as Boris left the room taking Marcy away.

"So, who will go with Boris?" Isaac asked the remaining three. "Dimple? You join him. That Rabbit hasn't given any blood since she's been marked; she's got plenty to spare."

With a glance at Canaan that might have been regret, Dimple obeyed their diminutive leader and disappeared down the hall. Rising carefully to his feet, Canaan grimaced, the invisible spear receding from his back. Marcy's screams for help sounded in his ears before she fell silent.

The silence was worse.

6

"Your behavior disgusts me, Canaan," Isaac said with disdain. "I knew you liked her, but look at yourself. That woman's done something to you." Isaac rose from his seat and slowly approached. "You're a magnificent being, perfect, gorgeous—one of the few left who haven't been ruined by the Dead Buzz." Isaac reached him and pulled his shirt until he dropped to his knees so they could speak eye-to-eye. "Elder Canaan, look at me."

He didn't refer to Canaan by his title often and Canaan turned his head.

"I was raised by the Fathers. Have you any idea what that was like? How secluded and sheltered I was for four decades? I might have seen four or five Rakum in all of those years, and then only from afar. Think about it. You're the only Elder I've seen aside from Rufus and in his condition, he barely qualified. Looking at you makes me think of how glorious our history has been. Looking at you gives me hope that those who remain might be glorious again."

Canaan nodded half-heartedly and Isaac exhaled, thinking, his mouth to the side. He opened the top two buttons of Canaan's long-sleeved shirt and tugged the left collar down to study his myriad of tattoos collected over the last three decades. A black flames-and-barbed-wire tattoo covered his entire shoulder from his neck, down his left arm to his fingertips. Isaac touched the ink over his muscle with his fingers and shook his head.

"They could all be like you, Elder Canaan," he mumbled, a sad sound welling from deep down. "Work with me. Help your brethren..."

Canaan watched The Last's hand run along his skin. The boy looked innocent enough, but Canaan didn't see him as he did when they first met, a pitiful orphan seeking shelter. Two nights ago, Isaac had duly demonstrated his power by effortlessly defeating the strongest of their kind. What did Isaac want from him? Canaan remained as still as possible and waited.

"What do I want?" Isaac asked. "What do I want? I want you restored! I want you at my side—not pining over some wrinkled old bat you've been shagging for forty years! I hate to see you defeated and miserable. I want to see you as you *were*—strong, proud, and unstoppable."

"I will try, Master," Canaan managed, forcing himself to not look away.

"To hell with trying! Look at what they've left me!" Isaac pointed in Beryl's direction. "Ta'avah rejected that one because he's too weak. He oozes failure. He's worthless!"

Canaan's eye flicked to Beryl who promptly looked away.

"And that one..." Isaac hooked his thumb toward Hoss on the other side of the throne. "He doesn't have an original thought in his head and no loyalty to me whatsoever."

Across the room, Hoss moved his bulk a fraction forward, his lips quivering, but then thought better of responding. It was a good call; Isaac was thoroughly worked up and liable to explode.

"And that imbecile, Dimple?" Isaac continued in a growl. "He's a loose cannon—I mean he marched up here and emptied that gun into Rufus without provocation or permission. Just BAM! BAM! BAM! BAM! BAM!" Isaac fired an invisible handgun as he spoke. He shook his head, ground his teeth, and then put both hands on Canaan's shoulders. "I should end them all. I could, you know? Do you realize how hard it is for me to *not* fry them, right now, just *poof?*"

Canaan attempted to see the kid's point of view, but didn't get very far. Even in his prime, he never had the scope of power that Isaac possessed. Instead, Canaan's mind turned to Boris, the one Rakum their leader favored and showed affection. Isaac smiled.

"Sure, I care about Boris," Isaac said. "He believed in me first. He serves me with a pure heart, with true faith." Isaac's eyes flashed and his hands came up to frame Canaan's head, fingers intertwined with Canaan's sideburns. "Is there any possible way that you could love me like that, Elder Canaan? You're the last Elder; if I had your loyalty, I wouldn't be so short-tempered. Understand where I'm coming from?"

"Master, I..." Canaan began, but didn't know how to continue. He wouldn't be able to lie, so how could such a question be answered? He cleared his throat and gave it a shot. "You told me once that you liked my anti-establishment ways..."

Isaac tilted his head to the side, no doubt recalling when he spoke those words. They'd been alone in Canaan's car; Canaan had given him blood for the first time, only a few hours before the Rabbit's posse confronted Rufus.

"And?" Isaac pressed, his hands sliding into Canaan's short curls.

"I want to be left alone, Isaac," he whispered, hoping he'd be permitted to use the kid's first name. "I left the brotherhood because I don't belong here. I don't believe in your cause—"

Isaac laughed and brought his hands to himself. "YOU'RE NOT HEARING ME," the boy king shouted. "I don't have a cause, Canaan! *I want to live!* To live life as I never could imprisoned in the Chamber of the Fathers." Isaac scoffed and rubbed his palms together. "Ta'avah—now *he* has a cause. Can you believe he's hoping to come here and take over my flesh? Think of it!" Isaac laughed again and turned away. "I've seen this as clear as day in Beryl's memories!" Isaac looked at Beryl. "Ta'avah possessed your brother to bide his time. He'll possess Father Theophilus, next. But he's not getting me! If he were flesh, I'd find him and crush him right now for plotting against me! How dare he? After he fathered me, raised me, and trained me to take over our people!"

Isaac's face grew red and Canaan wished for something to say to calm him.

"I'll show him!" Isaac shouted, shaking his fist toward the ceiling. "He thinks me an obedient infant who would bow down and allow him to take over my body. I'm not going anywhere! Father Damien taught me all I need to know to defeat him! Damien was a fool, but he left me the greatest legacy of all!"

Isaac pressed his lips together and somewhere in the house, a man roared with pain. He caught Canaan's eye. "I can rule the Rakum. I will. And I will have my way, even if I have to destroy you all." The agonized masculine cry rose, plateaued, and then died away. Chest heaving, eyes glazed, Isaac sunk into his throne and said, "I just killed Dimple."

The flat admission hung in the air for a few seconds before Canaan exhaled. Poor Dimple. He had saved Canaan's life, shot Rufus repeatedly moments before the Elder's attack on Canaan's nervous system turned into a lobotomy. Canaan had called out in his heart, asking Beth Rider's God to help him. At precisely the right moment, Dimple showed up with a gun.

God used Dimple to save Canaan.

Tonight, Isaac killed Dimple on a whim, with a mere thought.

"What was that?" Isaac said, zooming back to Canaan's side in a blur. "What are you thinking about? Are you BLOCKING ME?" he screamed, his chest out and adolescent arms flexing. "Elder or not, I won't put up with that!"

Canaan thought fast. "Dimple saved my life... I was remembering when Rufus attacked me."

Isaac narrowed his eyes. "I got that. Something else slipped by. What was it?"

Canaan thought of a white wall, void of décor. "I don't know, Master. I promise—I don't know. Maybe I'm still recovering. Rufus nearly cooked my brain."

Still suspicious, Isaac backed away and turned to crawl into his chair. "Beryl, you and Hoss put Dimple's corpse in the furnace. Then tap that Rabbit. Canaan, you stay with me."

Canaan clenched his jaw and when the other two were gone, he approached Isaac's throne. He had only just given blood; would he buzz off him again so soon? Canaan didn't know and realized he was also too weary to care.

7

Athens, GA
November 8th, 4 a.m.

Simon had been true to his word. A tall, middle-aged man dressed as the proverbial butler waited for him at the luggage corral. He introduced himself as Pinkston, asked if he had any luggage, and then led the way to the temporary parking.

"Mr. Miller asks if you need anything special to eat."

Javier regarded the man with a blank expression. What did Simon expect? Javier said no and the guy shrugged and opened the door of a black Lincoln Town Car.

"Then my instructions are to take you straight to the house."

Javier waited while Pinkston fell into the driver's seat and pulled the car into traffic. Was the guy Simon's chauffeur? Butler? The last time he read anything about Simon and his career, the kid had signed a two-year/12.5-million-dollar contract with the RedSox. Instead of asking Pinkston his questions, Javier remained silent and stared out the window. It was four in the morning and only a few cars accompanied them on the freeway. In a very short time, they pulled up to the deceased aunt's home.

Javier gawked at the size of Ruth Miller's foyer and followed Pinkston across the marbled floor. They passed a sitting room on the right with a large wall mirror sheeted with black satin. Pinkston continued on, turned down another hallway, and stopped at a closed door. He rapped on the wood twice and turned the knob to poke in his head.

"Your guest has arrived, sir," Pinkston announced and backed so Javier could enter the room.

Simon stood from an oversized oak desk covered with papers and waved a dismissal to the butler. Six feet, blond and fit, older, of course, but his blue eyes—even from the door, Javier read the same youthful enthusiasm and openness nineteen-year-old Simon possessed the first night they met. As soon as the door closed, Simon's face broke into a huge grin and he lunged toward Javier, arms wide.

"Javier! I can't believe it! You look… you look…" Unable to choose his words, Simon grabbed Javier into a bear hug and squeezed him tight. Javier had been mortal seven years, but hadn't hugged anyone since he last saw Simon at the now infamous Last Assembly.

Last Assembly… Javier swallowed. Since the Rakum race was founded, the Fathers periodically called Assembly, demanding attendance of the One Hundred Thousand. The one to which Jack Dawn brought Beth Rider became the last the Fathers would ever call.

Simon's embrace continued and after half a minute, he pushed back and abruptly turned away. Javier heard his breath catch.

"You're all grown up," Javier remarked, hoping to allow time for Simon to get a hold of his emotions. "You were a kid and now you're a man. A baseball superstar, no less."

"It's all crap," Simon whispered facing away and covering the hitch in his voice. "I'm washing up, my heart's not in it."

"What are you saying?" Javier took a step toward him. Whatever was bugging his friend had more to do with Javier than his love/hate relationship with baseball. Simon sniffled, blew his nose into his handkerchief, and turned around, his eyes red.

"You first. Why aren't you with David? Where's Roman?" Simon leaned back on the desktop behind him and blew his nose again. *"You could have called Beth Rider or Michael Stone. There are a dozen people you could have called."*

Javier shook his head, waiting for the correct response.

"Why haven't I heard from you in more than seven years?"

Javier shook his head again, this time with more fervor. "You told me to stay away. You made me promise."

Simon's eyebrows went up. "What?" he asked, thoroughly confused. "What question are you answering?"

Now Javier was confused. "You asked me why I haven't called you since we split up."

Simon shook his head and stood off the desk. "I didn't ask you that."

Javier watched his face to judge his intentions. "What? Yes, you did. 'Why didn't I call David? Why didn't I call Roman? Beth Rider?' Then you said, 'why haven't I heard from you in seven years?'"

Simon froze a few ticks of the clock and then looked Javier hard in the eye. "I thought you were mortal."

"What do you mean?" Javier asked, unwilling to jump into that topic before he was ready.

Simon narrowed his eyes. *"Did you just read my mind?"*

Javier's jaw twitched. It was a magic trick he hadn't used since he became a Believer. He heard Simon's voice clearly, but the man's lips hadn't moved; Javier's telepathy had returned.

"What does this mean?" Simon sent his thought precisely, obviously recalling the lessons Javier gave him nearly a decade ago. *"This has to do with why you called me, doesn't it?"*

Javier put his hands to his ears and turned to pace the room. "Please, stop."

"Okay, I'm sorry," Simon said aloud. He stepped to meet Javier where he stood and stopped him with a hand to the shoulder. "What happened?"

Javier turned and looked Simon in the eye, memories washing over him now that they stood face-to-face. They met when Simon was nineteen and so eager to serve, to donate blood, to spend time with the creature he adored. Now Simon was nearly thirty, taller, more muscular, with his yellow blond hair buzzed off in a military cut. And he had a man's experience, an adult's responsibilities — a house, a wife, a child.

Javier gasped, Simon's current information streaming to him via the physical contact. This was a new talent—the Rakum called it tactile telepathy and it had never been one of his gifts. He looked at Simon's hand on his shoulder and placed his palm upon Simon's fingers.

Jessica is two years old; Lisa-Marie wants a divorce. They live at the house in the Hamptons, while Simon stays in their apartment in Alpharetta when not on the road. He has a red dog named Jimbo and a goldfish with no name. Simon needs to call Stuart immediately.

"Who's Stuart?" Javier asked and Simon jerked away his hand.

"Why'd you ask that? I wasn't thinking about Stuart." Simon regarded Javier with suspicion, but Javier stepped back into his space and grabbed his forearm.

"He's nobody," Simon said telepathically and yanked his arm. Javier didn't let go.

Stuart Loudon, former Cow to Tork Furlong. Waiting for Simon's report on today's visit with his old Rakum master...

Javier had absorbed enough. He released Simon's arm and paced away. He'd heard of Tork. Why was Simon being secretive about a Cow named Stuart? Was he mixed up in something he shouldn't be?

"W-what's going on? Y-you touch my arm and can see into my life?" Simon stuttered. "What am I missing? Are you an Elder now?"

Javier reached the far window and peeked through the blinds to the dark street below.

Am I a Rakum Elder?

No. If he were, he'd be thirsting for blood. Javier looked down to his shirt and placed a hand on his gut. Nothing. Watching him closely, Simon crossed the room.

"What's going on?" Simon asked again, moving to stand in front of Javier, between him and the blinds. "Look at me," he hissed and waited for Javier to raise his head.

Javier looked instead at the tops of Simon's shoes. Brown patent leather. Funeral shoes. Appropriate. Simon fished around in his slacks, jingling coins, keys, whatever else men kept in their pockets.

"You're going to tell me, aren't you?" Simon whispered.

Javier trained his eyes to the carpet and Simon stopped fishing, his trinket in hand outside of Javier's field of vision.

"I think whatever happened to you is still happening," Simon whispered, then his voice fell telepathic. *"You don't know if you're a Rakum or not, do you?"*

Javier looked up and met his eye as Simon flicked open a pocketknife. With a maddening rush, hundreds of bloodlettings from hundreds of Cows flooded Javier's mind. Simon put the blade to his forearm and dragged the knife crosswise, opening up a gory wound.

Javier gasped. Nausea rose, then thick bile threatened to exit with power. Javier turned and ran from the study. He sprinted down the hall, made the left, bolted past the room with the covered mirror and propelled himself through the front door into the dawn. Pinkston called him by name, but Javier ran on.

The moon, still hanging high, was obscured by clouds, but he could see every pebble, lit up as if fluorescent, as if lit from within. It wasn't like when he was a Rakum. This was something different. Different, frightening, and much more powerful.

Javier ran on and tried to think of God. It wasn't easy.

8

Standing on his Aunt Ruth's wraparound porch, Simon breathed heavily; he'd been away from the gym too long. He had run after Javier on foot, but lost sight of him in less than a block. How could he expect to keep up with the guy? Not only did Javier have decades of training in stealth and avoidance, he had sprinted off at a shocking clip.

But didn't Javier look good…

Dark and mysterious, elegant and dangerous, like a Gypsy king from an ancient civilization. Simon smirked at his imagination. He used to pretend Javier was a guardian angel locked to earth by an ancient curse. He fantasized that out of all the people in the world, this prince of the night chose him—a goofy baseball player with a 2.0 GPA. Giving his blood never fazed him; Simon enjoyed it. But things were different now.

Frowning, Simon padded back to his bedroom, ignoring Pinkston's offers to be of service. He had a stash of Fireball in his dresser drawer and that was all the sleeping pill he needed for now. As he reached his door, two uncles rounded the corner behind him, heading for the kitchen, probably for coffee. Neither acknowledged him. A dozen relatives had come and gone since the funeral and only his aunt's brothers remained in the upstairs guest rooms.

Aunt Ruth had done right by him since he was very young. She raised him, paid his way through college, bought him his first motorcycle, and then a truck before he could buy his own wheels.

That motorcycle... A sad smile touched Simon's face as he dug the whiskey from underneath his BVDs. The motorcycle he crashed. And who was there to rescue him as he lay broken and bleeding on the side of that dark, winding road in the mountains above Atlanta? Javier d'Millier, an amazing creature he recognized on sight as something "other." It was deep, more than intuition. When he opened his eyes and looked into Javier's, their souls touched. It was impossible to fathom how deep their bond, and when they were separated after that horrible night in Nevada, part of Simon died.

But I'm better off... Simon told himself as he crossed the room to his bed and flopped atop the comforter.

Simon walked with God now. More than those weeping posers in Ruth's house, more than the chirping Protestants two doors down, more than the priests he passed on the way to the ballfield on weekdays. None of them knew God like he did. He'd seen God perform. Seen Him destroy a demon and put an end to an entire race of demonic underlings. The God of Israel was real and Simon had met Him. But...

Simon swigged the liquor, took a second pull, and waited for his face to tingle.

God. Where had He been lately? Simon's life was in the crapper—had the Big Guy noticed? Simon's Adam's apple wavered and he refused to admit he was close to tears.

His agent was stealing from him, his stats were down and his throwing arm ached with a hairline fracture. Was God hiding? And now, Aunt Ruth dies in her sleep. Had she been poisoned? Simon shook his head. The only one in the house at the time had been Pinkston and he made a horrible murder suspect.

Simon chuckled and massaged the gauze bandage on his arm. A former Army medic, Pinkston expertly wrapped it and didn't ask him how it happened. Ruth's lone employee was probably wondering if he still had a job. Simon would tell him if he knew, but he didn't. Not yet. Had Ruth left the house to him? If she had, Pinkston could stay on and Simon would move back in. He was going to go through with the divorce and Jessica was young enough to forget him and enjoy a new daddy. After all, he had heard Lisa-Marie had a beau all picked out.

Ruth's house was three floors and a basement, eight bedrooms with full baths and three half baths scattered downstairs, a giant industrial kitchen, two indoor solariums, offices, and three sitting rooms. The basement was finished with a game room including billiards and pinball machines, as well as a home theatre and a large guest suite. Ruth's house was big enough for Stuart's herd to assemble. With very little effort, her basement could be made light-tight for any Rakum guests they might have over. Stuart's Gathering was looking better and better. But what did Javier see of their plans, and what, if anything, did it matter?

If his former master returned, Simon would let him in. Maybe God sent Javier to help them figure out their next move. Simon looked at the ceiling and stared at the lazy swirling fan. His brain comfortably numb, he grinned. "What are You up to this time, Abba?"

Simon examined his heart. Why did it ache so? Why didn't he love his wife enough? She was beautiful—everyone said so. And the baby? She was perfect. But Simon couldn't hold her. Why?

Simon envisioned his heart as a two-chambered device; one half sat filled with God—to worship and serve all the days of his life. But the other half was empty, stripped bare; hollowed out by the scraping of a dirty scalpel. It was the place he kept Javier and the Rakum. Since God cleaned out his life, Simon dumped those things that reminded him of Javier. All those things he used to store in the other half of his heart.

Let God fill your entire heart, Simon, and then you'll be a whole person, just as He intended.

That was the voice of the *Ru-akh*, the Spirit of God. Simon heard Him plainly since he trusted in Yeshua as the Messiah. His advice was simple: *"Lower the barrier between the two chambers and God will flow to both sides of your heart."* Once God filled Simon's entire being, there would be enough love for everyone; for his wife and child, his friends and family, and for every child of God out in the world. But Simon held back. When Javier's people were scraped from his heart, the scarring went deep.

Simon closed his eyes and wept. He knew God was on the throne, ignorance was not an option, but he missed the old days. And he truly missed Javier.

9

Yazoo City, MS
November 9th, midnight

"**D**o you really think a locked door will keep me from wringing your neck, my brother?"

Ta'avah's voice rumbled with venom as he shouted through the doorjamb. Theophilus barely heard him, immersed as he was in a deep conversation with Elohim. He and the demon Ta'avah had slept the day away in the stolen basement and now that the sun had gone down, Theophilus came awake determined to clear the air with his Maker once and for all.

Less than a week ago in another stolen basement, former Rakum and equal, Father Damien, assured him that the Messiah still wanted him, still loved him, and still treasured him above all. If he would only repent of his rebellious deeds, the God of the humans would take Theophilus back, and oh, how he longed to desert the path he had chosen so long ago.

"Theophilus! You will consent! You belong to me, fool!" Ta'avah screamed and hammered the door with his fists. Miraculously, it held and Theophilus returned to his supplications.

Face down on the clean linoleum, eyes squeezed closed, Theophilus sought forgiveness from the One he had rejected millennia past. His reddish-gray beard rubbed the floor as his lips moved rapidly in prayer. When he had repented for everything he could think of, he returned to his initial prayer: *"Please, Abba, let me die."*

"OPEN UP THIS DOOR, THEOPHILUS, OR I WILL MAKE YOU SUFFER. YOU HAVEN'T KNOWN THE KIND OF PAIN I WILL INTRODUCE YOU TO!"

Ta'Avah's threats poured through the air with substance. Theophilus grimaced and spoke to God in his heart.

"Use me, Abba; use me to defeat Your enemy. He wants this body—let him have it. Let him have it after I've departed. It will decay and foil his plans. I give my life to You, Adonai. Do with me as You will..."

The sound of Ta'avah's abusive rants faded and within moments, the silky sound of singing voices filled his mind. Theophilus arose from his praying posture and lifted his hands to the dark ceiling.

"Abba! I am coming!" he called, although he no longer had a mouth with which to speak, for with the sensation of a gentle breeze blowing across his soul, he slipped from his flesh and became one with the Light. After two thousand years of running away, Theophilus returned to his Father's house and found peace.

▼ ▼

"THEOPHILUS!" Ta'avah cried once more and the wooden door splintered inward with a loud crash. Rushing down the steps to the cellar floor, he leapt to the old Father's side and yanked him off the ground. His flesh was warm, his eyes half-open, and Ta'avah shook him violently. "Consent! Consent!" he shrieked.

Meryl's body had carried him far, but a *Father's* body would enable him to locate and subdue Isaac Akaron. Ta'avah shook Theophilus again and this time the red-headed Rakum in his grasp telepathically whispered the magic words: *"I consent."*

In a flash, Ta'avah slipped from Meryl's body and with focused concentration, funneled his essence into the Father. Possessing another's flesh was tricky business. Even when the subject opened their vessel up to such intrusion, the invading spirit must fiercely and jealously adhere in an instant. Even a millisecond out of the flesh meant certain expulsion to the spirit realm. Ta'avah roared with victory as his last vestige crossed over, absorbed, safe inside Theophilus's skin.

"Now we will see who wins this battle!" he said moving the old Father's lips and getting a feeling of his limbs. He worked to balance on his new feet and held out his arms. Something wasn't right and a feeling of dread overshadowed his celebration.

"I consent," the voice repeated and Ta'avah screamed with fury. It wasn't Father Theophilus who invited him in, but the One who created them all, the One with whom he would never intentionally cross swords.

"NOOO!" Ta'avah yelped, shaking his head slowly and with effort. Theophilus's body was dead; he'd inhabited a corpse.

"I consent," the voice teased him and Ta'avah held his hands to his ears.

"This is not over! I will find that kid! I can use this body just as well. Watch me! I've done it before! I'll do whatever it takes!" Shouting as he jogged clumsily up the stairs, Ta'avah headed for the back door. The body would rot, but it would carry him around. The body would disintegrate, but not before he had his hands on the youth.

Trembling with rage, Ta'avah entered the garage and started the family mini-van. He was at least an eight hours' drive from Jackson with only five hours of darkness remaining. He needed a plan.

Peeling away from the suburban neighborhood, Ta'avah steered for the interstate. He'd work it out along the way. He had time. Rolling down all four windows to lower the temperature in the car, Ta'avah also turned on the A/C. A cool corpse rotted more slowly, rigor mortis could be delayed, perhaps postponed, until he reached a safe place to hole up. He'd locate a dark and quiet abandoned building a good two hours south, allow Theophilus's rigor to come and go, and then resume his trek to Jackson. It wouldn't be pleasant, but he'd done it before. Ta'avah laughed boisterously and thumped a Pinocchio bobble-head clinging to the dashboard. He knew exactly what he was doing.

10

San Francisco, CA
November 8th, 9 p.m.

"Why the mystery, Rafa? You think I don't know where you're taking me? I've known you my whole life, you can't hide anything from me," Santiago said with a laugh from the passenger seat, looking into the night and not at his driver.

Rafael smirked and turned off the highway down a poorly-tended asphalt drive. Now that they were arriving, he thought it best to offer Iago a little instruction as they entered such unknown circumstances.

"Follow my lead, amigo. The Elder has been hiding from the Brethren and may misinterpret my appearance. Also, I prefer you do not speak. *¿Comprende?*" When his friend nodded with obvious trepidation, Rafael gave him a kind smile and returned his attention to the crumbled drive. In the distance, a plantation-style edifice with six white columns and tall black-shuttered windows arose in the mist.

"*¡Madre de dios!* Is that a haunted house?" Santiago joked picking out the shape ahead of them. Rafael did not laugh.

"Elder Kilmeade's reputation has always been one of excessiveness; this is not his style," Rafael said thoughtfully in a soft voice. His exposure to the Elder had been limited to four separate meetings and in each of those, he had been one of many pups attending the Elder at Assembly. Still, if the man was sane, he would remember Rafa fondly. Mostly convinced, Rafael stopped the car a short distance from the iron gate barring the entrance.

On the other side, overgrown shrubbery did little to disguise the peeled paint on the house's exterior walls. Low flickering lights burned in a few of the downstairs rooms and as Rafael switched off his car, the front door opened fifty yards away.

"Is someone coming?" Santiago asked, squinting and leaning forward.

"Stay put," Rafael said and exited the car.

Two people headed toward them, a man and woman. The man was thin, fortyish with shaggy brown hair to his shoulders wearing jeans and a T-shirt. The woman was younger, wearing leggings and a too-small halter-top, her hair shorn off at chin-level. Rafael watched the two mortals walk casually to the closed gate. Hanging on to his patience, Rafael waited for one of them to make the first move.

"If you're sellin' somethin', we don't want any," the man drawled, not yet meeting his eye. The woman crossed her arms at her small bosom and with a snap of her chin, nodded in agreement.

"We need to see the man of the house," Rafael said, sending hypnotic suggestion.

The smidgen of information he'd heard about Elder Kilmeade's new life was that he took in strays. Rafael wasn't sure of anything else, his informants too nervous to divulge more. Maybe hypnosis would be enough to get them in. Rafael could break in, but that wouldn't be ideal. With a slack jaw and a sideways look, the man reached for the chains and the woman dropped her arms.

"What are you doing, Jimmy? You can't let these people in without checking with Mr. Star!"

The man slapped her hands away as she tried to prevent him from opening the locks. "Shut up, stupid! This is a friend of Mr. Star's. Stay out of the way."

"You're as simple as a nursery rhyme, ya jerk!" she screeched and turned back for the house. "I'm telling!" the woman called and sprinted for the front doors.

Jimmy shrugged. "Don't worry about Missy. She doesn't know your people." The chains slipped free and Jimmy pulled open the gate. "I do, though. I'm James DuPont. I served the Rakum fifteen years before Last Assembly."

Rafael nodded with approval; the guy was a Cow. He had thought that the wonderful humans who longed to give blood to Rakum were extinct and that Santiago was one of the last.

"Thank you, James," Rafael said with sincerity. "My name is Rafael."

The man smiled and his stubbled cheeks blushed red. "A beautiful name, sir. Please, call me Jimmy."

"Sir, is it?" Rafael asked and Jimmy inhaled sharply.

"Master, I'm so sorry, I meant no insult," he said and cringed as if somewhere in his past a Rakum slugged him for the offense. He shook his head with woeful eyes. "Mr. Star *insists* I don't call him that no matter how much I want to. I'm sorry if I offended you," Jimmy said wringing his hands.

"I'm not offended," Rafael said and briefly squeezed the man's shoulder. At the contact, Jimmy's eyes grew round and his lips parted. Rafael recognized the reaction; Cows desired affection and approval from their masters and apparently Kilmeade withheld his touch. "Come close." When the man stepped up, Rafa gave his cheek one slow stroke and closed the gesture with a wink. Jimmy exhaled forcefully.

"Oh, Master Rafael," Jimmy whispered and swallowed hard. "Thank you. Thank you." Then, working to disguise his sudden excitement, Jimmy waved toward the car. "I know your time is precious. Bring your friend, it's okay." He waited until Santiago reached their position and turned toward the house, keeping abreast with Rafael.

"I'm the only Cow here. My advice is that you pretend you're human." He glanced at Rafa as if checking to see if he'd stepped over the line giving advice to his master, but Rafael gestured for him to continue. "Everyone here sees Mr. Star as a wealthy recluse with a fondness for lost people. I was drawn here some years ago by my conscience, you know, as a Cow," he whispered the word before continuing. "But everyone else ambled in because they needed a place to crash or someplace to dry out. Okay, here we are." James touched the doorknob and looked back at Santiago. "You okay, man? You haven't said a word."

Rafael held up his hand. "He's fine. Take us to Mr. Star."

"Of course. Right this way," James said with a quick nod.

Rafael thanked him softly and they entered the house. The wide foyer had no furniture, but as they entered the first sitting room dozens of people lounged on chairs, sofas and beanbags, smoking, drinking, laughing, and sleeping. The atmosphere was subdued, quiet, and every face he looked into appeared peaceful, almost drugged. Rafael sniffed the air, but detected only cigarette smoke and incense.

"Rafael, sir," James said in a quiet voice, "at the end of this hallway, in the last room on the right."

Rafael proceeded down the hall. The odor of the humans was sorted out and he sought Kilmeade's distinctive scent. By the time he reached the door in the darkened hall, he picked up a very faint trace of the man's aroma and he wondered how he was able to suppress it. While he was reaching for the knob, the door opened in, pulled aside by the woman from the driveway.

"They're here, Mr. Star," she said, looking Rafael in the eye with a smug glint. He hardened his gaze and she paled, gasped, and bolted down the hall out of sight. A boisterous laugh emanated from within and Rafael entered the room. Santiago dawdled watching her escape and Rafael cleared his throat to bring the man around. Deep purple walls reflected no light and a black-lacquered chest of drawers on his right supported a dozen pillar candles flickering and smelling of frankincense.

Lying down the center of the king-size bed with his head propped up by his arms, Kilmeade watched them approach. The man looked exactly as Rafael remembered: movie-star handsome, veritably glowing with power and confidence. "Master?" Rafael whispered.

"Rafael Domingo Gonzales Ricci," the Elder said laughing, his pale gray eyes twinkling with humor. "Come close, old friend. Let me have a look at you."

Rafael smiled and ignored the fact that Kilmeade fabricated the rest of his name. Rakum were assigned a moniker during First Ritual and he had been simply *Rafael* for 245 years. Kilmeade's eccentric reputation tickled his memory as he stepped toward the bed and nodded a greeting in the way of their people. In a quick movement, Kilmeade swung his feet to the floor, stood, and met Rafael face-to-face.

Slightly taller, Rafael smiled on him. "It's good to see you, Master. You look well."

"You are even more beautiful than I remembered!" Kilmeade exclaimed. He scratched his chin sizing up his guest and then smiled showing white teeth with canines noticeably sharp.

"I am happy you think so," Rafael returned with a grin.

"But what kind of hello is that after all these years?" he cooed, forcefully grabbing Rafael into a tight hug. *"Oh, you smell goooooood, my brother,"* Kilmeade whispered so low only another Rakum could hear. *"Do you know how long it's been since I've laid eyes on one of our people? Oh, Rafa—"* he shuddered and placed a lingering kiss on Rafael's neck.

Rafael endured the affection and wondered again at the Elder's sanity. Such demonstrative actions weren't part of the Rakum code. However, he sincerely needed the man's healing touch applied to his best friend and so Rafael wrapped his arms around the Elder's back.

"I apologize for the intrusion, Elder—" Rafael began, but Kilmeade cut him off with a hiss in his ear.

"It's Mr. Star, my brother. Mr. Star. Kilmeade is dead." Still whispering low enough that Santiago couldn't make out the words, Kilmeade spoke with his lips against Rafael's throat. *"Rufus killed him in his sleep. Terrible tragedy. Despicable way to treat the greatest Rakum that ever lived."*

"Oh, yes, you're right," Rafael replied just as quietly. *"He was the finest Elder I'd ever met."*

Kilmeade chortled and moved one hand from Rafael's back to brace at the nape of his neck. *"Little brother, Mr. Star has a craving for your blood..."*

Rafael furrowed his brow and wished his back wasn't to his friend. What would Santiago make of their display? Would he keep his calm if the Elder began drinking his blood?

"Mr. Star is welcome to whatever I have to offer," Rafael said for Santiago to overhear.

"I'm frightening your Cow," Kilmeade whispered and drew his tongue across Rafael's throat.

"He'll be fine," Rafael answered aloud. "He will be still," he added for extra assurance.

"Good," Kilmeade said and pushed elongated canines through Rafael's skin.

Rafael made no outward sign of surprise, but he was curious. Rakum only sported fangs when they took a Dying Buzz. [12] He tucked the information away and closed his eyes, the sensation of being drained of blood turning his stomach. Behind him Santiago gasped, but obedient to the core, said nothing. It wasn't uncommon for a Rakum to buzz off his brother, but the taste could not compare with the blood of the mortals. Nonetheless, Kilmeade was sucking greedily and soon moaning with delight. More memories of the reclusive Elder burst forth in Rafael's mind.

A century ago, Kilmeade was chastised by the Ten Fathers for taking the Dying Buzz for an entire year while on assignment at a Rakum-controlled indigent hospital. Subsequently, he was exiled with Elder-candidate Canaan to determine if the physical and psychological effects of the transgression could be reversed. Kilmeade consumed only Canaan's blood for two years and completely recovered. If the Elder manifested fangs tonight he must still be drinking humans to death, at least periodically. Also, if the prospect of drinking Rakum blood excited him, Rafael reasoned, maybe two years of Canaan's offerings gave him a taste for what they would normally disdain.

The sound of Santiago's nervous shifting increased and Rafael willed him to remain quiet. Within another minute, Kilmeade closed his mouth against double punctures and pressed his tongue to Rafael's throat another long moment. Rafael ignored the swimming in his head and waited for the man to step back. Maybe with his gut full of blood, he'd be even more likely to help Santiago get well.

---

[12] Prohibited by the Ten Fathers, the Dying Buzz is the practice of drinking a mortal to death. It brings various side effects (euphoria, increased mystical and physical power, altered physicality of teeth, hair, nails, etc.), all short-lived unless the infraction is frequently repeated.

Finally, Kilmeade laughed low and breathy in Rafael's neck and ran the fingers of both hands into his hair. "For the love of all things pink, I needed that!" Kilmeade sought Rafael's eyes, their noses only inches apart. Rafael didn't know how to respond. "What do you need from me? I sense illness in your friend. Is this why you've come?"

He didn't seem upset at the prospect of helping an old Cow get well. Remaining as close as Kilmeade desired, Rafael nodded.

"Santiago's been getting sicker and the doctors can do no more. I recall you are a healer, we are at your mercy."

Kilmeade backed a few inches to consider Santiago standing a few feet away. "He was a looker in his youth, I can tell."

Rafael's smile went to the side. "He's still a looker, Mr. Star. Iago, come close," Rafael ordered. Santiago tip-toed up until he was standing next to Rafael and facing the Elder. Rafael dropped his right arm from Kilmeade's back and draped it about Santiago's shoulders. "What do you say? He looks exactly like Antonio Banderas, am I right?"

Kilmeade's grin remained as he lifted one hand to touch Santiago's cheek. "I sense the bond between the two of you. It goes deeper than the blood. Why do I see this man in your arms as a child?"

"He is a Legacy Cow, Master. His father and grandfather were my Cows. He was orphaned at five and I have tended him since then." Santiago's eyes grew misty and Rafael looked away.

Kilmeade huffed. "You've parented him," he said derisively. When the silence stretched on, Kilmeade sighed and asked Santiago, "Did you at least leave a son behind for your master?"

Rafael answered for him. "Iago's wife and daughter perished in a fire. He has not remarried."

"Then you better get busy, old Cow. You don't have much time left and you owe my little brother a son!" Kilmeade backed away from them both and sat on the edge of the bed facing his guests.

Rafael struggled for what to say, certain the Elder was toying with him. He knew what they'd come for; he'd hinted at it already. Rafael caught Santiago's eye and his friend wiped the water from his cheek.

"I can mate your friend to one of my girls here. Is that what you need?" Kilmeade asked his question through a ridiculous grin. "Assuming he can still perform. Are you sick down there, amigo?" Kilmeade asked gesturing toward Santiago's lower half.

Rafael inhaled, unhappy to hear his friend's illness mocked. He monitored his tone and squared his shoulders. "I ask you to heal his disease. He has prostate cancer that hasn't responded to chemo. The doctors have given him less than a year."

Kilmeade frowned. "He's used up, my brother. It would sap all of my energy to heal that sad pile of meat. Give him a vacation and pick him out a nice coffin."

Rafael's heart swelled in his chest; the pain of losing Santiago would be great. His face must have shown his discouragement, because Kilmeade stood and crossed to stand before him.

"Seriously, Rafa," Kilmeade said, his voice grave, "I can heal wounds, broken bones, correct imbalances, but disease?" He shook his head.

Rafael closed his eyes and concentrated on maintaining his composure. Kilmeade laid a heavy hand on his shoulder and shook him playfully.

"I see that your attachment to this Cow is extreme and I am not offended." Kilmeade lifted both hands to gently cup Rafael's face. "If you promise to stay with me, be my companion, I will cure him."

So he *was* able to heal the man? Rafael had no qualms about staying with the Elder if it meant Santiago's prolonged life. Could they both stay? He didn't wish to be separated after he was well. Kilmeade smiled.

"Both of you will stay. He stays for you, you stay for me. Do we have a deal?" Kilmeade watched Rafael's eyes and when he agreed with a nod, Kilmeade called for Jimmy in a loud voice. The door opened and Jimmy waited to hear his instructions.

"Take my brother to see Veronica," Kilmeade said and winked at both of his guests. "She'll feed you in anyway necessary. *She thinks I'm a vampire—so don't blow my cover*," Kilmeade whispered with a laugh and Rafael didn't know if he was joking.

For a moment, he wondered about leaving Santiago alone with Kilmeade, but what choice did he have? He had taken a risk by coming to see the Elder, but what if he healed the man fully? It would immensely ease Rafael's strained heart. Decided, Rafael sent Iago an encouraging glance and followed Jimmy out the door.

They found Veronica dozing in a pink-sheeted bed two doors down. She was plump, groggy, and happy to help Rafael in any way she could. Rafael closed the door behind him and let her do her thing.

11

When they were alone, Kilmeade regarded the quiet Mexican with humor in his gaze. He had no qualms for what he was about to do; who would care? Who'd try to stop him? It was every man for himself and after downing Rafael's incredibly strong Rakum blood, he felt invincible. He would keep Rafael close no matter what. Kilmeade motioned for Santiago to approach, which he did after a moment's hesitation.

"How old are you, my friend?" he asked, mentally measuring the man's age by his wrinkles and slightly stooped frame. He was a sturdy specimen, handsome and burly, a dedicated Cow Rafael could be proud of. When Santiago whispered his age, Kilmeade smiled. "Old man, I cannot roll back the years, but I will stop time from eating your body in this way."

"*¿Que?* I don't understand you."

"I think you do. You've served my little brother for more than four decades. You know there's only one way to save you now."

Santiago paled. "You're going to make me a Rabbit."

Kilmeade smiled.

"Shouldn't we warn Rafa?"

Kilmeade laughed aloud and grasped the Cow's shoulder. "Oh, he'll know the instant you transform. I ask you, are you willing to live on, or did you secretly desire death?"

Santiago shook his head, his eyes round. "I had resigned myself to die, but I want to live."

"And what of your master?"

"I will serve him until I draw my last breath, I promise."

Kilmeade chuckled. "You don't have to promise me anything. I'll extend your life to keep Rafael with me. I need him." Kilmeade laughed into his hand. "I *really* need him."

Santiago had no response and he stood ready for whatever Kilmeade would do next.

"This is going to hurt," he said and steered Santiago to the edge of the bed. With a swift motion, he whipped out his pocketknife and sliced his wrist deep. "Drink my blood, old Cow. Do it quickly."

The anxious Mexican knew what to do and he realized it would hurt. He took four urgent swallows and pushed away writhing in pain. Kilmeade put his wrist to his mouth as the wound closed and watched the man groan in discomfort. An Elder's blood leeched into a mortal like acid, but when it dissipated into the man's system, it would make him incredibly difficult to kill. Presumably, he'd live forever as Rakum Rabbit...or until he killed himself. Before Last Assembly, Rabbits ended their lives rather than be subject to the Rakum's insatiable lust. In fact, never did a Rabbit live more than a few months.

Unless you count the legend of the Lost Rabbit...

Kilmeade dropped his grin and considered the errant thought. Myths were based in fact so maybe it could happen. If a Rabbit was never tapped, would the Elder's blood eventually take over his system?

What does it matter now? The Rakum are over, Kilmeade smirked inside. This Cow would be a Rabbit with only his master to sup on his blood. Kilmeade chortled again, happy with his decision.

"You will be my little brother's personal pet—" Kilmeade began and looked at the opposite wall. By the sound of crashing furniture in the next room, he'd been found out. Rafael was on his way in and Kilmeade burst into a new fit of giggles.

Rafael stood so quickly from the chipped writing desk that it flew backward and slammed into the wall, shattering as if made of glass instead of pine. Veronica had been sitting in his lap and because of his movement she jumped with fear and fell onto the nearby bed. Blood ran down her throat from the wound he'd made with his knife, but her safety was not on his mind at present. The aroma that hit his nose turned his heart to ice.

Elder Kilmeade! What did you do?

Leaving the room, his hand crushed the knob and the wooden doorframe cracked as he misjudged the strength necessary to manipulate such common items. None of this registered as his anguished heart crushed knowing Kilmeade had turned his favorite mortal into prey, a Rabbit that his brethren would detect from miles away. Why had he put his trust in a Rakum whose every thought was for his own comfort? Rafael burst into Kilmeade's room with enough speed to knock the door off its hinges. The Elder watched with interest as he reached Santiago, putting his hand to his nose.

"*Why?* Why would you do this to me?" he asked Kilmeade while waiting for his friend to shake off the dizziness of becoming a Rabbit. "This man means everything to me; he is all that I have." Barely bottling a potent mixture of rage and despair, Rafael looked hard at the Elder a few feet away. "*Why?*"

"You said to save him. Look," Kilmeade said, no smile, but his eyes twinkled. "He is well. I fulfilled my promise."

Rafael screamed in fury, the sound welling from deep within and literally shaking the walls. The mirror on the room's bureau cracked before he'd spent his lung capacity. Several humans appeared in the doorway and he bared his teeth, scarcely in control of his anger. Kilmeade went to the door and shoved the onlookers gently out. In a mental fog, Rafael overheard the excuses he made for his obviously mad guest. As the Elder left the room, in his mind he heard a terse command: "*You will get a hold of yourself, pup.*"

Rafael slumped to the floor facing his friend, aware that because of the way he'd stormed in, they couldn't close the door for privacy. Santiago had no idea why he raged and Rafael uncovered his nose to explain.

"*¡Usted paria ahora!*[13] You'll never be safe again! Why did you consent? Haven't I explained what this means? Iago! Answer me!"

Rafael's hands became fists as the aroma of the Rabbit assaulted his senses. How long? How long since a Rabbit passed his way? Years, maybe a decade, and he was in no position to resist the hunger in his gut Santiago's new identity created.

Santiago leaned forward from his sitting position on the bed and grasped Rafael's upper arms. Rafael fell backward out of reach and sat on his rump on the carpeted floor.

"Don't touch me! What will I do?" Rafael covered his nose again and slapped his forehead repeatedly with his free hand. "What will I do?"

"Rafa, calm yourself," Santiago begged slipping to the floor before him. "The Rakum are gone; there's no one to chase me; be rational…"

Rafael met his eye and cringed at the sudden mental images of Rabbits he abused in the past. "No one will chase you? What about me? *Me,* Iago? I am a Rakum! I won't be able to resist you!"

Rafael inhaled deeply and reflexively narrowed his eyes; very soon, he

---

[13] "You are a pariah, now!" (Spanish)

would be at Santiago's throat and he loathed the loss of self-control as the Rabbit's scent mercilessly washed over him. Plus...wouldn't he have to share?

"My brothers, Iago...we have rules..."

"But the Rakum are no more," Santiago began and Rafael shook his head violently.

"Our Fathers are gone, *sí*, but WE STILL CHASE RABBITS!" He shouted the last phrase and Santiago jumped. Rafael worked to lower his tone. "Someone will come. They will come." Rafael blinked his eyes, a thousand what-ifs assaulting his senses. He'd have to protect his friend—could he? Would the Cow he called a son be collected by those now in control of their race?

Rafael growled in anger once more and sent his friend a pained glare. "*Mi hijo, amado,*[14] you have done a horrible thing."

"But the Elder said it was the only way," Santiago said, openly crying. He reached out closed his fingers around Rafael's forearm.

"*Iago...*" Rafael whispered and looked at the hand on his sleeve. His stomach lurched into his throat and he pulled his friend close until he was halfway in his lap. Their chests together and Santiago looking over Rafael's shoulder, he whispered to his friend the only thing he could think of as the blood lust overcame him. "I'm so sorry, *amado.*"

"*Esta bien*—" Santiago began, but was cut off by a lightning-quick stab of Rafael's knife, the blade puncturing his jugular in an instant.

Rafael covered the wound with his mouth and sated the monster within. Avoiding human blood was doable because he had Santiago; resisting Rabbit blood was not within his capabilities. From now until eternity, he'd be at his beloved's throat—son, friend, Cow—the carefree, self-controlled nights were gone. As he supped ferociously, he could only hope that over time he'd grow accustomed to the hunger that burned at his friend's new scent.

Santiago was unconscious when he pulled away, his throat wound healing within moments fueled by the poisonous blood he had ingested. Rafael rocked him in his lap, seeing in his long memory the same man as a boy frightened by a local dog and rushing to his arms for comfort. "*I'll watch over you, Iago, for as long as you live,*" he'd told the boy on more than one occasion. Rafael lowered his face into his friend's shoulder and closed his eyes. If only he had tears to cry.

---

[14] (Spanish) my son, beloved person

12

San Francisco, CA
November 9th, 3 p.m.

Kilmeade propped his feet on the footboard and stared at the dark ceiling. It was three in the afternoon and he and the pup Rafael were holed up in his sealed bedroom, one even Jimmy couldn't get into. He trusted the Cow who came to his aid back when Rufus attempted to kill him, but only to a certain extent; a human was still human and prone to mortal weakness.

James DuPont... Kilmeade closed his eyes, tempted to fiddle with the man's head, which he did sometimes during the day when he was bored. DuPont had an extremely open mind and could receive Kilmeade's simplest telepathic lob. This was a treat since before Rafael arrived and boosted his talents, telepathy had lost its luster. Today, he resisted bugging the Cow. Self-control would always be a very powerful tool for the Rakum that employed it.

DuPont had indeed been the first human to arrive at his rumble-down house, drawn to him by whatever drives a Cow's senses. Kilmeade had been in hiding two years and when Rufus's pogroms finally found him, DuPont helped Kilmeade fake his death. Today, as far as he could discern, no Rakum knew he lived. He had heard in stolen telepathic fragments that Rufus was bested a few nights ago, but the Rakum that stepped onto his throne seemed more dangerous than his predecessor.

Yes, Kilmeade thought with no small amount of weariness, *I'll avoid the brethren who bend the knee to this new leader until I know his intentions.*

Rafael whimpered in his sleep and Kilmeade shook his head. This one was hopeless. How had he survived attached to his Legacy Cow like a man obsessed? If the depth of his affection had been identified before the Fathers were destroyed, Santiago would be dead. How did the kid keep it hidden for forty years? Rafael mumbled a few sounds and Kilmeade rolled over, now facing away.

It is time to leave this place...

Bored with his little group of mortal disciples, at nightfall he'd take Rafael and his Cow and go. Maybe he'd take Jimmy, if he wished to accompany them. Kilmeade didn't use him as a food source, but he had proven to be a loyal and capable day man adept at disposing of the occasional drained body.

"You should have left him be, Master," Rafael said in a low voice and Kilmeade didn't turn. "I'll never get that odor out of my nostrils. My brethren will find us..."

"Good," Kilmeade hissed and rolled onto his back. "I have avoided your brothers too long." Kilmeade picked up the cadence. "Your blood has strengthened me." With a gentle exhale, he sought the pup's mental thread. Before Last Assembly, he need only desire to speak to a brother and it would happen. Had Rafa's blood awakened his skills as much as it had his spirit?

"Rafael, you and I will find joy again," he sent silently, testing their link.

Rafa turned his head, his eyes pained but impressed just the same. *"I hope so, Master..."* he replied clearly.

Kilmeade wiggled his eyebrows. "I will find your brothers telepathically, like the old days. Like-minded brethren, ones we can trust, ones not serving maniacs."

Rafael's mind filled with questions and Kilmeade turned to meet his eye. "Ask."

Rafael shook his head slowly. "Do you want to drink Rakum blood exclusively?"

"No, but my chosen diet is not your concern." Kilmeade paused to read more of Rafael's consternations. Momentarily, he found a likely reason. "Rafa, confess, did you leave your Elder too early?"

Rafael's face expressed surprise. "In my sixteenth year, Elder Bago perished in an avalanche. I survived on my own for eleven years. When the Fathers finally sent for me, they deemed me graduated."

Kilmeade narrowed his eyes recalling Bago's accident. He had taken in one of the Elder's proselytes at the Fathers' command, but to leave a fledgling Rakum alone before he graduated First Ritual was a cruel decision. To Rafael, he offered, "This means the Ten were impressed with you. Bravo."

Rafael's chin tipped slightly. "I have disappointed you, Master."

"No, still... you lack a few lessons Bago would have imparted had he had the chance. Be open to my teaching and you will learn what bits you missed. Understand?"

"Of course, I am grateful." Rafael exhaled slowly. "I should never question an Elder. This is where I slipped."

Kilmeade grinned and elbowed him as they reclined side-by-side. "Ask questions to seek answers, but never doubt my edicts. Learn you well, an Elder is *never* wrong."

The room fell silent and still Kilmeade discerned questions running past the youth's mind. He sighed and gently nudged him again.

"Ask," he sent telepathically.

"I heard the majority of the Elders are dead, the Fathers, too. Do you know if this is true?" he asked quietly.

"All of the Fathers have perished. And I sense only Elder Canaan survived. I cannot locate him, but I will... soon." Kilmeade hummed and thought to add more since the pup listened so closely. "A few days ago, Canaan and my brother destroyed Elder Rufus and put an end to his tyranny."

"Elder Rufus was destroyed?"

"Yes." Kilmeade's lack of details kept his response short.

"Mierda..." Rafael exhaled and then looked over. "You have a twin brother?" Rafael asked unaware as they all were of Kilmeade's fraternal twin.

"Yes," Kilmeade answered. A Breeder was never used twice and generally, twins were separated at birth to prevent development of human familial tendencies. However, being fraternal, Kilmeade and Roman enjoyed their youths together for the most part, keeping their birth relationship a mystery from all but the Fathers.

"I didn't know," Rafael said in a faraway voice.

"None of you could have known." Kilmeade pondered his long-held secret. The Ten Fathers were no more; why carry on the pretense? What if he went to see Roman, chat with him and rehash old times?

"Where is he now?"

Kilmeade sighed. "Roman follows the God of the mortals. Still, I wonder... what if I could bring him back to his former glory?"

"He transformed into a human," Rafael said simultaneously sorrowful and empathetic. Kilmeade nodded.

I could bring Roman home...

Kilmeade's heart quickened. Such an endeavor would require a *heap* of power. Power he could possibly develop if he consumed the most potent blood he could find—Rakum blood. His system learned to metabolize it in response to his twenty-four-month punishment.

"Master," Rafael whispered.

"Rafael," Kilmeade responded, mimicking his sad accented voice.

"I am concerned for Iago."

Kilmeade paused before he answered. The young Rakum beside him was suffering and his despondency turned Kilmeade's attitude in equal measure. What could he say to cheer the kid?

"Rafa, you are beautiful and precious," Kilmeade began and turned to lie on his side facing Rafael in the darkened room. He ran his hand down Rafa's arm to end at his wrist where he held him gently. "I haven't seen a Rakum in a very long time and your appearance has reinvigorated me in every way." Kilmeade took a cleansing breath and continued more animated than before. "I am a powerful being, the greatest of all our Elders, and it is time I came back to life fully."

Rafael's eyes widened and he nodded in agreement. "And you are more than gracious to invite me to remain with you. I should be chastised for my behavior and I regret my lack of trust. I will do better."

"I will not chastise you for being yourself." Kilmeade smiled. "Having you here brings back the past. If I close my eyes, I can almost imagine we're in my bunker at The Cave before everything went to hell." He sent Rafael a wink.

Rafael offered a sad smile, but Kilmeade grinned.

"Consider this. You and I both disassociated from the Brethren before the Rabbit mess. And we weren't alone. Other Rakum were sneaking about, doing things the Father's disapproved of, even before the debacle with the Rider book."

Rafael made a thoughtful nod. "I see what you mean, but what does it matter?"

"I don't know that it does. The Rider woman's book steered our brothers away from the Old Way at the same time many of us were already falling out." Kilmeade withdrew the contact with Rafa's wrist. "If Last Assembly never took place, I can count at least a hundred Rakum I knew personally who were subverting the High Father even never hearing about this woman's religion."

Rafael nodded and shrugged simultaneously. "I never considered..."

"Have you ever been to Alabama?" Kilmeade asked in a rush and Rafael shook his head. He then reached across Rafael to grab the man's cell off the far nightstand. "Tonight we will head for a college town in Alabama called Tuscaloosa. I looked it up on your phone earlier." After a few moments, he showed Rafael a screen of airline ticket deals.

"Flying, Master? On a mortal airline?" Rafael began and sat up, swinging his legs off the bed.

"We'll take two nights," Kilmeade answered, hoping to assuage the youngster's trepidation. Before the Rabbit trouble, the Rakum used their own exclusive airline to travel by night any time they needed free of charge. Nowadays, precise planning was required to assure a Brother didn't end up burned in the sun either by a delayed flight or not finding shelter between sunup and sundown. Kilmeade had flown across country several times since the debacle and assured Rafael he knew how to keep them safe.

As the pup Rafael leaned over his knees, periodically rubbed Iago's scent from his nostrils, and silently mourned for his favorite Cow, Kilmeade bought plane tickets. And because he could afford it, they would all ride first class.

13

Jackson, MS
November 9th, 6 p.m.

Beryl carried the scars of his association with the demon, Ta'avah, in his flesh on the favorite part of his body. He leaned into the bathroom mirror and gingerly plucked loose skin from his scarred cheek. As much as the tissue yearned to heal, Isaac's curse prevented proper regeneration. Beryl scowled at his reflection, careful to avoid any mental retaliation against their new leader.

Mere days ago as he pounded on Rufus's door to be rescued from the sun, Dimple pulled him inside at the last moment, blinding himself for three hours as a result. Now Dimple was dead, killed on a whim by their tiny Fuhrer.

Beryl shook his head. He had been burned over ninety percent of his body that morning and when he awoke the youngest, yet most powerful of their kind was laying hands on him to repair the damage. Isaac worked diligently until all that remained to be healed was Beryl's face.

Beryl stared at his reflection, wishing the deep red mass of burned tissue that covered his right cheek and eye would magically disappear. Yet there would be no healing; Isaac's word stood firm.

"Prove your allegiance to me and I'll consider removing that scar," their child-like leader had told him. "It won't heal until I say so. 'Til then, let it remind you of your hate. Ta'avah did this to you—work with me, fight for me, and together we'll fix everything that's broken with our people."

That was two nights ago. Since then, Isaac had been cleaning house. His first order of business was to destroy the two Rakum he disabled during the Takeover – the night he and the Rabbit's posse came in to destroy Elder Rufus. Two of Rufus's goons had tried to prevent him from entering and he snapped one's neck and shoved another's nose deep into his cranium after breaking his jaw. Both Rakum survived, but that same night, Isaac ordered them beheaded and their bodies, along with Elder Rufus's, to be incinerated in the furnace located in the bowels of the house. So who was left of Rufus's staff?

Beryl and Hoss both served under Rufus and now served Isaac in utter fear. Elder Canaan was also in residence, a practical slave to Isaac since the kid only had a taste for Rakum blood and the Elder's was the most potent. Being from the same pack but born two centuries apart, Beryl had history with Canaan. Recent events involving his woman had ruined any brotherly affection between them. And then there was Boris, the stoolie Isaac adored. Their motley bunch catered to the boy, desperate not to displease him. He was capricious and his moods fickle; his retaliation for disobedience was sudden and painful. This was new to Beryl. The Fathers did not assault the Brethren without cause. Isaac knew how to hurt a Rakum, how to torture him and make him beg for mercy. So very different from the Old Way.

"I need your head in the game, Beryl." Isaac's voice slithered in Beryl's mind. He abruptly turned from the mirror and left the bathroom. *"Get in here. I have a job for you."*

"Yes, Master," Beryl said in a low voice, knowing the kid would hear it even several rooms away. All the Rakum suffered a loss when Abroghia deserted them, but Isaac's strength multiplied daily and Beryl would do nothing to get on his bad side. He made his way to the kid's room—the same one Rufus claimed when he was in power—a sizeable study with a large cushioned armchair on one end and a desk on the other. Isaac sat cross-legged on the "throne," elbows on the armrests. When Beryl entered, he gave him a huge smile.

"Glad you could join us!" he said, sounding like a child on the playground. "You're going to help me help brother Canaan."

Beryl nodded to Canaan who grimly returned the gesture. Isaac had been draining his blood daily with no regard for how it debilitated a Rakum who was otherwise extremely powerful. Here and there, in weak moments, Beryl felt for him, but tonight he felt nothing.

"Canaan needs young blood, Beryl, and you have an excellent track record hunting the mortals."

Beryl nodded knowing his past was now Isaac's entertainment. When The Last healed him, he read his memories—all of them. Now The Last perused his personal history more easily than one read a newspaper. Isaac was an amazing seer and Beryl hated that he was subject to him.

"Would you rather have died? I'd think you'd be happy to live here with us, your brothers," Isaac said, a glint in his eye that could easily blossom into anger.

Beryl shook his head and hoped that was sufficient. It wasn't.

"I'm warning you, Beryl! You'd better placate me! I don't need you!"

Beryl startled and approached the boy's chair, falling to his knees. "Master, I'm guilty of disrespecting you and I don't deserve to live," Beryl reeled off, meeting the boy's eye with a sorrowful and begging gaze. "You are amazing and wonderful and I promise to serve your purposes. I swear my life to you..."

"That's more like it," Isaac said and smiled at Canaan, Boris, and Hoss. "Now get up. We have work to do. Tonight, you will bring Canaan some really young kids, eleven or twelve at the oldest. He isn't withstanding my appetite and the blood of the innocents will help him recover."

Beryl pressed his lips together. Many remarks came to mind, but none of them would please his master. *Control your bloodlust* was a good one. *Hunting children is the most dangerous game of all* was another. But aloud, he said, "What do you have in mind?"

"Hoss said he sometimes hunts at high school ball games. The children feel safe there and they like to sneak off in twos and threes. You and I will go find us some youngsters and bring them back here."

Beryl put a hand to his scarred cheek and Isaac hopped down from his chair.

"I'll put a Band-Aid on your face," he said as he approached. "We don't want to repulse the humans do we?" Being a foot shorter, Isaac reached up and pulled Beryl down by his collar. He placed his palm on his cheek and instantly, heat flared in his face. "That scar will return by sun-up," he stated flatly and then turned to Hoss. "What school do we hit, big guy?"

As if he'd been daydreaming, Hoss straightened his spine and cleared his throat. "Toss me your phone," he said and Beryl lobbed it over. Hoss opened a browser to the address he'd memorized and showed the screen to Isaac. "Emerald High School. It's a half-hour away in Pearl. I haven't hunted this one; it looks ripe. They play tonight at seven."

"What do you think?" Isaac asked Beryl and handed over the phone. Beryl scrolled through the site's photos. The children varied in ethnicity and socio-economic status; it was a good choice. He scrolled the first few message boards and ascertained that the entire city of Pearl would be in attendance, high school football on the top of their priorities. Beryl pocketed the device and nodded to all present. He didn't have to announce his findings, by a slight hum and irritating tickle behind his eyes, he was aware of Isaac eavesdropping on his every thought. *Oh, well, it saves me some breath.*

"Yeah," Isaac grinned and headed for the door. "Hoss, let me know when the delivery truck comes with my new stuff."

The kid put his finger to his temple indicating the Rakum should *think* it to him. In his day, Beryl had been one of the most telepathic Rakum alive; Isaac made his talent look like scraps. The delivery was for the largest flat screen television the store sold along with every imaginable accessory. Isaac had a taste for electronics and since he'd been in charge, he'd purchased quite a lot.

"You get changed," Isaac said to Beryl taking his arm to pull him into the hall. "You need to look like one of them. How do I look? Boris got this for me off a kid he grabbed at the park last night."

Beryl considered Isaac's faded blue-jeans and striped polo. "You're dressed like a nerd. Is that what you're going for?"

Isaac laughed. "*Precisely* what I was going for! Okay, let's go see what you have in your closet. You'll be my cool older brother. I've never hunted like this before—how exciting!"

Beryl resisted the urge to roll his eyes and headed to his bedroom. The Last was right behind him and he resigned himself to a night by the kid's side. At least for a few hours anyway he had his face back.

14

Athens, GA
November 9th, 6 p.m.

"That's Aunt Ruth's goy[15]," Simon said with humor as the butler walked away. They sat on the back porch sipping iced tea and watching the clouds pass over the moon.

"Goy, eh?" Javier chuckled.

"Aunt Ruth used to introduce him like that—'meet Pinkston, my goy.' Or 'and this is Pinkston, my goy.' One night when I was in town, he asked me what it meant. He thought it was a term of endearment, like she thought he was her paramour. He was so relieved when I explained it!"

Simon laughed and Javier appreciated the sound, thankful the tone of the evening was lighter than the night before.

"Were you okay last night? Where'd you go? You can stay here, you know, as long as you need to," Simon said, meeting his eye.

"I know, I made do." Javier had slept the day away in the train station, vomiting up air when the sun was at its zenith. Javier's eyes rest on Simon's bandage. "I'm sorry about last night," he said softly. "How's your arm?"

Simon smiled and touched the gauze with his other hand. "Stings like hell," he chuckled and rubbed the area. Javier got up from the porch swing and knelt beside Simon's wicker chair.

"A lot of things have happened since I saw you last and I don't even know where to start." Javier tugged at the bandage until the tape pulled up half-way and Simon winced. "You didn't use to be so sensitive," Javier joked and pulled the gauze free. The hasty puncture wound had scabbed over, but remained red and swollen. "Do you think you cut it deep enough?"

"I'm the one who needs to apologize," Simon murmured. "I don't

---

[15] "Gentile" (Hebrew)

59

know what got into me. I'm so embarrassed."

"We're both sorry, then," Javier said and covered the wound with his palm. He looked up from his kneeling posture and met Simon's blue eyes. "I'm not a Rakum, Simon, but I'm something else. You had that part right."

"Are you trying to heal that cut?"

"I want to see if I can," Javier said and concentrated on the wound as he did in the old days. After a few seconds, he knew it wasn't working. He shook his head and replaced the bandage. "I guess I can't."

"Well, thanks for trying."

Javier stood and returned to the swing. "Sure, and please, don't do that again."

Simon chuckled uneasily. Javier fell silent and Simon booted him gently with his toe.

"Was it bad-disgusting or bad-wonderful?"

Javier raised his eyebrows. "What?"

"Did you run off because you were grossed out or because you wanted my blood?"

Javier swallowed to bide his time. He wasn't sure what his reaction meant. He didn't lust for blood, *per se,* but he also wasn't disgusted at the idea of drinking it. God wouldn't want him to drink it—maybe that was supposed to be enough.

"You don't know, do you?" Simon merely thought the words and Javier picked them up easily.

"Let's come clean," Javier said, watching Simon's eyes. "I'll go first."

Simon nodded hesitantly. "Okay."

"The first two or three years after David and I got comfortable in our new lives, I started having bad dreams about my brethren." Simon was about to ask him to clarify and he beat him to it. "The Rakum who didn't choose God. *Those* brethren. I dreamed that they called to me. Sometimes I dreamed I rejoined them. When I woke up, I'd repent and ask God to take those dreams away."

"I have the dreams, too."

Simon didn't mean to share that thought, but it cascaded to Javier as if he'd spoken aloud. Javier chose to ignore it and continue his story.

"Last week, Roman picked us up and took us to Beth Rider's house in Montgomery. He said we were in danger and we were going to have to go to battle for God."

"Again? But the High Father was killed," Simon said, his eyebrows raised.

"Another Rakum rose to fill his shoes. A crazed Elder named Rufus. He kidnapped David's girlfriend and Jesse Cherrie's wife to draw us to Jackson."

"Okaaaay..." Simon said, but Javier discerned the man's mind was wandering, possibly pondering things better left alone.

Javier reorganized his thoughts and blurted, "Listen and pay attention. I lost my focus and made some unfortunate choices while in Montgomery." Javier looked to the night sky and swallowed before continuing.

"What could be so awful?" Simon asked, seemingly accusing Javier of being melodramatic. Javier turned to catch Simon's gaze and narrowed his eyes.

"It's bad. I took blood from this Rakum kid named Isaac, a true monster—a protégé of the Fathers." Javier waited for something to register in his friend's eye. "He was Abroghia's last offspring."

Simon's blank expression spoke volumes. He didn't understand the significance of what Javier shared, but he needed to. He needed to know why he shouldn't rip his flesh around Javier. Why he should help instead of hinder. Javier sighed.

"Isaac lived secluded in the Chamber of Fathers for forty years. In all that time, he drank only their blood." Again, Javier watched Simon's eyes, but he was still nonplused. "Isaac was being groomed to take over the Rakum when Abroghia's time was up. Understand? Isaac is stronger than the High Father..."

Simon shook his head a tiny degree. "Father Abroghia had a time limit?"

"Did you read Beth's account of her time with us? With them?" Javier corrected himself and despised that he had to, his mind walking two paths.

"No, I couldn't finish it. She wrote me all wrong—she made me sound so, I don't know...gay."

Javier laughed unexpectedly. "Geez, okay. At any rate," he chuckled again, "you should read it. Abroghia was a true demon. He had a limited time to do his thing here on earth and he planned for that contingency. His last offspring is much more powerful than he was in the flesh and completely self-serving."

Simon nodded and rolled his hands. "My point is, so what? You won't be seeing them anymore, right? They will do their thing and you'll do yours. Can't we co-exist like before?" Simon clammed up and Javier discerned he was walking down old paths, avoiding the way his new Master asked him to go. Javier tucked the information away and sighed.

"Maybe we will—who knows? I only wanted you to understand that I'm still working out what I am. I drank the kid's blood..." Javier lowered his voice even though they were alone.

"And?" Simon asked, matching Javier's volume.

"And when a mortal drinks from an Elder, he becomes a Rabbit. What happens when a Rakum-turned-mortal drinks from a Father?" Javier waited while Simon's eyes widened. "Essentially, I did that. I didn't know it at the time and I don't think Elder Canaan meant me any harm, but things are weird for me. I'm not like I was, but I'm not human, either."

"Who is Elder Canaan?" Simon asked, although Javier had read the man's name in his mind the night before regarding the Cow Stuart Loudon. Rather than pick a fight, Javier played along.

"He's an Elder I met as a kid and last week he helped us defeat Rufus..." Javier ended the recollection, unwilling to share more since Simon was showing much too much interest in the Rakum and not enough in Javier's problem.

"Where's Roman?" he asked with a tilt of his head.

"Can you stay on topic?" Javier snapped and then apologized at Simon's hurt expression. "We'll get to that. As for Elder Canaan, he got tight with that kid Isaac and I got tangled between them..."

Javier stopped talking. Simon didn't say anything either and silence enveloped the porch. In fact, the crickets had stopped chirping and the breeze had vanished. It was eerie. Suddenly alert, Javier sat up and looked around the yard. When the hair prickled on his arms, he rose to his feet.

"Who could that be?" he whispered, staring into the distance. Ruth's yard ended at a stone wall and on the other side of the wall similarly appointed estates were blocked together into a giant neighborhood of the wealthy.

Simon stepped beside him. "What?" he asked quietly.

Javier held up his hand and narrowed his eyes. Besides the power of his new eyesight, the street beyond Ruth's gate was well-lit and he didn't see anyone standing around. Javier sniffed the air and didn't catch any aromas that might tell him why he felt watched.

Simon grew impatient and touched his arm.

"I don't know!" Javier hissed under his breath. "I'm going out there."

"Where? Into the yard?" Simon asked, his sarcasm barely disguised. "Down the street? Going to get some Krystals?"

Javier glared at him, and unlike the old days, the guy didn't flinch. Instead, he stared back and crossed his arms at his chest. Javier turned and stepped off the porch.

"Well, I'll leave a light on for you," Simon called after him. "See you later." And then he was heard opening the front door before he said sarcastically, "Good talk, Javier. Good talk."

Javier didn't turn back, but made his way across the yard to the wall. He followed his senses, but it wasn't as he remembered as a Rakum. He was pulled from inside—as if an invisible rubber band tugged him in the way he should go. Javier steeled his nerve and followed the pressure from within. Was it God leading Him? Was it something else?

When Javier reached the high stone wall, he climbed it as easily as a Rakum and trotted into the next yard.

"Judas Priest! He sensed us! Shit!" Polly giggled as he turned on his heel and sprinted back to the car, running comically, knees high. Guap was right behind him, repeating, *shit shit shit*, but laughing even harder. They had parked one block away from the Cow's place and when they reached their goal, Guap hadn't yet unlocked the doors.

"ShitShitShit!" the stocky Latino Rakum grunted, although he was still chuckling. Once he balanced the key fob and pointed it to the Camry, it chirped happily and all four doors unlocked. *"STUPENDO!"*

"Go-go-go-go!" Polly shouted as he fell into the passenger seat. Guap got them in gear and Polly watched behind the car for the Anomaly.

"Anonomoly, amonoly," he murmured, playing with the word Stuart Loudon gave them for d'Millier before they embarked on the current recon. Stu had been collecting every Cow he could find and organizing them, all the way down to having directors, administrators, and secretaries. Polly and Guap were the only Rakum the enterprising Cow had located so far, which suited them just fine. No sharing. Polly grinned at the sudden memory of his last blood meal, ecstatic they found the guy after several years of struggling without the High Father's protection.

"Anomaly," Guap said, interrupting his thoughts.

That was what Stu said Javier D'Millier was now and Polly found the Cow's seriousness amusing.

"Anomonie," he said and smiled.

"A," Guap said and caught Polly's eye, pretending to teach him a new term. "Nom. Ah. Lee. Anomaly. Easy, man." Guap said, his accent not hindering him a bit.

"Anominoly," Polly laughed and sipped the flask before returning it to the center console. "The Anomenomi almost got us back there.

Shiiiiiiiiit."

"No, man, he sensed us then he ran off the wrong way," Guap replied and slowed the car to the speed limit. "He's not a Rakum—I got a good whiff of him. He's something else. Something we haven't seen before."

"Yeah, well, I don't get it – I *know* him. He *used* to be a Rakum." Polly watched the night speed by as he spoke. "I chased him around the Group Lair mercilessly. He was a hoot and bloodthirsty—DAMN. He'd drink anybody and anything." Polly howled until his breath gave out.

Guap grinned at his display. "Too bad, looks like he's one of those Traitors," Guap said thoughtfully. "Stu was trying to explain how he got that way, but when I look at that Cow all I think about is food." Guap grinned and Polly nodded.

"I know, I know," Polly laughed. "He's delicious!" Pounding the dashboard like a set of drums, he added with a chuckle, "Javier was so tiny, I used to chase him all over the place."

Guap shook his head and returned his attention to the road. "Well, he's not small anymore and we just ran like hell from *him*."

"Yeah, we did," Polly agreed, still drumming. "How far to Stu's hotel? I'm starving."

"Fifteen minutes," Guap responded and turned up the radio. "Stu will feed us. He always finds a way."

Polly cheered and then began to sing and drum even harder.

15

Emerald High School's Ray Rogers Stadium was packed with people of all ages coming, going, and cheering on both sides. Isaac and Beryl walked through the throng, heading for the darker far end. The Mississippi winter had finally rolled in and Isaac clutched his jacket collar. He flipped up the hood and glared at his companion who ignored the icy wind that lashed his face and neck. Beryl had a lot more experience being uncomfortable.

"I hate this weather!" Isaac barked and stepped lively to keep up with Beryl's long stride. "Slow down, you walk too fast."

Beryl slowed his pace. *"Big brothers hate little brothers, Master. If you struggle to keep up, it'll be more believable."*

Isaac frowned, but did as suggested. Beryl was infinitely more adept at hunting mortals and it was wise to bow to his skill. He had hoped that by sharing the guy's memories he'd also adopt his abilities. As it turned out, not so much. No big deal, Beryl would teach him. He might not always have servants at his command. Life was unpredictable; Isaac learned this the day the Rabbit Beth Rider destroyed everything he knew.

"There," Beryl said telepathically and stopped short. Isaac followed his line of sight and at the end of the crowded bleachers, three giggling pre-teens jogged into the dark shadows of the adjacent school building. *"I'm going to creep up and listen to them and gauge their weaknesses…"*

"Good. And hurry, I'm freezing," Isaac replied silently. Beryl shot him an irritated glance that instantly softened; the guy was learning. Isaac was young and inexperienced, but he was the only one sufficiently empowered to run the Rakum race. Even after Last Assembly, he disappeared with Father Damien who spent every waking moment teaching him the skills he would need to take over leadership of the flailing brotherhood. Isaac smiled at nothing; he was definitely up to the challenge.

"Listen," Beryl whispered and Isaac concentrated on the three youths speaking a dozen yards away in the shadows.

"...*I spent it yesterday at Target. What about you? Your mom gives you money for the game, right?*"

"*I had to give it to my stupid sister. She made me promise to pay her back today and I was afraid to not do it. Last time I owed her money and didn't pay on time, my daddy tanned my hide.*"

"*Well, I have three bucks. Wanna see if Gregory has any money? He usually does.*"

"*No, he stinks—I mean, he literally smells. Let's go ask your mom. She's in the stands, right?*"

"*She won't give me any more money. Dad lost his job and she's all depressed.*"

The trio started walking again, heading away, deep in conversation. Beryl pulled two twenties from his wallet and handed them to Isaac.

"*These kids look about twelve. They'll spook at me because I'm older.*"

"*Just tell me what to do,*" Isaac sent back, keeping an eye on the kids as they sauntered away. Beryl filled him in on the plan, assuring him it worked many times for him in the past. Isaac nodded when he was ready and Beryl headed back to the car. Plan initiated, Isaac proceeded toward the kids.

When he was a good twenty feet behind them, the one in the middle, an Asian girl with long straight hair took her hands out of her jacket pockets to playfully slap one of her friends. Isaac saw his chance.

"Hey, guys," he called and jogged up behind them. "Hey, I think you dropped this."

All three turned at the sound of his voice and none of them seemed alarmed. The girl's eyes widened at the sight of the two bills and she took furtive glances at her friends.

"What?" the boy on her right asked. He was the tallest of the three, but no taller than Isaac.

Isaac held the money out toward the girl. "Just now, when you took your hands out of your coat, this fell down from your pocket."

"Oh, yeah," the girl said and stepped closer to grasp the money. "My mom puts money in my coat all the time. I forgot." She caught her friends' eyes and they grinned.

Isaac put on a friendly smile and hoped it would get him an invitation to join them. The two boys didn't like him right off, but it had everything to do with his wholesome appearance, not that he wasn't human. The girl favored him a lot and she gave him a dimpled smile.

"Do you go to Jones High?" she asked, gesturing to the visitors' side of the stadium. Isaac nodded. "I'm Minji, and this is Fred and Hank."

"Hey," he replied. "So, are you guys heading to the front of the school? My brother said there's a fight going on there. S'posed to be pretty cool."

"Oh, yeah?" Hank asked, looking behind him. "I'd like to see that."

"Yeah, some kid named Gregory is getting his butt whooped," Isaac said and started walking. "I'm on my way to see it myself."

"Stinky Gregory's done messed up now!" Fred said and joined Isaac. The other two fell in, laughing and making jokes about their wayward classmate.

By the time they reached the school's quiet front yard, Beryl had parked the car and was leaning against the hood. The lot was surprisingly dark and the kids would only see his silhouette until they were closer.

Isaac touched Fred's shoulder and pointed to Beryl. "There's my brother. Let's ask him what happened."

The gullible kids scampered alongside Isaac, completely fearless. When they reached the BMW, Beryl gave them a bored look.

"What happened? Is the fight over?" Isaac asked him.

"Where'd they go? I can't believe we missed it!" Hank said.

"How'd they disappear so fast?" Minji asked.

Isaac waited for Beryl's signal and he opened the back door of the car. Taking one last look around the deserted schoolyard, Isaac and Beryl simultaneously rushed the youngsters and shoved them into the waiting car. Before they could begin to yell for real, both he and Beryl were loaded and the doors closed. Beryl peeled away from the school and joined the traffic leaving the stadium while Isaac silenced the kids with a powerful suggestion.

"Be quiet and I won't kill you," he sent the three kids telepathically. Years of watching television and horror movies hadn't desensitized the children to a real threat as they shivered and fell silent. Isaac relaxed in his seat in the front and caught Beryl's eye.

"Good job," Beryl sent silently.

"Great job, you mean," Isaac replied.

Beryl nodded. *"Canaan will enjoy this gift."*

Isaac nodded, smiling ear-to-ear and looked out his window. It was in his best interest to keep Canaan healthy. The only Rakum left more powerful than Canaan was one he wanted to drink from next—Theophilus. Then he'd explore powers he'd only dreamed of. Damien said he'd be able to transport himself great distances, disappear from human view, that he would even be able to *fly* if he continued on his current path. Flying. That would be sweet.

There had been a girl, her aroma hung in the air, but Canaan hadn't seen her. Yet the two boys Isaac gave him provided enough young blood for Canaan to feel like his old self. In fact, if Isaac would have allowed him to take it a tad further, he might have burst with joy at the invigoration the children gave him, but The Last wouldn't allow any of them to drink mortals to death. Such a thing transferred additional power and as such was not permitted.

It didn't matter—Canaan stretched and flexed and then roared as loudly as he could in the basement of the old house. The furnace simmered across the huge floor space and the two kids slumped unconscious and dying against the adjacent wall. Soon, someone *not* an Elder would come toss them in.

Canaan smiled again, his chest swelling with pride in his magnificence. He needed a mirror. He needed to see Marcy—she always made him feel like the king of the world.

"You can see Marcy now, Elder Canaan," Isaac cooed to him from upstairs. *"I'm excited about your recovery. Go show your woman. I'll leave you alone."* Canaan sensed Isaac disentangle from his psyche.

So... it was to be a conjugal visit. Canaan jogged to the stairs. Halfway up, he licked his lips and tasted the coppery aftereffects of his meal. He needed a shower and to brush his teeth; Marcy could never know he murdered two children to be reinvigorated.

But that's who I am. That's what I'm supposed to do, Canaan assured himself and headed for his own room upstairs, avoiding for the moment the suite that imprisoned Marcy. *I'll be a Rakum Elder and she can be a human.*

Feeling mostly justified, Canaan rushed through his grooming and put on his best cologne for his lover. She hadn't seen him since she'd been turned over and she had been bled several times by the Rakum in residence. Still, no one assaulted her sexually and Canaan had Isaac to thank for that. The Last wanted Canaan to like him, to *love* him, even. Leaving Canaan's favorite human alone was a huge move in the right direction. Canaan smiled and hoped Marcy didn't hate him too much.

"She's really pretty," Boris said to Isaac, his voice full of gratitude. "She's still crying, though. I don't think she's gonna consent any time soon. She's terrified of me."

In Boris's assigned room tied to the armchair the girl sniffled, too exhausted to cry any longer. Boris waved his fingers at her. Sitting next to Boris on the mattress edge, Isaac shook his big leg playfully.

"Does it matter that much?" Isaac asked. He was aware of the tenet about not taking blood from females unless they consent, but why did it matter? He was Master and he couldn't care less.

Boris shook his head, his eyes shining with respect. "It's flat, it's boring, um, like..." he looked up to the ceiling and clucked his cheek. "It's like drinking pond water when you want whiskey. Does that make sense?"

Isaac smiled at his favorite and shrugged. "Canaan's an Elder—I'll have him mark her for you. Rabbits don't have to consent, right?"

Boris's eyes grew wide. "Seriously? Master! Thank you!"

Isaac grinned, happy to make his favorite so joyful. "And here's my edict – this Rabbit belongs *exclusively* to Boris, for as long as she lives, no one but you may touch her."

Boris could smile no bigger and so he simply shook his head in wonder. "Master, Master—I don't deserve your kindness," he burbled and rolled up his sleeve.

Isaac accepted the offer. Boris was no Elder, but Isaac had developed a taste for him.

16

Athens, GA
November 10th, 1 a.m.

imon woke to see a dark figure standing over his bed. Instinctively, he gathered his strength and lunged out from under the covers. By the time he slammed into Javier's chest with his fists, he recognized his friend and apologized. Javier covered his mouth with a clammy palm.

"Hush!" he said in a harsh whisper and with a strength he remembered, forced Simon onto his back to be enveloped by the thick comforter. Javier was a silhouette with liquid eyes devoid of color in the dim lighting and Simon's pulse increased. He parted his lips to ask what was wrong, but Javier's hand only clamped down further. Without caution or care, Javier dropped his upper body atop Simon's causing him to exhale forcefully. Eyes wide, Simon panicked—he couldn't breathe.

"Javier, what's going on?" he shouted telepathically and glanced at the clock. *"It's one in the morning! What are you doing?"*

"Be still," Javier whispered. Chest to chest, Javier reached for Simon's wounded arm with his free hand. Ripping off the bandage, Javier yanked the wound to his mouth.

Simon gave a few tugs and when he couldn't get free, he maneuvered his pinned palm against Javier's side and shoved with all his might. Javier was not dislodged and Simon screamed against his hand.

"Shhh," he heard in his mind.

"You're scaring me! Stop!" he sent silently. When he wasn't released, Simon fought harder. Javier's strength was steel against him and the feeling of violation and betrayal stunned him. As a Cow, he'd given Javier his blood regularly, but that had been voluntary. Besides, Javier had always been gentle. At the moment, he was sucking blood violently from the still-tender wound and holding Simon down like an insect.

Simon continued to yell angrily through Javier's fingers as he began to swoon. How could his friend have drawn off enough blood to make him

70

dizzy? Surely only a few seconds had passed. Simon twisted his face inches to the left and caught the time again: 1:05 a.m. Five minutes had passed? Simon couldn't make sense of it.

His vision filling with white spots, Simon rolled his eyes to the dark ceiling. Javier wouldn't kill him; he was 100% certain of that. So, what was he doing?

The hand on his mouth slipped off and Javier jerked his lips from Simon's arm.

Simon gasped, "what's going on?"

"Be quiet," Javier whispered and pushed himself off Simon and found his feet. Looking down on him, Javier wiped his chin with the heel of his palm, his eyes dark and unreadable. Simon tried to stay awake and his laceration stung horribly, but soon his vision went completely white and he was out.

In the morning, Pinkston shrugged when Simon asked about their houseguest. Apparently, Javier left the house before dawn. He borrowed one of the extra cars and left a two-word message for Simon: "I'm sorry."

Simon slumped into the desk chair opposite Aunt Ruth's—now presumably his—desk. Grabbing up the handset, he started punching numbers. He was supposed to contact Ruth's lawyer and set up a time to sign papers. He was supposed to call his wife and get an update on their daughter's last well-kid doctor's appointment. And he was supposed to call his agent and let him know when he'd be back.

Simon grunted and punched Stu's number instead. To hell with what he was supposed to do—he wanted to find Javier. To help him discover whoever, whatever it was he was turning into. Stu could help. He was still a Cow. He knew people. The phone rang three times and went to voicemail. Simon sighed and left a message for him to return the call.

Stuart Loudon was an Aussie, transplanted twenty years ago by marriage and deserted by his American wife soon after. Ill-prepared for the internet boom, Stu's brick-and-mortar travel agency folded the next year, and he slowly became semi-transient. He discovered he was a Cow when he met a Rakum named Tork at a nightclub. He stayed near his Master for the next several years until—as they all were forced to do—he gave up waiting for Tork to return. The Last Assembly took all of their masters away and Stu made ends meet the best he could with odd jobs and gigs with the Turnip Trucks cover band.

Simon met Stu by happenstance at a sports bar three years after Beth

Rider "happened" to the Rakum race. Simon lowered his head onto his arms and allowed the memory to return. Stu would call him back soon and until then, why not think on better days?

It was Simon's second year of pro ball. The team lost by two runs and Simon joined his teammates for a few tear beers. The evening progressed as expected; one by one, each man who became too drunk to drive had a team representative quietly run them home. It was nearing 1 a.m. when Simon pushed away from the bar ready to call the driver. Simon said goodbye to the bartender and when he stepped off the stool, he ran into another patron.

"Oi! Watch it, mate!" the man said displaying his short martini glass even though it had been empty and nothing had spilled.

"Sorry, man," Simon said and noticed the guy wore the T-shirt of a local band. "Hey! I saw the Trucks in Louisville three months ago. Where'd you see 'em?"

The man put one hand on a bar stool and looked down at his shirtfront, taking a moment to focus. Then he smiled at Simon, pointing to his shirt.

"That's us, mate! I'm a Turnip!" he said and turned his pointer into a handshake. "Stuart Loudon." He removed his camel fedora and fluffed his hair with his free hand.

"Oh! Okay, I didn't recognize you. Simon Miller," Simon said and shook his hand, liking the shaggy man with the friendly eyes immediately. Ten years older, Stu sported dark blond hair past his ears and a forty-eight-hour beard. He was Simon's height, without the athletic physique.

"Sit down, let me refill that glass." When both were seated, Simon waved to the barkeep. "One more Bud, and for my friend...?"

"Martini, that's all. Next shout's mine, all right?" Stu said and thanked Simon. "You're a good bloke, Simon Miller. You were here with the team, right?"

"Guilty. We come here when we lose to Kentucky."

"You lost? That's crap," Stu said sincerely.

"Ahhh," Simon waved his hand, dismissing the entire topic of baseball. "Tell me about the Trucks. How'd that get started?"

Stu began a tale that thirty minutes later mentioned, "Master Tork," and Simon's radar pinged.

"Did you just say, *Master* Tork?" Simon had asked, his head to the side. Stu froze in place, expressionless, and Simon repeated himself in a conspiratorial whisper. *"Tork was your master?"*

Stu swallowed the last drop of his martini and pushed off the stool, never losing eye contact. He looked for a private table and because of the hour, there were plenty. Simon followed him away, a small smile on his face. He only called Javier master around other Rakum, but in private, Javier never wanted to hear it. Still, just because a stranger in a bar says he has a master doesn't mean it was necessarily a Rakum. Yet what else could it be? Simon was still smiling when Stu sat across from him trying to think of what to say.

"Did you call him 'master' all the time or only in private?" Simon asked, his expression as neutral as he could manage. Although he and Javier intentionally dropped all contact, he still thought about their time together. The chance to connect with another Cow seemed too good to be true. Stu answered after a few thoughtful seconds.

"Always. You?" he asked, also keeping his expression unreadable.

Simon blushed and lowered his eyes. "Nah, Javier hated that. We were friends."

Stu's face lit up and he exhaled audibly. "Javier? Yours was called Javier. Oh, god, I'm so glad we met here tonight," Stu said excitedly, his voice low even though no one was nearby. "Where is he? Master Tork disappeared. Just vanished!"

Simon nodded and proceeded to fill Stuart in on the entire Beth Rider Rabbit calamity, leaving God's amazing deliverance largely out of the tale.

For the next two years, they kept in touch via email when Simon's busy schedule allowed. Only recently, when Aunt Ruth died, did he contact Stu and ask him if they could catch up in person. And now seven long years after Last Assembly, Javier showed up out of the blue behaving strangely. Simon wanted—no, he *needed*—another Cow's sympathy.

Simon sat up and redialed Stu's number. Humming a tune, he waited and this time his friend picked up on the third ring.

"So what did you find out?" Stuart asked.

"I'll be getting the house. Got the word last night and it'll be official in a month," Simon replied. "Ya'll can start coming. My uncles are here, but come anyway. I don't care if they see you arrive. It's my house now, not theirs."

"Right!" Stuart said with glee. "I'm already in town at the Hampton. Gimme your address and I'll be there this morning."

Simon rattled off the information, glad to know his friend had arrived. Now maybe he'd help decode Javier's spouted tale.

"Stu, what do you know about an Elder named Rufus?"

"Rufus? He was bad news. Got it on good witness that Rufus was the oldest living Elder and he tried to bring things together for the Rakum after the High Father left. Why?"

"Where is he now?"

"One source told me he was offed last week. That it had to do with the same blokes who ruined everything to begin with." Stu's voice turned hard. "Somebody ought to do something about them."

"Hey, don't forget, I was with them so don't lump us together. We did it for everyone's good," Simon said, questioning himself along the way. *You're slipping, little Simon, don't be bad, little Simon,* his conscience sang. Simon blocked it out. "Anyway, who's in charge now?"

"I don't know. What have you heard?"

"I might know who's going to take over for them. I had my visit from Javier."

"You beauty… what happened?" Stu's joy could be felt through the phone.

"I'll tell you when you get here. Hurry. We have a lot to do before the rest of the herd arrives." Simon shuffled the papers on his desk and found the one for which he'd been searching: his contract with the Sox.

"I have news for you, too," Stu said and his voice became even more animated. "I found us two masters."

"Two Rakum? Who are they?" Simon asked with trepidation. Not all Rakum were nice to Cows. Could Stu tell the difference?

"Don't sound so paranoid. They're wonderful—the good kind. I'll tell you more when I get there." Stu disconnected the call and was gone.

Simon stared at the desktop and thought about what Stu said. Stu had known only one Master and as far as Simon knew, never had a bad experience with him. But Simon had been attacked and nearly killed by twin Rakum during Last Assembly. If it hadn't been for the healing efforts of Stone's friend Jesse Cherrie, Simon would have died.

So, they're not all bad, Simon told himself, again ignoring his conscience that tried to remind him God abhorred them *and* the demon that spawned their race.

I need to snap out of it and stop being so dramatic! Simon shook his entire body and punched his agent's number. He expertly put on a weary, sickly voice. How much would it cost him to break the contract? He had over eight million dollars in the bank; Lisa-Marie would take half and Ruth's house was worth at least a mil. It might work out okay. Plus, he'd be with Javier again—then his heart would be whole.

As his agent's answering machine clicked on, Simon scratched at his bandage, surprised that it didn't sting or itch. He mumbled a message into the phone and peeled back the paper tape over the wound. To his amazement, the wound had healed. Not like before, when healed by Javier-the-Rakum, completely erased as if it had never occurred. No, this time, Javier-the-Mystery left a scar of the deepest purple. Simon ran his hand over it numerous times, studying the slick surface of the otherwise normal scar tissue.

Not a human, not a Rakum, but something else.

Simon looked to the ceiling and sighed. Would God stop him if he began to fall in love with Javier all over again?

Save me from myself, he prayed and wrestled God one more time.

17

"Boris, your gift is ready," Isaac said as he led his favorite into the basement holding area. The two boys' bodies were long gone, but the girl remained. Moments ago, he had watched with interest as Canaan marked her. She had writhed and screamed like an actual rabbit in a trap as his blood leeched into her pure system. When she quieted, it was done, and Isaac telepathically heard Hoss and Beryl come to attention at her scent. It made him happy to deny them—all except Boris, who deserved this and more.

"Master, again..." Boris stopped speaking as they reached the cold floor of the cellar. A small form stood in the far corner with her back to the door. Boris shivered. "I don't deserve this."

Isaac laughed. "You're the *only* one who deserves it. You're the only one I trust." Isaac watched Boris lick his lips and make a few furtive glances his way, as if the gift could be revoked any second. "You want her, don't you? Go ahead, then."

Boris surged forward and grabbed the youngster by both arms. She screamed and then fell silent, stunned by the ferocity of his attack.

Isaac waited for Boris to finish, thinking about his own next meal. During his last sleep, he dreamed that Father Theophilus was dead. Isaac had been foretelling the future with incredible accuracy since he was eighteen so there was no doubt it was true. Canaan had been providing blood every day and last night's double feast on the two boys increased the Elder's vigor and vastly improved his attitude. Still, Isaac would need to let up on the guy. If only there were more Elders—

"Elder Kilmeade..." a distant voice whispered deep within his consciousness and Isaac closed his eyes to concentrate.

Someone—a Rakum grunt he did not know—had just spoken to an

76

Elder in the present tense and Isaac picked up the communication. It happened to him more and more every day and since he'd defeated Rufus and conquered Canaan, his every ability magnified each time he used them.

Elder Kilmeade... Isaac pondered the name, waiting for more impressions to filter in. He blocked out the sounds of Boris enjoying his Rabbit dinner to concentrate fully. His mind toyed with the Kilmeade memories belonging to Canaan and Beryl—both transferred to him earlier, but Isaac shooed them away, seeking fresh revelation. Within a few moments, another hazy transmission trickled past.

"The car is out front. Everything is prepared."

Isaac furrowed his brow to call up a mental image of the speaker and a dashing Latino Rakum appeared in his vision. Tall and muscular, he spoke respectfully to another. This one not as tall, but similarly built, with longish, auburn hair and eyes as pale as a storm.

"How is your nose?"

"I'm fine, Master. I apologize again for overreacting."

"What's done is done. Come, we have a long trip ahead of us."

Immediately, Isaac realized this Elder was the Apostate Roman's twin. Isaac inhaled deeply and in his excitement, he lost the connection and his eyes flew open.

"Boris!" he shouted and sprang to his servant's side. Boris was finished with the girl and she dangled unconscious from his massive hands. "Come! We have much to do!"

"Yes, Master," Boris answered with urgency. When it looked like he might leave the child on the floor, Isaac gestured to her with one hand.

"No, bring her. She's yours. Let's go!" Isaac scooted up the basement stairs with Boris right behind carrying the Rabbit over his shoulder.

Rafael slipped into the driver's seat only after Kilmeade was comfortable on the passenger's side. Iago and Jimmy sat in the rear, both men lost in thought. Rafael couldn't meet his friend's eye anyway; he'd buzzed off him again as soon as the sun went down. Afterward, Iago swore up and down that it was fine, *he* was fine, but none of that helped. Rafael did not like being out of control and since his Cow had become a Rabbit, staying off him would be impossible.

In Rafa's peripheral vision, the Elder's fingers flew to his temple. A tiny grunt sounded and then Kilmeade lowered his hand and pursed his lips. Rafael waited as long as he could, but recognizing the gesture, asked him about it when the Elder offered no explanation.

"May I ask...who was that?"

Kilmeade rolled his head to the left and met Rafa's eye. He didn't speak for a long minute, as if formulating a proper response. When he finally did reply, he faced front and put both hands on the dash.

"The Last was just here," Kilmeade whispered shaking his head. "This kid isn't like anything I've ever encountered."

Rafael nodded, his own telepathy tweaked ever since coming in contact with the Elder.

"His telepathy is different. Unique. It's as if he's *here* when our minds touch." Kilmeade shook his head. "He'll be translating soon."

Rafael started the car, his spirits lower than ever. *"He's only fifty years old; if he translates at that age, he's more powerful than the Fathers,"* he sent telepathically.

Kilmeade rubbed his face and leaned into the leather seat. "Take us to the airport, pup. I do not have the power to block that one. All we can do is stay away from him." After a moment, Kilmeade added in a low voice. "He has my beloved brother Canaan with him."

Rafael made no sound, wondering how the Elder knew.

Kilmeade answered quietly. "When he *visits*, I see him as well. It isn't crystal clear, but I saw Canaan being held by force. Curiously, before tonight..." Kilmeade chuckled then and looked out the window, "the Last had no awareness of my existence. *Shew...* he's certainly excited now."

"Does he want to destroy you?" Rafael asked as he steered them toward the interstate.

"*FFfffft,*" Kilmeade responded with his lips. "Not at all. He wants to own me." Kilmeade rolled his eyes in Rafael's peripheral vision. "Oh, I sense his need, too. He wants me very, very badly."

"Will he restore us? He is a Father, if the legend is true..." Rafael said with a flicker of hope that the kid might set things straight. No matter what rumors and telepathic warnings his spirit received regarding the youth, deep down, Rafael wanted order among his kind.

Kilmeade shook his head, staring into the night. "No, my pet, put away that naïve optimism once and for all. Isaac Akaron offers the remaining Rakum only subjugation and misery."

"I appreciate the advice, Master," Rafael said morosely, not caring if the Cows in the back heard their conversation. They were in the same boat and may as well know the obstacles ahead. Rafael caught Iago's eye in the rearview mirror for a split-second and looked away. A glance at Jimmy found him fast asleep, not a care in the world.

"What do you see of The Last's next move? Anything that might help us?" Rafael asked.

"This Rakum is a child with a child's needs," Kilmeade said with a shrug. "His immediate plan is grandiose no-holds-barred self-gratification. He wants what he wants and he wants it now."

"What does he want?"

"The blood of the Elders, electronic gadgets, and enough Rabbits in the house to keep his closest minions happy."

"Iago is a Rabbit," Rafael said without planning to. Kilmeade agreed with a small sound. Looking out the windshield, Rafael recovered enough to continue. "It doesn't make sense, his plan. Buy stuff, tap Elders, and make Rabbits?"

"He is a child, after all," Kilmeade chuckled without smiling and crossed his arms. "On a happy note, if it comes down to it, his immaturity could be a significant weakness. Only age and wisdom can best him; those things he lacks and cannot attain by force or theft."

"Maybe we won't encounter him, then," Rafael mumbled and concentrated on the road. Kilmeade grunted in agreement and said no more.

18

The rigor had passed, but the green and yellow discoloration on Ta'avah's stolen torso disturbed him. He was a powerful entity and should be able to control the bacteria and microbes ruining all of his hard work. Ta'avah cranked the air conditioning to maximum and steered the dead man's mini-van down the interstate. In three hours, he'd confront The Last and assume his body. It was the plan all along, to breed a Rakum the Ten Fathers could prepare for such an eventuality. Ta'avah simply did not expect it to arrive so soon. Ideally, Isaac would be fully-grown before he assumed his flesh. Elohim must have enjoyed surprising Ta'avah by dispatching an unassuming Rabbit to decimate the Rakum race.

Meh, it's not ruined. This is exactly what I planned, Ta'avah told himself and grinned with dead Theophilus's swollen cheeks. *See, Elohim, I still win. I'm still here and tonight, I'll start again. All You've done is move up the timeline. I'll soon get Isaac's body. He's young and more powerful than any being that ever walked this earth—*

Ta'avah abruptly ceased his internal ramblings. Challenging Elohim and the deity of the One He sent had always been fun, but he was coming too close to actually garnering a reply from the Creator. Ta'avah didn't want that so he pressed the gas and increased his speed.

To his internal organs, he commanded the bacteria to fall dormant. Whether they would or not, he'd know in a couple of hours if his belly distended and his face continued to swell. *I only have to hold this body together a few more hours...*

Flashing lights and then an abrupt two-burst police siren snapped Ta'avah out of his reverie.

"Pull over and keep your hands where I can see 'em. This is the police!" an authoritative voice hollered via loudspeaker.

Ta'avah punched the gas. He had been traveling seventy-five already, but now he needed the stolen vehicle to get him as far away from the cops as possible while he came up with a plan. How had they snuck up on him? If he had time to think, he would have blamed Elohim—how else could there suddenly be three marked police cruisers directly on his tail? Ta'avah cursed as he topped out at ninety-five and the police had no problem keeping up with him in their Dodge Chargers.

"Pull over!" the voice commanded.

Ta'avah caught a glimpse of the men in the first cruiser, their faces set and frowning behind tinted glass. They were probably hoping to apprehend the murderer of the stupid little family in Yazoo City. Ta'avah needed an escape and he was in no shape to face off with six-plus armed police officers. Theophilus's decomposing flesh was less cohesive than ever and all the power and concentration he could muster was not preventing the tissues from dissolving.

"Last warning, pull over!" the voice shouted as the nose of the number-one cruiser dipped dangerously close to the mini-van. Ta'avah swerved, barely maintaining control of the car. Then with no other options, he exited the interstate and violently hit a dirt side road, kicking up dust in the frigid air. The police were mere yards behind him, but if he could just get a quiet moment, he could translate.

CRASH!

The number-one cruiser slammed into the mini-van's rear and Ta'avah stomped the brakes, yanking the wheel to the left. His vehicle spun several times and came to a stop facing the authorities. At the same instant, Ta'avah had a plan. Kicking open the driver's-side door, he flung his body onto the cold ground face first, arms and legs spread wide.

"Freeze!" a booming command sounded. "Keep your hands where I can see them!"

Ta'avah did as he was told and called out in an accented old man's voice, "Please help me. He almost killed me. Please..."

"Don't move!" the same voice shouted moving closer.

Flashlight beams danced across his face as one cop exclaimed with surprise at his grotesque appearance. "Sir, stay where you are, paramedics are coming!"

A different man approached Ta'avah's facing side, 9mm drawn, finger just to the side of the trigger. He scowled and covered his nose before asking in a shout, "How did you get this van?"

Ta'avah rolled his eyes, his fluid-swollen cheek pressed to the near-frozen grass. He mumbled a few words in Hungarian and as he predicted, the police assumed he was incoherent.

To him, the far away officer shouted, "Don't move!" But the one looking at him lowered his weapon and drew close to where Ta'avah lay, flashlight illuminating his drooling mouth.

"Oh, God," he mouthed. "Sir, are you sick? Were you attacked?"

Ta'avah mumbled off a few more sentences in Hungarian and coughed, spitting up greenish bile.

"Shit! Murphy, this man is really sick!" the officer said and jumped back, gun at half-mast. "He's not our killer. Get those paramedics over here!"

Ta'avah rolled his eyes again, hoping he appeared more insane than ever and within seconds, gentle hands were turning him onto his back and carefully lifting him onto a gurney. The medics began their initial examination even as he was loaded into the waiting ambulance. Ta'avah assumed an expression of terror and pain and did not resist as the medical personnel attached an IV and sticky ECG monitoring pads on his chest and distended upper abdomen. One attendant said aloud that the patient appeared to be decomposing, but the senior medic hushed her and they sped to the hospital.

Now...

Ta'avah tuned out the frantic chatter as the crew desperately sought a heartbeat and attempted to push fluids into a dead body. With incredible focus he relaxed his reanimated limbs, commanding his mind to think on one thing and one thing only—the house where he left Meryl's body. Taking only a few seconds, his inner eye traveled to the front door of the home he and Theophilus invaded three nights ago. Yellow police tape blocked the entrance. He sent his view into the house, then up the stairs. At the master bedroom where he had gleefully ravaged the dead man's wife, he listened to the house. It had been emptied of corpses and no police presence remained.

Back in the ambulance, Ta'avah smiled. In another moment, he disappeared out from under the attendants' careful hands and found himself translated to the very basement where he had assumed Theophilus's unfortunately dead body.

Triumphant, Ta'avah opened the cellar door and walked to the back of the house. It was nearly 11 p.m. when he stepped into the cold night. His disintegrating flesh wiggled as he broke into an easy jog between the large two- and three-acre homesteads. A few dogs barked, but no mortals saw him as he covered a mile in a short quarter-hour to sneak into a quiet horse barn at the back of one of the larger properties. The smelly beasts were indoors, their puffs of breath whispering into his ears, but none were alarmed at his sudden presence.

Ta'avah found an empty stall and knelt in the straw. Yellowish fluid seeped from his nostrils and he snarled. He was going to need new flesh or he'd be back in his spirit prison very soon. Closing his purple-tinged eyes, he quieted his frenetic mind and sought out his brethren across dimensions.

"Zahdone! Rah-keel! Zara!" he sent to the space between worlds knowing they would hear him. Whether or not they would respond was another thing. It took a very long time for any of the spirits he called upon to answer. So long, in fact that Ta'avah allowed his melting Rakum Father's body to lie back on the prickly stall floor while he waited.

Finally, his brethren wisped about, laughing, gawking, and in a thousand entities, poking fun at his condition. When Ta'avah sensed Zara, Prince of Sickness and Disease near, he summoned him by name.

"Zara! You see me! Come!"

The specter came near, materializing as a milky shadow above him. *"You are very entertaining, Ta'avah. I don't see what you think I can do for you, though."*

"Get me another body! You can bring someone here, you could try," Ta'avah barked in the spirit.

Zara, one of three entities Elohim expelled from heaven with him, along with Rah-keel and Zahdone, only laughed with derision. *"Sure, let me just snap my —oh, wait, I don't have any fingers!"* he laughed.

"Stop wasting time, Zara! I am so close to resuming my reign on earth—I will share it with you. Help me and I will appoint you in the flesh as my second hand. You can get me a flesh if you try!"

"Can it be an animal?" a new voice asked.

Ta'avah shook his head in his mind's eye. *"An animal has no voice, idiot!"* he shouted, now addressing Rah-keel, Prince of False Witness and Gossip.

Rah-keel shrugged. *"I can get you into an animal. You could get close to your target and then let Zara send a disciple to speak for you. If, that is, you also give me the same deal as Zara. Together, Zara and I could get you to your target."*

"You're heading to the boy?" Zara asked. Ta'avah nodded, knowing the view of the world of the flesh was fuzzy and indistinct from his dimension. They could watch, but only truly experience when a flesh permitted them access.

"What of Zahdone?" Ta'avah asked and received only silence. *"Why is not Zahdone present?"* The other spirits had no answer and Ta'avah considered their proposal. If they were true to their word, which was not

guaranteed, it could work. Having no other option, Ta'avah grunted his consent. The Rakum Father's flesh would not be able to rise out of the stall.

"*Send a dog. Can it be a dog?*"

"*A cat,*" Rah-keel answered and Ta'avah sighed, not in a position to argue. Within seconds, an orange and white tabby strolled into the stall and sniffed Ta'avah's rotting hand. Possessing an animal was the simplest of all spirit tricks and with determination, Ta'avah forced his essence into the smaller flesh.

Instantly, he came fully alive, full of strength and vigor. He tried out the feline limbs and leapt onto the stall door ledge. His spirit brethren were still with him and they laughed and cheered simultaneously.

"*When you get to the boy, call me. I have disciples in every mortal city—one will help you,*" Zara said and faded away. Rah-keel and the thousands of spirits that had come for the show faded into Ta'avah's consciousness and he looked around the dark barn with new eyes.

He had animated a feline before, so without much study of the mechanics, he slipped out into the night. Forty miles or so to Jackson on cat paws. Undaunted, Ta'avah trotted into the trees. He would be careful, he would find food along the way, and he would stay out of sight, but he would make it to Jackson—and the seed he had raised up for this very purpose. Everything was going to plan as it always did, no matter the interference of Elohim and His messengers.

Ta'avah nodded the tabby cat's head; he was a very powerful and capable spirit and within forty-eight mortal hours, he expected to meet his goal. Being a cat for a while was a small price to pay to regain his throne.

19

Jackson, MS
November 10th, 10 p.m.

"Canaan!" Isaac bellowed down the hallway even though the Elder would have heard a soft whisper or telepathic request equally well. Sometimes it was simply more fun to shout.

The burly Elder responded instantly with his mind and body, arriving in Isaac's private chamber within seconds.

"That was fast. I should yell for you more often," Isaac joked and Canaan half-grinned. The *new* Canaan was much more enjoyable and Isaac told him as much.

"I appreciate your concessions, Master, I sincerely do," Canaan responded, referring to his woman, no doubt. "What can I do for you?"

"You know a Cow named Stuart—he showed you a business card once," Isaac said. Moments ago, a borrowed memory from Canaan's past arrived vision-like in Isaac's subconscious. It came with a prophetic vibe revealing Stuart Loudon had become very important to his plans for the future. Anxious to be found helpful, Canaan nodded even as he pulled up his memory of the event.

"Yes..." the big Elder said. "Stuart Loudon, Tork's Cow, an Aussie. I found him on the way to Jackson." Canaan looked at Isaac. "You saw him. In the truck at the rest area. That was Stu."

Isaac grinned remembering everything the Elder remembered. Canaan had corralled the Cow into a pickup and buzzed off him before coming back to actually be buzzed *upon* by Isaac. He laughed at how things had changed since the night they headed out to destroy Rufus. Now Isaac ruled them all.

"Would you like me to find him?" Canaan asked.

Isaac smiled. The big goof had no idea why he wanted to see some scruffy Cow, but he wanted to please. *This* was good.

"Here's the thing. I've seen this Cow's plans. He's been single-handedly collecting Cows and seeking Rakum to serve. He calls it 'The Gathering,'" Isaac said laughing. "We're gonna call it 'The Cow Club.'" Canaan stood expressionless awaiting more so he continued. "Find him and have him take you to his collection. Then examine his herd and bring the best ones to the house."

Canaan nodded, but Isaac saw questions in his eyes.

"Don't look so surprised. As a reward for your loyalty, you who serve me here will want for nothing. Elder Canaan, you shall have innocents—as many as you can gobble down. Boris, Hoss, and Beryl will have Rabbits. And I want them to have *gorgeous* Rabbits, so choose wisely." The Elder seemed to understand and he added with a flash of inspiration, "Take Beryl with you—the two of you will choose for us six perfect specimens to start. Then leave Stuart to his Cow Club. We'll throw him a bone now and then to keep him in line."

Canaan smiled and Isaac grinned back. The guy was truly joining ranks.

"Elder Canaan," Isaac said using a serious tone as his spirit soared with a new sense of satisfaction, "no one has touched your woman since that second night. And no one will. She is no longer available to anyone but you." Isaac did not discern any change in the Elder's expression, although he expected relief. Undaunted, he continued, "She must remain here, though. I forbid her to leave."

"I understand, Master. It will be as you say," the Elder said, tipping his chin in a miniscule bow.

Isaac stared at him a few moments; was he hiding something? Waiting while the seconds ticked by, Canaan held the exact same poker face and waited as well. When neither of them had moved or spoken for a full minute, Isaac sighed. If the Elder was being deceptive, he couldn't see it.

"You and Beryl should plan to go soon—tonight or tomorrow night—whichever is safest," Isaac said and gestured toward his bedroom door. "I'll be watching you. If you need help, I'm not far away." Isaac touched his temple.

"Thank you, Master," Elder Canaan said and again tipped a tiny bow.

Isaac sent him out and silently called for Boris. He wanted to begin his new adventure with the one Rakum who truly loved him. Boris lumbered in, his huge frame diminishing the doorway as he passed through. Isaac met him across the floor and grasped his left hand.

"Close your eyes and empty your mind," he told the big Rakum. Boris did as he was told and Isaac closed his eyes, too. "I will use your telepathy to magnify mine. Just go blank—imagine you're in a white box, nothing but white on all sides. Are you there?"

"Yes, Master," Boris said as Isaac picked up the same white expanse through his inferior's eyes.

"Okay, I'm going to find that fantastic Kilmeade..." he whispered and concentrated on the last transmission he'd shared with the Elder. In what seemed only seconds, he developed a hazy vision of the handsome Elder settling into an airliner's cushy First Class seat. As soon as their minds touched, the Elder looked him in the eye. Isaac smiled, amazed at himself once again.

Still standing in his own bedroom, holding Boris's big brown paw, Isaac gave the Elder a wink. "Where ya headed?" he asked, counting on the man's mind to give him whatever answers he needed.

"I am on my way to find my brother, Roman," Kilmeade said with a focused telepathic thought. The Elder didn't attempt to lie, which told Isaac the man had already discerned his great power.

Isaac said, "I want you to come to Jackson. Bring all those with you— they'll be safe. I have plenty of room. What do you say?"

The Elder looked to his right and waited while the swarthy and dashing Rakum with him settled at his side. Isaac saw immediately that this one could not see or hear what he discussed with the Elder. Once Kilmeade determined the same thing, he shook his head.

"I do not wish to come, Master," Kilmeade sent over, as polite a declination as possible. "I wish to find Roman. I have my mind set on it. I will not deviate from my plans."

Isaac frowned, but wasn't immediately incensed. This Elder had brass, true individuality. If allowed some rein, he might come to see things in Isaac's favor. Then Isaac got a flash of the Elder's deepest desire and he smiled ear-to-ear.

"Oh! Okay. I understand – yes. This is good. Proceed, I'll back you." Isaac squeezed Boris's hand and the big Rakum squeezed his in return. "Go to Roman and try to convert him. If your blood isn't powerful enough, bring him to me. I am certain mine is. I will help you."

The Elder seemed surprised at Isaac's offer, which pleased him even more. This Rakum was self-serving as they were born to be. This was a Rakum Isaac understood and no matter how delicious he would be to buzz, a tiny measure of patience is all it would take to use the Elder's plans to further his own.

Shortly, the Elder nodded and closed his eyes. The vision faded and Isaac squeezed Boris's hand again.

"I want to go to *Tuscaloosa, Alabama*—" he said, sounding out the town's strange name. "That's where they're headed. It'll take them two days to get there, so we can wait until tomorrow." Isaac grinned then and beckoned Boris to follow him with one finger. "First..." he said and entered the hall.

Isaac passed a few closed doors and when he reached the last one on the right, he smiled at Boris, who grinned knowingly back. With his hand on the knob, he asked Boris for his cellphone. *"Watch this,"* he said silently and shoved open the door to Marcy Haddle's room.

"Catch!" he shouted and tossed the phone at Canaan's old lady. It slammed into her cheek and she yelped. "Keep that phone handy, Rabbit," he hissed and the woman paled instantly. "Your man's going on an errand for me. I want you to call him often while he's gone. If he doesn't do precisely as I asked and return home quickly, tell him that I'm going to explode you from the inside out. He'll believe me—he knows I'm capable."

"Oh, God!" the Rabbit whimpered, making herself small on the bed's dingy comforter.

Isaac smiled. "Yes! I'll be your god. I accept!" Chuckling, Isaac left the room and led Boris to the stairs.

"She's funny," Boris said, laughing in a deep baritone. When they reached the foyer, he paused and waited for Isaac to notice.

"What is it?" Isaac asked.

"In your vision earlier, if I may, I saw Elder Kilmeade," Boris said. "Everyone said he was dead."

Isaac smiled wickedly. "He's a crafty one. He even hid from me until now," he said and softened his gaze. "Boris, he is perfect, just like Canaan. I want him here with me. He needs to join us." Isaac's smile faded as his mind wandered.

"He will come, Master," Boris replied. "He is a loyal Rakum, very popular at Assembly. Rumor had it he was killed for refusing to serve Rufus. Yet he would serve *you*. You're a Father and Elder Kilmeade holds the Rakum above all else."

"Yeah..." Isaac said softly. Rufus killed thousands of their brethren before he was destroyed. Isaac wasn't shy about murdering insubordinate Rakum, but he wasn't insane. That was the difference. Gravely, Isaac said, "Tell me more."

"He was liked by everyone," Boris began with a smile, happy he could offer something useful to his god. "At Assembly, he would allow me—and any grunt that wished to do so—stay with him, right in his bunker. He taught us rare Elder stuff and willingly gave good counsel." Boris lowered his eyes as if he spoke too long. Isaac prompted him to continue. "Elder Kilmeade had no use for anything not one-hundred-percent Rakum; he didn't suffer humans and he didn't coddle Cows. I have seen this with my own eyes."

"You're saying that he would never put up with this stupid Rabbit religion?" Isaac asked.

Boris shook his head. "No way."

"Excellent!" Isaac impulsively wiggled Boris's hand. "Tell me more."

Boris nodded his bald head and started talking.

20

Tuscaloosa, AL
November 10th, 9:30 p.m.

J avier had spent the daylight hours in the Athens bus station, snoozing in a chair near the wall, periodically changing benches to make it appear he wasn't transient. The sun still caused him great discomfort, and he decided he would wait to drive home after sunset.

He had borrowed a car from Simon's garage, intending to run it back in a few days. Pink handed him the keys to a black BMW and told him Simon suggested it in particular. Now ten minutes from his and David's condo in Tuscaloosa, Javier attempted to clear his mind of the many evil thoughts that had assaulted him since he attacked Simon so violently. Picturing himself with his fingers like claws on the poor man's body, Javier could not believe it truly happened. What had come over him?

Javier thought back to why he left Simon's so abruptly at their second reunion. Ironically, the one where he came to apologize for running off the first time. But it couldn't have been helped. Javier had sensed being *watched*. It wasn't a sensation like before, like when he was a Rakum. He didn't know who or what awaited him in the dark. It made no sense. Javier had felt an impulse to *flee*—to run, which disgusted him to the core. Never in his life had fear dictated his actions. Even more disconcerting, it wasn't that whoever or whatever was watching him was trying to kill him—rather, Javier had been compelled by an unknown force to run for his life and not being in control of his fear was scarier than whatever caused it.

I am not in control, Javier told himself. *I'm not in control of my life, my situation... hell,* he thought miserably, shaking his head in the borrowed car, *I'm not even in control of my body.*

Mortified again that he actually drank blood, that he stole it, raping his friendship as surely as biting Simon's wounded arm. It was a violation the boy—the man—would never forget.

But he'll forgive me. Javier had no doubt.

Simon had found God seven years ago, but he was still acting like a

Cow, even though he had been delivered from the addiction by faith. Javier sensed his yearning and watched his adoration of what he wished Javier still was return to his blue eyes when they spoke.

Javier pulled into his assigned parking spot at their unit and switched off the car. There was a chance David would be home. Since Roman left him at the ER, five days had elapsed. They would have been trying to find him, but as he had no phone they were aware of, they hadn't spoken.

Javier exited the car and considered the front window. It was dark. As the huge church clock two streets over chimed the hour, Javier strode to his door. If any of them—Roman, David, Canaan or Isaac—were at his place, what would he say? How had they handled Rufus? Did they all survive? Javier was no longer angry with Roman for his deception regarding poor Isabella. In fact, since he had been so fiercely concentrating on himself, he barely gave his former Elder and the battle with Rufus thought.

Feeling guilty for his selfishness, Javier opened the door and headed straight for the landline next to the answering machine. Not too surprisingly, the contraption was blinking and Javier hit the button.

"Javier, it's Beth. If you get this message before we find you—stay there and call me. The guys are going nuts trying to find you and I told them I'd leave a message at your house. Please call me and tell me you're okay. I had a dream about you and I want to believe it is true—that you are fine. Better than fine—that you are healed and going home. So call me..."

Javier stared at the machine, processing Beth Rider's words. After a moment, he shook his head and dropped his keys on the coffee table. A familiar scent hit his nose.

Chloe Bushman, David's girlfriend. She'd been kidnapped by Elder Rufus. He should return Beth Rider's call and ask for a full report, but...

The young woman's scent was strong. Was she in the house?

At the threshold of the quiet sitting area, Javier held his breath. His bedroom was off to the right and David's to the left. Javier paused to concentrate on what lay behind the closed doors. It was incredibly weird to be able to "feel" beyond his eyesight. He'd never been mystically amazing, as many of his Rakum brethren were, so he didn't know if the nuances were normal, but right now, with a strange "third-eye," he could see into whichever room he focused on.

David's room was empty. Curious, now that he was even more certain he wasn't alone in the apartment, he looked at his own closed door. In a hazy mirage, he recognized Chloe Bushman lying on his bed fully dressed on top of the covers. At least one mystery solved—the girl had been rescued. Javier swallowed hard.

Chloe Bushman was a freshman at the University of Alabama and for the past several months, David's sweetheart. Why was she in his room? Even more curiously, why was she in his bed?

Javier unlocked his feet and stepped toward the door, his emotions soaring. He was infatuated with the girl no doubt, always had been. Since David first brought her home. He couldn't help himself. She was the carbon copy of his first love, Isabella. Javier's breath hitched as the girl's name crossed his mind. A week ago, he learned that his most trusted friend murdered Isabella in her sleep and allowed him to believe he'd done it. One hundred and thirty years later and he remembered everything about her. Javier put his hand to the doorknob.

This is a bad idea, Javier, he told himself, pausing before turning the knob. *You can still back away. Come back later, when she's gone.*

Then what? He wanted to know why she was here and why she was in his room. Maybe she'd been hoping he'd come back and surprise her.

Yeah, right, she wants to be attacked in her sleep like Simon. Think, Javier! Come back later!

Javier looked around the dark living room. He wasn't talking to himself, not really. Someone else was talking to him, offering him advice in a most intimate way. Javier imagined Chloe's reaction at seeing him; she might be afraid or she might be overjoyed. He had a fifty-fifty shot.

Don't do it. You'll be sorry.

Javier smirked, finally acknowledging the voice that spoke in his spirit with such familiarity was his conscience, and his conscience was spurred by the Holy Spirit of God. Javier sent up a prayer in his heart, more a message really. *"I'm going in. You brought her here so this is on You,"* and he turned the knob.

Could she be any more beautiful? The original Isabella had been sixteen, half-starved and wan from blood loss. Her modern double glowed with health, her fair cheeks sprinkled with freckles and her waist-length dark brown hair flowed around her head on his sham-covered pillow. She was dressed as always in low-rise Levi's and a snug T-shirt. How did she make such simple clothing so enticing?

Chloe stirred and Javier instinctively backed, closing the door quietly with him inside. When the latch clicked, her eyes fluttered open. Chloe rolled to the nightstand and clicked on the bedside lamp; Javier held his breath. What would she do? What did he want her to do? Was he physically attracted to her? Sure. Could he be dangerous to her? Maybe. He thought of Simon's blood pouring into him the night before and he frowned. He didn't thirst for blood then and he didn't now. So there should be no issue...

Chloe sensed she wasn't alone and jerked her eyes his way. Instantly, her face erupted into a grin and she leapt off the bed and into his arms.

"Javier! Oh, my God! You're okay!" Chloe's voice in his ear caused him to wince, but he returned her embrace and tried to match her enthusiasm. "Roman said you broke your back!"

"And you've been rescued. Where *is* Roman?" Javier asked.

Chloe gushed her answers. "In Memphis, to stay with you at the hospital. But look at you!" Chloe said and leaned out of his arms. "You look better than ever. Oh, my God!"

"I'm happy you're okay, too," Javier offered. "So the battle was a victory, I assume?"

Chloe searched his eyes. "You haven't heard?"

Javier shook his head. "Can you give me a run-down of what happened in Jackson?"

Chloe inhaled and rattled off her reply. "That night—the night you were hit by a car—Michael Stone and David rescued me and Selene. You know her, right?" Javier nodded and Chloe continued. "Roman showed up with a really young Wraith named Isaac and another I didn't see. Roman told me in the car his name is Canaan."

"Wraith," he mumbled, thinking. Chloe never used the term Rakum, but instead used the word Beth Rider substituted in her novel that started the entire avalanche. *Wraith* was creepier somehow and Javier found it fitting.

"Yeah, and then Roman got Damien out of the house. He told us that Isaac and Canaan destroyed Rufus. They brought me home and Roman, David, and Damien went to find you." Chloe fell into him again and held him tightly. "I overheard that Damien is your real father. Is that right?"

Processing the news, Javier only made a sound of affirmation.

"He became human only a week ago and he's really looking forward to seeing you again. On the way home, he talked about you a lot. Kept saying how he wanted to see you through God's eyes."

"Is that so?" Javier whispered conflicted on the news. What would it be like, meeting his blood father in human form? *Am I even human anymore?*

"Roman is going to be so happy to find you all healed up," she said into his chest. Javier made no reply recalling he still owed Roman that apology for his shameful behavior.

Chloe sighed contentedly and Javier considered his hands overlapping her narrow back. How long since he'd held a woman like this? It had been years—and not at all since he'd been mortal. Chloe's body fit nicely in his arms and her cheek was pressed against the lapel of his leather knee-length coat.

"You're okay. It's a miracle," she said and then mumbled, "Thank God," through quiet tears.

Seconds ticked by and Javier sought a proper reply. The information regarding his broken back was new; had he healed from that? Even as a Rakum, the spine took much longer to heal than other major joints and bones. He finally uttered the most human thing he could think of in his current mind-numbed state.

"I guess it wasn't as bad as he thought."

Chloe nodded her head against him. "You have no idea how worried we were." *Why can't I let him go? Javier never liked me much—he sure is being polite. Let him go, Chloe!*

At the girl's telepathic relays, a small smile touched the corners of Javier's mouth and he relaxed his posture to melt further into her arms. Chloe responded by turning her face to his, only inches away.

"I always liked you, Chloe," Javier said with a small smile. "I apologize for my behavior before. I was going through a lot of stuff that had nothing to do with you."

Chloe's face went blank, no doubt wondering if he'd just read her thoughts. Javier took the opportunity to touch his lips to her forehead. No harm in that, just a small peck between friends. That done, Chloe still didn't pull out of his arms.

"Did you just read my mind, Javier?" A test thought went out from her as she gazed into his eyes and Javier didn't reply. A capable Rakum would use telepathy to control a human under his thumb. Javier had no such desire. Plus, he wasn't *reading* her mind so much as hearing what cascaded forth. He played no active role, so he wasn't to blame. Was he?

"How did you heal up so fast?" Finally suspicious, Chloe leaned away and repositioned her arms from around his waist to around Javier's neck.

"What are you doing in my room?" Javier redirected with a question of his own.

Chloe looked over her shoulder to the mussed bed and blushed. *What was I doing in here? I have no idea,* she thought.

Javier had his answer.

"I was supposed to stay home, but I didn't want to. My parents are out of the country and they don't even know I was kidnapped," she said when she met his eyes again.

She was so lovely and even though since Isabella he'd not been much of a romantic, he wanted very much to kiss her lips. Yet those were David's, right? Javier didn't ask anyone: not himself or the Lord. He didn't want to hear another warning to leave.

"You seem strange…are you okay?" Chloe asked and in her mind, he heard, *he was always a little strange, wasn't he? But he is so hot…*

There was the reason Javier's inner voice warned him to leave. David's friend harbored feelings for him that she kept secret. Those unspoken thoughts lined up with his—that could get them into trouble.

Javier leaned a few more inches out of their embrace and lowered his chin. "I'm fine. Just making plans, gotta contact Roman and David and let them know I'm home."

"Javier," Chloe asked him, stressing the "hah" for comical effect, She batted her eyelashes and he reacted with an easy smile. "Since you don't hate me after all, can we sit and talk? I have a lot of questions. David answered some of them for me, but not nearly all of them. What do you say?"

"Rakum questions?" Javier asked, searching her eyes. What did she really seek from him? She was sexually innocent; he discerned that right away by the limited scope of her fantasy thought-life. She was hearts and candy and long caresses, nothing more. Javier wasn't the one to satisfy that part of her.

"Well, sure. David's ashamed of it. But you're not, right? You seem like you accepted the way things are and that's that."

Javier licked his lips. Chloe had seen up close and personal what the Rakum were capable of and she wanted to see more. A week earlier, he'd fought with David about the girl. Javier sensed even then that Chloe Bushman had an aberrant attraction to the supernatural and he'd accused her of being a Cow. He'd used a different euphemism that she didn't understand, but David had and he flew into a rage. Looking at her now, huge eyes misty with emotion and an eagerness for adventure, he knew it was true—if the Rakum had come across Chloe before Last Assembly, she would have been somebody's pet. But what was all of that to him now? He wasn't a Rakum.

Javier's stomach rumbled then and Chloe heard it.

"I can make you something to eat. Have you had dinner?" she asked softly, clueless to his mental brainstorm. Javier smiled at her kindness and Chloe interpreted the move as a yes.

"Good!" Chloe said and turned from his grip. "Let me go see what you have in the kitchen." She took two steps for the door and Javier caught her wrist.

"Don't make me anything to eat, Chloe." Javier thought about his next words carefully and then spit them out. "What did you want to ask me? Go ahead. I'll answer if I can." *Get out. You're playing a dangerous game. Why are you so thick-headed? Do you want to hurt her? She is not for you...*

Javier shushed his conscience and allowed Chloe to lead him into the living room. She asked questions and made observations about the Rakum all the way to the couch. When she sat, she pulled him down with her close enough that their knees touched. She hadn't paused in her current topic and he sensed a growing emptiness in his middle. She gesticulated with her hands, describing what she'd seen while in Rufus's clutches, and Javier found himself mesmerized by her voice and the cadence of it. The emptiness grew.

"David wants me to forget that he was ever a Wraith. How about you? Have you let it all go? What's that like, letting something like that go?" Chloe asked leaning forward, her hand on his right knee, so innocently playing with lions. Javier cleared his throat and tried on a smile.

"It's not easy. It's a process," Javier said softly. "I doubt David will ever completely release his past. We can use our past tribulations to make us better people for the future," Javier said, happy his answer sounded wise.

"Yeah, that makes sense. I just can't get over it..." Chloe's voice waxed philosophical and her gaze grew soft. "David said you're over a hundred years old...but look at you. I would peg you at thirty, thirty-five at the most...it's so weird..." Delicate fingers moved from Javier's knee to his cheek and her touch expanded the growing void in his center.

"I feel even older than that," Javier mumbled low. "And you seem all of twelve years old. An innocent, a baby—somebody's baby." Without thinking about what he was doing, he lifted his outside hand and cupped Chloe's neck, tucking his fingers beneath her silky curls.

"I'm twenty today..." she said, her voice dreamy.

"Happy birthday," Javier whispered and reality gave him a nudge. "Your parents went out of town on your birthday?"

"I'm not a baby anymore. It's time I grew up," Chloe retorted softly.

Javier recognized that tone; he heard it every time a blood donor looked into his eyes for any period of time. He wasn't a Rakum, but he had hypnotized David's girlfriend. The emptiness crawled up his throat. This talent was used to draw a human's blood. He didn't want that, did he?

Why won't he kiss me? Chloe's thoughts rambled. *I might be too young for him. I might be gross to him. I really have no idea what he likes or anything about him. If he doesn't kiss me soon I think I'm going to die.*

Javier pulled Chloe close and touched his lips to hers. Just barely making contact, he remained and she did the same, and their breath intermingled between them.

"I don't kiss you because David kisses you..." Javier sent the sentiment telepathically and her response was to inhale sharply and pull back.

"I thought you said you were human now," Chloe began, her eyes wide with no desire to leave.

"I never said any such thing." Javier shook his head. "Come close."

Javier pulled her to him, his hand at her neck. He fixed his gaze on her throat—things were so different now. As a Rakum, with a Cow close enough to buzz, his head would swim, his gut would knot, and a lust for blood would fill his soul until he sated it with a drink. As a human, he was repulsed at the thought of consuming blood. What was he morphing into? He didn't lust, but he was growing quite fond of the idea of biting her neck.

Like a vampire.

Javier's teeth seemed sharper at the mere thought.

"Javier, I-I'm feeling faint," Chloe whispered. Javier stared at his thumb sitting peacefully on her skin just below her ear, her hair feathers on the tops of his fingers. He lifted his other hand and laid it on her thigh. She started at the contact. Had David never touched her leg? A flash in her mind of lying in a red satin bed with Elder Rufus hit him and he realized that at least to some degree, she equated her time with the crazed Rakum with what was currently happening.

"I'm not like Elder Rufus," he whispered. Chloe made a small sound of agreement and was silent. "I'll catch you if you faint," he murmured and put his lips to her throat. The vacuum that had begun in his middle had reached his brain and consumed him. When they were Rakum, they awaited consent to drink from females. What were the rules now? And was that what he was about to do?

"Chloe, I want to do an experiment. I want to kiss your neck. What do you think about that?" Javier asked telepathically.

"I trust you, Javier," she whispered, "I've always trusted you."

Javier opened his mouth wide against the soft skin of her throat. He laid his tongue on her skin and he waited to see what might happen. As a Rakum, he would have used a knife to open a wound; Rakum do not have fangs like Dracula. Whatever he was now fueled his movements, and he rolled closed his eyes to wait.

Chloe shivered, sending another terrified image of herself in Rufus's arms, and Javier sent her a few soothing words. *"I'm changing into something else, Chloe, and I won't hurt you, I promise. If you want me to leave, just say so and I will be gone. Do you understand?"*

"Please, don't leave me," Chloe whispered, clinging to him, her fingers gripping his arms.

Javier sensed a curious tingle in his gums and his conscience lit into him anew. *It's not too late to leave, Javier. Go now. It'll be okay.* Javier was resolute and he heard his inner voice backtrack in response. *You had a chance to leave and you dismissed it. You're playing with fire and you're growing fangs. Tonight you will see what you have become. You are what you eat. Remember that.*

Javier ate a part of Isaac.

Isaac ate a part of the Fathers ...for decades.

The Fathers were monsters, pure and simple.

Chloe's body rose to meet him and he wrapped his arms around her. She may have whimpered, but he was listening too closely to his own heartbeat and considering the advice of his conscience. The emptiness that numbed him began to subside, from the top of his head, sliding down his spine, and trickling its way down his back, past his pelvis, all the way to his toes. And then it was gone.

Relieved, Javier opened his eyes and pulled away from Chloe's neck. Touching his tongue to his palate, he tasted copper. Languidly focusing on the girl's face, he saw blood running down her neck, from just under her ear into the collar of her T-shirt. Chloe's head lolled to the side and Javier snapped to attention. She wasn't breathing. He'd hurt her after all.

21

Athens, GA
Hampton Inn
November 10th, 10 p.m.

"That's a lot of Cows, Stu," Polly cooed as he, Guap, and Stuart Loudon peeked into the Hampton Inn conference room. The enterprising Cow had rented it for the week. His famous "gathering" was in full swing and some two hundred men and women chatted, sat, drank, and laughed in the banquet hall. The general energy emanating from the crowd was optimism and Polly anticipated quite a welcome when Stu got around to introducing them.

Guap stood opposite, peeking in the other side of the threshold. "How did you find them all? This is amazing," he said, true wonder in his tone.

Stu grinned with pride. "A website. A simple website with a few specific Google search terms and BAM! I had forty-five the first week."

Polly had draped his arm across Stu's shoulders and he squeezed him briefly. "You done good, my man. Really good."

Stu blushed and tried to keep a straight face. Polly liked that he was gushy—he liked gushy Cows.

Guap backed from the doorway and motioned for Polly to do the same. "Tell Stu about his Anomaly."

"Oh, sure," Polly said and pulled Stuart so all three of them were several feet from the room. "The guy is definitely not a Rakum, but he used to be. I know him. He's also not human." Polly shrugged. "He was aware of us and he bolted. That's all we know."

Stuart nodded. "Master, that helps heaps. The guy who lives there said Javier attacked him the next night. *Attack* attacked him," Stuart said, miming biting his own arm.

"Damn," Guap whispered. He shrugged at Polly. "I have no idea what he's become. I hope he's not simply loco. If I could get closer to him, I might be able to discern, but..."

"I know, me too," Polly said. They had both lost a great deal of power since Last Assembly.

"Simon thinks Javier will be back," Stu said quietly. "Master Polly, do you know Elder Canaan? He called me tonight. He wants to see the herd."

"D*aaaaaa*mn, Stuey!" Polly said clapping his back hard. "We definitely want to see *him*. Mention us. He knows us."

Stu smiled. "I will, Master."

"Awesome," Polly nodded. "This is just great. Life is *gooooood!*"

Stu exhaled with barely bottled excitement. "Masters, it's nearly ten. You ready?"

Polly and Guap nodded.

"Okay, here we go."

As they had planned beforehand, Stuart entered first, receiving a huge round of applause. Polly and Guap listened as he gave them the rundown of how many Cows had assembled and how many were still due to arrive. He gave them a few dates to remember. Then he stressed the importance of secrecy. Finally, he built up Polly and Guap to the crowd, assigning to them much more amazing supernatural powers than they actually had. That was Guap's idea, saying it was best if they were kept unaware of the extent of the Rakum's loss of vitality when their spiritual High Father deserted them. Then the room grew quiet and the sound of chinking champagne glasses filtered into the hall.

Polly and Guap gave each other a knowing grin; Stu had insisted everyone in attendance drink eight ounces of champagne at 9:30, and now they had to finish a second glass before the Rakum would be introduced. This was to hopefully prevent any uncontrolled emotional outbursts as it was well known that Cows were the most unstable of all humanity.

"All done? Good," Stuart said from the dais.

The crowd remained silent and Polly absorbed the anticipation in the Cows that awaited them. They were hungry—no, *starving*—for Rakum attention. It had been a good idea to tranquilize them a little with the wine.

"You've waited long enough, brothers and sisters. May I present Master Guap and Master Polly," Stu said and Polly entered first, jovially shoving Guap aside as he crossed the threshold.

"Hello, my beauties!" he said and waded into the throng. "Call me Master Polly. You may touch me, go ahead," he said and held his arms out from his body. Dozens of hands caressed him all over and dozens of tongues praised his name. Across the room similarly adored, Guap enjoyed the same experience.

"Damn! It's good to be a Rakum," Polly sent to Guap who agreed with a boisterous laugh.

The Cows loved on them until an hour before dawn. It was *real* good.

100

22

Chloe's heart had stopped and he was the cause. Javier jumped into action, barely thinking. A flash memory of waking up next to a very dead Isabella flooded his mind as he scooped Chloe's still body off the couch and laid her on the carpet. Javier began chest compressions; as a Rakum he'd been an amazing healer, but as a human he needed mortal skills to help anyone in medical distress.

Rhythmically, Javier compressed Chloe's ribcage, carefully measuring his output to avoid cracking her ribs with his unstudied new strength. When she did not respond after fifteen compressions, Javier bent to her open lips and filled her lungs with his own breath. Instantly, Chloe coughed, sputtered, and opened her eyes.

Stunned, Javier remained as he was on his knees and hands, hovering over her, inches from her face. Chloe took a few deep breaths and then met his eye.

"What? Did I pass out?" she asked in an embarrassed whisper.

Realizing it was agape, Javier closed his mouth and rolled over to lie on his back. Chloe rose to a sitting position, crossed her legs and faced Javier.

"What's wrong? What did I do?"

Javier didn't react. She had no idea that she'd died and been brought back to life. What good would it do to tell her? Then Javier offered a cautious smile and Chloe's expression softened.

"I must have passed out," she said with finality. Chloe reached for his nearest hand and clasped it in both of her own. "I'm okay, see?"

She rotated her head both ways and Javier noted a miniscule wince. One of her hands went to her throat wound and her fingers came away tacky. Chloe stared at them in the low light and then turned them, red side out, for Javier to see.

"Did you bite me?"

"I did," Javier whispered, not liking the admission in the least.

Chloe touched the punctures tenderly checking for fresh blood, but they no longer leaked. She unlocked her legs preparing to rise and Javier grasped her wrist.

"Wait," he whispered and pulled her lower to the carpet. She didn't pull back and when close enough, he touched her wound. The disrupted skin was healing quickly, much like it had for Simon earlier. Had his saliva accelerated the process? Come to think of it, had his *breath* brought her back to life? Javier's mind raced as Chloe popped up and disappeared into his bedroom. Water ran in the sink and then she locked the door.

Javier turned over and closed his eyes. He had indeed consumed at least two pints of Chloe's blood; it sat heavily in his stomach, slowly leeching its vitality into his system. None of the experience was like that of his Rakum days. Why had he taken it, and how? Javier poked a finger into his mouth; his teeth felt normal at first blush, but when he pressed his canines, they seemed sharper than before.

At least Chloe's alive, he thought and allowed his hand to drop back to the floor. The toilet flushed and he remained as he was on the carpet lying flat on his back. What was Chloe thinking? What did it matter? She hadn't died, which seemed of paramount importance for the moment.

"Hey," Chloe said as she re-entered the living room and dropped to the floor next to Javier. "Look, it's already healed."

She turned her head to the side, but Javier didn't have to see. Chloe lowered herself until she lay alongside and propped up onto her elbow. With her free hand she touched his hair, moving it absently, deep in thought.

"I'm sorry, Chloe," Javier whispered, not allowing his voice to carry.

She shrugged. "I'm not hurt so what's the big deal?" she said and did not continue until he met her eyes. "When Rufus kidnapped me, he was horrible. I was terrified every waking moment. But I'm not afraid of you, Javier. I feel safe—safer than I have in a long time."

Doesn't David make you feel safe? Javier wanted to ask, but he held back. He didn't want to mention his roommate's name, unwilling to derail the conversation in that direction. As in, why had he allowed David's girlfriend to get so close and why wasn't he pushing her away? Javier frowned and returned his attention to the ceiling.

"I don't understand what's happening to you," she replied, her cool palm now on his forehead and then cheek. "Have you changed back into a Rakum?"

"No, something else, I think." Javier studied her face and slowly shook his head. "You are a remarkable young woman, Chloe Bushman." He chuckled softly. "I see why David finds you so fascinating."

"Do I fascinate you?" she asked. Then she lay down, draped her left arm over his chest and rested her chin on his shoulder.

"Hmm," Javier mumbled and rearranged his arm to snug her close.

"I don't think you're evil, Javier," she said in a low voice "I think whatever is happening to you will be a good thing in the end."

Javier huffed. "God, I hope so."

"No, I'm serious," she reiterated.

Javier turned his face her way and without forethought, pulled her to him. So many times, hundreds really, he had fantasized of the moment when David's Chloe might fill in for his lost Isabella. It was happening; he wasn't a kisser, but their lips were touching; he wasn't a romantic, but the kiss deepened; he wasn't sexually wanton, but he'd already risen to one elbow and draped himself on top of her.

Javier's inner commentary was strangely silent and Chloe hadn't voiced any objections. Javier opened his eyes and ended their kiss, still holding her tightly to his chest.

"Should I stop?" he asked purposing to normalize his breathing, although she would notice his arousal. Chloe didn't answer, but rather pulled him to her again, shivering with conflict. Javier waited a full minute for his conscience to object, but when he heard nothing, he scooped David's girlfriend into his arms and carried her to his bed.

Stop me, dammit. Please.

But no one—and no *One*—did.

23

Athens, GA
Hampton Inn
November 11th, 9 a.m.

"Beryl, you awake?" Canaan nudged the pup's arm. They'd tucked themselves into the hotel's bathtub to avoid the floor. Beryl didn't respond, but he was awake. Neither of them could sleep. Four doors down, the Cow sat waiting for them, waiting for the sunset and waiting to be milked. Canaan sensed his need as soon as the man returned to his room. Now that they were mere hours from contacting the guy, Canaan was glad Isaac had allowed him to go. Sitting around the miniature tyrant's prison was driving him bats.

Canaan's mind flashed on Marcy. Isaac had commanded she be left alone, but only after she'd been accosted seven separate times by the other Rakum in the house. When Canaan approached her since, she recoiled in disgust and fear. Also, he hadn't gotten his conjugal visit.

Canaan nudged Beryl again. "I know you're awake."

"Stop it!" Beryl barked and elbowed Canaan much harder than necessary, disregarding his senior status. Canaan had grown accustomed to it since Isaac had demoted him publicly several times over.

"Are you still sore that I shot you?" Canaan asked. He didn't truly care if the Rakum was angry, but he was bored as hell. Plus, he'd only planted a .45 slug in Beryl's gut because he and Meryl attacked Marcy. He had been completely in his rights.

Beryl's scarred face pinched and he glared at Canaan in the low light. "You incapacitated Meryl. I blame you as much as Ta'avah."

Canaan shook his head. "Blame yourself, buddy. You swim with sharks, you gotta be prepared to have a leg bit off." He didn't need to elaborate. Every Rakum knew not to cross an Elder; swift and merciless punishment was the normal outcome of such foolhardy action. That got Canaan to thinking about the other Elders. Isaac hinted he had located Kilmeade alive. Besides Rufus and Roman, there were ninety-six others. Where were they? Dead? Mortal and in hiding? His telepathy was coming back online since he'd been with Isaac, but he couldn't see who was left.

When Beryl stopped responding and had closed his eyes to lean back against the cool tile, Canaan nudged his arm with a balled fist. "When Rufus sent you to get Marcy, how many Elders remained?"

"I don't want to talk about it," Beryl mumbled.

"When Rufus sent you to get Marcy, how many Elders were left?" Canaan asked again in the exact same tone.

"You and Kilmeade. We thought Kilmeade was dead so we lied and told Rufus you were the last one." Beryl spoke in a monotone.

Canaan discerned he was ashamed of his behavior under Rufus and shame was a very unRakum-like emotion. Canaan wanted to jibe him about it and make him feel worse, but more than that, he wanted to know how the Elders died. "What happened to them?"

Beryl opened his eyes and looked at Canaan briefly. "They're dead, okay? Meryl and I didn't want that—*Rufus* did. Get it?"

Canaan dismissed his attitude and asked again. "What happened to my brothers?"

Beryl sighed. "More than half of them went Apostate. They were human. Meryl and I killed thirty of those ourselves. Rufus killed the Elders who were intact. They would not submit, so he killed them. When he couldn't go out any longer, we lured the last few to Jackson just like we lured you."

Canaan took the back of Beryl's neck in one big hand. "How many Elders are alive tonight?"

Beryl closed his eyes. "You don't have to read me—why would I lie? I told you. Two—you and Kilmeade. Roman is the only mortal Elder that survived. I have seen ninety-six Elder corpses with my own eyes. Look at them if you want to. My mind is open."

Canaan didn't dig that deep, but he did not release Beryl right away. After a long minute, he gently squeezed his neck. "The hundreds of our brethren you and Meryl ended and the hundreds you had a hand in destroying, were killed under orders."

"I know," Beryl said tersely, but Canaan read regret in his eyes.

"You're a Rakum Captain. Nut-up and let that shit go," Canaan said sternly holding the pup's gaze. He had done many things in his life on orders that he would never initiate, yet he regretted nothing. Witnessing

Beryl's weakness would eventually become unbearable. Maybe he could educate the kid a little.

"I'm fine," Beryl huffed frowning, but Canaan saw through his bravado. Beryl no longer enjoyed anything and had not been happy since Meryl died. For reasons he didn't want to discover, Canaan cared that Beryl was unhappy.

Beryl looked at him suspiciously. Probably because of their tactile contact, he had heard the gist of Canaan's last thought. Neither spoke and as Canaan withdrew his hand, Beryl's gaze softened.

"I lied before... I don't blame you for Meryl's death. I saw you wanted to heal us. I know you care about the Brethren," he whispered and looked away. "Let's doze. I don't feel like talking."

Canaan watched him exhale and lean back again, closing his eyes. After a full minute, Canaan poked his arm.

"Did you read Beth Rider's book?" Sure, Isaac wouldn't like them to speak of it, but it was 9 a.m.; surely their tiny ruler was asleep...

"Guard your thoughts!" Beryl hissed.

"He's asleep," he responded and repeated the question.

"Yes, I read it," Beryl said frowning.

"I wish I had," Canaan said. "I spoke to their God." Canaan waited for a reaction and got none. *"He spoke to me, too,"* Canaan whispered and this time Beryl turned.

"What did He say?" Beryl asked barely audible.

Canaan understood his unease; if Isaac discovered them speaking of the God of the mortals he'd probably fry them on the spot. Canaan leaned in. *"He said, 'turn to God.'"* Beryl shook his head woefully and Canaan narrowed his eyes. "You heard from Him, too?"

"No." Beryl looked at his knees dangling over the edge of the tub. "But I *did* ask Him to help me..." Beryl cut himself short and winced. Canaan didn't sense Isaac with them, so the guy's nerves were just twitchy.

"When you were locked out of the house?" Canaan asked. He'd surmised as much already. How else was he dragged in at the last second?

Beryl nodded. "I could say the same thing about you," he chided looking at Canaan's profile. "How is it that Dimple would come upstairs and shoot Rufus right before he melted your brain? I figured you'd been praying, too."

Canaan huffed, a sad smile on his face. "There must be something to it. He must be stronger than Isaac, do you think? I mean, He bested Abroghia..."

"I guess He's the strongest of all, but..." Beryl lowered his voice again and shifted his gaze forward, "but you never know what He'll do. It appears He's in control of everything and we all do His bidding whether we want to or not. I don't like it."

Canaan chuckled uneasily. "Beth Rider told me I was a puppet. That folks who follow Him are used by Him voluntarily, but everyone else is used as a puppet."

"That's retarded," Beryl said still looking dead ahead. "I'd know if I was some giant being's puppet."

"That's what I said." Canaan fell silent.

In the quiet, Canaan sensed Beryl wasn't saying something, guarding his words from Isaac with urgency. "I don't buy it, Beryl."

"Don't buy what? That's what the book said," Beryl replied.

"No, not that. I don't buy that you're not interested in knowing Him better, this God of the mortals. You want to know if He'll help us out. You want to get away from Isaac as much as I do, no matter what."

"If you don't shut your m—" Beryl stopped short and squeezed closed his eyes. Canaan watched him a split second before a knife sliced through his mind as real as steel. Canaan and Beryl both stifled screams that would have certainly attracted the mortal authority to the hotel room in which they hid.

"If you two morons don't stop that whining, I will silence you for good!" Isaac's mental voice was raspy and full of fury. *"One more word about this, and you, Canaan, will be lobotomized, and Beryl will be dead. Period!"*

"Yes! We understand! Yes, Master!" Canaan yelped, breathless, hearing Beryl make similar promises. Within moments, the pain subsided, and both men held their heads in their hands. Isaac was still there, his presence as palpable as if he stood in the room.

Neither man said anything else. Canaan watched the color of the light fade as the hours passed and Beryl dozed off to sleep against his shoulder. It sucked big time and there was nothing to be done to fix it. At least nothing Canaan was willing to spend time pondering.

It wasn't completely miserable. Kilmeade had arranged for their party to be taxied to a property he owned in Oklahoma City, a good halfway point from California to their destination in Alabama. During the night, it was a popular local tavern, but at 4 a.m. sharp, its patrons and workers departed, leaving a delightfully dark storeroom for the Rakum to hole up in until sundown. Iago and Jimmy were there as well, but slightly more comfortable, lying across soft booths in the back of the establishment. The business manager wasn't a Cow, but he respected Kilmeade as an eccentric and magnanimous investor and he didn't bother them when told to avoid the place until evening this particular day.

Rafa had tapped Iago again and was miserable about it, *again*. Kilmeade stepped over to him in the dark room and knelt where he sat on the cold floor.

"My poor, tragic pup," he said affectionately and stroked the younger Rakum's hair. "Stand," Kilmeade said while rising himself. Rafael did as commanded and apologized for his behavior. "Don't apologize anymore, Rafa, I know you can't help it. This is your nature and I adore a Rakum who can be himself without restraint."

"I appreciate your understanding, Master," Rafael said, now standing face-to-face. "May I ask you a question?" he asked and Kilmeade nodded. "Before Iago, I had only come across a Rabbit twice, and both times, the Rabbit killed himself before I'd been there three nights."

Kilmeade opened his mouth to interject, but Rafael held up his hand, respect in his eyes.

"No, Iago would never end his life because of his devotion to me. He serves me with his whole being."

Kilmeade nodded with approval.

"My question is will I eventually grow used to it? Will I learn to control my bloodlust? It's been a few nights now and I am blind with it from sunset to the moment I tap his blood again. This is misery for me."

Kilmeade tempered his response knowing he didn't have good news. Speaking as gently as possible, he put a hand on the pup's shoulder.

"You are aware that I am nearly four hundred years old," Kilmeade began and Rafael nodded. "That said I have never heard of an instance where a Rakum grunt overcame his lust for a Rabbit." Kilmeade offered a sad smile. "This marking procedure was designed, if you will, with a purpose—to make certain, beyond the shadow of a doubt, that the mortal who earned the mark would never have peace. This means the pups can never stop chasing them."

Rafael's face grew red and his eyes were as miserable as before. After a few deep breaths, he expended a long exhale. "You knew this and still made my very favorite person into an irresistible drug."

"Yes," Kilmeade said and placed his other hand on Rafael's opposite shoulder. "I did it because I am your Master. Because I am an Elder. And because that is our *way*. I *like* you, Rafa," Kilmeade continued, kneading Rafael's shoulders. "I mean—more than a Rakum should *like*. That is why

I'm trying to educate you a little, proselytize you a bit. Will you learn?"

Still red-faced, Rafael nodded. "Yes, Master," he said, his voice shaking. "Thank you."

"Good. If we switched places, think on this very hard. If you were the Elder, what would you have done? Do not answer until you have given it the proper thought. There is only one correct answer, so wait for it and allow it to come."

Kilmeade ignored the pain that continued to flash in the pup's dark eyes and watched him concentrate. He was doing it—imagining himself an Elder in Kilmeade's circumstance, long without Rakum companionship, presented with a delightful youngster and a sick Cow in tow. It really only took the kid a minute to reach his answer.

"Tell me." Kilmeade moved his hands to gently cup Rafael's throat, his thumbs hovering over the man's Adam's apple.

"Master, I would have done the very same thing," Rafael said, his voice stronger, with conviction.

"And why is that?" Kilmeade asked.

"Because I would take what I wanted and make sure my will was done in every aspect of my life."

Kilmeade grinned and kissed Rafael's mouth.

Encouraged, the youngster added, "If I were an Elder, I would design my entire existence around my own desires and judge harshly anyone who disrupted my life."

"Excellent," Kilmeade said sincerely. "That is exactly how I live my life. I always have. I have been in trouble with the Fathers for it, but even they found my way charming. I am what they made me and I am the perfect Rakum Elder."

Rafael allowed a tiny smile. "You are, Master," he said and accepted the embrace Kilmeade initiated.

"And I like this—I will hold you, I will drink your blood, and I will keep you with me, because I can and because it's what I want," Kilmeade said softly and nuzzled the pup's warm throat.

"Whatever I have is yours, Master," Rafael sent silently.

Kilmeade smiled and then didn't stop until he was satisfied.

24

Chloe's ringtone jostled her out of a deep sleep. The morning sun caressed the room in an enchanting glow and the room smelled of men's cologne. On the second ring, she recognized it as David's assigned tone. Fuzzy-brained, Chloe yawned and stretched her entire body. On the third ring, she remembered whose bed she lay in. Chloe sat bolt upright and snatched the phone off Javier's bedside table.

"Hey, Sunshine. Did I wake you?"

Looking to her left where Javier slept like the dead, Chloe put her feet to the floor and tiptoed into the bath.

"Hey, Dave, what's up?" she asked, keeping her voice low.

"Are you okay? You sound funny," David said.

Chloe turned on the shower. "No, I stayed up late. What's up?"

"Javier's still missing. The police made us wait to file a report. It's so stupid—he disappeared from a hospital!" David sounded tired and irritated. Chloe chose her words carefully.

"Javier's home, Dave," Chloe said. Could she hide that she'd slept over? She rushed a follow-up. "Came in late last night, I saw him."

"What? He didn't call us. *You* didn't call us?" David barked, then his voice muffled as he spoke to whomever he was with. "How is he? What about his back?"

Chloe bit her lip; a lot had happened in the past twelve hours, but his back was fine.

"Chloe?" David pressed, at least two other voices asking questions near him.

"He looks totally normal. It must not have been as bad as they thought."

"Where are you? At my apartment?" David asked and Chloe didn't like his suspicious tone.

110

"No, I'm home," she lied and tested the water temperature.

"Okay, let me call you back. I'll try the apartment."

"Are you guys heading back now?" Chloe asked, peeking out the bathroom door at Javier on the bed; he hadn't awakened.

"*I know!*" David said to the side and then to Chloe, "Yes, we're coming. I'll call you from the road."

Chloe said a quiet good-bye and ended the call. Javier hadn't been roused by her conversation or movement about the room. Clutching the hem of her T-shirt, she realized that she was fully dressed. Javier must have played the gentleman all night, for certainly she'd realize if she'd had sex for the first time. Last night's entire adventure blurred in her memory. She recalled an unreal sensation of her boyfriend's roommate gently nuzzling her neck and then that same man drawing blood from her throat. He must have bitten her, yet she hadn't felt any pain.

Chloe darted back into the bathroom, locking the door behind her. Upon examination, her neck sported two small, purplish scars raised in the contour of her skin. They were smooth to the touch and didn't sting. So what had happened? She'd passed out and found herself on the floor with Javier leaning over her. Chloe turned off the noisy shower, flipped off the bathroom light, and peeked into the room. She blushed as she remembered her reckless behavior; she had taken her flirting dangerously far. Thankfully, Javier had resisted. Why had she so ruthlessly seduced him?

In the other room, the landline rang. Chloe tiptoed to the bed and sat, looking upon Javier asleep and as yet, undisturbed by her movements or the sound of the phone. He wasn't a Rakum; the sun fell on them both and he was fine. But he said he wasn't human; after all, he'd bitten her neck like F. W. Murnau's *Nosferatu*. Javier barely breathed and she concentrated on his chest-falls to determine he was alive. But of course, he was; his skin tone was just as dark, like creamy coffee, his jet-black hair mussed, and his perfect mouth partly open.

What was it about him? Even before his recent change, Javier had always been David's opposite. Now that she had the facts about David's former life, her eyes were opening regarding her attraction to both men. Was there something wrong with her—being attracted to inhuman blood-drinkers? How could God approve of such a thing? Needing answers, Chloe licked her lips and gently tapped Javier's shoulder.

"Javier," she whispered. When he made no response, she shook him more vigorously. "Javier, wake up."

"Blinds," Javier mumbled.

Chloe wasn't sure she'd understood. "Javier," she said, beginning her update, "David just called. They're headed back."

"Close the blinds," he said more clearly and Chloe did as he asked. The mini-blinds twirled closed and the sheer curtains pulled together, but the room remained sunny. She went back to the bed and sat against Javier.

"Did you hear what I said?"

Javier languidly lifted his arms, shoved the thick comforter to mid-chest, and made a grab for the pillow beneath his head. Moving in half-time, he tugged on the corner until it flipped over and covered his face. "What are you trying to tell me?" he asked through his self-made sunshade.

"David called," Chloe said and touched his bare shoulder. "They're headed back."

"Ugh…" Javier moaned and fell silent.

Chloe prodded his arm. "Javier, are you okay?"

"I'm fine," he said, his voice raspy. "The sun makes me nauseous."

Chloe looked at the window and then at the clock read-out. It was only 9:30 in the morning, which meant he had a long day of discomfort ahead.

"I'm sorry," she replied, then more softly, averting her eyes, "and thank you. For being a gentleman. With me. Last night."

Javier peeked at her a moment before replacing the pillow over his face. "You're welcome."

Chloe didn't speak for a few seconds, wondering what would happen when David returned. Were things different now? Then she remembered something Javier had tried to tell her last night. After a few false starts, he never completed his confession.

"Javier," she said and waited for him to indicate he'd heard her.

Javier exhaled with a sigh of resignation.

"Javier…" She moved her hand down his arm a few inches. "You wanted to tell me something last night. You said, 'I messed up. I need to tell someone.' What did you mean? Does it have anything to do with why you're acting so weird? With what's happening to you?"

"Tonight," he said. "Let's speak tonight."

Chloe's face heated with displeasure. Didn't she deserve better than being shut out? Chloe grabbed his pillow and yanked it into her lap.

"Javier, talk to me. You owe me," she said hardening her tone. Javier groaned and flopped his right arm over his eyes.

"Tonight," he repeated, but Chloe punched his arm and shouted his name. Javier peeked from under his arm. "Chloe, I'm sorry, I can't do this now. I'm sick."

"You're not so sick that you can't tell me what's going on. Talk to me!" she barked, glad that her nerve remained strong. Ever since she survived Rufus's torture, she felt as strong as an ox.

Javier moaned and touched the sheet over his middle. "I'm sorry about last night."

"Sorry for biting me?" she asked more softly than intended.

He nodded. "I should've had more self-control."

Chloe kneaded the soft pillow in her lap and waited to see if he'd say more. Within a minute, he did.

"Last week, before my fight with Roman, before we left Beth Rider's house…I-I…" Javier didn't finish. Chloe touched his shoulder.

"You did something you wish you hadn't, right? What was it?" Chloe had surmised that much from his ramblings and half-sentences. "Go ahead. Don't you trust me?"

"Yes," Javier said and covered her fingers with his free hand. "Yes, I *do*." He sighed and rubbed her fingers.

"It's my fault, you know, what happened last night," Chloe said quietly, "you did everything you could to get me to object. I came on to you. I'm horrible…" Embarrassed, Chloe lowered her voice to a whisper. "I like you. Maybe too much. Is there something wrong with me?" And only to herself she finished with, *Why do I only chase monsters and not normal men?*

Javier frowned. "I hypnotized you. It's not your fault."

"Maybe so, but I could have said no," Chloe said. "I knew what was happening."

Javier cracked a weary smile and squeezed her fingers. "You remind me of someone I knew a long time ago."

"Somebody nice?" Chloe asked quietly.

"An angel, an innocent, a victim of my people." Javier grunted and shook his head. "My *former* people."

"What did you do in Montgomery that you wish you hadn't?" Chloe pressed gently and then changed position to be lying next to Javier staring at the ceiling fan.

For a bit, Javier didn't answer and then covered his face with his arm again. "I was mixed up, angry, disgusted with everything. I wasn't fitting into my mortal skin, I never felt natural. It was so damn easy for David!" he hissed and then softened his tone. "I was weak."

"What happened?" Chloe asked, unable to guess what he might say.

"When Canaan arrived at Beth's house, I was alone. He seemed so perfect, so at peace. I looked at him and wished for the old days."

"Yeah," Chloe agreed wistfully. "You know, I saw a photo of him online when I Googled his wife, Marcy. He was very, even in a photo, knowing what I know, well..." Chloe blushed.

"Don't be embarrassed. Satan made the Rakum that way, and he's an Elder, so multiply his spiritual output times a hundred."

"What?" Chloe's brain had fuzzed a little at the mental distraction. *What is Javier saying about Satan?*

"It doesn't matter," Javier said and shook his head. "The Rakum are supposed to attract you, mankind, all of us. Drawn to be beautiful to draw us away from God." Javier rubbed his face. "God help me, I did it myself for more than a hundred years."

Chloe knew it was wrong, but she wanted to see him that way. If only she could go back in time and meet all of them—Roman, David and Javier as Rakum. She mentally spanked herself and changed tracks. "You're saying, seeing Canaan made you regret being saved?"

"No—I thank God for yanking me out of hell. No, looking at Canaan made me long for what I *knew*, what I was good at, what made me most at ease...does that make sense?"

"Yeah," Chloe said honestly. "I mean, all the Wraiths in that monster's house were powerful and scary. From what David told me on the way home after, Canaan was heroic and brave—if you used to be anything like that it's completely understandable that you might miss it."

"Chloe, that Rakum is an Elder. I was never anything close to being as powerful as he is. You need to realize that no matter how heroic or amazing..." Javier said and paused as Chloe blushed and started to interrupt him. "No, listen. The point I'm trying to make is I would have done anything to please Canaan that night and all he wanted was my blood. I shouldn't have, it's not the way of God's people to consent to such a practice, but I did. I gave it up, didn't even want to resist."

"Was that so wrong?" Chloe hadn't resisted Javier last night when he asked to try his experiment. She knew what she was agreeing to. In her heart, she knew he was going to drink her blood, like Rufus, only gently. Why was Javier so bent out of shape?

"You don't understand," Javier continued, his voice strained. "My sin was wanting to please Canaan more than God. And I knew Canaan wanted me to convert back. He thought if I took his blood, I'd be returned to the fold. He thought his blood was powerful enough to make me a Rakum again."

"Is that what you wanted?" Chloe asked, barely audible.

"Yes, no, I don't know. It doesn't matter now. Later that night, he convinced me to drink blood from The Last."

"That kid?" The one they called The Last started up on Rufus even before the Elder showed up. He had taunted Rufus mercilessly and showed no fear. Chloe sensed that this youngster had somehow taken over the Rakum, but she didn't understand how or why.

"Isaac is an abomination, heartless, self-serving, and completely evil. I took his blood at Canaan's request and I haven't been the same since."

"I don't understand. You're in the sun; you're not a Rakum…"

"Isaac has power beyond my comprehension. I don't think anyone except maybe the Fathers knew his true strength. He might be unstoppable. I took his blood and it did something to me, something that I haven't yet figured out."

Chloe considered his words, realizing from her knowledge of the Rakum that he was in a pickle.

Overhearing her thoughts, Javier sighed resignedly. "Now you understand my problem."

"You're in the sun, but you also drink blood—"

"No, that's not right," Javier interrupted, his voice hardened. "It's not like before. I don't lust for blood; I can't even taste it. I'm supposed to be channeling this new energy into something useful, but I don't know what that is…"

"Like God allowed this to happen so He could use you in some way?"

Javier turned his head and looked at her from underneath his arm.

She shrugged. "What about that Isaac—will everything be cool now? Will he leave us alone? Is it over?"

Looking her right in the eye, Javier said nothing. Yet Father Damien had prophesied to him about Isaac more than a hundred years ago. Hadn't he warned Javier that this aberration of Abroghia's would one day try to kill him? Javier emptied his mind, not willing to rehash the prediction today. One thing was certain, it wasn't over, and at least one major battle remained between the spirit of evil behind the Rakum and the Spirit of God behind Beth Rider.

25

Like every morning when she awoke in her new hell, Marcy sat up from a nightmare dripping with sweat and cursing Canaan. Given a few moments to collect her thoughts, she eventually settled back down to the sheets and looked at her watch. 9:30 a.m. The monsters were sleeping, weren't they?

Where was Canaan? She wouldn't let him touch her when he visited her last night. For the first time in forty years, she refused his affections. She half-wanted him to fly into a rage and force her, but he didn't. He remained her gentleman prince, no matter how many curses she spat in his face until he left her room, head down, and eyes sorrowful.

Marcy sat up and grabbed the cell phone the devil Isaac beaned her with. He had warned her to call Canaan often and she hadn't called at all. Canaan had apologized, but she was still furious with him for turning her over to his bloodthirsty brethren. Her face grew red with the memory of the huge Black Rakum called Boris drawing her blood the first night, and then Dimple, and Beryl and Hoss—all the monsters she hated with her entire being, touching her, putting their sticky mouths on her—on Canaan's princess! How could he allow it? Those Rakum, disgusting and smelly and full of all things evil...

Marcy flipped open the low-cost Tracfone and scrolled the contacts. Canaan was second, right after Beryl. She frowned.

I should call the police.

Marcy sat up and clutched the phone with both hands.

"I can call the police!" she whispered and looked warily around the room. The Rakum *might* be sleeping, but the whole house was painted dark—if they wanted to, they could walk about all hours. For the first time in almost a week, she asked God for help.

"Please, please, please..." she whispered and punched 911. Immediately, a woman picked up on the other end with a practiced identifier. Marcy spoke fast. "Help me! My name is Marcy Haddle. I've been kidnapped! They're holding me at 144 Sherwood Lane upstairs in a bedroom. They might come get me any minute so listen. I am a Tennessee Park Ranger and one of these guys has my sidearm. They are extremely dangerous. Send lots of reinforcements!"

"Ma'am, I have dispatched officers to your location—"

"Send LOTS!"

"Ma'am, where are your kidnappers now? Are you alone?"

Marcy looked at her closed door. It wasn't locked. The bloodsuckers had full and easy access to her whenever they wanted. "I'm alone in this room," she whispered, "but they are probably in the basement..."

"Ma'am, would it be safe for you to leave the house right now?"

Marcy pictured herself walking to the front door. Why hadn't she considered it? Six nights and six days she remained in the house voluntarily—why? Was it because of Canaan? To the dispatcher, she had no real answer.

"Uh... I don't know," she stammered.

"Ma'am, remain where you are if you're not sure. The officers will reach you in a few minutes. Listen for them."

"How many did you send?" Marcy asked, still whispering and wondering how long she had before one of the household monsters burst into her room to punish her.

"Ma'am, are you injured?" the dispatcher asked, ignoring Marcy's question.

"Uh, well..." Marcy frowned. Every injury they had inflicted healed on its own in moments. Her rescuers would find no wounds on her because she was a Rabbit. She looked at her watch; four minutes had elapsed. Did she hear sirens?

"Ma'am, the officers are at the security gate, but it's not locked. They're going to push it open..."

"Oh, God!" Knowing that help was so close caused Marcy to unhinge. She ran to her bedroom door and flung it open. "Hurry! Help me! Please!"

"Ma'am, the officers have gained entry. Do you see them?"

Marcy looked down the dark hall both ways and then tip-toed to the top of the stairs. The house felt empty, quiet—dead. Marcy ran down the steps. "I'm at the front door! Should I open it?"

"Yes, ma'am, the police should be there. I advised them your situation." Marcy closed the cheap cellphone and whipped open the door.

Meeting the eyes of the police officer, Marcy lost consciousness. Thankfully, she was caught before she hit the marble floor.

Still as the dead, Isaac and Boris lay stacked under the basement floorboards and listened to the chaos up top. Ten minutes ago, he, Boris and Hoss had been shooting pool in a closed off portion of the basement. This extra space had been used as a larder by the previous mortal owners, but Rufus, and now Isaac, used it to plan, relax, and play pool or cards as far away from the sun as possible. In his time at the stolen estate, Rufus had already installed several carbon steel locks on the door and reinforced the wood with an iron frame, but the room had been open when all three Rakum heard Marcy Haddle say aloud, "Help me! I've been kidnapped!"

Trying to preserve his servants, Isaac sent Hoss up to silence the Rabbit and secure the house. How he ended up confronting police had to have been his own carelessness. When the sirens were at the security gate, Boris threw all the locks and shut off the lightbulb overhead. Then he stomped the floor in different spots until he heard an echo.

"Here, Master, hurry—" he had whispered. *"Elder Rufus hollowed this out to hide cash. We can both squeeze in."*

In the pitch-black underground darkness, Isaac listened to him pry up floorboards with his fingernails until the two of them could crowd under the floor. Boris insisted Isaac lie underneath him, swearing to take apart any mortal that tried to get to him. It was going to be daylight for another eight hours and Boris' tone and furtive movements revealed his anxiety.

"You did well," Isaac said to him telepathically as he replaced the boards on top of them, easily re-securing the nails with a combination of careful physical manipulation and telekinesis. He lay atop Isaac, his back to Isaac's front, and both of them slowed their breathing to the minimum to await the exit of all mortal authority.

"Master, forgive me for crushing you," Boris began silently, but Isaac hushed him.

"Shh shh, you have done excellently, and rest your mind, my friend."

"My Rabbit—Master, they will see her. I left her in my room," Boris sent.

"Let the mortals do their thing, let them have those Rabbits for now, but don't be concerned for our safety. I have seen our future. We will not be discovered and at nightfall, we will leave here. Shh shh..." Isaac soothed him and Boris's frantic mind went quiet.

Isaac listened to the gunshots, the shouting men, the instructions as those same men traipsed through the house. They entered the basement and clomped around the space in heavy city-issue work boots. Because he could, Isaac sent out a powerful delusion to any mortal that lay eyes on the special room door where they had hidden themselves under the floor. Not a single officer of the eleven that came through the basement over the next eight hours saw that door. Boris and Isaac snoozed some, silently shared plans, and waited for the moon. Let Canaan's idiot woman go with the police. Isaac would deal with her later. Everything in its time, Isaac thought to himself and smiled. The future was bright and he feared nothing.

"Weirdest thing I've ever seen... Juster emptied his piece in the guy before he dropped."

"Was the guy high on coke?"

"I dunno, but when we got him on a stretcher and rolled him outside, he melted."

"You're pulling my leg."

"Kelly, shut your mouth!"

"I'm serious as a heart attack—the guy turned into black oil and red shit.

"That little girl said they were vampires."

"That makes sense..."

"Kelly, idiot! Don't you have paperwork to file?"

Marcy looked around the gray-walled hospital room and focused her eyes on a circle of five uniformed officers huddled fifteen feet away at the wide door. A man in a suit with a crooked tie physically shoved two of the men away as he entered and the group dispersed, sending Marcy strange looks until they were out of view. The suit pulled up a chair next to Marcy's bed and gave her a grim smile.

"How do you feel, Ranger Haddle?"

A Jackson PD detective's badge hung around his neck on a long leather thong and up close, Marcy picked out a mustard stain on the front pocket.

"What happened at the house? Did ya'll get the guys who kidnapped me?" Marcy had overheard the snippets of conversation as she came to, but making sense of it didn't come easy. At her question, the detective frowned.

"Ranger, I'm Detective Pouncey. Tell me what happened."

Marcy's mind raced unsure what to say, or if she should say anything.

"Who is the child? Was she with you?" he asked and Marcy whipped her head around to read his eyes.

"A child? I didn't know they had anyone else. Is she okay?"

The detective jotted something on his pad and returned to her gaze. "A girl, preteen, she's stable, they have her in observation. What happened?"

Children, Canaan? Marcy paled. *Calm, calm, calm. I need to calm down...*

Marcy closed her eyes. Maybe the girl had nothing to do with Canaan. Marcy was safe, free from the Rakum's clutches. Now she needed to give them a believable story and, bastard or not, Canaan was her lover. She thought fast.

"Detective Pouncey, where's my cell phone?"

"It's right here." He pointed to the table beside the bed. "We took the numbers off of it and some interesting texts. This isn't your phone at all, is it?"

"No," Marcy said while reaching for the cell. "One of the goons gave it to me. I guess it never occurred to him that I'd use it to call you guys." She caught the officer's eye. "What happened to them? To Isaac? To Hoss?"

"Only one man was found in the house. I'm afraid he didn't make it."

The earlier conversations came together in her mind and formed a fairly solid picture of what happened to the Rakum. Whoever it was attacked the police, they fired their weapon into him, he fell unconscious, and when they wheeled him outdoors to the waiting ambulance, he burned to death in the bright Mississippi sun. Marcy's lips parted—which one was it?

"Was it a boy?" she asked, then kicked herself. If it had been Isaac, the detective would have said a *boy*, not a *man*.

"No, ma'am," Pouncey said looking at a notepad. "Male, 6'3", approximately thirty, dark hair, dark eyes. Was a different child than the girl with you?" the deputy added, now alarmed anew. He motioned to an officer near the door to come over. "Do we need to issue an Amber alert?"

"God, no!" Marcy said and waved the other officer away. "No, I said boy, but he's not a boy." Marcy thought fast to cover up her big mouth. "I'm fifty-six years old, hell, you're a boy as far as I'm concerned."

Detective Pouncey slow-blinked a few times, deciding what to say next. Marcy had no intention of blabbing again and she waited for him to speak. Finally, he sighed and continued his original line.

"Okay, sure. Hoss and Isaac, you said? Are these the men that kidnapped you?" Pouncey asked and Marcy nodded. He jotted another note on his pad. "We haven't recovered your firearm. Another team has been dispatched search the house."

Unconcerned with her Glock, Marcy mumbled miserably, "God,

Canaan...", and averted her eyes. Isaac and Boris were loose somewhere, and where was her husband?

"Ranger, I need you to tell me what happened. From the top," Pouncey said patiently.

Marcy closed her eyes. Canaan, her love, her husband, her hero. She grimaced with her next thought. Big, bad Canaan, former terror to all inferior Rakum, now servant to the youngest one of all. But what to tell this detective? If Canaan returned while it was swarmed with cops, he might tangle with the authorities. He might fight back and be shot. The blood left her face and she gasped. Without answering the detective, she found Canaan's number in the cell phone and pressed send.

"Ma'am, who are you calling?"

Marcy waved her hand as the phone rang a third time. *Come on, Canaan. Come on!* Maybe he thought it was Boris calling. Maybe he was asleep and couldn't hear it.

"What?" Canaan's said on the other end, his voice hard. Marcy's heart leapt in her throat.

"Canaan! Oh, God! I called the police! They cleaned out the house." The detective leaned forward, uncomfortable with Marcy's use of the phone, and she hissed at him to chill out. "It's my husband! Just a minute!"

"You called the police?" Canaan asked, his voice incredulous. Then he whispered, *"Is Isaac dead?"*

"I wish!" Marcy crawled out of the hospital bed on the opposite side so Pouncey couldn't reach her. "No, it was Hoss. The police killed him. They didn't see Isaac or Boris. Canaan—there was a *child!* A little *girl*—somebody's *baby!* Did you..." Marcy stopped, recalling the police surrounded her conversation. Canaan hadn't responded anyway. Into the phone, she said, "Please, come and get me, Canaan. Please."

"Ranger Haddle, I'm going to have to ask you to hang up or put me on with your husband..." Detective Pouncey stepped around the bed and Marcy shuffled into the corner.

"I'm proud of you, Marcy, you did good," Canaan said sounding a little like his old self. "But you're a big girl and I'm trapped. Can you see the windows? It's high noon. I'm not going anywhere."

"Where are you? I can come to you," Marcy whispered, even though the detective was right next to her now, his fingers touching the phone as he politely asked her again to cease speaking.

"Marcy, go home. I'll find you."

Click.

Marcy pulled the phone from her ear and stared at the display. *Go home. Of all the—*

"Ranger, ma'am, who you were speaking to?" the detective asked, removing the phone from her hand.

"Canaan. Just Canaan. He's my husband. He didn't do anything wrong." Numb, Marcy walked back to the stiff bed and sat down.

"I see. Canaan precedes a person named Beryl. Who is that?"

Marcy shook her head, not sure what to say and who to finger for the job. They were all monsters, but Beryl had been sent on a mission with Canaan. She shouldn't point a finger at him while he was with her beloved.

"Ma'am, I'm going to need these answers if I'm going to help you. Please, if you can, tell me what happened."

Marcy lay back on the bed and closed her eyes. She'd make up something believable, leaving Canaan and Beryl in the clear. Then she'd go home and wait for Canaan to come.

What else could she do?

Marcy sighed and began her tale.

26

US-22 S, Three hours to Tuscaloosa
November 11th, 6:30 p.m.

The boy was livid and Roman had no luck getting him to open up. Since the phone call to Chloe Bushman earlier that morning, David had said very little. At the moment, he sat silently in the rear of the truck staring out the window, frown lines etched into his brow. Roman would give anything to be able to read his mind.

No! He hastily reprimanded himself, not even aware that he had innocently wished for the powers of the devil that he once possessed as a child of Abroghia. Next to him in the passenger's seat Damien grunted and gestured to the exit sign.

"Pit stop, please, Roman."

"Of course," Roman said gently. His beef wasn't with the old man who in another life had been his god and Father. No, his irritation flared against the youngster in the rear, a former Rakum grunt, an inferior that he would have squashed for his insolence a mere seven years ago.

"Stop it, Roman!" he nearly shouted, but was able to keep his internal raging silent. The stress of the past few days had eaten away at the camaraderie the three former Rakum enjoyed when first delivered from the Rufus in Jackson, Mississippi. All three of them had previously been transformed into mortal men when they admitted their faith in the Creator of the universe, the God of Israel. This afternoon, as they raced home at just above the speed limit, Roman held his angst in check knowing his companions were consciously doing the same thing.

Javier d'Millier. Roman swallowed and shook his head as his adopted son's name came to mind. Their current distress was due to his lack of concern for anyone but himself. Five days earlier, when he, Javier, and Elder Canaan were bound for Jackson to rescue Chloe Bushman and Selene Cherrie, Javier provoked a fistfight with Roman. On the side of the busy interstate at ten o'clock at night, Javier came at him with ferocity, and

123

although Roman did his best to avoid harming the boy, Javier eventually lost his balance and fell into traffic. His injuries were severe and Canaan stooped down to heal his concussion before the ambulance arrived. However, the enigmatic Elder assured Roman that Javier had suffered a broken back. How had he walked out of the hospital that very night?

"The McDonald's, please," Damien said softly as the yellow arches appeared at the top of the exit ramp.

Roman nodded and steered the truck in that direction, his mind still reeling on Javier's ability to walk after the injuries Canaan described. Had the Elder healed his back without realizing it? That was a question David posed earlier, but Roman disqualified such a possibility. As a former Elder himself, one that excelled in diagnosing and healing Rakum *and* human ailments, he knew such a mistake was impossible. A Rakum doesn't guess, he *knows*, and when Javier was carried off by the EMTs, he was paralyzed. *Then…how?*

"I won't be long," Damien mumbled as he hopped out of the truck.

Roman watched him go. The former Father had been healed of cancer and a strained shoulder by still-Rakum Father Theophilus before they left Rufus's estate. He moved like someone in his 40's. How long would that last? The man looked seventy, but was born 2000 years ago. How long before the sorrows of the flesh caught up with the old guy? Roman sighed; there were many unanswered questions and all the prayer in the world hadn't provided answers for even a fraction of them.

"Javier's with her, I know it."

It was David's voice, edgy and angry from the back seat, finally ready to explain his behavior. Roman turned to watch his face. David had been a young Rakum when he became a mortal man—barely seventy. Today he looked twenty. His reddish-brown hair was short and spiked, and his dark green eyes became murky as his emotions churned within. Roman softened his expression, hoping to encourage the kid to elaborate on his comment regarding his roommate.

"Somehow, he got to her… *Dammit!*" David cursed and struck the window with his fist. "I should have gone home with her. Why did I come out here to get Javier? Why did I care? Why did I listen to you?"

Roman winced inwardly for he had asked David to come and it was his idea to send Chloe Bushman, who still lived with her parents, home. He thought David's easy-going companionship would ease everyone's burdens once they rejoined Javier in the hospital and waited for him to be discharged. But when they arrived, Javier had already left—disappeared, actually—and had returned home without calling them.

"You think Javier is with Chloe romantically?" Roman asked. David nodded one quick tip of the head and looked away. "And you know this how?"

David regained Roman's gaze, his scowl evident. "Plain old human intuition, *Dad*," he said stressing the last word as an insult.

Roman bit his tongue, reminding himself that of all their newly-mortal brethren, David had always been the most kind. He had rarely seen the boy incensed and it was very likely he never had been this angry before. David was probably so unfamiliar with such hateful emotions that he frightened even himself. Roman empathized and his face showed it, for David's stern expression wilted.

"I'm sorry, Roman, you didn't deserve that. I just can't get the image out of my head..." He trailed off.

"The image of what?"

"Javier and Chloe together," David said in a near whisper, his eyes wet. "I thought he hated her—all this time—so rude to her, so dismissive. But it was an act, wasn't it? You know him better than anybody—why was he so broken up about her getting kidnapped? You know something, don't you, sir. Please tell me."

Some of the old submissiveness had returned to David's demeanor and Roman's heart softened further.

"David, I can't tell you if Javier and Chloe are together, but I will tell you that he never hated her." Roman paused, preparing to tell the shameful story once more. "When he was a kid, barely twenty years old, he was obsessed with a girl who looked a lot like your Chloe. Her name was Isabella and Javier grew so attached to her that I was ordered to end her. I arranged it so that he would believe he accidentally killed her by taking too much of her blood." Roman lowered his voice. "Last week, he discovered my secret."

"*Oh...*" David said barely audibly.

In his eyes, Roman read that the kid understood his motives—his *Rakum Elder* motives. The Fathers had commanded the heinous deed and Roman carried out their orders.

"He blames you?" David whispered. Roman nodded. "That explains why he's avoiding us, not contacting us, not wanting us to know his movements." David sat up in the seat. "What is he up to? Did he do all this just to get to Chloe before me?"

Roman chewed his lip in thought. If Chloe figured into the equation, it would only be in a sideways fashion. The main factor that rolled around in his mind was Javier's amazing recovery from a brutal list of injuries. And wasn't Canaan tight-lipped about the entire affair? They were no longer in touch, but the hulky Elder's demeanor around Javier had been suspicious. Every furtive glance and every queer nod between the two ran past Roman's memory. They had a secret and now he feared it fueled Javier's current moves.

"What are you thinking, sir?" David asked respectfully.

Roman met his eye. "Chloe may be involved by proximity. I do not believe she's Javier's main objective. I've known him his entire life and something else is bugging him."

"I don't understand," David added.

"Javier's back was broken, David, I'm certain of it."

"And he walked out of the hospital," David replied. Roman nodded. "And nobody saw him," David said, his voice growing softer. "He snuck out of the hospital, stealthy, just like you taught him…"

"No mortal man," Roman said pacing his words, "could have healed from those wounds in a matter of hours and then slipped out from under a hundred watchful eyes as he did."

"He's no longer mortal?" David whispered, the possibility dawning in his eyes. "But how?"

Roman shook his head. "I'm only guessing, but he spent plenty of quiet time with Elder Canaan, and Canaan was tight with Isaac."

"Javier…" David said and turned his gaze to the early evening sky.

Damien returned to the truck and slid into his seat carrying three cups of cola and a big bag. "Three hours until we get to Tuscaloosa. Eat up and we won't have to stop for food."

Roman thanked him. From the back seat, David waved his hand, refusing Damien's offer.

"Okay, okay," Damien said, his voice weary, "I'll just have to eat it myself."

Roman smiled and unwrapped his cheeseburger. He'd scarf it down and then hit the road. Damien chatted about the people he'd seen inside and a fight that broke out between two of the store's employees, but Roman was still thinking about Javier.

Damien was gleeful about seeing Javier in the flesh God gave him, in the light of day, which was never possible when they lived as Rakum. As Damien rambled on, Roman nodded in all the right places, and in his heart prayed for answers regarding Javier. And of course, for protection for Chloe Bushman, a girl he recognized as a supernatural junkie upon their first meeting. *God help her,* he prayed, and finished off his meal.

27

The tickle that woke Isaac from a deep, dreamless sleep nudged him again, deep in his middle. Not his gut, no, not really—the more he concentrated on it, the more he decided it wasn't a place in *him* at all. Rather, it was a parallel place. *Metaphysical, interdimensional, spiritual...* The words bounced around his mind as he examined the odd tingle, ethereal fingers lightly touching the nerve endings along the length of his torso. The only place the sensation wasn't experienced was his head; the remainder of his body, including his extremities soon were wholly shivering with the vibration of whatever was coming. At that moment, a flash appeared in his mind's eye, more vivid and more three-dimensional than any vision he'd had so far.

Isaac's eyes flew open and the events of the morning came flooding back. Boris still lay upon him, both of them facing up, and the big guy was dead asleep. Isaac listened to the house and by picturing every room, hallway, and even the outside, he effectively could "see" there were no humans or Rakum about. He shifted his arm and poked Boris.

"Let's get out," he said quietly. The huge Rakum snapped awake and immediately began removing the boards above them. Once he was out, he reached down and pulled Isaac to his feet.

"Your delusion worked perfectly, Master," he said, pointing to the secured door. "Will you teach me this trick?"

"Of course. There is nothing I won't teach you, my favorite," Isaac said and squeezed his hand. "Boris—I was dreaming just now and I believe I'm about to have a gigantic vision."

"Oh, Master!" Boris said, and Isaac smiled. He didn't even know why he was excited, he just was, and such devotion was much too rare. Isaac slumped to the smooth concrete floor and tugged on Boris's sleeve until he joined him. Once they had been seated and quiet a full minute, Isaac sensed the vision returning and it was going to send him into ecstasy.

"Here it comes, my friend," he whispered and squeezed Boris's hand. He switched to telepathy and giggled as the curious tickle spread in his core. *"I want you to see it with me. Try it. Look! Do you see?"*

Isaac pointed to what now filled his entire view: a dark surgeon's table framed by a room cut out of the very rock. It was The Cave, the old Rakum Headquarters, which Boris would recognize. Without question, he was seeing the past, but it existed right now in the room he occupied. Did Boris see? He looked to the big man's profile and for the first few seconds, Boris stared into the far corner of the small room, squinting and huffing with frustration. He was trying too hard. Isaac placed his hand on Boris's leg.

"Gently, gently, my giant friend," he whispered telepathically, and Boris calmed and relaxed his shoulders. *"Good. Soften your gaze, open your mind, listen—"*

Isaac stopped speaking as the breeder on the steel table before him screamed in agony. She was bleeding profusely and the Rakum physicians were poised to save the infant and disregard the mother. It was common enough that the breeders died in childbirth, but Rakum newborns were as fragile as the humans they mimicked and all care was taken to keep them viable.

At his side, Boris stiffened and rolled to his knees. "I see, Master!" he said and fell silent. Isaac grinned and patted him playfully.

"Watch with me. Shhh..." Isaac and Boris trained their eyes to the spectacle before them that had occurred more than fifty years ago.

The woman on the table was pale, her long yellow hair damp and dripping off both sides of the table in strings. Her wrists and ankles were bound on four corners with thick leather shackles and she wore no clothing in the cold, damp underground birthing suite. She screamed and cursed until her throat gave out. Then the breeder gasped, helpless and dying as the doctors steered the mewling new brother from her womb. When the infant slipped free, the woman strained, seized violently, and fell still. As Isaac and Boris watched, the physicians feverishly worked over the infant on an adjacent table. After only a couple of minutes, shoulders drooping, they whisked the baby to the far side of the rock-carved room and held it up to a darkened window.

"It is a brother, Father; he does not live," the taller of the two doctors said to the figure on the opposite side of the glass. Isaac squinted his eyes and tried to guess the Father's identity as the vision proceeded.

From the opposite wall, a wispy, man-shaped specter entered the room unseen by the Rakum working there. Isaac and Boris watched as it floated toward the breeder on the table and then toward the lifeless infant in the doctor's arms.

"Zahdone, Prince of the Air," a voice whispered in Isaac's mind. Within moments, but seeming to take minutes in the slowed-down-world of his waking dream, the black spirit drew near to the doctors.

"Zahdone, the Powerful and Mighty, so wondrous and beautiful, none can compare..." the harsh whisper came again, but Isaac didn't dare glance at Boris to see if he heard. The ghostly apparition came to rest over the child and hovered above, its shape shifting like gravity-defying sand.

"I'm sorry, Master," the shorter physician mumbled and reached for the dead Rakum child in his partner's hands. As he made contact, the spirit called Zahdone melted out of sight at the baby's chest. The tiny bundle suddenly screeched and writhed, slipping from the doctor's gloved hands. The second doctor reached forward with unnatural speed and grasped the child by the heel before he hit the stone floor. The physician looked up to the glass and re-presented the infant to the dark figure of their Master.

"He lives, Father Abroghia! Your seed lives!"

A chuckle erupted from the dark room on the other side of the window. "Brothers, meet Yitzhak Akaron, The Last," the Father said, his peculiar voice rumbling through the cavernous space.

The vision wavered in ripples and morphed until Isaac found himself alone in a shadowy room where the only light came from a slit underneath the door. Boris was no longer present and Isaac looked around the space with interest. A familiar shape loomed behind him—his bed? One nightstand, one lamp in the corner, all thrown into the deepest shadow—and didn't they shimmer as if not truly there? Isaac grinned and shook his head in wonder.

"Yes? I am here," he said with his mouth, although in the odd mirage the sound did not enter his physical ears.

"Beautiful boy, perfect and unblemished," a feathery voice whispered across Isaac's mind. *"Share your thoughts, I will hear them,"* it said and Isaac became aware of a sensation of warm air embracing him from head to toe.

"Mighty Zahdone?" he asked, not sure what to do or say.

The entity speaking chuckled. *"Master, it is time. Awake."*

Isaac opened his eyes and considered the specter's words. Zahdone, Powerful and Mighty, had entered that dead infant's shell. That infant was *him*, Yitzhak Akaron.

Isaac's mouth dropped. "I am Zahdone."

An explosion of light, sound, and movement disrupted and then dissolved Isaac's current vision until he found himself standing in the small basement room in his own dimension with Boris beside him still on his knees staring with eyes as big as saucers.

"Master!" Boris said. "You disappeared!" The big man fell onto his face, arms out in worship whispering, *"Master, Master, powerful and mighty..."*

Isaac-Zahdone reached down and caressed his bald head. "Hi, Boris," he said, his voice different now; it rumbled around the room with substance without any effort on Isaac's part. "I am here," Isaac said smiling. "I am awake."

Athens, GA

How did he get here and why is it so familiar? A minute ago he was dozing on his bed, killing time before he was supposed to go see Stu. But then this place...

Simon spun in a circle, taking in the room. Damp stone walls, no windows because he's underground; filtered light easy on sensitive Rakum eyes; two 60's-style couches with a small fridge between them; five cot-like twin beds lining the far wall, close enough together for their inhabitants to bump knuckles; it was a dorm room. *A Bunker.* Off to his left, a doorless lavatory. In there, a shower was running. Simon's heart dissolved within him—he was back in The Cave, the Rakum Headquarters, destroyed seven years ago when Beth Rider showed up.

I'm dreaming! Simon! Wake up before he comes out! But no matter how often he blinked, the room remained.

Simon stepped for the couch just as he had seven years ago. He went to the fridge and looked inside, just as he had seven years ago. From the shower, a voice called, "Watch for my brother..."

Simon inhaled sharply. Meryl!

Meryl the Deceiver who lured Simon to this place.

Meryl the Beautiful Devil who seduced Simon away from Javier and now had him in his lair.

Wake up! Wake up! His brother is coming! Simon screamed inwardly, but continued to relive each step all over again.

"Oh, my..." A silky masculine voice trickled from the doorway. "Where have you been hiding?"

Simon spun around. Meryl's clone walked in and scanned Simon's body as a lion eyes a lamb. Beryl, identical in every way, approached with greedy hunger in his eyes. Simon spooked and fell into the couch. The

Rakum stood over him, hands on his hips, half-sneer on his mouth.

"You look like you need a hug. Do you need a hug, little Simon? I'll hug you..." Beryl falls into the couch beside him and wraps a strong hand around his thigh. "Come on. You let Meryl hug you..."

Oh, God, please let me wake up...

Simon needed to wake up before Meryl comes out of the shower. That's when it gets really bad.

"Simon, is my brother scaring you?" Meryl walks in dripping wet, yanks on a shirt he grabbed off the cold floor and Beryl gets up to stand beside him. They're facing Simon on the sofa, they're talking about *sharing* him, both taking his blood at the same time. Can he hold up? They don't care. Each twin takes an arm and hauls Simon to his feet.

It's only a dream... It's only a dream...

Meryl wants to touch him, to feel his skin under his fingertips. Beryl knows this and jerks the hem of Simon's shirt over his head. Simon has no strength; it's as if his arms and legs are made of lead. Meryl had punctured his neck earlier. Beryl rips off the bandage, opens his mouth wide and bears down so viciously that Simon goes to his knees.

I can't do this again... Simon, WAKE THE HELL UP!

Simon wanted to be brave, the water on his cheeks was involuntary. Meryl drops to his knees beside them and wipes Simon's cheek with a finger, tastes the tears, and grins with that angelic face.

"Even your tears are delicious, little Simon..." Meryl's voice fades out as he turns Simon's arm, shoves a small knife into the crook and brings the wound to his burning tongue.

"We'll make you last a long time, Simon. Don't you worry. You'll last and last and last..."

That one he hears in his mind; which twin sent it, he can't tell. They sound identical in his head. But it doesn't matter. They are having their way with him and his life is slipping right out of his body. *God won't wake me up. Why won't He wake me up?*

Simon floated away and stored up his despair.

28

S haking off the nightmare of a half-hour ago, Simon strolled down the carpeted hallway of the Athens Hampton Inn and stopped at Stu's room. He didn't dream of the twins' attack often, but recent events were screwing with his subconscious. Simon shook the wicked memories loose and concentrated on tonight and Stu Loudon.

Earlier, the Aussie came to the house and filled him in on all the details up to then—the Cows, the two Rakum, Polly and Guap, and finally, now that his website was running so well, he shared how he planned to direct the search terms to the Rakum. If any of their former masters thought to search for Rakum Cows, with very little further digging, he would find them. Since novelist Beth Rider refrained from using the true term for their race in her books, anyone who searched it on the internet would find only Stu's Gathering. Simon couldn't help but be impressed. He still didn't want to meet any new Rakum yet—not until Javier was beside him making him feel safe.

Simon checked his watch and wondered where Javier was at the moment. He had left him a text when he woke up, but received no response. Tonight, he'd call him. Why not? The guy owed him an explanation. Simon knocked on Stu's door. His Aussie pal asked him over to meet a couple of the chief Cows and said they could also get dinner. Stu opened the door wide grinning like a loon.

"You made it! Come in," Stuart said and jogged around him after closing the door.

"You sure look swanky," Simon said noting his attire. Wearing a jazzy pin-striped suit, Stuart had gotten a haircut and shaved his perpetual five-o'clock shadow. "Is Beyoncé coming?"

"*Ffff*, right," Stuart replied. "Although, she's probably a Cow, too." He grinned and pointed to the mini-fridge. "Want anything to drink? I have some Colas and those tiny Vodkas."

"Vodka? Are you drunk now?" Simon asked laughing. "You sure are hyped up. Where are our new friends? I'm starving."

"Oh, sure," Stuart said checking the watch at his wrist. He stepped jerkily to the window and looked at the horizon.

"What are you doing?" Simon also walked to the window and looked out onto the parking lot. "I assumed they were in the hotel already."

"Well, we'll see them later. I had a better idea." Simon yanked the curtains closed and grinned. "Sure you don't want any vodka?"

Simon frowned; something was off. "What did you do?"

Stuart smiled and lowered his chin. "I got a phone call from the Rakum in Jackson." His eyes flashed and the odd smile remained. Simon's mouth fell open, but Stuart continued. "They called *me*, Simon. *Me*. They knew about the Gathering. They asked if I wanted to meet with them. *Me, Stuart Loudon*. Isn't that amazing?"

Simon processed his words and frowned. "How did they know? How'd they get your number?"

Stuart sent him an irritated glare. "What does that matter? They called *me*, out of all the Cows in the world. They're headed here now!"

Simon stopped breathing and out of old habit looked at his watch. The sun had been down ten minutes tops. Depending on how far away they spent hidden from the day, they could arrive within the hour.

"You should be over the moon, what's your problem?" Stuart asked interpreting Simon's reaction. "Fair dinkum, Simo, stop being such a blouse about it."

Simon shook his head. "Stu, I told you, they're not harmless just because things are different now. And the ones in Jackson? How do you know you can trust them? You don't!"

"What happened to your love of our masters?" Stuart pressed, jittery hands clasped in front of him. "Does this have something to do with you being a God botherer now?"

"No, it has to do with you jumping the gun and bringing dangerous, frustrated and angry Rakum right to our doorstep! What happened to sussing them out? To carefully allowing these two 'nice' masters you found help determine who to inform?"

Simon had lost his temper while admitting to himself that he recognized Stuart's excitement—he'd had it too, back before he'd become a child of God. But right now, as much as he was beginning to feel the old way for Javier, he didn't feel allegiance to all of them. The realization hit him then—he was no longer a Cow. Not like he had been. Not even close. And he was nothing like Stuart Loudon—sweating, panting, and practically palpitating at the thought of being *milked* by a Rakum. Simon was suddenly queasy and deep down, a warning claxon told him to leave without delay.

"I gotta go," Simon said and turned for the door, not prepared to explain himself in the short time they had.

"Simo... *maaaate,*" Stu said following him to the door.

"No, it's okay, I'm just not ready for this. It's cool," he said and hoped that was the end of it. He needed to go; what was he to do if the Rakum arrived while he was there and took his blood by force? Stuart had no idea what he was in for if his bloodthirsty guests turned out to be the mean sort.

"Simo, Guap and Polly want to meet you. You'll be safe."

"They aren't all NICE!" Simon barked, panic creeping into his heart along with the memory of Beryl's and Meryl's attack. Stu had no idea of that kind of terror. "They aren't all like Tork or Javier!" Simon stepped up to his friend and took his upper arm in his fingers. "Some of them are awful to Cows. You did a bad thing giving away our location!"

"You're bonkers!" Stuart shouted back and broke away. "You've lost your love for your master's people." Stuart turned away from the door. "Just go. I knew you were nervous, but this is ridiculous!"

Hand on the doorknob, Simon frowned. "Look, Stu, no hard feelings, eh? I'm sorry. I didn't tell you everything about my experience with the Rakum. I loved Javier. I truly did. *I still do.* But there were other Rakum who almost killed me. I'll call you tomorrow and you tell me how it went."

"All right, mate, I'm sorry, too."

"No, you don't need to apologize," Simon said smiling and turned the doorknob. "Be careful." When he faced forward to leave, he was inches away from colliding with a Rakum he recognized.

"Simon Miller. What are the odds?"

Simon inhaled sharply and stumbled backwards. Despite a new and disgusting burn on the Rakum's face, there would be no denying his identity as one of the twins. Whether it turned out to be Beryl or Meryl mattered little, because Simon feared them equally. He sensed Stuart come up behind him and greet his visitor just before his knees buckled. He was passing out. The Rakum reached forward in a blur and caught him under his armpits.

"I'm happy to see you, too, Simon," the Rakum said and gently maneuvered him to the deep sofa. "You are a sight for these old eyes."

Simon grimaced and fought the nausea that accompanied his sudden fear. Stuart had unwittingly invited the worst Rakum of them all right to their doorstep. Who would save him this time?

The twin laid him on the couch and knelt over him. Simon looked into his face, noted his half-perfect, half-scarred visage, and put his hand to his mouth. The Rakum gingerly touched his forehead and ran his fingers through his hair.

"I have thought of you often, little Simon. Meryl and I enjoyed you so," Beryl whispered, licking his lips. "You're older," he grinned, "but still my type."

So... it was Beryl. Simon leaned over and vomited on the floor.

Ten minutes later, after Beryl forced Simon to wash up and brush his teeth—unfortunately with Stuart's supplies—he sat him on the only bed in the room. In shock and unable to resist or react, Simon remained where he was placed and allowed the Rakum to remove his shirt. As if from miles away, he heard Stuart reacting excitedly, causing Beryl to hiss for him to quiet.

"My brother is right behind me, moron. Be patient," Beryl said to the Aussie.

"Is it Elder Canaan?" he asked and Beryl nodded without taking his eyes off Simon. Stuart spun around and opened the door to look.

"Canaan's a healer," Beryl said to Simon. "I promise not to leave you bleeding all over the place."

Simon's pulse increased. Elder Canaan was the one Javier told him about. The one Javier liked and respected. Would he help?

"Ask God to help you," Simon heard distinctly in his spirit.

What could God do?

The Rakum was leaning in now, knife in hand, and about to press it into his neck. If Simon called out to God, would He miraculously cause Beryl to stop what he was doing?

The knife punctured his skin and Beryl whispered in his ear, "I've missed you, Simon. Did you miss me?"

Why don't I call out to God? Simon asked himself as Beryl fixed his lips onto his neck. *Please stop, please stop, please stop,* Simon repeated in his mind, still not able to call for help from anyone, spiritually or in the natural.

"Come with me, Simon. Meryl is dead. Things are different now with us. We have a new Father and he will let me keep you to myself," Beryl said in Simon's mind, his words musical as before. *"It wasn't my will that you be so ill-treated at Last Assembly. Let me take care of you, I will make you happy."*

Simon didn't reply aloud or in his mind, but remained as still as possible, feeling his blood drain out as it had before. Beryl said he would keep him, take care of him. Would he love him as Javier had?

"You show me how to love, Simon, and I'll do the best I can," Beryl replied.

135

Simon jerked. What did it mean that he was just overheard telepathically by Beryl? Had he slipped away from God?

Beryl pulled back and used a handkerchief to apply gentle pressure to Simon's wound. *"Ahhhh... I've missed you,"* Beryl sent silently, eyes closed, obviously buzzing on the stolen blood. *"I'm not offended that you switched sides,"* he cooed, his telepathic voice dreamy. *"Tastes different, I like it..."* Then after nearly a minute, *"Come with me, Simon,"* Beryl said to him silently, locking Simon's gaze.

"Javier's going to be mad," Simon gasped not planning his words. "He isn't going to allow you to take me away..." Simon coughed as the weakness consumed him.

Across the room, he was aware of the door opening and Stuart's excited greetings to their second Rakum visitor. But Beryl wasn't done. He took Simon's chin with his free hand and forced him to look him in the eye.

"Javier is over," Beryl whispered as Simon tried to hear Stuart and the new visitor's chatter at the same time. "He's not even a Rakum. I *am*, I'm here, and..." he gestured to the other Rakum, "Elder Canaan will back me up—you're coming with me."

Simon grimaced and gathered what little strength he had remaining to push against Beryl's chest. The Rakum tightened his jaw, snarled, and stood away from him as Simon passed out.

"Javier? What about Javier?" Canaan said and approached the couple with Stuart on his heels. He heard d'Millier's name spoken before he even entered the room and once inside, Stuart wouldn't hush long enough for him to hear what Beryl and the blond guy were talking about. Now the mortal had passed out and Beryl was fuming. Canaan jabbed Beryl's shoulder and asked his question again. "What about Javier?"

"I don't know, okay?" Beryl snapped and crossed to the window.

"Who is this kid to Javier d'Millier?" Canaan asked and threatened Beryl with a glare.

"He's Javier's Cow. Javier deserted him at Last Assembly, okay? Now back off!" Beryl snapped, his tone harsh, shrinking from the threat of being pummeled by an Elder. Canaan balled his fist to pound him when Stuart touched his elbow.

"Master, I'll tell you about Javier."

Canaan turned to face the Cow and the guy visibly shivered, almost useless in his excitement. Milking him would calm him down and would ease the hunger in Canaan's middle, but hearing about Javier seemed much more pressing. Canaan put one hand on Stuart's shoulder and squeezed hard enough to help the guy concentrate.

"Spill it," Canaan said.

Stuart winced from the pressure and burbled, "Simon's master contacted him. Came to see him. He was different—confused. He freaked Simon out."

"How?"

"He was acting weird. Walking about during the day, but took his blood at night. Master Polly said he's no longer Rakum, but also he's not human…"

"Polly?" Canaan asked smiling. "As in, Polly and Guap?"

Stu nodded effusively. Canaan remembered the two genial pups with the laughing eyes and terrible, unfunny jokes. He'd sensed more Rakum in the region, but was out of practice discerning their identities. Stuart made an impatient sigh and Canaan tilted his head to the little man.

"Where is Javier now?" Canaan asked. When the Cow didn't answer quickly enough, he squeezed his shoulder harder. Stuart fruitlessly shrank back. He *was* concentrating though.

"Ow! I'm sure his number is in Simon's phone!"

Canaan released the Cow and leaned over the snoozing man on top of the covers. The guy was shirtless and wearing relaxed-fit blue jeans. Canaan fished through his front pockets and then roughly flipped him over, locating his cell in his back pocket.

"Be careful with him," Beryl said from the window.

With a mischievous grin, Canaan rolled the youngster off the bed altogether without meeting Beryl's eye.

"Dammit, Canaan!" Beryl hissed and jogged over to lift the man back onto the mattress.

"Shit," Canaan chuckled and crossed to the desk. "He's not made of glass." He scrolled through Simon's contacts and found Javier filed under JDM.

"Javier d'Millier," Canaan said under his breath and pressed send. He sank into the chair and Stuart lighted at his feet on the floor, eyes wide, his gaze unwavering. As the phone rang a second time, the Aussie touched the top of Canaan's shoe. Finally exasperated with the anxious Cow, he lifted his other foot and shoved Stu away with just enough force to convince him to keep his distance. Then the line connected.

"Simon, what's wrong?"

Canaan smiled and looked up to the ceiling. "Javier! You sound well.

Seems Isaac's blood worked some magic in you last week."

There was silence then Javier's voice returned strong. "Elder Canaan? What are you doing with Simon's phone? Where are you? Did something happen to him?"

Canaan lowered his gaze to see Beryl carefully straightening Simon's arms and legs on the thick bedcover. "He looks fine, but Beryl has taken quite a liking to him," he snickered good-naturedly.

"Beryl! Oh, God! Where are you? Is Simon in Jackson? How—"

"Don't piss yourself, Javie," Canaan laughed. "We came to him. He's hanging with a very interesting group and Isaac wants to know what they're up to. Did he tell you what they were doing? Did you hear about the Cow Club?"

"Please, Canaan, did Beryl hurt him?" Javier's voice carried enough pain that Canaan dropped his smile and thought of Marcy, alone and terrified with only monsters to keep her company.

"Simon's fine," Canaan said his voice low as he gave their location. "When can you get here?"

"I'm four and a half hours away!" Javier shouted. "I'm leaving now— I'm counting on you to protect Simon."

Canaan's impish grin returned as he watched Beryl assume a possessive posture next to the guy on the bed. "But Beryl likes him so much," Canaan said with a laugh and Beryl nodded. "I'll protect him. Come on over—we'll wait for you."

"No, we will NOT!" Beryl said and stood up.

Canaan pursed his lips and he sent Beryl a silent threat: *We might be getting chummy and all, but I'm your master. Don't make me squash you in front of these Cows.*

Beryl's jaw twitched. Cursing, Beryl collapsed onto the mattress beside the kid and crossed his arms.

"Ya big baby, I have a passie you can suck on," he teased grabbing his crotch. To Javier, he said aloud, "Hurry up, Javie. Beryl buzzed off him once before I got here."

Javier abruptly disconnected the call and was gone. Canaan laughed and got up to heal the kid's wound. Things were finally getting interesting.

29

Jackson, MS
November 11th, 7 p.m.

In the small basement cubby, Isaac-Zahdone gently convinced Boris to stand. It was difficult for the big Rakum to maintain eye contact and Isaac nodded with understanding. Looking at Zahdone in the flesh was akin to how they saw Father Abroghia—a pure spirit prince with only the thinnest veil of flesh between them. That explained why a mere handful of Rakum ever saw Father Abroghia in person, period.

Thinking of Ta'avah, Isaac-Zahdone smiled. Father Abroghia did not see him slip into the infant that night. Fifty-two years and the arrogant jerk had no idea he had spawned a true competitor to his throne. Isaac-Zahdone beamed with glee.

"You were wise to follow me, my delicious giant," he said to Boris telepathically. Boris averted his eyes, but Isaac-Zahdone recognized that the Rakum's heart burst with adoration. He purposed to dim his countenance and caressed Boris's thick forearm. "Of all the beings on this planet, Boris, you are safe under my gaze. Try again—look upon your god."

Boris carefully lifted his eyes and smiled. "Master, you are shining."

Isaac-Zahdone grinned. "That's because I'm awesome," he laughed and playfully nudged Boris's arm. "It's time to leave this house and we aren't coming back, so gather all the money we have and bring the car around," he said. Without question or delay, Boris leapt into action.

Isaac climbed the basement steps after Boris and went to the foyer to wait. Canaan's old Rabbit had spoiled his ready-made Rakum headquarters, but he was *awake*. The work of a stupid woman couldn't come near to interfering with his destiny; he was Zahdone and his millions of minions would help him choose the next path.

"Show me Canaan and Beryl," he commanded the air and closed his eyes.

Isaac grinned as the image wavered into place. Before his awakening, he had been able to see Elder Kilmeade as they spoke, but this was ever so much more clear. Below him, in his strange from-the-ceiling view, Beryl was caressing a blond man, whispering idiotic things in his ear. Isaac smirked and looked for Canaan. The muscular Elder was heading down the hall toward the hotel room door. Both men appeared to be on-task, which was nice.

Isaac blinked and said, *"Show me Kilmeade."*

Instantly his mind was transported, now viewing a black Lexus SUV with four occupants rolling down a dark side street and nearing a well-lit city. Isaac's view morphed and warped until he was inside the car, looking at those in the front seat, as if he were a fly on the dashboard. Smiling again at the wonders of his minions, Isaac listened in, actively blocking any ability of the Elder to sense his presence.

"I was there, Master. Iago was with me," the younger Rakum was saying to the Elder, both men lit by the yellow glow of the dash lights. Classical violin music pumped through the Bose sound system and the camaraderie between the two Rakum was palpable. "I was not affected," the Rakum finished, his finger tapping the wheel in time with the radio.

"I, too, was present—me with hundreds of my pups. We listened, we lived," the Elder replied and Isaac pondered their topic.

"It puzzles me still how so many of our brothers became mortal after that night, Master. I can't understand it," the grunt said, eyes never leaving the road. The two well-disciplined humans in the backseat paid the Rakum no attention and Isaac nodded with approval; these brethren lived by the Old Way and were not contaminated by the Rabbit's stupid religion.

Oh! Isaac grinned, *and that's what they're talking about...*

"It is about choices, pup," the Elder said, his voice neutral. "When you've lived as long as I have you awake to what exists beyond the physical world. We collided with the other side that night at The Cave. We *collided* head-on," he said with emphasis and shrugged, looking out the window. "Some emerged unchanged, like us, and some with a new heart *and* a new body."

The respectful Rakum grunt had questions, but refused to ask them. Isaac grinned again, happy to see such unspoiled brethren.

In the foyer of the huge house, Boris lumbered past Isaac carrying a leather satchel. Without a word, but a quick nod, he opened the front door and headed for the driveway. Isaac watched him go and had a new request for the spirits that served him.

"Show me Ta'avah," he said, barely able to hide his pride at his ability to

spy on the one who thought he controlled everything. Isaac was surprised his mind's eye traveled only a mile away, gliding from the foyer, over the cold brown grass in the front yard, past the broken security gate, and through the forest that encircled the acreage. Then the vision slowed and lighted on a tree branch above a pile of logs cut for burning. An axe lay on the top layer and an orange and white cat hunkered next to it, watching the night. Isaac peered around the clearing, about to ask the air for clarification, when several thousand invisible demons pointed at the cat and laughed.

"Maio-maio, Ta'avah! Catch a mouse, Ta'avah! There's a lightning bug! Here, kitty-kitty!" the voices chanted and a few of the more boisterous ones manipulated flies to pester the cat's ears. It pawed and snarled before it glimpsed the limb above it and Isaac locked eyes with his former Master. Instead of fear or dread or even excitement, Isaac felt only derision.

"You couldn't manage the Theophilus vessel?" he asked, his voice melding with the myriad that rained upon the cat below.

"ZAHDONE!" Ta'avah shouted in the spirit, but Isaac ignored him and prepared to leave the clearing, laughing at the confusion and surprise he sensed in his former Father.

"You're too late, little cat," he sang to the demon Ta'avah inside the feline. *"I'm gone. Have fun in that kitty cat,"* Isaac cooed and allowed the vision to fade.

Boris honked the horn as he pulled the Hyundai to the curb. Isaac-Zahdone danced to the car and leapt in, screaming for joy as he shut the door.

"LET'S FIND OUR BRETHREN!" he shouted.

"Yes!" Boris agreed and put the car in gear. "Where to?"

Isaac clapped his hands together. "We will meet with Elder Kilmeade in *Tuscaloosa,*" Isaac said, stressing the name in a heavy Southern accent. "Head that way and I'll divine the street address as we get closer."

"Yes, Master," Boris said and punched the GPS in the dash as he carefully steered the car through the crashed gate. "Says it's a little less than three hours away. Are you hungry?" Boris asked.

"I'm always hungry, but later," Isaac responded and looked out the window, certain that once he reached the Elder, the man would give up his blood. After all, his minions said he would and why would they lie?

Ta'avah looked all around the tiny clearing.

This can't be happening! his mind screamed. He commanded his minions to report and none appeared. He called out for Rah-keel and Zara and neither they nor their followers answered back.

So, it is to be war between us? Ta'avah shouted without words, the cat-host's back arching in response to his mood. *Then let it be so!*

Ta'avah hopped off the woodpile and ran to a tall straight pine. With feline agility, he zipped up the bark, taking huge strides, until he found the uppermost branch that would support his weight. From his vantage point seventy-five feet in the air, he was above the surrounding trees and looked down on the neighborhood, the Mississippi pasturelands spreading out before him like a green and brown blanket in the moonlight.

I don't need those ingrates. I am the great and mighty Ta'avah! Prince of the air! I will do this MYSELF! his mind screamed at no one as he settled the cat's balance and concentrated on listening to the world below. The position of the moon told him it was nearing eight and during the window of midnight to 2 a.m., his human worshippers would summon him by one of his many names. Every mortal village since the dawn of man sported those who followed the princes of the air. He would listen and wait for one or more of them to call.

Then I will have a flesh to tote me around. It may not be a full possession as I had before, but it will be enough to get me to Yitzhak... Ta'avah pictured a worshipper, tall, goth, wickedly handsome, who would summon him tonight, invoking him, begging him to appear. It was easy, it would be fun, and he would have revenge on his despicable brethren. Ta'avah would wait. Determined, he nodded his cat head and purred.

30

US-459 E
November 11th, 8 p.m.

Forty-five minutes into the long ride to Athens to rescue Simon from Beryl yet again, Javier's cell phone came alive in the cup holder where he'd dropped it. He had only given the number to Simon and more recently, Chloe; was it her turn to bring him trouble? Javier hadn't bothered to program the BMW's Bluetooth so he answered the phone and put it on speaker.

"Uh, Javier? There are a bunch of people here," Chloe said on the other end. She didn't sound alarmed, which was refreshing. Maybe there wouldn't be a second emergency tonight. "One of them is a Rakum Elder," she finished.

"What?" Javier barked not completely in control of his tone. "What are you talking about?" Canaan was in Athens, wasn't he? Javier almost shouted for Chloe to explain herself, but she handed off the phone to the visitors.

"Javier d'Millier," a voice said amicably, "you remember me, don't you? I am a friend." Javier concentrated on the voice. It wasn't familiar in the least. "Elder Kilmeade," he said and then added, "Elder Roman's brother."

"Oh, God," Javier sighed, but he didn't have enough information yet to panic. To the Elder, he calmed his voice. "Elder Kilmeade, what are you doing at my house? Chloe didn't invite you in, right?" Javier asked, remembering the custom. If it was to be a pure visit—no threats to life or liberty intended—the Rakum would wait to be invited.

"I am a gentleman," Kilmeade replied with humor.

"What do you want? Were you looking for me or David?" Javier asked, his brain racing to find memories of Kilmeade; there were very few.

Kilmeade laughed. "I'm sure you are both delightful, but I came for

Roman. This is where he is headed. I sense he is near. We would like to wait inside your abode, if you please. As a courtesy."

Javier sped down the interstate, the opposite car headlights periodically blinding him as he worked to drive and solve problems simultaneously. *I can trust Roman's brother...* And Chloe had said, *people.*

"Who is with you, sir?" Javier asked, purposefully not referring to him as "Elder" again.

Kilmeade sighed and handed off the phone. Just before Javier lost patience and re-asked the question, a new voice came on the line.

"Mr. d'Millier? My name is Santiago and I serve Master Rafael," the man said with a Spanish accent. "We have traveled with Elder Kilmeade and his Cow from San Francisco over the past two nights and you can imagine, two of us are exhausted. If you would permit us to wait inside your home, you can rest assured no harm will come to anyone there or arriving. Honest, sir, we have no intention to do anything but see Elder Kilmeade's brother."

Javier was stunned into silence a few seconds downloading the new information. Two Cows, a Rakum grunt, and a Rakum Elder had traveled across the country to *his* house. Had they come by plane? Javier knew the dangers of flying when you are morbidly allergic to the sun. Impressed, the more he thought it over, Javier was inclined to let them in. Would Chloe agree? He asked the Cow to give the phone back to her. In a few moments, she said a tiny hello.

"Chloe, are they on the stoop and you're in the house?" Javier asked, wondering how much of them she saw and how much of her *they* saw. Rakum, Cow, or mortal, a young woman alone needed to be protected. "Did they just ring the bell like normal people?"

"Yep. I saw four heads through the peephole and called you after one said his name had the word 'elder' in it," Chloe said, keeping her voice low.

"How do you feel about them?" Javier asked, now wondering why she didn't simply return to her own home. Her presence only complicated his already difficult circumstances. "They want to come inside and wait for Roman, but if you're uncomfortable, they can wait outside."

"No, they're very polite—and if you say they're harmless, I'm certainly not worried. Are they harmless?" Chloe asked, still at a near whisper. Javier smiled, the two Rakum were surely listening to their every word no matter how quietly she spoke.

But were they harmless?

"It's really cold out and one of those men looks sorta old. He's shivering, too. I say let them wait inside. I'm not scared," Chloe said.

"Hand the phone to the Rakum called Rafael." Javier waited, heard her crack open the front door and low voices discussed the chilly air.

"Javier," Rafael said, his voice strong and accented. "You needn't fear us, I give you my word."

Javier checked his speed, glanced at the GPS for the distance remaining to Simon's and sighed. "Rafael, listen, I have an emergency in Athens, Georgia, and I won't be home tonight. I am counting on you to wait for Roman and then leave right after. I do not permit any of you to stay after that. Got it?"

"Thank you, Javier. We will do as you say," the Rakum said.

"And Rafael, that young woman, Chloe, is familiar with the Rakum, but she is *not* a Cow and you two *must* stay away from her—understand?"

"Of course," Rafael said and Javier was as satisfied as he was going to be nearly two hours away from home.

"*Señorita,*" the older man with a Spanish accent sounded through the closed door. "Mr. d'Millier welcomes us."

Chloe put her hand to the knob. David was due back with Roman any minute and knowing that gave her much needed backbone.

"Ma'am, we prefer to not stand on the stoop any longer," another voice said, a tad of impatience hidden in his tone. Chloe guessed it was the one who referred to himself as Elder. He was bossy, she could tell from his first word. "I can open this door without your help."

Chloe smirked and steeled her nerve. "No need," she said and unhooked the chain. Since the quartet arrived, she'd been speaking to them through a crack in the door, chain *on*. When she pulled open the door, she looked up. Standing at least 6'4", a handsome dark-eyed, raven-haired Rakum towered over her, gave her a brief glance, and ambled in. She turned to see him pass and when she faced front, she made way as a second man, also Latino, not as tall, older, and immaculately attired in a tailored suit, approached. He stuck out his hand and bowed his head.

"Good evening, *senorita,* I am Santiago. This is my master, Rafael." He gestured toward the man who entered first and was already in the living room down the hall. He then stood to the side and looked out the door. "Behind me is Elder Kilmeade and behind him is Mr. DuPont."

Chloe hugged the wall with her back and waited while the third man entered. Taking his time, he reached the threshold and shook his coat, sending icy droplets in all directions.

"I much prefer West Coast weather, my friends," he mumbled and met Chloe's eye. "Oh, my! I have been dying to see more of you than a sliver through a portal."

Kilmeade stepped toward Chloe and she tried on a smile. It wasn't easy; his bright gray eyes caused her head to swim. Kilmeade was tall with wide shoulders and classic American good-looks. He wore his silky reddish-brown hair to his shoulders and his long canvas coat covered dark blue jeans and a thick burgundy sweater. He searched her eyes and Chloe's tongue went numb.

"Have you never seen a Rakum Elder in the flesh, my sweet?" he mused, grinning. "You're staring."

Chloe didn't answer. She'd seen Elder Rufus, but he looked like a horror movie monster. Kilmeade laughed quietly and pulled off his leather gloves, one by one, his eyes never leaving hers.

"Beautiful child, what is your name and are you spoken for?" Kilmeade reached for her hand. Chloe blushed and decided to start with her name and hope the rest of his question was rhetorical.

"I'm Chloe Bushman, Javier's...uh, friend."

"Friends, eh? That's so sweet." The Elder pressed his lips to the back of her hand and a jolt of electricity spread from the contact to her core before filtering away. Even as the fourth man closed the door and left them alone in the front hall, Kilmeade held her fingers and stared into her eyes. When he finally stood, he threw her a debonair smile.

"Tell me you're single," he said reaching out to touch her hair. Chloe forced an answer hidden in a cough to clear her throat.

"No, sir, I'm not," she said and backed against the wall. The Elder's face fell at her words and her stomach lurched. Had Javier been correct back when he accused her of being like a Rakum Cow? She shuddered and waited for Kilmeade to make a move toward the others. When he didn't move, she forced out the words, "Please, make yourself comfortable in the den. The guys should be here any minute."

"Mmmm," he murmured. He looked to be heading away, but he stopped and turned to face her, now blocking her view of the living room. "You have a curious scar under your ear, my love. Do tell; who bit you there?"

Chloe's hand went to her throat. A week ago, when the horrible Rufus attacked her and bit her neck, he healed the punctures perfectly. Last night, when Javier came too close in a similar manner, she was left with two rosy red scars where his teeth had pressed through the skin. Chloe assumed her hair hid the new wound from sight, but perhaps when Kilmeade touched her moments earlier, he actually moved it aside to see her neck more clearly. When she didn't answer, Kilmeade lowered his gaze and his voice.

"Whoever it was had curiously sharp teeth."

Chloe swallowed hard at the memory of Javier lulling her into a swoon more casually than she would have thought possible. The Elder had not given up and he awaited an answer.

"Whoever it was didn't heal you in the way of the Rakum," Kilmeade whispered and took a step toward her. "I, on the other hand, can heal any wound easily. Shall I demonstrate?"

Chloe stopped breathing; he wanted to bite her. Why hadn't she objected? Chloe thought to ask God for help, but the Elder interrupted her with his soft words.

"I don't prefer mortal blood, angel, but... are you about to consent?" Kilmeade closed the distance between them. "That changes everything. Oh, you're about to swoon. I will catch you."

Chloe blinked her eyes several times and focused on her breathing. She didn't want to consent, but he was correct—she was becoming lightheaded. She objected silently with her palms to the front of his coat.

"Master, may I ask what you find so fascinating?"

The Rakum from the living room had joined them in the hall, and his face appeared over Kilmeade's shoulder. The Elder placed his hands to Chloe's upper arms and he answered his friend without turning.

"This child is a blood donor. See for yourself," he said as one hand moved aside her long curls. The one called Rafael narrowed his eyes and shook his head.

"That's no Rakum bite—even one on the Dying Buzz. It would have healed clean."

"I agree. What do you make of it?" Kilmeade asked his cohort, running his thumb over the scar. Chloe shivered and tried to tell him to back off. All that came out was a sigh. Kilmeade smiled into her face. "She hasn't spent much time with our people. She's not a Cow. Oh, wouldn't it be sweet if she were."

"You're addling her brain, Master. At any rate, you heard Javier. She's his. We are to leave her alone." Rafael returned to the other room as he finished speaking and Kilmeade shook his head.

I'm his? Chloe wondered at the meaning.

"Are you his, Miss Bushman?"

"I'm... we're friends," Chloe stuttered. "You're making my head hurt," she said then, but her words barely carried.

"Tsk-tsk," the Elder whispered. "What *is* Javier now, angel? Is he a

human with sharp teeth? When he served my brother, he was such a delight. Strange events have taken place, yes?"

Beginning to feel more like herself, Chloe wondered what to reply. She had a few answers, but not all of them. Kilmeade gently held her shoulders as she leaned against the wall.

"Javier is something else; he doesn't exactly know what," Chloe said, sounding stronger. Then she remembered something the Elder said about his brother. "You're Roman's brother?"

Kilmeade smiled. "Don't you see the resemblance?"

Chloe pictured Roman, thinner, older, and more serious—no, the two didn't compare. As she hesitated, Kilmeade chuckled.

"Roman takes life much too seriously."

Chloe had no reply and held the Elder's gaze. Three long seconds passed in silence, during which Kilmeade massaged Chloe's ego deep inside her consciousness. *You are beautiful, precious, matchless...* adjective after adjective rolled through her mind in Kilmeade's distinct voice.

"Stop..." she whispered holding his gaze.

"Stop what?" he replied innocently as the eerie silent compliments continued.

The Elder was right, she hadn't spent time with any Rakum that weren't trying to hurt her. His presence in her mind was as three-dimensional as a hand and an embarrassing tingle began to grow in her middle. Was this behavior an Elder thing? He grinned then as if overhearing her thoughts.

"You delight me," he said in her mind and abruptly yanked his mental connection free. Chloe exhaled, blinked, and managed a sensible remark.

"They'll be here soon. Roman, David, and Father Damien."

Kilmeade clasped his hands at chest level. "Father Damien? He, too, is now mortal?" Chloe nodded her head and Kilmeade rolled his eyes, made another *tsk-tsk* noise, and turned around.

She watched him walk to the living room before she backed into the kitchen. Determined to stay out of sight until David arrived, the Elder's unspoken sentiments repeated in her mind. *You are beautiful, precious, matchless...* Chloe tried, but there was no forgetting them.

31

Athens, GA
Hampton Inn
November 11th, 9 p.m.

Canaan changed the channels on the television with telekinesis to cook Beryl's goat, which worked again and again.

"You're impossible!" Beryl barked and rose off the couch. Canaan watched to see where he was headed and he went into the bathroom. At least he wouldn't have to warn him off the Simon kid for the millionth time. Javier's young friend was dozing on the bed and had completely recovered from the bloodletting due to Canaan's excellent healing and rejuvenation skills.

Leaving the TV on a Bruce Willis flick for the moment, he rolled his head to the right and met eyes with Stuart Loudon sitting on the floor facing him. The man's behavior had normalized since Canaan buzzed off him, but he was still the most fixated Cow Canaan had ever encountered. Stories of the sort circulated for decades and Canaan found it amusing. He grinned at his own thoughts and Stu leaned forward as if about to speak. Before he did, he closed his eyes tightly and put both hands to his ears. Canaan tilted his head, not yet truly curious, but when Stuart made a sound of discomfort, he reached down and touched the Cow's shoulder.

"You okay?" Canaan asked and the Cow nodded, but his grimace remained. Canaan waited a few ticks of the clock and stood, bringing Stuart to his feet along with him. "What is this, then?" he asked, pointing to the man's face. And then he was fine again. His normal expression returned and he dropped his hands. When he met Canaan's eye, he exhaled and apologized.

"That's never happened before—Master Polly just spoke to me—*in my mind*," Stuart said, his eyes round.

"Polly?" Canaan asked and called Beryl into the room.

"He asks if he can come—he and Guap. They're in the hotel and want

149

to see you." Stuart smiled. "I love it. I just love it!"

"Ponder it later, Stuart," Canaan said in a terse tone, positioning Beryl on his right once he returned. "Tell them to come."

Stuart looked at him, eyebrows raised. "How, Master? How do I, um... call him back?"

Beryl reached around Canaan, yanked Stuart to him by his wrist, and then pulled him chest-to-chest.

"Come now!" Beryl said into Stuart's ear and roughly pushed the Cow away.

Canaan laughed. "I don't know if it works that way, Beryl," he said and helped Stuart right himself. "There ya go, Stu, you're okay. Beryl's a bit of a bully tonight."

Knock-knock.

Canaan and Beryl looked at the door and then at Stuart. When he didn't move to open it, they both shooed him with their hands. Stuart nodded and jogged to the door to look through the peephole.

"It's them!" he said to Canaan and opened the door.

"Master!" the first Rakum said when he caught Canaan's eye. He threw himself to his knees and bowed low on the carpet.

"Polly," Canaan said with a wink.

"You take my breath away! I don't know how to behave around such a great Elder," he said and although he was laughing as he spoke, Canaan discerned the respect in his tone. Seconds later, his compatriot entered, went down to both knees, but instead of putting his face to the carpet, he raised his arms in the air and looked Canaan in the eye.

"Elder Canaan, Master! You are as beautiful as I remember!" he said smiling, also emanating sincere respect.

"Guap—still *muy guapo,* I see," Canaan jibed and nodded before gesturing for the two men to stand. "I don't think you've met this scarred bag of juice. This is Beryl from Jack Dawn's pack," Canaan said and motioned for Beryl to step up. Guap and Polly nodded to him and returned their focus wholly to Canaan, which he liked—a lot.

As his name indicated, Guap was indeed very handsome, and Canaan had always liked the astute moniker. Wearing a pink silk dress shirt and dark grey slacks, Guap was 5'8", thick with muscles, and as bald as a cue ball. He sported a thin mustache on a very expressive face. Polly was taller, but not by much, with dark chocolate skin, a slender build and muscled like a cyclist, evident through his fitted yellow exercise suit.

Stuart closed the door and Canaan shooed him away. "Go into the bathroom and don't come out until we come get you," he said and Stuart disappeared in the smaller room without argument.

Polly giggled. "Good boy, Stu!" he called toward the bathroom once the door closed. "Good boy!" Then Polly caught Canaan's eye, grinning. "He loves to be petted when he's a good Cow. Guap will pet him, won't you, Guap?"

"If Elder Canaan doesn't mind, then, yes, I will pet the Cow," Guap said, his accent making his statement even funnier.

Canaan didn't know if there was more to the joke, but he laughed anyway. These two were extremely likable and they respected his position as Elder. Beryl disregarded him because he witnessed him humbled night after night by Isaac, but these two—they still lived by the Rakum code of authority, ravaged as it was the past seven years.

"How exactly do you pet a Cow?" Canaan asked.

The stocky Hispanic Rakum thrust his chest out, his butt back, and stroked his own forehead, saying, "Pet it right here, between the eyes. Puts a Cow right to sleep."

Polly laughed at his partner and soon Canaan was laughing even louder than they were. Beryl turned away and crossed to the bed. He sat next to Simon and grasped his wrist.

Canaan dropped his smile. "Beryl, I warned you. You just couldn't keep your hands off that kid."

"I checked his pulse, that's all," Beryl replied, but Canaan shook his head. He'd been listening to the man's heartbeat since they arrived and Beryl had no hearing deficiency.

"You don't need hands for that, moron," Canaan growled finally ready to punish Beryl to save face. "Go sit with Stuart in the bathroom," Canaan told him, "and I'll call you when Javier gets here."

"You don't—" Beryl began and stopped. Canaan glared at him and sent the tiniest jolt to the man's spine.

"Ya feel that? I'm infinitely stronger than you'll ever be, little brother," Canaan sent to Beryl privately and he didn't look away. *"Do not question me in front of others, understand? I will NOT be humiliated by YOU."*

Beryl spun away and stomped to the bathroom. Canaan watched him until he slammed the door and then turned back to Polly and Guap. Each had dropped his cheery demeanor and Canaan flashed them a big smile.

"Don't let Grumpy Gus ruin our night," Canaan said changing the subject. "Polly, you favor Father Amos."

The pup nodded, his easy smile returning. "Father Amos covered the breeder for both of us, believe it or not, three years apart," Polly said throwing an arm around Guap's shoulders.

Canaan grinned at the memory of the Old Way. Whenever the High Father's target Rakum population of 100,000 was reduced for whatever reason, one of the Ten would impregnate a choice female Cow to produce a new Brother. Amos had been Eurasian so depending on the Breeder, the offspring born to him would result in a mix of ethnicity. All of that was now over. Only the Fathers were fertile, so with them gone, the end of their race was in sight.

"I suppose you heard that Father Amos was slaughtered by Rufus," Guap offered quietly.

Canaan inclined his head. He knew of a few specific upper-level assassinations by Rufus, but for the most part he had kept his head down and avoided them since Last Assembly. Even before then to protect his mate, he handed off most of his Elder duties to Kilmeade.

"Master, we didn't know any Elders remained," Polly said. "When Stu told us you were coming here, I nearly pissed my pants."

"Oh, he wet his pants, trust me," Guap said smiling.

"Ass," Polly shot to his friend and then turned back to Canaan, his grin in place. "After Last Assembly, Guap and I got out of there as soon as it was safe. And it's been a miserable and *lonely* seven years."

"Lonely for the Brethren," Canaan surmised and the grunt nodded.

"We didn't eat the dead, but there were lean months." Polly glanced at Guap who picked up the telling.

"We found Stu by complete accident and I'll tell you—happy days are here again. You have *got* to see this Gathering he's collected. I mean, the Cows are out there, but their senses are dulled. They still want us badly. Stu gives us real hope."

"Have you met our new leader?" Canaan asked wanting first to hear what they knew before he chose what to divulge. Hiding the pups from Isaac wasn't even an option—already, Canaan sensed him snooping in on them much like the Fathers did in days of old.

"No, we're told he's young," Polly replied.

"He's The Last," Canaan said and both Rakum did a double-take before responding.

"*The Last* the last? As in High Father Abroghia's last offspring?" Guap asked.

"No longer a legend," Canaan said keeping it short. If he spoke about Isaac too long, he might reveal his unhappiness and he had been working overtime to show the tiny Father that he would play ball.

"Will he see us?" Polly said and looked to his friend, then he looked to Canaan, eyebrows raised.

152

Canaan exhaled slowly before replying. "He'll call you when he wants to see you. He knows you're here," Canaan said and tapped his temple. At that moment, Canaan's phone rang. It said unknown, but he sensed it was Isaac. He cleared his mind and answered. "Master."

"Those two Rakum are dim bulbs," Isaac said and laughed. His voice was different, deeper, and somehow more pronounced; Canaan did not want to ask him about it.

"They mean well," he said, knowing Guap and Polly would have overheard their Master's remark. "They want to meet you."

"I know," Isaac said offhandedly. "I called you so you'd have this number. Text their info to me. Boris and I are on the road."

"I will do it," Canaan said.

"Your Rabbit called the police," Isaac said, his voice harder. "The Jackson house is over. Hoss is dead and Boris lost his little Rabbit. All of this makes me extremely unhappy."

"I heard about it, Master. She called me afterwards," Canaan said, knowing a lie would be detected. "I promise to make it up to you." After a pause that felt much too long, The Last spoke again, his voice flat.

"Elder Canaan," Isaac said, using his title, "complete your current mission and join us. I'll have an address for you later tonight. I don't care about that woman or her betrayal. If you do what I ask, I'll forget she even exists."

"It will be as you say, Master," Canaan said softly, turning his back to the two Rakum watching on.

"And I want to be able to read those two with you," Isaac said. "Tell them to sit down and you will be my telepathy repairman."

Canaan gestured to Guap and Polly with two fingers and motioned they sit on the couch. Canaan sat on the coffee table facing them and set the phone on the surface at his thigh.

"Polly, look directly at Elder Canaan," Isaac said, not bothering with introductions or preamble to their activity. "Imagine you're looking in a mirror."

The Rakum did as commanded, both of them with curiosity and excitement written across their faces.

This might feel weird," Isaac said to Canaan telepathically and in a moment's time, he experienced an alarming weightlessness in his middle. He did not react and after another three seconds of staring into Polly's eyes, the other Rakum blinked, looked away, and grinned ear-to-ear.

"Awesome!" he said and got to his feet excitedly. "Our Master is SO YOUNG! HOW ADORABLE!"

Guap's head bounced up and down. "Do me, do me..." he whispered and he looked at Canaan hard. In half the time, Guap jumped to his feet and whooped, slapping Polly on the back of the head with joy. "He will set everything right!"

While his inferiors were marveling at what had just occurred, Canaan turned his attention back to the phone. Isaac had disconnected the call, but his new rumbling voice came across Canaan's psyche loud and clear.

"Remember what I said and stay on task."

Canaan promised he would and sensed his new Master slither away. Guap and Polly asked permission to tell Beryl about what had just happened and Canaan consented. While they expounded on Isaac's telepathic abilities, Canaan cleared his mind, happy he hadn't thought about Javier the entire time Isaac was there.

32

US-22 E
November 8 p.m.

"Elder Kilmeade is alive," Damien said thoughtfully, disconnecting his last phone call and dropping the cell in the center console. "He is waiting for us at David's. He wants to see you, Roman. Miss Bushman said he came specifically seeking you."

Roman couldn't speak; surely, he had misheard. When the call came in over the Bluetooth and Chloe's number showed on the dash, he had sent it to Damien to handle. Never would he have guessed her news would surprise him to the core.

"She didn't ask to speak to me?" David said from the rear, but Roman barely heard him. His eyes glued to the road, Roman's heart sent thanks to God. Sure, Kilmeade was still a devil, but he was alive. Damien and David launched into reminiscing about what they knew about Elder Kilmeade and Roman blocked them out. Instead, he allowed his memories to cascade forth, his heart beating with anticipation at seeing his brother.

As teenage grunts, being fraternal twins and first-rate telepaths, they were able to keep their blood connection secret. For decades, they traveled the world as Rakum comrades. Eventually, they were each promoted to Elder months apart and thus separated by the Fathers to settle different areas of the North American Continent. In 1833, at 200 years old, Kilmeade was sent to establish a Rakum presence in New York City and Roman to the villages of southeastern Canada.

Roman grinned, his face lit by the dashboard lights. Kilmeade in New York caused quite a disturbance sixty-five years later when his brother was found guilty of breaking one of their leaders' most stringent prohibitions—drinking a mortal to death. Roman kept his eye on the road ahead and sent his memory back to that night in 1887 New York.

... *"Why, brother? Why do this?"* Roman had asked his brother more than a century ago....

"I am what I am and I always have been," Kilmeade muttered around elongated canines spurred by his lengthy indulgence of the Dying Buzz. He winked one eye and scrunched his face. "And it feels *fantastic...*"

Roman shook his head and marveled at his appearance. Hunched-over and more muscular by inches, Kilmeade's shoulder-length auburn hair now drizzled down his chest on either side as long as a woman's. His formerly smoke-gray eyes were an unnaturally bright robin-egg blue and his lips ruby red.

Roman snickered. "And what does young Canaan think of this face?"

Kilmeade giggled and shrugged one oddly-rounded shoulder. "He prefers my old look." His brother leaned against the painted wall. "The pup removed my mirrors if that gives you any clue."

Roman nodded, unable to drop his grin. "There are no mirrors in the cabin," he said stepping closer to examine Kilmeade's skin texture. He'd never seen the advanced effects up close. His brother moved into his hand and closed his eyes as Roman stroked his cheek.

"I'll warn him," Kilmeade purred, enjoying the attention. "That kid worships his own reflection." Kilmeade opened his eyes and Roman stepped back. "What do you think?"

Roman crossed his arms, his eyebrows arched. "I think you should worship your image a little more. This buzz is destroying you."

Kilmeade shrugged. "Truth be known, I ended my experiment a month ago, but the Ten had already passed judgment." His brother sighed with no evidence of despair. "I look forward to the challenge."

"The hospital assignment became too predictive? Repetitive?" Roman asked telepathically and his brother nodded with a tiny grin. *"Don't worry; your secret's safe with me."*

Roman turned away to look about the dingy office space. Kilmeade had always been one for constant stimulation, where Roman preferred long, thoughtful introspection. Still, by no means did his twin lack intelligence; if anything, Kilmeade exceeded all living Elders in terms of mystical power and scope of cognitive ability. This is why the Fathers tolerated him; Kilmeade was more like them than any of their kind.

"Are you venerating me, my brother?" Kilmeade joked, peeking into his thoughts. "Bow down. I much prefer my subjects bow."

Roman chortled and clasped his hands behind him. "Young Canaan will be your master for two years. How will your ego manage?"

Kilmeade shook his head slowly, his stringy hair bunching with every move. "He is a superior companion—even better than you, my fair twin."

Kilmeade stopped short and Roman's eyebrows went up, seeing what he almost said. *If the Ten truly wanted to punish me, they would have paired me with someone else.*

Roman shook his head. "The Fathers don't coddle—"

Kilmeade's grin went to the side and they both looked toward the door as Canaan entered.

The Elder Candidate nodded to Kilmeade with a small bow. "Master." He sent Roman the same greeting and stopped a respectable distance away. "Elder Roman's pup is wandering the campus."

Roman nodded at Canaan's brief report; both Elders had telepathically watched him sample Javier's blood minutes ago in the barn. Javier had been held closer than any other proselyte Roman trained. This seemed to have made him more like Roman than the Rakum population at large. Out of curiosity, Roman asked him his opinion of the youth. For the first time, he would hear another Rakum's thoughts on his accidental protégé.

Canaan's face shined with humor at the question. "That one is special, Master. Brave, inquisitive, and tough."

"You forgot delicious," Kilmeade added touching his temple to remind him he missed nothing.

Canaan shook his head with a wide grin. "That he is. Like none other." When he faced Roman, he offered another small bow. "Elder Roman, Javier is clear evidence of your superiority raising up proselytes."

Kilmeade stepped close to Roman and wrapped his arm around his shoulders. "One day, he may be every bit as great as I am!"

Roman endured the embrace with a roll of his eyes. His brother's need for tactile stimulation exceeded Roman's and with the Dying Buzz dampening his self-control there would be no stopping him anyway.

"Aye, Master," Canaan agreed and turned to leave. "Aye."

Roman watched him go, still under his brother's wing. An internal nudge informed him the sun was a mere ninety minutes away and he hadn't had a blood meal. Kilmeade walked him toward the door, pulling him along.

"Canaan's favorite ward is the orphanage," his brother whispered in his ear as they entered the hall. "Go with Poppy. The children are frightened of my face," he giggled. Within a few seconds, a stout man rounded the hall corner and strode toward them. Roman had been introduced to Kilmeade's Cow who was also the groundskeeper. Without a spoken word, Poppy nodded to his master and then to Roman, indicating he'd lead the way.

Roman followed him and Kilmeade sent images of the many children of various ages available to tap for their blood. Rubbing his palms together, he sent a telepathic greeting to Javier. The pup should join him; this was to be their new assignment and they would discover its rewards together.

"Companionship is everything," Kilmeade sent him then. *"Treasure those you can enjoy, my brother. Most of them, we only tolerate."*

Roman grinned at his twin's advice and told Javier to hurry.

33

Jackson, MS
Jackson Marriott
November 8th, 8 p.m.

"Ten hours, Beth! Ten friggin' hours! I might as well have been kidnapped all over again!" Marcy barked into the phone. Pretty and perfectly-behaved Beth Rider would absorb her angst as she had before the crap hit the fan for all of them, so Marcy didn't hold back. "And do you think the police believed me? That Pouncey—patronizing, son-of-a—"

"Did you at least hear from Canaan?" Beth asked, her voice even smaller than usual across the hotel landline.

"What do you think? He's off with that monster, Beryl, doing whatever the tiniest and most dreadful monster of them all told them to do!" Marcy uttered a few choice curses into the phone and closed the curtains to the parking lot.

"Did you get a hotel room? You shouldn't try to drive home this late," Beth said in her mom voice.

"Yeah, which they shoulda paid for," Marcy retorted, still angry at the world. It was a six-hour drive to her apartment *if* she could rent a decent car so late. She opted for the hotel the trauma CNA suggested. Marcy shook her head; it had been altogether a horrible experience.

"Hang in there," Beth said kindly. "Canaan loves you with his whole heart. Try to be patient and keep praying."

"Pray for what? This should be over!" Marcy shouted. "They just finished destroying Rufus! That should be enough!"

"*Should be* and *is* are two different things," Beth said.

Wasn't there the tiniest bit of irritation in her voice finally? Marcy's mouth turned up in victory.

"Roman is on his way to see Javier and I'm hoping they're done, but if Canaan's in danger, we'll help him. He came through for us and none of

159

us will sit back and let bad things happen to you or your husband. Plus, we're sisters now."

Marcy's grin fell. This woman barely knew her, but because they were both marked as Rabbits, and because Marcy came to know God while sitting in Beth Rider's living room, and because they used her man to take down Rufus, she was going to risk her life and lives of her loved ones all over again? Speechless, Marcy turned from the window and fell onto the hotel bed.

"Don't forget you can come here if you want to," Beth said. "We will fight for the two of you, you know we will."

Marcy sighed. Beth had a very young daughter and so did Selene, the woman who was kidnapped by Rufus along with the Chloe girl. They would help Marcy if she asked, but they had so much to lose, and dammit, out of character, Marcy's heart worried for their safety.

"Beth, look, I'm sorry I'm so crabby," Marcy said, her voice softer. "You guys were good to Canaan when he needed help and he doesn't deserve what Isaac is doing to him. It's a nightmare. *Isaac* is a nightmare."

"Do you want to tell me about it?" Beth asked, probably trying not to pry, but Marcy had no qualms sharing the gory details.

Beth Rider had been marked as a Rabbit, kidnapped, accosted, tortured and bled plenty when in the Rakum's clutches. There wasn't anything Marcy could say to surprise her. Plus, the petite Bible warrior truly helped Canaan in Montgomery, gave him much needed guidance when he wanted to destroy Rufus for threatening their way of life. How was he, or any of them, to know that Isaac would be worse than the Fathers and Rufus rolled together?

"Oh, honey, if your husband told you what kind of problem the kid was then you can imagine he's being really evil to Canaan. And I'm afraid that…" Marcy stopped, unable to say what she feared most about tonight.

"What, Marcy? Canaan will be okay—I know it."

"Beth, there was a little girl in the house—" Marcy said and then whispered, *"she'd been abused."*

"Oh, God," Beth said.

"And I heard them talking—she didn't have any injuries, nothing," Marcy said and clenched her jaw tight. Her eyes were trying to water and she did not want to cry. "I think Canaan marked her and that means *what if it was him?"* Marcy paused again.

Did she have to say more? At one point during her hospital stay, the girl—a tearful Asian-American pre-teen—had been sitting in an interview room before Marcy was ushered in. She heard the child say three things.

"He made me drink his blood," "he stabbed my neck," and the third was garbled by tears and the detective's follow-up questions, but the impression was she had been sexually assaulted. *She was just a baby!* Marcy couldn't even think it. And although she tried, the police wouldn't let her speak to the girl about anything.

"Marcy, listen to me. Listen," Beth said, her voice stern. "Canaan may have marked her under orders, but he would never rape a little girl. *You know that.* Isaac couldn't make him do that—no one could. This is Canaan we're talking about."

Marcy sniffled. Beth was right. Canaan, the incredibly powerful Elder who, in his day, had a thousand Rakum under his command, a hundred Captains and Lieutenants, and every mortal he subjugated bowed to his will. With all that, never once in forty years had she seen him be cruel or unjust with an innocent.

"Oh, God, Beth, you're right, you are," Marcy said in a rush. "Boris, Hoss and Beryl were also there—any of them could have hurt that poor girl. My Canaan wouldn't—you're right."

"Marcy, do you want me to come there? I will, really," Beth said, sounding like she might be getting her purse to leave as she spoke.

"No, seriously..." Marcy shook her head in the quiet room. "I'm going to get some sleep and first thing in the morning, rent a car. Once I'm home, everything will seem normal again. I'll wait for Canaan from my own little kingdom."

Beth made a little laugh and shortly, Marcy ended the call. The clock on her iPhone showed 8:30 and she switched on the television. It might be a long night, but at least there were no Rakum about.

▼▼

US-59 N, 8 p.m.

Boris piloted the car with precision, behaving as if he carried the most precious cargo in the world. None of his concern got past Isaac, the big Rakum continued to be unbelievably attentive and responsive to Isaac's every perceived need. One hour into their journey eastward, Isaac had been fantasizing about his newfound power in Zahdone when an odd sensation tickled his inner ear. Boris took notice of the change in Isaac's countenance in his peripheral vision and his brow furrowed.

"Master, do I need to pull over?" he asked, his foot hovering over the brake pedal.

"No, no, Boris," Isaac said and closed his eyes. "Just shhhh..." Isaac cleared his mind and waited for the experience to repeat.

First came a tiny whisper of someone calling his name from far away. Before his awakening as Zahdone, he heard telepathic snippets like flakes of paint falling from the walls of his mind, but now he was hearing a voice with clarity—somewhere, a Rakum he had never connected with was trying to reach him telepathically.

"Master Isaac," the stranger's voice repeated. Isaac was very close now; such spiritual ears would take some getting used to. Isaac wondered, *do I need Zahdone to show me how to use this?* How could he turn this close-by sound into a vision?

Then it hit him anew: *I AM Zahdone...*

Isaac nodded to no one and said in his mind, *"Show yourself, Rakum. I will see you now."*

Appearing slowly, like a photograph developing in a film tray, a Rakum appeared. He stood in a dark corner in a place with a low ceiling illuminated by a bulb hanging outside Isaac's view. When the Rakum looked up, he locked eyes with Isaac and fell to his knees.

"Master, I am here to serve you!"

"Excellent, I accept!" Isaac said smiling. This young Rakum was dark-skinned and comely, dressed like a mortal teenager, wearing Converse sneakers and faded blue jeans. "What's your story?" Isaac asked, already peeking into his open mind.

"Before Last Assembly—" he began and Isaac held up his hand, having received the entire history from the man's mind before he could articulate it. This Rakum discipled under Jack Dawn since First Ritual, he was called to serve Elder Rufus after Last Assembly, and when he heard Rufus was dead, he sought to serve Isaac.

Isaac grinned, excited about his new reach of mental ability. "Kite?" he ascertained and the Rakum replied in the affirmative, still on his knees. "There's more—tell me." Isaac plainly saw the man had more to say that did not cascade to him as the other information had.

Kite took a deep breath. "Before we gathered in the Great Hall to hear the cursed Rabbit," he said and spit to the side before continuing, "I saw her at the doors to the Chamber of Fathers. She and Michael Stone held the Staff of Abroghia—"

Isaac's eyes grew wide. He hadn't even thought about the staff. The Rakum regarded it as a fearsome extension of the High Father's power. Isaac had seen it daily when under the care of the Ten. His heartrate increased at the thought of holding it. Oh, how he enjoyed watching from his hiding place when Father Abroghia reprimanded and sometimes brained rebellious Rakum with it. The staff was ancient—weighing more than forty pounds, it was six feet long and carved of cedar salvaged from the ruins of Solomon's Temple in Jerusalem. Spanning six inches across at the top, it tapered to one inch at the tip. The greatest insult of all? The staff was engraved with Abroghia's true name, his spirit name—*Rakah Ta'avah*. What fun it would be to overwrite that with Zahdone.

"You've had it all this time?" Isaac asked Kite curious. Would it be useful in the hands of a mere grunt?

"Master, I'm ashamed to admit, I fled," Kite said, his voice tight as if he expected chastisement, but Isaac waited for him to continue. "Later, Elder Rufus commanded me to retrieve the staff from the ruins of The Cave. It took more than six years, but I have it. I have it, Master, and I will bring it to you."

Isaac grinned and nodded happily. "You have done well, Kite! You're in Mississippi?" Isaac asked as the answer to his question came as quickly as he thought to inquire. The Rakum nodded. Isaac didn't ask, but he received a stream of consciousness from Kite regarding a Rabbit he sensed had been marked by Canaan and carried a "do not touch" edict from a Father. This signature is what led him to call out to his new master tonight.

Isaac was elated. "The directive on the Rabbit was that of the Fathers?"

"Oh, yes, Master, and I instinctively knew it was you," Kite said, his eyes huge. "I am superbly spiritual, Master, and when I detected that Rabbit, I heard your name chanted by a thousand voices in my mind."

"Oh, you *are* wonderful, Kite!" Having caught on to how his new mental acuity worked, Isaac didn't ask the next question aloud. Instead, he simply wondered, *do you know where this Rabbit is right now?* Isaac sensed an affirmative reply and he grinned.

"Kite, collect this woman for me. Take her to your safe place and hold her there until you hear otherwise. I'm in transit and the house in Jackson is compromised."

"Yes, Master, I will do it," Kite said.

"Kite, with the Rabbit, show Elder Canaan respect. You may buzz off her, but don't terrorize or assault her. Do you understand?" Isaac watched his eyes and his thoughts as he nodded and replied yes. He had been yearning for the Rabbit since he awoke for the evening.

Isaac pondered a moment about how his verbal mark lay on the woman as strongly as Canaan's. An Elder's mark is his blood, an actual three-dimensional substance. Isaac's edict had been applied by word and will—was he *that* powerful? That his *very word* carried his essence? Ready to burst with joy, Isaac clapped his hands together.

"You're an excellent Rakum, Kite. Get the Rabbit, hole up, and wait for instructions." Isaac blinked and returned his consciousness to where his body sat in the passenger's seat. To Boris he said, "I just had a new kind of vision. What did *you* see just now?"

"You stared into that corner, Master. Your lips moved, but I heard no sound."

"I am so awesome!" Isaac giggled. "How far to Tuscaloosa?"

"Couple of hours, Master," Boris said grinning. "How about some tunes?"

"YES!" Isaac blurted and turned up the XM radio as loud as it would go.

34

Tuscaloosa, AL
November 11th, 9 p.m.

There he was—alive and well, looking exactly as he did during Last Assembly where he scooted Roman and Javier past security to meet up with Beth Rider for the night that changed everything. Roman gripped the steering wheel, unmoving and unblinking.

"You sneaky little devil," Roman mumbled to no one. Kilmeade must have faked his death, which would be his style. Sifting through a cacophony of emotions, Roman climbed out of the truck.

Damien and David walked toward his brother. Kilmeade offered a perfunctory nod to David, but to Father Damien, he bowed low in exaggeration, playfully mocking the man's loss in status among the Rakum.

"Welcome to the Outcasts, Father Damien," Kilmeade said in a booming voice.

Roman instinctively looked around the quiet quad, but only their group stood outside in the chilly air.

"You look good for one who has been to heaven and to hell and back again."

Damien responded too low for Roman to hear and ambled into the house behind David. Roman continued toward his brother who waited with an amused grin.

"I could eat you up, brother," Kilmeade said as they came within a few feet of each other. Roman put out his hand, ignoring the double meaning in the odd phrase. Kilmeade disdained the offered shake and grabbed him into a hug. "Put that away, I'm not a mortal."

"And a Rakum would embrace?" Roman chuckled, pressed against Kilmeade's chest. "Brother," he then whispered, "it is very good to see you again."

"And you," Kilmeade replied, his lips against Roman's brow. "You're

165

different than I remember," Kilmeade chuckled.

"I regret none of it," Roman asserted and remained in his arms until released.

When Kilmeade stepped back, the two scrutinized each other. As fraternal twins, they were the same height, and shared similar hair color and eyes, but their facial features varied greatly. Kilmeade's high cheekbones and perfect chin placed him in the camera-ready category, where Roman had always considered himself more the scholarly-type. And his twin's personality had always leant itself to excessiveness and extravagance. Since his Elder-hood, no matter where the Fathers stationed him, Kilmeade always managed to ferret out the luxury in his appointments.

"I am saddened I can no longer read you," he said and dropped half of his grin. Still he winked fondly. "And," he said inhaling dramatically, "you don't smell precisely like one of them, my brother. What's it like?" he asked and winked.

The wind cut between the buildings and Roman visibly shivered.

"Cold? Does the icy wind pain you? Do sprains and strains daily torment your joints?" Still grinning, Kilmeade put ungloved hands to Roman's shoulders. *"Do you no longer drink blood?"* he whispered.

Roman shook his head and stepped out from under Kilmeade's hands. "Brother, such talk—leave it. I'm a new man and there is no going back. Why are you here?"

"First, I wanted to find my brother—here you are," Kilmeade answered and stepped back into his space. Roman did not back away. "Now, I will play it by ear." He gestured behind him. "I have a pet Cow and a pet Rakum who has a pet Rabbit. What else does a man need?"

"Kilmeade..." Out of old habit, Roman looked behind to the empty street; any Rakum grunt who caught a whiff of Kilmeade's Rabbit would come right to their door. "He'll attract attention."

"Meh," Kilmeade scoffed, brushing imaginary dust from Roman's lapel. "I'll deal with that if it comes up."

"It's not safe," Roman began and stopped. Kilmeade was still a Rakum Elder and his power would protect those with him. Kilmeade smiled and puffed out his chest, guessing what Roman privately concluded. "It's still a bad idea to travel with a Rabbit. Rufus is dead, but there's a kid..."

Kilmeade nodded. "We've met up here," he said and tipped his head forward. "You are wise to be concerned about him."

Roman nodded and shivered anew. Kilmeade grinned, twirled him into a half hug and pulled him into the house.

"Brrrrrr," Kilmeade purred in his ear and positioned him in front to walk down the narrow hallway to the living area where the group was stationed. "We will revisit that topic. Meet my pet, Rafael."

Roman stopped at the entrance to the living room and took in the occupants. Rafael was tall, muscular and dark, and he lounged in a recliner, kicked back with one arm up and behind his head. The Rakum nodded to Roman a greeting, regarding him with a mixture of expressions Roman did not bother to decipher.

Still standing close behind him, Kilmeade grasped both of Roman's shoulders and spoke in his ear. "Did you know my delightful Rafael before? In your past life?"

"Recollection fades in this flesh, brother," Roman said, yet searched his long memory as Kilmeade waited, amusement in his eyes. "Rafael," Roman then whispered. The name rang a bell. Roman sighed and gave the comely Rakum a steely glare. "I recall him and as his weakness regarding a Legacy Cow."

Disregarding the accusation, Rafael looked away.

"Take it easy," Kilmeade joked. "That's my pet."

Roman shook his head. "Brother, did you come here specifically for me?" Then Roman whispered with admiration, *"On a mortal's airliner?"*

"Of course!" Kilmeade replied. "Roman, my brother, come with us. I'm not offended by your mortal shell or your nearly-human smell."

Roman smirked at his brother's rhyme. "Kilmeade, I have my own troubles. I came to speak to Javier. Any word on when he's returning?"

"You may want speak to his little friend about that," Kilmeade whispered and moved to stand beside Roman in the threshold. Chloe had been conversing with David privately and she entered the living room then, passed Roman giving him the smallest smile, and scooted into the kitchen, spooking past Kilmeade.

Roman caught his brother's eye. "What did you do?"

"Me? Nothing." Kilmeade giggled into his hand. "Are you aware that your pup Javier has sprouted sharp teeth?" Kilmeade tapped his own oddly-sharp canine. "He bit that innocent girl, mm-hmm. She won't talk about it, but I'm certain he took her blood." Kilmeade touched his nose. Roman's jaw dropped.

"You must be joking," Roman said, his mind racing.

Kilmeade shook his head. "No, and she is infatuated with him." He shrugged his shoulders. "But..." he added and looked back to Roman, "she'd be in love with me if she had let me bite her. That child has it bad."

Roman didn't respond, his mind working over how a *human* Javier might grow fangs and lust for blood. Had he taken Canaan's blood? Or maybe even Isaac's? What would such ingestion do to him?

Kilmeade put a hand to Roman's cheek. "What are you thinking? *I truly miss reading you,*" he whispered the last few words and cupped Roman's chin. *"I miss you dearly, period."*

Roman nodded and covered his fingers with his own and lowered them. "I miss you, too, brother. Though, that emotion is more human than Rakum, you must admit."

Kilmeade shrugged again. "I am what I am and always have been," he said. "Javier concerns you, then?" he asked in a low voice. "It is obvious he is not mortal as you thought."

Roman met his brother's eye and said nothing. Just then, behind him, Chloe shouted incoherently and stormed out of the apartment. David followed her, yelling, "Chloe! Wait, let's talk about this!"

Kilmeade laughed into his hand and Roman caught his eye.

"What?" Roman asked, knowing his brother would have heard their entire conversation. Kilmeade smiled and took Roman's arm to walk with him to look out the front door. He gestured toward David who was now leaning on Chloe's VW Beetle. She sat in the driver's seat and had locked the doors.

"It is as I said," Kilmeade whispered close to Roman's ear, *"that girl loves the pointy teeth. Your friend, David—no points."* Bursting into a new fit of laughter, Kilmeade tugged Roman back into the house.

Roman pressed his lips together, wishing he could help David, but what could he do? The problems the kid had now were of a romantic nature and Roman had no authority in that department.

"This is just great," Roman said frowning.

At that moment, Rafael stood and disappeared into Javier's bedroom, presumably to use the john. Roman inclined his head to Kilmeade and changed the subject to something his brother *did* know about. "Your pet Rafael, I assume we're safe with him?"

Kilmeade nodded with a wry smile. "As safe as you are with me."

When Roman sent him a frown, Kilmeade plopped into the second recliner on the opposite side of the couch and kicked open the footrest. He closed his eyes and began humming a horror movie theme. With a grim humorless smile, Roman sent up a prayer for wisdom and guidance.

35

The Texaco was two miles from their destination and Isaac waited while Boris filled the gas tank and ran inside to pay. When he returned to the driver's seat, he pulled the Hyundai to the side of the building instead of getting back on the road. Isaac didn't have to ask what he was thinking, so instead he asked, "Are you hungry?"

Boris didn't answer, still scrolling through the iPhone they'd purchased for the drive east. Rakum didn't *need* human blood to survive, but consuming it gave them pleasure and transferred a power that normal foods did not supply. Boris buzzed his new Rabbit last night, but since then, neither of them had eaten anything—solid or otherwise.

Isaac intuited that Boris was busy tending to something important for his master's wellbeing. Still, he didn't like being ignored. When ten seconds had elapsed, Isaac gave the big Rakum a nudge.

"Tell me if you hunger for blood. I want to hear you say it."

Boris gave him a tiny nod. "Master, like you, I'm always hungry," he said and grinned. "But I can't think about food until I secure the day for you. I think I have it," he said and pointed the phone screen to Isaac. "This man is bragging online about a huge underground shelter he built last year and he lives just three miles south of our location."

Isaac considered their options. It was early yet, but his favorite was correct—they should have their safe place chosen well before sunup. Again, he was reminded that being the all-powerful and mighty Zahdone went only as far as his experience in the flesh allowed. He looked again at the tiny images on the phone. The shelter looked clean and the man looked young and gullible. He gave Boris the nod.

Boris smiled showing white teeth and put the car in gear. Once they were underway, he parted his lips to ask Isaac a question and stopped

169

himself. Isaac noticed and sought his mind, thus learning a new parameter of his mental prowess: intentional reading happened intentionally. If he didn't actively seek his companion's thoughts, they would stay in his head. Isaac grinned, happy to be self-taught such incredible matters. He reached across and touched Boris's arm.

"Ask me. I don't want you to be like them—you know, *afraid*. I know you love me so ask me anything."

"Thank you, Master. There's a Rabbit nearby. I'd sure like to find him. He's close." Boris licked his lips as he spoke. Isaac closed his eyes and concentrated a few seconds. When he had zeroed in on the one Rufus detected, he opened his eyes.

"I'm sorry, that's the Cow who came with Rafael from California. He won't be there when we arrive, they'll insulate him from me in their weakness," Isaac said, a snarl on his face. "Why a Rakum would attach himself to any of them amazes me."

Boris nodded and sucked his teeth. "Well, shit. I didn't realize he was with them."

"I'll get him back for you, Boris, if you want him. And don't worry—your little Rabbit can't get away from that mark. When this blows over, we'll go get her. I promise."

Boris smiled. "Thank you, Master, I would like that very much."

Isaac sent him a nod and watched the pastures zip by in the night. He concentrated on Elder Canaan and again hit a wall. He pulled at Beryl and the same barrier that stopped him the night before held him back now from seeing or communicating with them. Isaac closed his eyes.

"Zahdone commands you to see Canaan!" Isaac sent into the spirit dimension. A myriad of shapeless entities responded to his directive, but none returned with a report. Canaan and Beryl had disappeared.

Isaac looked at Boris's profile and then out the windshield. He wanted Boris's advice, but didn't want to let on that he might have a weakness. So Isaac kept it to himself. Eventually, he'd figure it out. He was still fitting and tailoring his new Zahdone clothes anyway.

Boris slowed the car and gestured to an iron fence that sat across an immaculately tended drive. The gate was open and Boris turned in, crawling toward the bend in the asphalt driveway.

"Boris, will I be in the way if I come with you and watch you work?" Isaac asked. He had no real-life experience physically overcoming mortals for their possessions and Boris did. Plus, he had enjoyed his hunting excursion with Beryl more than anything so far.

"Would you like to help?" Boris asked with a gleam in his eye. Isaac nodded his head. "Okay, Master, here's what we'll do…"

As Boris divulged the plan, the car reached the house and he switched off the lights, leaving the engine purring. Boris closed his eyes and after a minute, he whispered, *"Do you hear more than one heartbeat here, Master?"*

Isaac had been seeking a headcount, too, and he waited for Boris to meet his eye. "One man and one dog," he said smiling. Then added, "A little dog."

Boris grinned. "Okay, let's do it."

His eyes shining with excitement, Isaac hopped out of the car and ran to the front door. He pounded it with his fists and cried out, "Help! Please, help! Anybody home? Help!"

The porch light came on and a portly man, thirtyish with mousy brown hair, opened the door, alarm in his round face. He wore a baggy white button-up shirt with khakis and his five-o-clock shadow was several days old. To the man, Isaac looked all of thirteen. Isaac played up the puppy-dog eyes when he read concern in the homeowner's face.

"Son, slow down, what's wrong? I'll help you," the man said, his eyes searching the dark night behind Isaac. So far, he hadn't seen the car parked against the front flowerbeds.

"My chauffeur is sick—can I use your phone? Please, he has a heart condition and I've known him since I was a baby. I need to call my dad. Please, mister?"

Isaac's frantic voice hyped the homeowner's energy and he opened the door wide leading Isaac to a front room, all the while trying to calm him with his words.

"Shhh, shhh, let me call him for you. What's your Dad's name and number?" the man said and lifted a landline handset off its cradle. Isaac couldn't make tears like a mortal boy so he hitched his breathing and sniffled.

"B-B-Boris…" he stuttered, sensing his friend had entered the house and locked the front door behind him. The yappy terrier hopped to work and filled the air with barking.

"Travis!" the homeowner shouted, covering the phone's handset. To Isaac he said kindly, "Go ahead, son."

Boris entered the room behind the man and Isaac ceased his frantic crying. "Oh, look, Mister… he's okay." Isaac pointed behind them.

The man whipped around and stood stock-still as he locked eyes with Boris only fifteen feet away.

Isaac expected his giant friend to attack, but Boris was grinning. He held an 8" x 10" gilded frame in his hand and he showed the image to

Isaac. The homeowner looked on, holding his breath. Isaac grabbed the item and sitting at a circular table in what appeared to be a posh restaurant was the homeowner and the Rakum David Walker. Isaac looked at Boris who grinned again. Then they both looked at the chubby homeowner who fell to his knees between them, his eyes filled with confusion.

"How do you know David?" Isaac asked the man.

The homeowner looked into both faces again and parted his lips. In the photo he was younger, and Isaac guessed it was taken before Last Assembly. The terrier stopped barking and sat in the floor licking its feet.

Boris picked up the slack when the man couldn't speak.

"What's your name?" he asked, his deep voice echoing in the large room.

"M-Maury, Master," the man said and Boris beamed at Isaac.

"Nice to meet you, Maury," Boris said and stepped up to gently lift the man off the ground. "Call me Master Boris, and this is Master Isaac."

Maury jerked his head to Isaac, his eyes incredulous.

Isaac laughed. "You didn't know I was a Rakum?" he asked. All this time, he assumed Cows would see him as they saw all of his brethren.

The man shook his head. "Please, don't be angry," Maury said in a tiny voice.

"What do I care?" Isaac laughed and looked around the room, from the gaudy furnishings to the high ceilings. "You must be a very rich man," he said and then asked him, "Are you? Very rich?"

Maury shrugged and nodded his head. "I inherited this a few years ago. I've been trying to find Master David. Do you—"

Isaac waved his hand. "He's dead, but Boris is alive," Isaac said and touched his shoulder, turning his body toward his favorite. "And Boris is hungry."

"Oh, god," Maury whispered and rolled up the sleeves of his loose shirt. "I'm embarrassed—I'm not, I mean, with David I stayed so healthy, so clean, so pure. Master Boris," he said, stretching his arm forward for Boris to grasp. "I'm high. Marijuana. I might even be hallucinating."

Boris laughed. "I'll leave a scar for you so you'll know I was here." Taking the proffered wrist, Boris fished out his knife.

"Oh, god," Maury said, his eyes glazing over. Before his knees buckled, Boris caught his arm and maneuvered him to the closest sofa.

"I don't mind a little weed, Maury," Boris said as he stuck the tip of his knife into the crook of the man's arm.

"Maury, we need to stay here tonight in your underground bunker," Isaac said as Boris slurped noisily, causing him to smile. "What do you say about that?"

Maury had closed his eyes, but he was still conscious, his weakness more from the cannabis than the buzzing. "I say, whatever I have is yours, Master."

"Good answer. We might be bringing some of our brethren with us tonight," Isaac added.

The man smiled drunkenly and nodded. "Makes me... the luckiest... man... in..." he said, then fell off to la-la-land.

Boris finished and fell face-forward into Maury's chest, humming pleasantly to himself. Isaac grinned and rubbed his bald head. He'd wait for the buzz to pass, but then they needed to make plans. And more importantly, Elder Kilmeade awaited.

36

Roman would have to leave David to his misery for the time being. As he prepared to join the Rakum and Damien in conversation, he was stopped by a light touch on his sleeve.

"Mister Roman, sir, I am Santiago," Rafael's Cow said to Roman, his tone formal. He offered a low bow worthy of a Rakum Elder and Roman ignored the gesture with a tip of his chin. "This gentleman with Elder Kilmeade is James DuPont." Santiago gestured to a quiet and lanky man who leaned against the wall behind the sofa. James smiled at Roman, his hands in his pockets.

Father Damien sat on the couch watching them all intently. Behind him, the front door slammed and Roman caught a glimpse of David entering the small kitchen.

"David, are you okay?" Roman called, but received no reply.

"Are you going to fix everyone's problems, Mr. Mom?" Kilmeade asked Roman, a smirk on his face. "Join us in here, brother. Let's have a chat with what used to be our Father."

Not offended by Kilmeade's words, Damien caught Roman's eye and pat the sofa cushion next to him.

Kilmeade launched several verbal jabs at Damien, marveling repeatedly and in several different ways how strange it was to have discourse with one of the Ten Fathers and have him be just a "little old man."

Rafael sauntered back in and scowled briefly in Damien's direction before settling into the recliner. Santiago and James walked to the hallway, waited for consent from their masters, and exited for the front of the condo. It was time to get some answers; Roman gathered his thoughts and prepared to dive in.

▼ ▼

At the dinette table, David rest his head on folded arms, angry, sad, and miserable. Chloe hadn't admitted anything, but she also refused to speak to him about Javier and what they did or *did not* do together before he and Roman arrived.

"How about a beer, amigo?"

David sat up at the voice behind him. He'd met Iago when he first arrived, but they had no dialogue since. Standing in the doorway was the other man introduced as Jimmy. This man didn't make eye contact, but stared at the floor, swiveling the toe of his canvas shoe.

Not feeling particularly like hosting, David hooked a thumb toward the refrigerator. "Help yourself," he said and looked at the wall to discourage conversation.

"Gracias," Iago said and grabbed two Coors, tossing one to Jimmy. He motioned to the chair nearest him. "Do you mind?"

David shrugged and Iago dropped into the chair.

"We are waiting for your friend, Javier d'Millier, is that correct?" the man asked and David's mouth became a thin line.

The mere mention of his roommate's name now threw him into a rage. David's fists curled and he set his water glass down too hard. Iago jumped.

"Oh!" the man said putting his palm over his heart. Then he *tsked* and shook his head. "Is this about the girl?"

"She's pretty," Jimmy said from the door in a low voice, his eyes still on his shoe.

David looked at him a moment, trying to decide his angle, but the man had nothing else to add. To Iago, he nodded, unsure if he wanted to discuss his problems with a stranger. Also, somewhere deep in his mind, he was reminded that Iago and Jimmy were both Cows; that used to *mean* something to him. Now, it only shamed him, reminding him of the life he'd lived for so long.

"Ah, amigo, trust me, it will all work out in the end. You love her?" he asked and sipped his beer.

"Iago, do you know who I am? Who I was?" David asked ignoring his line of questioning.

"I know enough," Iago answered, nodding his head.

"Then you should know I don't want to discuss anything with you," David said. Conviction stabbed his heart at his rude behavior, but his anger was winning the moment and his frown remained.

"Is it weird for you?" Iago asked, his voice soft and respectful. "Being so close to a Cow, a Rabbit even, and…well…nothing?"

Out of character now and wishing he could stop himself, David hardened his gaze. "Is it weird speaking so casually with me, knowing I used to be your master?"

Unaffected by David's evil tone, Iago thoughtfully paused before shaking his head no. "It would be odd if we knew each other before."

David looked at his hands on the tabletop and had no reply.

"You look nothin' like a Rakum," Jimmy said then from the doorway. "I never woulda known it if Iago hadn't told me."

David regarded him with a glare.

Jimmy shrugged with a derisive chuckle. "What? You look like my kid brother. I can't wrap my mind around *why*."

"Why I don't look like a Rakum?" David asked, wary about engaging the idiot in conversation.

He shook his head and switched to leaning on the opposite side of the threshold. "Why you gave up *that*—" he said and pointed to the living room, "for this," he finished gesturing up and down David's body.

David's fury simmered, the Cow Jimmy adding fuel in heaps. He could launch into a testimony about how God saved his life and filled him with joy, or how in his short seventy years as a Rakum he contaminated and spoiled every human he touched, but he didn't. Instead, he sipped his water and looked back at his hands. He needed to get out of there.

Jimmy filled the silence with a new question.

"What about the bite on that little girl's neck? Was she your Cow?"

"No, dammit!" David said, sorry for his reactionary response, but the man rubbed him the wrong way with every word. "You don't know what you're talking about."

Iago backed him up. "I'm sorry, David, but it's true. My master said your girlfriend had a bite." He touched the side of his neck. "Right here, and not from a Rakum."

"*A bite?*" David's voice hissed and he hated the sound. "I don't understand. Not from a Rakum?"

Iago nodded. "Your friend Javier bit her with fangs and the wounds healed differently. Not like a Rakum. Rafa said he'd never seen anything like it."

David stood up from the table. "That's impossible," he said and walked to the threshold, moving Jimmy aside with a swish of his hand. "I can't talk about this with you." David looked down the hall where Roman, Damien, Kilmeade, and Rafael sat chatting animatedly, leaning forward. "I gotta get out of here," he mumbled.

Stepping down the hallway to the living room opening, he held out his hand to Roman, purposefully not meeting the other men's eyes.

"May I have the keys, please."

Roman met his gaze, paused a millisecond, and then nodded with something that looked like understanding. He dug in his pocket and tossed the keys across the room to land in David's hand.

"Thanks. I'll be back."

"Be careful and take your phone," Roman said sounding every bit like a mortal father.

David nodded and left without a remark from Damien or either Rakum in the room. He passed Iago and Jimmy, grabbed his coat, and left the house. He'd drive in circles if he had to, but he didn't want to see Javier, he didn't want to have to look at the Rakum at the apartment, and he didn't want to make small talk with the pitiful Cows in the kitchen. David drove toward town and sighed too furious with Javier to pray. It was going to be a long night.

"That one was never much of a Rakum, was he, Father Damien," Kilmeade said rhetorically when David closed the front door. Damien responded anyway.

"All of our children had varying degrees of Abroghia's spirit, but even as a Rakum Father, I saw some more human than others." Damien looked directly at Kilmeade as he spoke the rest. "Each of you has a soul, gifted at conception by God. That soul longs to be re-joined with its original element—the Holy Spirit—and only ceases to long when the flesh dies. This is why many Rakum were saved, because when they were made aware of this longing, they consented to its leading."

"Father Damien—do you still want to be called *Father*, Father?" Kilmeade asked, a twinkle of humor in his eye. "I have no such longing, and I never have."

Damien didn't miss a beat. "Call me whatever you like, my son," he said with a kind smile. "It is not my place to reveal this longing to you, only to inform you it exists. Your heart knows I do not lie."

Roman rolled in his lips, understanding Damien's meaning. For millennia, the Fathers dealt out judgments and laws and they did not lie, deceit being something saved for the Rakum population alone. The Fathers spoke their minds without reservation at all times because of their absolute power and authority. Kilmeade and Rafael wouldn't like the truths their former Father shared, but they did not truly doubt him.

"Kilmeade, in any event, I am happy to see you are well. And you, Rafael, look as if you haven't suffered too badly this past seven years," he said looking toward the other Rakum. Roman looked on with interest to see how the youngster would respond.

"I am well," Rafael replied still looking away.

"I am going to address you as Father Damien; your *humanness* does not offend me," Kilmeade said, now reclining, footrest kicked open with arms up and head supported on his hands. "Please ignore Rafa—my pet is sulking. Tell us about Isaac."

"Yitzhak Akaron, yes," Damien said with a sad nod.

Kilmeade inclined his head with a half-grin. *"The Last Laugh,"* he said in a chuckle. Rafael searched his face and Kilmeade grinned. "I get it. In Hebrew, his name means *the last laugh.*" He looked back to Damien. "Clever."

Damien smiled. "It's appropriate, no? At the time, we did not understand that Abroghia was making plans for our future. Abroghia fathered the last Rakum with much intention, never revealing to the rest of us that he had foreseen the end of his reign and was preparing a new vessel to occupy when the time arrived. We were aware Yitzhak would one day *lead,* but never did we assume Abroghia intended to *be reborn* inside him." Damien paused as Roman took a stance against the living room threshold, at rapt attention.

"Did he foresee the Rabbit woman and her book?" Rafael asked softly, joining the conversation.

Damien gave him a kind shake of the head. "No, my son, he thought he had a few hundred years left. You see, of the Nine, I had Abroghia's ear. I was the second Father called and our personalities complimented each other, we both had intense interest in prophecy and science. When Yitzhak was thirteen, we moved him from his group lair into our Chamber and because Abroghia trusted me to do the best tutelage, I took him under my wing."

"The legends of The Last began when he was so abruptly separated from the others," Roman shared thoughtfully. "I remember hearing the proselytes that shared his lair greatly feared him."

Damien nodded. "Yes, his extrasensory powers were exponentially more advanced than any youth we had ever seen. It became impossible for the proselytes to maintain amity. I brought Yitzhak to live with us and we kept him isolated and secluded, even from other Rakum. Under Abroghia's orders, we discipled him to be a Father, but with such specialized circumstances, I don't think even Abroghia had a notion as to how super-powerful he would become. By his twentieth birthday, he outperformed all of us in clairvoyance and foretelling."

Kilmeade whistled quietly and looked up to the ceiling.

"No, we didn't see it as a problem at the time," Damien said to Kilmeade interpreting his reaction. "We had no reason to worry, none of us knew, in clean hard facts, that Abroghia was in fact a demonic spirit that planned to one day use that youth's body to resurrect himself. Who could have predicted that?" Damien caught Roman's eye. "I was the most prophetic of the Ten and I never saw any problem in making Yitzhak stronger than us all."

"Demonic spirit," Kilmeade said derisively.

"You have much to learn," Damien said to Kilmeade, "and before The Last arrives, I will share with you as much as I can. After I'm gone, perhaps my words will be more meaningful."

"Why does Isaac hate you so much?" Roman asked, sorry to sound harsh. When they rescued Father Damien from the basement a week ago, Isaac made it plain he loathed the former leader. "Is it because you became mortal?"

"He feels I abandoned him and in a lot of ways, I did." Damien looked at his hands. "After Last Assembly, I took Yitzhak with me and continued to disciple him. But the seed planted by the Rabbit in The Cave began to grow and I started seeking the God of the mortals. I eventually revealed myself to a monk who accepted me as I was, broken and evil, and he lovingly taught me about God."

"Broken and evil," Kilmeade whispered with a smirk and was silent.

"Is that where you became human?" Rafael asked.

"No, that didn't happen for years, but it was the time I left Yitzhak to fend for himself. We parted ways and I didn't see him again. Over the next few years, I moved around from monastery to monastery and monks who knew I was a blood-drinker kept me from the sun and taught me the ways of God during the night. Eventually, I moved across country and settled in Tennessee, still a Rakum Father, never giving in to the Truth God planted in my soul."

"DAMIEN," Kilmeade said loudly, but not angrily. "You're making me insane with this strange language. Just please, *please*, tell me about this magical transformation. What words did you say to make this happen? Rafa and I certainly don't want to accidentally ruin our beautiful lives with a few mystery phrases."

Roman smirked and lowered his eyes, pleased with the way Damien was handling their Rakum element. Roman had been an Elder and the power he gave up to be with God, he remembered well. Damien had been a *Father*—there existed no being in the flesh more powerful and capable than a Rakum Father.

"One day you're our god," Kilmeade said, "and the next, you're a slave to an invisible deity?"

"Let me correct you, my son," Damien said, his old man voice thin but strong and his eyes shining with affection. "One *second,* I'm your god, and the next *second,* I meet the one true God," he finished and smiled again. "You, Kilmeade, of all my Elders, would be the one to appreciate the tale of how I became mortal. You, who bucked and flounced, constantly testing the limits of The Ten Fathers' patience."

Kilmeade did not disagree and leaned forward.

"You consider yourself the consummate Rakum—one the Fathers could be proud of, brag about, and otherwise favor," Damien said, his smile genuine and Roman detected the affection in his gaze.

Kilmeade blew on his knuckles and winked at Roman.

Damien laughed. "Not all of us favored you, Elder Kilmeade. Father Damien *did,*" he said touching his chest briefly. "And Father Theophilus, Father Yuri, and Father Kin. These spoke up for you when you committed your worst crimes."

"I appreciate that," Kilmeade said with a grin. "I am what I am."

"We knew about Doctor Penny," Damien said, his eyes drilling into Kilmeade's face. Kilmeade flinched and turned to catch Roman's eye.

"Who's that?" Roman asked.

"You wouldn't know about her. None of your brethren knew, yet you can't hide from your Fathers. We watched you, Kilmeade, and some of us were hoping you might succeed if only to add knowledge to our arsenal."

"What? Who was Doctor Penny?" Roman asked, now extremely curious, which must have been Damien's intention. Roman looked at the back of Kilmeade's head, but he wasn't offering answers.

"Elder Kilmeade was trying to procreate," Damien said meeting the eyes of all three present.

Kilmeade grinned and looked briefly at Roman. "If I had known they knew about that, I would have gone into hiding."

"What? Why?" Roman asked him, incredulous. Only the Fathers were fertile and in over three thousand years of their history, no one had ever disagreed openly with that edict. Kilmeade said nothing and Damien continued.

"We watched with interest, the science was new. Genetics was born, DNA was being studied as the basis of organic life."

"What were you thinking?" Roman asked him.

"I am highly intelligent, as you know," Kilmeade said with a mock-evil chuckle.

"You wasted your time..."

"Brother," Kilmeade said to Roman, an odd glimmer in his eye, "we experienced some degree of success."

"Ffff," Damien huffed. "I wouldn't agree."

Kilmeade's eyebrows went up. "Hmm, I guess you didn't see *everything* then."

Now Roman was too curious to remain silent. "What happened, Kilmeade? What's the big secret?"

Rafael also leaned forward in his seat.

"No, I didn't make a bunch of little Kilmeades," he said and laughed. He danced his ten fingers across his lap, watched them, and laughed again. "Not exactly..."

"What is it Damien didn't see?" Roman grimly asked.

Kilmeade reached into his pocket and pulled out a keyring. Untethering a small silver key, he tossed it to Roman. "I've moved it many times over the years, but now? Manhattan, Grand Central Terminal, Locker 1191."

Roman held the key in his open palm and tried to read his brother's expression. Damien and Rafael didn't speak, their minds probably racing to find the proper questions. When Kilmeade only sat back, smugly nodding his head, Roman sighed. "Okay. What's in the locker?"

"My babies," Kilmeade said smiling. "Doctor Penny and Elder Kilmeade's science project, preserved, awaiting the proper technology to bring them to life." Kilmeade crossed his arms behind his head grinning with satisfaction at being the center of attention.

"Impossible," Damien said, but Roman detected doubt in his voice. "Wait," Damien muttered and closed his eyes. "I recall when Doctor Penny gave you that key. It was to her loft, no?"

Kilmeade only grinned.

"You transmitted a lie to your Fathers?" Damien asked, his mouth squeezed into a tiny smile. "You fox," he said with affection and looked at Roman. "We saw the key, but we didn't watch the doctor. If she stored those items and gave Kilmeade a key, it is feasible he fooled us."

Roman exhaled wondering what it could mean. "Are we talking cloning?"

"No, silly. I may be old, but I still have the moves," Kilmeade said with humor.

"Rakum aren't fertile," Rafael said, his voice tapering off as if he shouldn't have spoken.

Kilmeade did not chastise him. "*Au contraire,* my pet. For decades, I suspected a metaphysical reason for our infertility. When I found a Cow who was also a preeminent scientist, I learned our seed is present, yet it refuses to reproduce." Kilmeade raised his hands into fists. His right hand moved toward the left and then flicked away in the opposite direction. "That's what it looks like under the microscope." He looked to meet Roman's eye and repeated the gesture. "Why would it do that? With *sentience.* When no organic solution presented itself, we returned to my earlier theory—something metaphysical was going on. So Doctor Penny used her own alchemy against the curse, if you will, and some of the seed took root."

"No. What?" Roman's mind now galloped back, years, decades, three centuries, to every female he lay with—every time he did so, his seed had run in the opposite direction? His expression must have been grim, for his brother chuckled pointing at his face.

"Billions of Rakum seed for millennia refusing to take root! Oh, the Fathers and their alchemy!" Kilmeade tossed back his head and laughed riotously.

"Damien," Roman said, not happy in the least, "did you know this? About the seed and the egg?"

"No," Damien said, his face ashen. "This is Abroghia's work. We drew every ounce of our power from him. You all sensed it." He looked at Rafael, being the least in the group. "You recognized High Father Abroghia was truly higher?"

Rafael nodded slowly as the news of the evening dawned in his psyche.

"Now they are yours, Uncle Roman," Kilmeade said, breathless with his fun. "Do with them as you wish."

A clock somewhere in the house chirped the quarter hour and Roman checked his watch. Damien shook visibly and straightened in his place on the sofa.

"Take care with that key," he said and Roman nodded, reining in his thoughts that scampered like wild cats across his mind. Kilmeade was the one to bring the group back on topic.

"So you knew about my experiments? I'm happy I wasn't squashed," he said with a grin. "Thank you for your favor, Father Damien."

Damien beamed, knowing all present were aware how close Kilmeade came to severe judgment. "We convinced the Ten that your curiosity and determination was to your credit as an Elder. Father Theophilus took responsibility and swore to Abroghia that he would encourage you to use your medical tendencies and modern science to find ways to strengthen us in our weakness."

Kilmeade grinned. "I have no weakness."

"The sun, Kilmeade. Your weakness is the same for all Rakum," Damien said and Kilmeade's cocky expression fell. "And since Theophilus convinced Abroghia that we needed this research, you were forgiven."

"I would thank him if it were possible," Kilmeade said and fell silent.

"Are the Fathers all deceased?" Roman inquired aware only of Theophilus's and Damien's fates.

"As of last week, only Theophilus and I remained alive," Damien said and crossed his arms over his knees sitting forward on the couch. "When I last spoke with Theophilus I had already transformed. We spoke of God and he listened."

"Be that as it may," Kilmeade scoffed, "I'm confident Father Theophilus's light has been extinguished." He touched his temple. "There is but one Elder alive, aside from yours truly."

"Elder Canaan," Roman volunteered.

Kilmeade nodded. "And the Rakum youth stronger than all the Fathers combined."

"Which brings us back to Isaac," Roman said.

"Indeed," Damien whispered and frowned, looking into his lap. "It is a blessing that his training was cut short."

"He cannot read you," Kilmeade said and gestured to Roman and Damien. "It frustrates him that your *condition* blocks his intrusions. Yet, as far as I can tell, his power among Rakum is limitless."

"You've spoken with him, then?" Damien asked and Roman noted fatherly concern in his gaze. Damien loved the Rakum as a "boy," when that word didn't even come close to describing him.

"He has visited me in the way of the Fathers," Kilmeade said with a wry grin. "He's a pretty boy and young, young, young. It's your blood that has done that, eh? The Father's blood?"

Damien nodded slowly.

"He has plans of his own," Kilmeade said matter-of-factly. "He will come *here*, to this house, if I stay. He wants me, my blood, and my allegiance. Both Elders that remain, he wants to keep us close."

"Wait. He's coming here?" Roman said and stood to his feet. "I have to get David back," he said pulling his phone from his pants pocket. He reached for Father Damien's elbow. "Let's go. We will find somewhere else to wait for Javier."

"No, I will stay—" Damien began, but Kilmeade interjected, coming to his feet.

"Roman is right, Father, you are not safe around Isaac. His plans…" Kilmeade paused, looking for the right words. "His plans are about his own comfort and he will destroy without prejudice any Rakum or mortal that displeases him."

"David, we need to leave, come pick us up," Roman said into the phone. To Kilmeade he asked, "Do you want us to help hide you?" He guessed Kilmeade's answer as he began his reply.

"For a Rakum, there's no hiding from The Last." Kilmeade shook his head. "*You* hide and contact me later. Don't tell me where you are because my thoughts are not private."

"God help us," Roman said gravely and put his hand on his brother's shoulder. "I don't want to lose you again. Be careful."

Kilmeade shrugged. "I'm completely safe with the little Father."

"You can't assume that," Roman disagreed.

"Yes, I can. He's addicted to Rakum blood and an Elder's is the most powerful with the Fathers gone," Kilmeade said and Rafael came over then to stand at his side. Kilmeade draped an arm about the Rakum's shoulders and shook him playfully. "Keep in mind that there will never be any new Elders or Fathers—*ever*. The way I see it, The Last must keep Canaan and me alive to satiate his ravenous belly."

Roman shook his head. "I didn't realize." His mind went back to their trip to Jackson to battle Elder Rufus and the strange looks between Isaac and Canaan—they were swapping blood the whole time. And what did Javier do? He wanted to ask Damien about it, but he held his tongue.

"Isaac has never ingested human blood," Damien added. "In the group lair, he only drank from the proctors. Since age thirteen, we, the Fathers, fed him directly from our veins. The only one who never nursed him was Abroghia and I understand now why."

Rafael tentatively touched Damien's arm from the side. "I do not follow."

"Abroghia was a demon, Rafael," Roman answered, catching the younger Rakum's eye. The man knew nothing about spiritual things and Roman's mouth made a tight line. "Kilmeade, you need to read Beth Rider's book regarding her time with us. It is no longer safe to live in blind faith to something you don't understand."

Kilmeade offered a slight nod. Roman had followed the Rakum code for nearly four-hundred years and only the last few decades, had he begun to pick up on the parallel world of spirits. Now that God and his angels had burst through the veil, none of the Rakum could pretend that other world didn't exist. If Rafael didn't learn all of this quickly, he wouldn't survive under the new regime and even Kilmeade needed to fully understand his new master's make up.

"David will be out front in a few minutes," Roman said to Damien. "We will keep our distance from Isaac for now, do you agree?"

Damien's chin dropped. "I want to see him so dearly."

Kilmeade gave Damien a victorious smile. "I can find out if you're in danger." He held up a finger and closed his eyes. Roman watched his brother's eyebrow twitch once and then he was back, his grin falling. "You should stay and wait for The Last if you would like to die," Kilmeade said, no humor in his voice. "Those are Isaac's exact words. I think he's hoping you'll stay."

"God help us," Roman said. "We're out of time. Jimmy, Santiago, you're with us. Let's go to the curb." Roman didn't wait to see their expressions. He exited the apartment and walked to the street to wait for David. Within a minute, the two Cows had joined him, wordlessly obeying their masters' edicts to stay with Roman. Damien was last to the curb and he stood behind Roman, wringing his hands with a forlorn expression.

"You will get to see Javier, Damien. He'll be home tomorrow. That was your main goal, eh?" Roman said, hoping to cheer him and not certain his words had merit. Would they see Javier and was he still human? Damien didn't respond and Roman was glad of it.

37

Tuscaloosa, AL
November 11th, 10 p.m.

The black Dodge pickup pulled to the curb and Damien could just make out David's head and shoulders dwarfed by the truck's size.

"You can sit up front, Damien," Roman told him, ushering Jimmy and Iago to the back seat of the crew cab.

Damien planted his feet and waited for Roman to notice. He couldn't leave, feeling in his spirit that no matter what Roman was thinking, he did not have a monopoly on God's purposes. When he hadn't moved, Roman finally turned.

"Damien, please, we need to hurry," Roman said, his urgency sounding more like fatherly responsibility than any sort of fear. "I need to keep you safe. I need to keep all of us safe."

Damien gave him a kind smile. "Listen to yourself. Did you hear what you just said? It is not up to you to keep everyone safe. We're not here to be safe and I was never going to be safe in this flesh."

"Damien," Roman said, disagreeing, but Damien continued.

"The moment I discarded the Rakum Father, I was immediately aware that my purpose was to bring as many Rakum with me to the Light," Damien said, seeing the beginnings of understanding in Roman's bright eyes. "I received an old man's flesh, riddled with cancer, and God used Theophilus to scare that disease away—that's when I knew for sure that He was going to use me a little longer. I will stay here with Kilmeade and Rafael, and I will make sure they know about our true Father before Yitzhak arrives."

Roman had no words, but his eyes wavered with tears he barely contained.

"You know it's true, I see it in your face," Damien said and pulled Roman into a warm embrace. "You always made me proud as a Rakum

186

Father and since my transformation, you have filled my heart with joy."

"Father Damien," Roman said, his voice cracking and falling back to the old title, "I need you, just a little longer. Javier needs you. David needs you."

Damien ended the hug and shook his head, catching Roman's eye. "Listen, my son, these words fall from your mouth because you love me. Your heart says loudly, 'go, and be strong.'"

Roman rubbed both eyes, cleared his throat, and stood straight. When he had taken a deep breath, he put out his hand. "Go, and be strong, Father. And God be with you."

"And also with you." Damien turned for the apartment and did not look back. Within a few seconds, he heard the truck door close and the engine rev as they pulled away. God would carry Roman and David to their next challenge. For him, he needed to get inside. Time was short and Yitzhak was on the way.

Kilmeade and Rafael were sipping beers in the living room when he returned. They occupied the two recliners and Damien again sat on the couch between them. The mood was decidedly more somber and Damien wasn't quite sure how to begin his tale. Thankfully, the previous topic hadn't left Kilmeade's mind.

"The Last is at least an hour away, Father Damien," Kilmeade offered. "If you feel so inclined, I will hear now about the magic that can make a Rakum Father into a tiny old man."

Damien smiled good-naturedly. "I'm still six feet tall," he laughed. "But I will tell you."

"Very good," Kilmeade said and leaned back.

"The tale begins with a woman named Lorna," Damien said seeking Rafa's eye, but the younger Rakum looked away.

"Females can be very persuasive," Kilmeade offered with a smile.

"This one truly was," Damien agreed. "I had money, so after my time with the monks, I moved South. I bought a house in an established neighborhood and blended in, playing the lonely widower longing for attention from the local widows." Damien winked and Kilmeade nodded his head.

"I'm sure you were very popular," he said chuckling.

"I had plenty of girlfriends," Damien laughed and then settled forward over his knees. "I lived comfortably, drawing blood only when I could swoon a consenting widow while watching a DVD." Damien shook his head. "Like most of you, I hid from Rufus. I purposed to avoid using my advanced powers; when I did, it drew attention. Once while searching for the other Fathers, I came across Canaan." Damien paused and caught Kilmeade's eye, knowing the two shared a bond.

"An excellent Rakum," Kilmeade whispered with a wry grin.

"When our minds touched, we both learned we would need to avoid telepathy altogether to stay off the radar of the collective unconscious." Both Rakum nodded before he continued. "The night I transformed, this woman Lorna visited uninvited and when she came in, I discerned she knew a Rakum in her past. By the time I jogged her memory with my directed conversation, I knew they had been intimate."

"Did she know you were a Rakum?" Rafael asked at rapt attention.

"I told her I was a Father and she knew what that meant. Kilmeade, you know Dae Kim," Damien said and the Elder nodded without expression. "He held this consenting Cow as a lover a few weeks in the fifties. At any rate, she told me she was no longer a Cow, but had become a follower of God."

Kilmeade sighed. "She talked you into it."

Damien shook his head. "No, it doesn't work that way. She told me that her God—Jesus—was knocking on the door of my heart." Damien put his palm to his sternum. "The strange thing was that I had been sensing an actual knocking deep inside, as if some unknown force stood and knocked—the analogy was incredibly accurate." Damien stopped his tale and studied his hands in his lap. He had been terrified of that knock; how could he express it to the two lost souls before him without frightening them away?

"I don't feel anything like that," Rafael said as if to himself.

Damien exhaled. "I told Lorna I heard Him knocking and she said He loved me desperately. She promised me that if I would open to Him the tiniest crack, He'd do the rest of the work."

"You opened the door?" Kilmeade asked and sat up.

Damien nodded. "That very night. She prayed for me to hear Him and when she left, I bowed my head and said to the Creator, 'I want to know You. Please come in.'" Damien's voice choked and he gathered control of his emotions. He wiped his face with both palms, avoiding the men's gazes, not ready to see what they thought. The seconds ticked by and he stared at the water glistening on his knuckles. What could they be thinking?

Kilmeade spoke first, his voice low in the quiet house. "When you said those words, the door opened and you became mortal. Is that how this happened?"

Damien looked up, braving Kilmeade's expression. It wasn't as bad as it could be—the man was curious, not insulted or unbelieving.

"I opened the door and Jesus Christ walked through it," Damien said, feeling as if his face must be shining with joy.

"What did He say to you?" Rafael asked in a whisper and Damien looked at him. The Rakum was sitting over his knees mimicking Damien's posture.

"He said, 'I love you, Damien. You are My son and I knew you before you were born,'" Damien replied. "I dedicated my life to Him and He filled me with unimaginable joy. I became whole, when for two thousand years, I never knew I was incomplete without Him." Damien turned to Kilmeade. As a Father, he had been privy to the Elder's entire lifespan and recognized the man considered himself quite a force. More than that, though, Kilmeade was a thinker, more so than all of their Elders.

"Yes?" Kilmeade said aware of the sudden scrutiny.

"You will search inside you and find you knew Him all along," Damien said softly, not planning his words.

Kilmeade scoffed without rancor and Rafael mumbled, "I don't want to be mortal."

The room fell silent and only the clock ticked across the room, reminding Damien of his heartbeat that may soon cease its noise. Before he became too morose, he gently clapped his wrinkled hands together.

"Rafa, Kilmeade, now that you've heard my story, He will knock at your door. What you do is up to you."

Kilmeade closed the footrest and stood. He looked as if he was about to offer an opinion on the current topic, but turned for the front door instead. "Isaac is here," he said.

"I am ready," Damien mumbled sincerely and sent up a prayer.

38

Javier punched Simon's phone number again to see if someone would pick up. Every half-hour, he tried the number and it went to voicemail each time. Now he was sixty miles away and all the prayer in the world gave him no peace regarding Simon's condition. Just before he gave up, a familiar voice said hello.

"Simon!" Javier said, pulling the phone to his ear. "Are you okay? I'm about an hour out."

"Everything's just *dandy*, Javier," Simon said, his voice full of grit. "Your friend Canaan really stepped up a few minutes ago when Beryl started harassing me again. A real hero."

Javier discerned the sarcasm, but didn't want to hear the reason Simon was so angry. What could he do? He couldn't get there any faster.

"And there are four of them here now, Javier. FOUR jolly Rakum holding me captive, and where are you? How could you leave me like that? I needed you and you disappeared—TWICE!" Simon screamed the last word. He was hysterical; something was dreadfully wrong.

"Put Canaan on," he said. When Simon balked, he repeated himself, much more firmly. "Put Canaan on the phone NOW."

"This Cow needs a baby bottle, Javier," Canaan said into the phone after a short wait. "He's completely hilarious." Canaan laughed and Javier heard him teasing Simon with his hand over the cell.

"Canaan, I asked you to protect him and he doesn't sound right," Javier said, his voice sterner than intended. After all, Canaan was a Rakum Elder and accustomed to great respect. All their history, past and recent, did not erase that fact. "Please, Canaan, I am counting on you," Javier added to erase his transgression of before.

"Seriously," Canaan said to Javier, his tone flatter and spoken directly into the phone, "Simon is beside himself and it really isn't anything we're doing to him." Canaan said a few words to someone on his end and when he came back, his voice echoed as if he'd taken the call into a smaller space. "It's true Beryl tapped him once when we first arrived, but since then, I've kept him away from the guy."

"I appreciate that, but what do you think has him so upset? He said there are two more Rakum there—are they threatening him?"

"Guap and Polly?" Canaan said and guffawed into the phone. "Yeah, right! No, not at all. Anyway, they're playing with *me*. Maybe your Cow is jealous."

"He's not my Cow, Canaan, please. He's my friend and I'm worried about him. I will be there in…" Javier checked his in-dash GPS. "…in another forty minutes. Just try to calm him down. He said he was captive—let him go home. There's no reason for him to stay there."

"Simon?" Canaan said obviously to the side. "You go on home. We're not holding you here. Go on." To Javier, he said, "I told him. Guess what—he wants to wait for you. See? He's irrational." And then Canaan added, "like a Cow."

Javier disconnected the call and stiffened his jaw. Simon had truly flipped out, his senses overloaded. At least he was almost there, and he hadn't heard from Chloe—*Chloe!*

Javier found her number in recents and hit send. She picked up on the first ring.

"Are you there yet? How's your friend?" she asked.

"Still a little to go. How about you? What's happening at my house?"

"I left a little after Roman and David got there," she said and Javier asked her for more. "I got in a fight with David—he thinks, well, he thinks we are an item now."

"Chloe…" Javier said and took a deep breath.

"Look, I understand. You and me, whatever we are is a tiny drop in a giant ocean of what's going on right now," she said, her voice fairly even, although Javier heard pain in admitting she might not be as important as she wanted to be. "Go help your friend and find out what God is doing in your body—see? I can think about someone besides myself. Proud?"

"Yes, I'm very proud. I don't know what will happen when this is over, but I'm relieved you went home. If I could proceed the next couple of nights knowing you're safe and *not* with any of the Rakum, I'd be very thankful."

"You pretty much just said exactly what I was thinking." Chloe's voice faded with their connection and when she crackled back in, he heard, "Roman wants you to call him. Bad company was headed to your house and he had to leave."

"Bad company?" Javier asked.

"That's what he said." Chloe gave him the phone number. "I know you're driving so I'll text it to you when we hang up."

"Thanks and listen—" Javier said as he changed lanes for his exit ahead. "Be careful and lay low until I can see what's going on."

"I will, I promise," she said and was gone.

Javier merged onto the highway leading into Athens. Once he set the cruise control, he dialed Roman's phone. He didn't take time to plan what he would say, but he owed the man a giant apology for many different transgressions of late. Roman picked up on the first ring.

"Roman, it's Javier," he said.

"Thank God!" Roman said, his voice smooth and sincere.

"Right off the bat, I'm sorry for the way I acted last week. I'm sorry for picking a fight and I know you did only what you were ordered to do to poor Isabella." Javier paused and then spit it out. "In Montgomery, I was weak and stupid and I took blood from The Last. I'm mortified and embarrassed, but if I don't come clean I'm afraid I could somehow stint God's efforts to help us get out of this mess."

"Shhh, Javie, shhhh," Roman said using the nickname he gave Javier as an eight-year-old. "Apology accepted and listen, God isn't affected by how we get along and I'm sure with all of us working together with His purposes as our goal, He will give us victory just like He did before."

"I know you're right," Javier said controlling his emotions. "You've seen Chloe..."

"Save it, Javie, shhh," Roman said gently. "You can tell me later."

Javier exhaled with relief realizing by his response that his former Elder knew about her bite mark. "Thank you. I will need you to help me figure this out, but first I need to know what happened at my place."

"Yes," Roman said. "Suffice it to say, David and I are fine. We left before Isaac got there. Kilmeade insisted he would kill us if we stayed."

"How *is* Kilmeade?"

"He's... well, he's healthy," Roman replied, choosing his descriptor.

Javier discerned the tremendous affection in his voice and then realized Father Damien had not been mentioned.

"Damien's not with you?" Javier asked, knowing the answer by the pause on Roman's end.

"I'm sorry," Roman said finally. "Damien feels God wants him to stay behind and he would not be dissuaded."

"But," Javier uttered surprised by the ache in his heart at the news. *That wasn't the plan,* Javier said in his heart.

"Also," Roman said, his voice very soft, "Isaac will kill him tonight. Kilmeade said as much."

"But…" Javier had no words, disappointment flooding his mind.

The pot doesn't tell the Potter what to do.

Javier's throat constricted with a mixture of emotions at the errant sentiment. Shouldn't the Potter *care* if He broke the pot's heart? Or was Javier being selfish? If God assigned the old Father the task of sharing the truth with the Rakum, who was Javier to disagree?

"Chloe said you needed to rescue Simon," Roman said then, plucking him out of his pain. "What happened?"

Javier sighed and changed tracks, setting Damien on hold. "I'm almost there, so in short, he's friends with a man who's been gathering Cows with a website. He finally attracted enough attention that Canaan and Beryl went right to them."

"Beryl?" Roman asked, gravel in his voice.

"Yes," Javier had no need to say more. At Last Assembly, when Roman was still in full Elder mode, he broke Beryl up against a cinderblock wall when he threatened them in The Cave. Plus, Beryl and Meryl had been dangerously infatuated with Simon from the get. Simon had his weak moments, but Javier's need to protect him had not waned from the first night they met.

"Okay, Javie, we're praying for you, and please call me as soon as you have something to report. Let me know if I need to come there. As much as you need to protect Simon, that is how I feel about you a million times over."

Javier had no doubt what Roman said was true so he promised to call him as soon as he determined the next move.

"Roman, listen," Javier said, his tone grim. "You're in the same town as Isaac so *you* be careful, okay?"

"Absolutely," Roman said and was gone.

Javier dropped the phone into the console and concentrated on his breathing. Anger, white and hot, threatened to the surface and such negativity was much more readily available than he ever remember it to be. Was his transformation causing a change in temperament?

Who am I so mad at? Javier breathed in, out, in, out, but the blood rushed to his face and his chest constricted with emotion. *Pray, Javier, pray,* he told himself, but truthfully—the *Person he was angry with was God.*

God, who decided to kill Damien before Javier got his one-on-one. Javier frowned as the recollection of his first and only meeting with Father Damien streamed back although it occurred more than a century ago.

I can't believe I fainted...

He had been so nervous anticipating the meet that he passed out and the Father had actually carried him back into the house. Javier's frown lifted only slightly as he recollected how Damien compared himself to his blood-son without embarrassment, saying they had identical tendencies toward empathy and emotionalism. But hadn't the most amazing part of that visit been the prophecy?

"You will suffer a tragedy before you leave the hospital, but when you settle in your first situation as an adult Rakum, you will find life easy. You'll never be without Cows and Elder Roman will remain at your disposal for as long as you live. Your bond is stronger than any I've seen amongst the brethren."

When he offered his advice, Javier had nodded eagerly.

"Be easygoing and do not seek trouble," the old Father had said. *"When trouble finds you, Roman will protect you. One day, you will get in over your head and if you're not careful, you will take everyone you call friend down with you."*

Javier must have been awestruck at the portents and Damien added one more piece to recall when the time came.

"When this happens, a promised one will simultaneously emerge. It will come to pass that High Father Abroghia will father the last Rakum and imbue him with the combined power and might of the Ten Fathers. He will be called Yitzhak and he will take over the Rakum for a time. He will be bloodthirsty and deadly, and if you do not beware, he will kill you."

"Is Isaac looking for me already?" Javier thought. *"Will he try to kill me?"* There were no answers from above or inside. He shook the memories away with effort as he pulled into the hotel parking lot. Weaving his way to an open space, he poured cool water on his hateful emotions regarding the loss of his blood-father.

"Abba, I repent of my anger," he prayed and switched off the car. *"And I pray Damien does whatever You need him to do."*

Javier gripped the steering wheel with both hands and looked up at the building looming in the dark night before him. *"And go with me. I'm not as brave as You think I am."*

The cell phone rang and he read Simon's number. Instead of answering it, Javier jogged toward the lobby.

Jackson, MS   11 p.m.

What a cruel trick of the devil, Marcy thought, relatively calm despite her current situation. The Rakum attached to her arm looked like a teen model, a fair-skinned African-American, his course hair cut short against his scalp. And didn't he look *sweet?* Huge puppy-dog eyes, bright hazel and shining with life, a well-shaped nose flared with purpose, full lips ready to pout and complain as adolescents are wont to do. But this creature was none of those things. This face was a mask given by Satan, enabling him to deceive poor little Marcy Haddle when she allowed herself the smallest distraction from her troubles. Thankfully, so far, this Rakum had handled her carefully.

I should have known better... Now that she was a Rabbit, escaping their clutches would never mean the end of the chase. *Thanks, Canaan!*

"Ow!" she blurted by reflex and quieted again. The *darling* young Rakum was sucking greedily at her inner elbow and now and then, an untrimmed fingernail pressed like a claw in the sensitive underskin of her arm. Other than that, she felt no pain; hadn't he been unusually cautious? Marcy sensed it had a lot to do with Canaan's status as Elder. Their world had turned upside down, but an Elder was infinitely stronger than any grunt.

Tonight, she answered the knock on the door and didn't fear the face in the peephole. He'd given her the lamest story: *"Can I use your phone? My mom's using ours and I need to see if Daddy's out of surgery."*

Marcy smiled sadly and shook her head. She had been thinking about a million other things when she let him in. Once inside, it was immediately apparent by his self-carriage and basic other-worldliness that he was a Rakum. Too late, of course. He had calmly closed the door as he entered and introduced himself as Kite. He knew Canaan from days past and admitted he was collecting her for Isaac.

From the start, he hadn't attempted to intimidate her and as a result, Marcy was taking the attack well. Plus, she found comfort in blaming Canaan every few seconds. Hadn't it been Canaan who marked her as a Rabbit in her sleep after she refused his offer to do so? The Rakum still chase Rabbits; who sat in the leader's chair had little to do with that fact.

The Rakum ceased feeding and remained as he was, leaning over her arm, buzzing on her blood as Canaan used to do before he marked her. Marcy looked around the hotel room, wishing she was home. Back when she and Canaan lived each night to the fullest where she worked five nights a week and Canaan romped around until her shift was over. Absently, she thought of her captain; she learned of his concern that she'd disappeared, and witnessed via phone call his relief when she escaped. He said they would hold her job—would she go back?

"Rabbit," the Rakum said, his voice husky as a lover. "Tell Elder Canaan I was gentle." Kite languidly straightened his spine.

"Why? Nobody else ever is," Marcy retorted, her voice more angry than she intended.

Kite dropped contact with her arm. They sat side-by-side on the bed and he leaned back and rested on his palms.

"Tell him. Elder Canaan should hear it from you. We're gonna be working together and he's a big dude." Kite raised his eyebrows and finished his smile. "I wanna stay on his good side."

To ask him to *not* drink her blood was a waste of breath. "I'll tell him," she said, her voice flat.

"I wrestled Elder Canaan once at Assembly. He pounded me into the ground," Kite said with humor.

Marcy turned to catch his eye once more; he was laughing. "You enjoy this memory?" she asked.

"Oh, definitely," Kite responded and sent her a wink.

Marcy rolled her eyes.

"Where's your gun? I heard you shot Beryl in the nuts."

Marcy flashed her eyes rearward to him and frowned.

"What?" he asked, the picture of innocence.

Marcy stood, and in a blur, the Rakum was beside her, his fingers firmly about her left wrist. *Don't forget he's a Rakum, Marcy,* she told herself and closed her eyes to concentrate on slowing her heartrate.

"Rabbits sometimes run," Kite said, maintaining his grip.

"If you want a good report with my husband," Marcy said when she thought she might maintain a strong voice, "don't ask me about that night."

Kite sighed and swayed his shoulders in tiny increments, looking all the more like a little kid. "Who remains with Master Isaac besides Elder Canaan?"

That question was easier. "Beryl and Boris."

He nodded. "I picked up that Meryl was missing or dead."

Marcy shrugged her shoulders.

"Okay, then. Who else? Just Beryl and Boris? What about the guys in the house? Gage, Hoss, Dimple. We had fifteen before Elder Rufus was attacked."

"I only know about Dimple and Hoss," Marcy said her voice hard. Both of them were viciously brutal when they took her blood and she was glad they were dead. Keeping her answers short, she said, "Isaac killed Dimple my first night there and Hoss was killed by police yesterday."

"And you ran away, naughty Rabbit," Kite said with a mischievous grin. "My Elder would have tortured you to death for that. Lucky for you, Master Isaac likes Rabbits and he *loves* Elder Canaan."

His statements all seemed rhetorical so Marcy said nothing.

"Call Elder Canaan," Kite said.

"Why?" Marcy asked trying to read his bright eyes.

He hardened his gaze, reminding Marcy he wasn't just a visiting youngster. She took a step toward the desk, but Kite held her in place. She pointed to the cheap cell phone she had picked up in the drug store next door; the cops had kept the one Isaac threw at her as evidence.

Kite laughed a little and opened his fingers. When she crossed and picked up the phone, he pat the mattress by his leg. Marcy sat precisely where he requested and he smiled again.

"Good Rabbit," he purred and motioned for her to make the call.

"Thanks a lot," she mumbled and selected Canaan. She had texted him with the number, so she wasn't surprised he picked right up.

"Cee, are you in the hotel?" he asked, his tone as serene as if they were on vacation, not under duress from a miniature maniac.

Marcy controlled her inflection and said, "Isaac sent a Rakum to collect me."

"What the shit?" Canaan barked, his humor evaporated. "Are you okay? Do I know him?"

Marcy blinked slowly, very willfully maintaining composure. "His name is Kite."

"Put him on the phone," Canaan said and she handed the cell to the Rakum.

"Master, I did *not* hurt your woman, ask her," Kite said as a greeting. "I'll take good care of her. Master Isaac told me to secure her until he lands somewhere. I have a good shelter, a clean place. Trust me. Where are *you?*"

"You don't get to ask me anything, you little turd. Put Marcy back on," Canaan said, which Marcy could hear from her seat beside Kite.

"Canaan, I'm really tired of this," Marcy said when the phone was in her hand again. She wiped her eye, consciously daring it to cry for real. "Are you safe?"

"Hon, everything is going to work out fine," he said and Marcy thought he believed his words. "Beryl and I are on an errand for Isaac. I'm real sick that he sent someone to get you, but you'll be safe. I will call you tomorrow night. We will be together soon."

"Oh, so this little Rakum sucking my life out equals me being safe," she stated flatly and not as a question. "You've changed, Canaan, I don't think I know you anymore."

"Cee," he began, but she cut him off.

"Forty years and you never let a single one of them *touch* me, your *princess*, remember? Now you let them paw me, put their filthy lips on me, and you think nothing of it. This is not what my Canaan would allow!" Marcy shouted the last and Kite removed the phone from her hand to shut off the call.

"Come on, Rabbit," he said standing and pulling her up by the wrist. "I'll watch over you and I won't buzz off you again until tomorrow night. How about that?"

Marcy looked at him, sniffled, and cursed Canaan aloud.

39

Kilmeade sensed Isaac had arrived and for his own reasons, stood on the stoop without knocking. He smirked and flashed his eyes at Rafael who stepped to the door. Once positioned in the center of the living room facing front, he requested Father Damien stand behind him. When all three were ready, Kilmeade directed Rafael to open the door.

"Hey!" The Last said cheerfully when the door came open.

"Welcome, Master," Rafael said and bowed low, averting his eyes. Kilmeade had suggested this greeting since it was the one the Rakum used when presented before the Fathers in days gone by. Rafael finished with a coached phrase, "I am Rafael. Shall I call you, 'Father,' Master?" Rafa's voice did not reveal any of the anxiety Kilmeade knew brewed inside him.

The Last crossed the threshold and put both hands onto Rafa's bowed head, running his fingers in the man's dark hair. "Rafael, you are a beautiful Rakum," he said and moved his hands to manually lift his face. "What do you feel like calling me?"

Kilmeade took one step forward to grab The Last's attention and when the youngster looked his way, he proffered the same respectful bow, saying, "The pup and I can see you are more than a Father. Shall we call you 'Father Isaac'?"

Isaac abandoned Rafael and approached Kilmeade, his eyes shining. "Elder Kilmeade!" he said and stepped right into his space, forcing Kilmeade out of his bowing stance. "I don't care what you call me as long as you mean it." He reached up to cup Kilmeade's face in his hands. "I'm so happy you're alive, you have no idea," the boy said.

Rafael now stood upright and he had not left his station at the door. Standing beside him and at least two inches taller was a Rakum Kilmeade recognized as Boris, one of Elder Rufus's pups. Kilmeade made no attempt to speak to Boris or Rafa, his focus solely on the tiny king before him. He flashed The Last a friendly smile.

"I am very happy to be alive, Master," Kilmeade said and slipped off his thick cashmere sweater in one swift move. Underneath he wore a plain white T-shirt and he presented his arm to The Last. "Whatever I have is yours," he said and without hesitation, the boy covered his inner elbow with his mouth.

No one made a sound and Kilmeade didn't look at the other men in the room. It didn't hurt and he wasn't dizzy when the little Father had had enough and pulled away, buzzing deeply, his eyes glazed.

Sporting a lazy grin, Isaac held Kilmeade's arm with both hands, and pulled him past Father Damien to the couch. Kilmeade gave no resistance and settled beside him, thighs touching, and waited for the kid's buzz to pass. In his peripheral vision, he noted Rafael and Boris had not moved and Damien had backed up to the wall, watching everything. When the clock sitting on the side table chimed the hour, Isaac rolled his eyes and leaned into the cushioned sofa back. With an audible sigh, he pulled Kilmeade's hand to his mouth.

"You honor me, Elder Kilmeade," he said and he kissed his hand noisily. "I won't forget that. Look—" he said and pointed toward the door. "That's Boris, but I see you know him already."

Boris unlocked his feet and lumbered into the room.

"Boris, you look well," Kilmeade said. "Have you practiced what I showed you the last time we met?" Kilmeade sent Isaac a wink and he smiled even bigger.

"What? What was it?" he asked Boris eagerly.

"Ah, the *krav maga!* Yes, see this…" Boris replied and assumed a half-squat, his arms coming out from his body, tense and ready for battle. Kilmeade chuckled as he displayed the first position.

"Well done," Kilmeade said and looked to the door. Rafa hadn't moved. "Master, you met my pet, Rafael, when you entered. He's a little star-struck. Allow me to encourage him inside. Come in, Rafa," Kilmeade said when Isaac gave him a tiny consenting nod.

"*Your pet*—I like that," Isaac giggled.

"I pet him with my teeth as often as I can," Kilmeade said deep into Isaac's baby blue eyes, noting his every move mesmerized the youngster.

"Yeahhhh," Isaac responded and moved his hand toward Kilmeade's mouth. "You have teeth like mine?" His fingers touched Kilmeade's lips so he opened wide. The Last gingerly rubbed his thumb against Kilmeade's slightly sharper canines. "Boris said you have this as a holdover to your transgression of the Dying Buzz."

Kilmeade nodded, allowing his eyes to twinkle with humor. The Last withdrew his hand and used the same fingers to push up his upper lip. "Shee? I have'em, too," he said with a comical lisp.

"They come in handy, Master," Kilmeade said.

"Does your pet mind?" Isaac asked and looked over at Rafa still a distance away, but Kilmeade answered for him.

"It wouldn't concern me if he did."

"Yeah!" Isaac laughed. "You're right. I love it. You're *very* cool, Elder Kilmeade. Hey!" he then said excitedly. "Maybe that makes Boris my pet. Whatcha think?" He held his free hand outward for Boris to grasp. "Boris? Would you be my pet Rakum?"

The big Rakum grinned. "Of course!"

Isaac laughed with him and watched Rafa enter the room and stand near the couch on Kilmeade's left. Boris settled in the living room entrance, effectively blocking the exit.

"Master, I don't want you to kill Father Damien," Kilmeade said and Isaac turned to read his expression. Kilmeade sent him a little shrug when he raised his eyebrows with a question. "Why make small talk and fill the air with empty words? Even with my poorly-developed extrasensory skills, I can see that you are more than a Father in power and stature. That means your every word is precious."

"What do you mean?" he asked.

"The Fathers did not use many words," Kilmeade explained, realizing the youngster before him didn't have the same experience as the rest of them and he was never called before the Fathers in the formal sense. "Also, the Fathers were *scarce*. We did not see them but once, before we graduated First Ritual. Any other time, if called before them, it would be for a chastisement."

"Really?" Isaac said, his chin tilted to the side. "I say consider yourself lucky. The Fathers spoke to me a lot, *for hours,* every day for forty years. I thought they'd never stop talking."

Kilmeade noted Isaac hadn't looked at nor acknowledged Father Damien, but that observation gave him no peace. Isaac had a calculating and ruthless nature; all Kilmeade could hope to do was keep the youngster distracted.

"Your immense power can be partially attributed to the schooling you, alone, received. The very power of our people was poured into you with every word spoken," Kilmeade said, his voice soft and lilting. "The Fathers' words carried substance. In your ears, each word transformed into three-dimensional food for your spirit."

Isaac's eyes narrowed in thought, processing Kilmeade's teaching. "You've provided confirmation on something I am beginning to understand on my own, Elder Kilmeade," he said. "Did you know that Father Damien was assigned my care after the Rabbit destroyed our lives?"

"I heard that information just tonight," he replied. Kilmeade did not look at Damien leaning on the wall behind Isaac, but he wanted to. He wanted to encourage him, but already, he saw telepathically that Isaac was mentally devising the former Father's method of execution.

"He betrayed me—his own seed, his proselyte, his future Master and god. He deserted me for a pitiful mortal shell," Isaac said and dropped his hand from Kilmeade's fingers.

"Master," Kilmeade said as low as possible, hoping Isaac would look at him to hear the rest. It didn't work. Isaac rose to his feet and crossed the room to stand before Damien.

"Master, I like Father Damien," Kilmeade said, his words meaningless to The Last, as he expected, but he could only speak the truth. Anything less, Isaac would discern right away.

"Kilmeade, don't weep for this human," Isaac said, for the first time dropping Kilmeade's title. "You told him he would die if he stayed, and he stayed anyway. This is what he wants."

"Yitzhak, may I speak?" Damien asked.

Kilmeade rose to his feet to listen and watch Isaac's movements.

"Depends, traitor," Isaac said, his voice bitter. "If I don't like your first few words, you'll know it."

Damien swallowed, met Kilmeade's eye a brief second, and then nodded his head. "I'm sorry I deserted you the way I did. If I could do it all over again, I would never have left you behind. I would have done things differently."

"Damien," Isaac said crossing his arms at his narrow little-boy's chest. "I see through you." Isaac turned halfway to catch Kilmeade's eye. "Elder Kilmeade, allow *me* to teach *you* something. Stand here."

Kilmeade stepped to Isaac's left where he indicated. He then gestured Rafael over with two fingers.

"You, too, pet. You can probably learn this, if you're bright enough."

Rafael stepped into place, and if he objected to the insult, Kilmeade read nothing on his face nor in his head. A distant hum vibrated in the furthest parts of Kilmeade's mind, almost as if an invisible train headed toward them. In his mind's eye, this train brought with it incredible revelation. Good news or bad, all he could do was wait for it to mature, and he focused his attention on Isaac's profile.

202

"Kilmeade," Isaac said, eyes still fixed on Damien before him, "every word you have said with your mouth matches your thoughts. Because of this, I will ask you a special question. Are you ready?" Isaac turned his head to catch Kilmeade's eye.

"Yes, Master," Kilmeade said with the tiniest nod.

"Who do you say I am?" Isaac asked, his face devoid of expression.

Kilmeade considered the question carefully, discerning that his answer was of the utmost importance. The train was closer to the station now, and Kilmeade relaxed his mental barriers to see if it would come on in. With a slow-building white light, it arrived, and Kilmeade set about sorting through a myriad of impulses and images it delivered. Every iota of the information had to do with the diminutive Rakum before him, and looking into Isaac's eyes, the answer unfolded itself in such a way that Isaac saw it the very same time. The boy smiled and winked. Kilmeade's mouth dropped open.

"I want to hear you say it," Isaac said, his voice soft.

Kilmeade searched for words, but none came forth. His revelation, the boy before him was *exactly the same* immense spiritual power as Abroghia. He wasn't "like" the High Father—he was *more than*. Flustered, Kilmeade exhaled and shook his head.

"I fear my spiritual ears are muted, weakened by my own laziness and avoidance of our people. I can see you, Master—in the spirit, but I cannot hear your name."

"Zahdone," Isaac said strangely reserved.

Kilmeade fell to his knees and dropped his eyes. "Yes! I hear it now. Zahdone, powerful and mighty, none can compare! I hear it, thank you, Master." Kilmeade reached out for Rafa's wrist as he stood on Isaac's other side. Gripping it tight, he sent the images to Rafa through touch. Rafael fell to his knees, too, but he looked at Isaac's profile, wonder and surprise in his face.

Isaac turned away from Damien to put a hand on each of their heads. "THIS is how you treat your god, guys. I could get used to this," he said to Boris who grinned nodding.

In his mind's eye, millions of entities praised the boy king and when he focused upon them, Kilmeade understood they worshipped him as their prince. Having only an elementary understanding of the spirit dimension, Kilmeade was at a complete loss. Rafa had zero awareness of such a realm and he looked as if he might lose consciousness. Kilmeade squeezed his fingers to ground him.

Isaac turned to Kilmeade. "Now you understand me when I say, I can see right through this *human* in Father Damien's skin. Nothing spiritual is hidden from me. I see the unseen as well as the seen. Are you impressed?"

"Beyond words," Kilmeade said, barely audible.

"Yes, Master," Rafael said, his voice shaking. Kilmeade discerned fear in his pet and then overheard frantic worries for Iago.

Isaac smirked and removed his hand from Rafa's head. He repositioned himself to place both in Kilmeade's hair, who knelt before him. "This human *murdered* Father Damien. See him how I, Isaac-Zahdone, see him."

Kilmeade did as ordered and turned his face to where Damien stood against the wall. At first, he saw only the man, Damien, with whom he had been conversing all evening. But then, like scales falling away from his eyes, he saw white light in the shape of a man. Confused, Kilmeade turned to look once more at Isaac who also seemed be made of light. But when he concentrated on the differences of the two light-beings, he noted that Damien's light-man emanated beams outward from the center, where Isaac's drew light into it, flowing in. Kilmeade turned back to study Damien's emanation and as he did, the head turned to him. At that moment, two things happened simultaneously—first, an unfamiliar, yet all-consuming joy encircled his heart, and second, a voice as gentle as a breeze whispered across his spirit, *"Remember Me, Kilmeade, you are My son and I love you."* At those words, the vision evaporated and he was looking only at a sad old man with his hands clasped at his chest.

"Remember Me?" Remember what? Who? Kilmeade's mind flirted with something vague from his past. But Rakum have perfect recall; how could he forget anything? How could anything be hazy in a Rakum Elder's mind? Answer: it couldn't. Unless a memory had been expunged by the Fathers. Kilmeade regarded Isaac. Had he heard that voice?

"What about it?" Isaac asked while gesturing for Kilmeade and Rafael to stand. "You heard a voice telling you to remember?"

Kilmeade's mind raced, unwilling to admit what he had heard. Something unnamable warned him that he wasn't supposed to communicate with the spirit in Damien, that Isaac would be displeased. The same unnamable abstract told him his memory had been erased. *When? Where?* Kilmeade searched his long memory for circumstances, unable to prevent Isaac from seeing it all.

"Kilmeade, what did He say?" Isaac pressed, openly threatening him by stepping closer.

"I don't..." Kilmeade began, and stopped. Nothing made sense. Why would Damien's white-light being say such words to him and had his memory been altered by the Fathers in the past?

"Yitzhak," Damien said then and stepped off the wall. "I will tell you what He said. Don't blame Kilmeade—look. He is completely without guile. He doesn't understand what you and I already know." Father Damien caught Kilmeade's eye and smiled. "You just saw Messiah Yeshua, the one true God—"

"SHUT UP, TRAITOR!" Isaac boomed. The walls vibrated at the sound and somewhere in the house, glass shattered. Isaac grabbed Damien by the throat with both hands, reaching up since he was a head shorter and the man immediately began to strangle.

Damien's pained eyes sought Kilmeade's and as their gazes locked, he heard the white-being's voice again, this time Damien's lips moved soundlessly with every word.

"Zahdone, you have no power except that which my Father in heaven gives you. You cannot take my life because I give it up freely…"

Isaac screeched and squeezed the old neck tighter, claiming aloud, "Die! Die! You are dead!"

"I give my life for Kilmeade and Rafa, my beloved sons," Damien said aloud, meeting Kilmeade's, then Rafael's eyes.

"THIS IS IMPOSSIBLE!" Isaac shrieked, his thumbs depressed several centimeters into the old Father's Adam's apple. And then, as if he had never resisted at all, Damien's neck snapped and his eyes went dark.

Kilmeade said nothing. He watched the old man sink down the wall and puddle on the floor like a six-foot doll. Rafael also remained silent, his eyes darting from Isaac, to Kilmeade, to Damien and back.

Isaac remained where he was, facing the dead man, his chest heaving. After a minute passed, Boris stepped up and gathered the body off the floor and dragged it into the closest bedroom. He reentered the living room and waited for the next command.

Kilmeade became aware that Rafa was holding his breath and trying to catch his eye. He wasn't ready to look at him. Not yet. In 380 years on the planet, he had never seen such a sight—or had he? Now the last Father had perished; no one remained to ask the burning question: had Kilmeade met that white-light being in the past and had his memory of the event removed? He began to replay the scene in his mind and Isaac abruptly turned and left the room. Kilmeade and Rafael watched him go and heard the front door close softly a few moments later. Boris stood conspicuously across the room and when Kilmeade looked his way, he gestured for the exit.

"Follow us to our day place, Master."

Nodding, his mind still numb, Kilmeade got his feet moving and passed Rafael toward the hall. Rafael filed in behind him and Boris brought up the back.

"Poor Javier has a dead man in his bedroom," Kilmeade sent to Rafa. His pet didn't respond and that was probably best. Isaac was listening and he didn't need to be reminded there were more traitors about.

40

Jackson, MS
November 12th, Midnight

"Oh, great spirit Pawsa! Show us your power! Reveal yourself to your servant!" Eric cooed, swaying back and forth and holding the bloody towel in front of him. He had used a cube steak from Winn Dixie for blood, but the girls didn't know that. Reka and Luella giggled and he enjoyed the sound. Both girls were wasted and he hoped if he could only evoke Pawsa like he had last week, one or both of them would take him to bed. Jeanette Spencer French-kissed him last month simply from hearing *the rumors* about his mighty spirit guide. It seemed Pawsa made pretty girls blind to his oily hair, infected pimples and terminal body-odor.

Pawsa revealed himself when Eric was seven, directly after watching a TV marathon of *Ghosts and Witches of Nassau County* with his older brother. The first time Pawsa appeared, he came as a rat. He had tip-toed right up to little Eric, sat up on his haunches and waved his paws. Last week, Pawsa came as a raven and swooped down on the group—they had eleven that night—causing Beverly Grant to wet her pants crying. Eric was only eighteen and not the oldest there, but because his was the only spirit that would show up on cue, he was named coven leader.

Tonight, they had six, and only he, Reka, and Luella were still awake. The other three had fallen out an hour ago, drunk on chocolate vodka. Eric did a line of coke, but hadn't had anything to drink; at eleven when Reka passed him the bottle, a loud voice in his mind commanded him to refuse. He did and hoped that meant come evocation time, Pawsa would come bigger and better than ever.

"Where is he, Eric?" Reka asked, slurring a bit and still sipping vodka. "We want to see Pawsa."

"Yeah, where is he? You promised," Luella added, leaning forward, causing a deep scoop in her shirt.

Eric grinned at the sight and turned his face to the ceiling. "Oh, mighty Pawsa! Come and show us your power!"

"You can have the same power as Pawsa! Would you like that?" a familiar voice said in his mind and Eric closed his eyes.

"Yes, great Pawsa! I hear you!" he said aloud.

"All it takes is your consent! Pawsa will use your body to make you great! You won't believe how amazing you will be!"

Eric opened his eyes to peek at the girls. They had both assumed his pose, eyes closed, legs crossed, faces to the ceiling, chests out. *Oh, those beautiful T-shirts,* Eric thought. With Pawsa's help, he'd be allowed to take those shirts right off and do as he pleased.

"Great and mighty Pawsa! Use my body! I am yours! I consent!" he said and opened his arms wide to the air around him.

A rush of cold wind swirled through the room and both girls screamed, at first with surprise, but then with fear as the room filled with black flies.

"Eric! Eric!" Luella yelled, hopping unsteadily to her feet. Reka jumped up and leaned on her friend as both backed to the door. Eric paid them no mind; from his toes, to his shins, knees, thighs, groin, up his lower back, and into his neck and head, a tingling of pure pleasure filled his soul.

Arms still wide to the room, he shouted, "More, Pawsa! More of you! I want more of YOU!"

From far away, he heard the girls screaming that the door wouldn't open and he should help them get out. Screw 'em; Eric had never been happier in his life.

"I will show you something amazing—want to see?" the voice asked, silky and sweet as honey dripping into his ears.

"YES!" Eric yelled, eyes still tightly closed, his face to the ceiling. "YES!"

"Open your eyes and see your master!" the voice said, and Eric did as he was told. Before him, created entirely of black flies, stood a man-shaped entity, arms akimbo, featureless face slightly tilted to one side, as if measuring him up in the same manner. Eric stared at the apparition, marveling and awaiting instruction. The women continued to struggle with the jammed exit and when they saw the fly-man-specter, they screamed with more gusto than before.

"Eric! Help us! Somebody, HELP!" they shouted, banging on the door, all intoxication shocked out of their system.

"Step forward, Eric, step into your reward," the voice said as the fly-man spun away, now facing the wall with its back to Eric. *"Step into your master*

and become ONE. I will show you great and mighty things you do not know!"

"Yes! Great Pawsa!" Eric called and without fear, took a giant step directly into the center of the swirling flies. For a split second, maybe less, a thousand tiny beaks stabbed his flesh, but the fleeting pain was replaced by the greatest pleasure he had ever known. Eric fell to his knees and toppled over onto his side, gasping with the orgasmic pulse that rushed through his system. When it passed, the flies were gone. Breathless with delight, Eric rose to his knees and then stood to face the girls ashen-faced, exhausted, and terrified.

The shorter one, Luella, stepped toward him, maybe for comfort, maybe for some other reason. Eric needed more than anything in the world to crush her throat and watch her eyes go dim. In a fluid movement that he didn't know he was capable of, he rushed to meet her, took her slender throat in both hands and began to squeeze. She gasped, Reka restarted her scream machine and Eric smiled. Oh, the pleasure that coursed through him—with every breath Luella missed, he gained a new wave of ecstasy. It didn't even take sixty seconds and she had less strength than a baby against him. Eric laughed with joy when her eyes dilated and she went limp in his hands.

"No! Please! Eric! What are you doing? Stop!" Reka sputtered, her back to the impossibly-locked door, cried-out and essentially losing hope after watching the amazing new Eric end her friend.

Eric looked her over, her soft curly hair, her alabaster skin, her shapely waist and long legs snugly poured into her fashionably ripped blue jeans. What did he want to do now? What did the Great Pawsa want?

Blood.

Blood.

Blood.

A million voices chanted in his ear the same word over and over. Eric shoved his hands in his pockets, he had nothing sharp, not even keys—his lame-ass parents wouldn't buy him a car after he wrecked the first two. His eyes fell on the girl's small handbags and he dumped them out. No ink pens, no pocketknives, nothing pointy or sharp.

Blood.

Blood.

Blood.

Eric searched the small room with his eyes. Candles, matches, pillows, a blanket. DAMMIT, I gotta get that blood!

Eric jumped toward Reka and covered her mouth with one hand, flipped her back to him and hugged her close with his free arm. Oh, he needed that blood so badly, he felt he would scream. Her hair tickled his nose and he removed his hand from her mouth to move it aside. She released one short yelp before he clamped her quiet once more. Her throat was only inches from his mouth; he could see the individual hairs standing up on her pink skin. If only he was a vampire!

Bite.

Bite.

Bite!

So Eric did. His blunt teeth didn't puncture, so he ripped and tore and dragged them across her flesh until it gave way. The jagged laceration didn't flow blood as a puncture would have, but the voices were appeased.

YES!

YES!

YES!

Eric lapped up the blood and when it ceased its dribbling tide, he squeezed the life out of her as he had the other one. Pawsa was *very* happy with him, sending jolts of pleasure through his very essence as he touched the knob the girls couldn't open earlier. It wasn't locked, it wasn't jammed. Eric walked out of the room past his unconscious coven and left the house. Jimmy's truck was in the back and he got in and cranked it up.

"Where to, Master?" he asked the air and as gentle as a lover, the mighty Pawsa whispered to him a new adventure.

Ta'avah sensed Zara and Rah Keel's minions exiting the vicinity, traveling to the next summoning, clamoring toward whomever would call any of their millions of names. It was all any free spirit wanted, to be called by name and asked a favor. From the dawn of man, Ta'avah and his brethren only sought to teach the flesh how to be fulfilled, how to avoid the prison of Elohim.

The Eric flesh was young, but pock-marked, flabby, and physically unattractive. Ta'avah comforted himself with the realization that the most beautiful flesh ever created was only two hours away and soon to be his for eternity.

41

At the Broad Street Hampton Inn, Javier passed the front desk walking, but jogged down the hallway where Canaan had directed him on their call. Beryl was trouble—had been seven years ago, and from Javier's conversation with Canaan earlier, he was still obsessed with Simon. Then there was Canaan—Javier liked him, had history with him, but the guy was a Rakum and that meant his agenda would rarely run congruent with Javier's. When it came to Simon's friend Stuart and the other two Rakum, Javier had no idea what to expect from them. He reached the room and knocked twice. Canaan's large frame immediately filled the door.

"Javier," he said and ushered him inside. "It's about damn time. Look at poor Simon," Canaan said with a smile. "He's a mad little fella."

Across the room, Simon sat shirtless on the foot of the bed, arms folded, ankles crossed, and his face a mask of anger. Standing beside him with his hands in his pants pockets, Beryl glared at Javier, daring him to protest.

"He's safe, see?" Canaan said, one hand on Javier's shoulder.

"He doesn't need to be half-naked, Canaan," Javier said under his breath, knowing it was Beryl that removed his shirt when he attacked him hours ago. "The man's a professional ball player, for God's sake!" Indignant, Javier grew livid and glared at Canaan. "He's not a Cow. Don't treat him like one!"

With a mock look of surprise, Canaan raised his hands in surrender and gave Beryl a pointed look. Beryl huffed, picked Simon's shirt off the floor and tossed it in his lap. In angry jerks, Simon pulled it on.

"Better. And Beryl's standing too close to him," Javier barked, calming a little.

"Give him some space, B," Canaan said quietly, eyes on Javier, amused grin in place. Beryl took three steps away and crossed his arms at his chest.

"Thank you. Wait a minute..." Looking around the room, Javier asked, "Where are the other two?"

Not at all concerned with Javier's histrionics, Canaan winked and said, "Oh, they'll be back. They went out for a little dessert."

Javier pretended not to get the inference and moved toward Simon.

"Hold up, little brother." Canaan tugged him back with his hand once again resting on his shoulder. "What's happening with you? I've heard some interesting things." Canaan pulled him close and sniffed his hair. "You smell different. Stu said you walk in the day *and* drink blood? So, spill."

Assuming it was Stuart, Javier looked at the man sitting alone in the furthest chair and then back at Canaan. "I do not drink blood."

Canaan laughed and inhaled again, close to Javier's head. "Yes, you do. What's going on?"

"Canaan," Javier whispered, *"Help me out. I need to get Simon out of here. You owe me."*

"I can hear you, moron," Beryl said, his voice harsh. "And please—*please*—try to take him from me. I am so sick of you apostates. *Please,"* Beryl moaned and stepped up to stand between Javier and the bed. "Canaan can make me stay off him, but no one's going to keep me from taking him with me if he wants to go." Careful not to touch him, Beryl turned sideways to look into Simon's face. "Tell him, Simon. Tell Javier you want to go with me."

Afraid Simon might say yes, Javier elbowed Canaan's arm. "Canaan?"

Canaan draped an arm about Javier's shoulders. "You can take Simon with you if you—"

"No, he CAN'T," Beryl asserted still not attempting to touch the man.

Canaan continued as if he hadn't spoken. "—tell us what happened to you. What did Isaac's blood do to you?"

Javier wriggled to free himself from the Elder's grip, then gave up and dropped his shoulders.

"You took blood from The Last?" Beryl asked, incredulous and disgusted. Canaan shushed him with his hand.

"What's going on? I'm sensing some strange things..."

Javier sighed, his eye on Simon, who stared straight ahead, frowning. "Look, I don't know exactly," Javier said. "Chloe says my back was broken."

"Like a twig," Canaan said nodding.

"Well, I had no idea I was injured. I woke up in the hospital completely restored. When I went outside, the sun didn't hurt me. I'm different, but I'm still figuring it out. Now, please, let me check on Simon."

"Keep your pants on, Kemosabi. What about your teeth? Do you have fangs, Javier? The story is, you have fangs now." Canaan's finger headed for Javier's mouth, so with an irritated sigh he showed him his teeth. Canaan pressed his canines and nodded. "Isaac has teeth like that, Javier. You inherited his fangs, then. What else?"

Javier huffed. "I told you, Canaan, I don't know."

"You took Simon's blood?" Canaan asked and Javier glared at the Cow on the floor listening to every word.

"It's true, Master," Stu said to Canaan's back. "Simon said so."

"Shut it, Stu," Canaan said quietly and then turned back to Javier. "What of it?"

"Canaan," Javier pleaded, "do we have to do this now?"

Javier hoped Simon would at least look up and meet his eye, but his friend refused. He appeared uninjured, beyond that, Javier could tell nothing. And what was Canaan's angle? With all the questions, were they going to be allies or enemies? When Rufus was alive, they had joined forces wholeheartedly, but now? Could he trust him? And what of Beryl? The Rakum across the room hated him and heard every word he whispered. Javier paled; were either of them able to read his mind? He wasn't reading them and he was grateful.

"Huh," Canaan chuckled, recognizing the look on Javier's face. "I'm not reading you, but your urgency says a lot. Where's the fire?" he chided and squeezed the back of Javier's neck. "What's your hurry? Are you missing an appointment?"

Javier closed his eyes and when he opened them again, he looked hard at the Elder. He had reached the end of his patience. Hopefully, ingesting Isaac's blood gave him the ability to stand his ground with Canaan. No time to test his theory, Javier put his pointer finger to the Elder's broad chest.

"Canaan," he said gritting his teeth, "you and I can swap stories as soon as I check on Simon. Now release me."

Canaan dropped the contact, a secret smile on his face. Javier stepped away from him and pointed at Beryl.

"You move away from Simon or I'll move you myself." Javier watched Beryl's fawn-colored eyes, glassy and emotionless as a shark.

Barely moving his mouth, Beryl said, "You think you can move me, *human,* try it."

Javier exhaled and crossed to the bed. He and Beryl were the same height and weight, but when they were young Rakum, Beryl learned hand-to-hand combat from Elder Jack Dawn, where Javier spent his youth in seclusion with Roman and library full of books. Hoping their past had nothing to do with their present, Javier reached for Simon's upper arm.

"Simon, come on, stand up," he said softly, seeking the man's eyes. Beryl was behind him now and Javier heard him begin a snarl that ended with a grab from behind as Beryl pinned his arms at chest level.

"You have a death wish, you always have!" he barked and lifted Javier off the ground.

Javier growled deep in his throat and lifted his feet until they were on the edge of the bed. With all his might, he pushed off, sending Beryl flying backward in a violent rush. The Rakum's body slammed into the chest of drawers, knocking over the television set before he collapsed into a pile on the hard floor. Javier had landed backward on top of him and he crawled off quickly, expecting retaliation. But Beryl remained still, apparently unconscious. Javier rushed back to Simon.

"Simon," he said and attempted to turn the man's face with a finger to the chin.

"Whooo, Javie," Canaan said, laughing at the sight of Beryl on the floor. "Great move!" Canaan shook his head. "B is gonna be so embarrassed when he comes to."

Javier ignored both Rakum and tried again to meet Simon's eye.

"Let me see the baby," Canaan joked and reached Simon's opposite side. He grabbed hold of Simon's upper arm and abruptly lifted him to a standing position. Simon stood on his own two feet, but refused to look at Javier.

Now that he was standing, Javier squeezed Simon's cheek, shaking his face. "Snap out of it!" he said sharply and Simon averted his gaze again.

"What a turkey. I'll fix him," Canaan said. He lowered his chin and spun the kid around to face him. Then he grasped both upper arms and shook Simon hard. Javier stood close, but didn't intervene. The move had an effect, because Simon's marionette stare turned into something akin to fear. After four hard shakes, Canaan violently yanked Simon close and put his mouth to his ear.

Javier leapt forward, thinking the worst, but as his hands landed on Simon's forearm, the Elder was only whispering. When Canaan leaned back, Simon swiveled his head to Javier and met his eye.

"Turns out you're not a very good friend, Javier," he said, his voice shaking.

Javier slapped Canaan's hands off his arms and yanked Simon into a hug. Simon initiated plenty of hugs in the years they knew each other, and Javier realized at that moment that this was the first time he made the gesture.

"It's going to be okay, Simon," Javier said quietly. "I make a lot of mistakes and I never should have left you alone. I'm here now." It took a few seconds, but Simon relaxed his angry posture and embraced Javier in return.

Behind him, Beryl moaned. Jerking his gaze that way, Javier determined the Rakum was still out, but would come around soon. Canaan padded over to Beryl's position on the floor and nudged him with the toe of his boot.

"You're on the ground, buddy," he said. To Javier he whistled and shook his head. "You really scrambled his eggs. You can add that to your list. That's not *humanly* possible."

"I warned him," Javier said numbly, ending the hug with Simon to look at Beryl. The Rakum rolled onto his back, knees bent, and fluttered his eyes.

"I'm sorry for the way I behaved," Simon said, eyes downcast. "I'm just not myself. I keep screwing everything up."

"Hush that," Javier told him and they both watched Canaan tap Beryl's side again with his toe. The Rakum moaned, swatted at Canaan's foot, and remained where he lay. Javier looked at his watch and handed Simon his jacket. It was time to get going and Javier hoped to be gone before Beryl came to and the two Rakum strangers arrived.

"Stu, catch!" Canaan said and tossed an empty beer can across the room at the dozing Cow in the corner. Stuart startled to attention and the can bounced off his chest before he scooped it up and walked it to the wastebasket by the desk. Canaan chuckled at his blind obedience as Stu came near and stood by awaiting another directive. Canaan had forgotten the guy was there, he was nearly invisible. If it weren't for his eagerness to give his blood, he would never have noticed him at all. But Javier... Canaan watched with a half-grin as the guy he'd always thought of as a smaller version of himself moved Simon toward the door. Canaan shook his head and walked with them.

"This power you have, does it have something to do with, well," Canaan stopped before he said the word Isaac hated. But Isaac hadn't checked in with them since Javier arrived. Emboldened, Canaan finished his thought. "Did your God give you this power?"

Stopping a few steps out, Javier met his eye. "I can't say for sure, but it feels like His work. I need to get Simon home. Move out of the way, or He'll probably help me move you."

Javier sounded apologetic and Canaan wasn't offended. He stepped aside and touched his shoulder as he passed. "Let us come with you, Javier. Look—" Canaan paused to gather his thoughts. He didn't want to appear weak, but he wanted Javier's help. He exhaled and continued. "Look, your God saved my life last week. He saved Beryl, too."

Beryl moaned and Canaan walked to his side. Lifting him roughly off the ground by his arms, Canaan dropped him on the bed and looked at Javier. "Let us come with you."

With his palms against Beryl's half-scarred face, he barely showed any effort and the Rakum sputtered to consciousness and jumped to his feet. Canaan grabbed his bicep and held him in place as he finished his thought to Javier.

"I'm not sure what all you know, but I'm with Isaac under duress. His power over us is absolute—"

"Canaan! He will hear you!" Beryl hissed, putting his free hand to his temple. Canaan shook him roughly and he quieted.

"That's another thing, Javier. Since you got here, Isaac hasn't been in my head." He looked at Beryl. "Think about it, have you felt that pipsqueak in your business the past thirty-minutes?"

Beryl's face went lax and Canaan winked.

"Isaac is a monster," Canaan said, then looked between the room's inhabitants. Nothing happened, no ping, no twinge, and no pain.

"Isaac is a tyrannical dipshit," Beryl said, paused, and then exhaled, smiling. "You're right. Isaac's not here."

"Yes!" Canaan bellowed, pointing. "YOU'RE DOING THIS!"

"What?" Javier said.

"He can't see us because of you!" Canaan whooped again. Finally, relief had arrived and in the form of an apostate he liked probably a little too much.

42

J avier opened the door ignoring whatever had Canaan so excited. But he was going nowhere, the door was blocked. Standing at the threshold, hand upraised to knock, two Rakum grinned when they saw him. Javier sighed. He hadn't gotten out quickly enough after all.

"Anomenomie! How fun!" one of the two shouted with a laugh. "Call me Polly," the Rakum said and surged into the hotel room pushing into Javier, one hand cupping his neck and the other pressed into his chest. "You are one oddball character," he continued and pulled Javier close enough to sniff his hair.

"Stop that!" Javier said and pushed away, all the while Canaan guffawed behind him. In the shoving match, Simon had been released; he frowned, crossed his arms, and backed a few paces from the action.

"Just expanding my brainpan," Polly said and moved in to sniff him again. "Not a Rakum, not human—let me see."

"Stop!" Javier barked, but there was no threat present with the overly-demonstrative Rakum. When he had a second long whiff of Javier's hair, he pushed himself away and whirled around to the second Rakum entering behind him.

"Guap! You were right! You called it," Polly said and pointed at Javier, who was straightening his shirtfront. "Sniff him!"

Guap didn't step into Javier's space, but remained as he was by the door. He pushed it closed with his heel and nodded to his buddy. "I smell him just fine from here," he said with a wink to Javier. "You have a lovely aroma. Very earthy. Call me Guap."

Javier narrowed his eyes at their behavior.

Canaan chuckled. "Javier, these two, you would have loved them if you weren't so, you know..." He pointed up and down Javier's frame. "...not Rakum."

"Master, are you guys heading out?" Guap asked noting the group's proximity to the door. "What did we miss?"

"Yeah, let's see," Canaan said surveying the heads in the room. "Simon, your house is near here?"

Simon nodded.

"What are you thinking?" Javier asked, suspicious again of Canaan's motives.

"I would like to go there with you and talk," he said, then pointed to the Guap and Polly. "I have your number. Steer clear of me and when I need you I'll call you."

Both Rakum nodded as if they had expected as much.

Then Canaan pointed at Stuart. "Simon will call you when he wants to see you again. I do *not* want to see you anywhere near his house while I'm there. Understand? I will break you in half if you cross me, Stu—do you believe me?"

"Elder Canaan," Simon said softly.

Approving of the Elder's opinion that Stuart was bad for Simon, Javier did not object.

"Yes, Master." Eyes wide, Stuart stepped backwards until he met the far wall.

"Stuey!" Polly laughed, "don't be scared. Come here." Polly crossed over to him and grabbed him in a one-arm hug. "Don't worry, Elder Canaan, we will keep Stuey occupied, right, Guap?"

"Always," Guap said and then gave Canaan a respectful thumbs up. "Master, we remain at your disposal."

Canaan turned back to Javier and raised his eyebrows. "Walk outside with me, at least hear me out," he said, stepping past Javier to pull open the door. In the hallway, he pulled Beryl along like a dog on a leash.

Javier waited for Simon to start moving forward and he left the room after him. In the long hall toward the stairs, no one spoke and Javier assumed Canaan was getting out of earshot of Guap and Polly. In the parking lot, Canaan led the foursome to his Cadillac and then leaned upon the trunk, facing Javier. He released Beryl who stood by, eyeing Simon with an unreadable expression. Had he finally given up on coercing Simon to his purposes? And if he hadn't, would Simon do his part to resist?

"This is what puzzles me. Shouldn't you be trying to help us? Me and Beryl? Aren't we hell bound?" he said, barely keeping a straight face at his last two words. "Beth Rider gave me the impression that you guys were compelled to rescue the poor deceived Rakum," he said with false anxiety.

Javier opened his mouth to answer, but Canaan's cell phone rang. Canaan pulled it from his jeans pocket, looked at the Caller ID and flashed a smile. "It's High Father His Majesty King Isaac." Beryl smirked at the extended title.

"Speak of the devil," Javier said without emotion.

Canaan sent him a wink. "You heard me before—he can't read us when you're around. As soon as you stepped into that hotel room, Isaac stepped out." Canaan looked at Beryl. Beryl looked off, but nodded in agreement. "That's gotta mean something," Canaan said. He touched the green icon and put the phone to his ear.

Javier heard Isaac's voice from the speaker and Canaan didn't try to prevent him.

"Are you guys done?" Isaac asked. "What's going on over there? You know I could—"

Canaan grinned at Javier and disconnected the call.

"Canaan!" Beryl said, eyes flashing. "Don't antagonize him."

"What do you say, Javier?" Canaan said ignoring Beryl.

Javier's eye twitched, the Rakum's question hit him in the gut. At what point did his mission become about himself, anyway?

"Look, Javie," Canaan continued, using the moniker he had used when they were on the same team. "You want me to come clean?"

"Yes, Canaan," Javier said with undisguised sarcasm, "that would be a nice change. What do you want?"

"I told you Beryl and I serve Isaac under duress. You know me—I don't like dictators. For whatever reason, by whatever power, your presence blocks Isaac's intrusions. If you would allow us to be near you, we might have enough private time away from him to plan our coup."

Javier blinked slowly and then looked up at the cold stars above them. Canaan sighed and he looked back at him, unaccustomed to that sound coming from the Elder.

"Isaac has Marcy." He shrugged, but did not sound at all nonchalant. "She's a Rabbit, but she's taken a lot of abuse. I want to get her free even more than I want to free myself."

"Oh, dear Lord, I didn't know," Javier said.

"We can't beat him, Canaan!" Beryl interrupted his voice higher than he probably preferred.

"You can," Javier said without planning to. "Look," he continued after a visible sigh, "there's nothing God can't do. I think he's going to use me as a weapon against Isaac. That's not a prophecy, just a guess. If Canaan wants to be on the winning side again, who am I to stop him?" Javier looked at Simon. "Are you with us, Simon? Can we go to your place and talk this out?"

Simon nodded, his eyes tired. "It'll be sun-up in five hours," he said and inclined his head to the two Rakum. "They'll be safe in the basement. Cover one window, you're fine."

Javier nodded and looked back at Canaan. "I'll make sure of it. What about Beryl?" he said watching Canaan and not trying to deal with the other Rakum.

Canaan grabbed Beryl in a half-hug and squeezed him tight, then planted a noogie in his hair with his knuckles. "Beryl's with me. We're two peas in a pod, right, B?"

Beryl struggled to get loose and when he had flailed long enough, Canaan released him. He squared off with Javier and put a hand to his scarred jaw.

"Look at my face," Beryl said, his voice dripping with acid. "Isaac won't allow this to heal. He put a curse on me, it won't heal." Beryl closed his eyes and exhaled slowly. When he reopened them, he barely controlled the rage in his tone. "I can feel it, Javier. Twitching, itching, longing to replace this charred tissue, and at the same time, I feel Isaac working against it, full-time, abrading the flesh with every millimeter that replenishes…"

"Beryl, let me see your face," Javier said, his mouth a straight line. He stopped mere feet from Beryl and held his gaze. "Jesus is a healer. He is the reason any of the Rakum can heal wounds and disease—Jesus healed first. He is also the God of the Universe. With absolutely no effort, He can break that curse Isaac placed upon you."

"I'd like to see that," Beryl said under his breath.

"You could see it tonight. Right now," Javier said not offended by the Rakum's doubt. "Let's begin this way. God rescued you last week, right?" Beryl nodded slowly. "Let's hear it aloud. You want God to heal your cheek and you won't even admit He helped you out a week ago?"

Beryl met Canaan's eye, then Simon's before looking back at Javier. "It's true. I asked the God of the mortals to save me and at that moment, Dimple yanked me into the house and I didn't die."

Javier sighed. "So who saved you? Dimple or God?"

"I-I'm not sure," Beryl said and Canaan chuckled softly.

Javier lifted his right hand to Beryl's scarred cheek and the Rakum did not move away. "I'm going to ask God right now to break this curse Isaac put in your flesh. If He consents, you will know once and for all who runs the show."

"And if He doesn't?" Beryl asked. At rapt attention, Canaan and Simon appeared to have the same question.

"If He doesn't, then He has a reason for leaving your face scarred up. I'm just a man and His thoughts and His ways are high above my own. I can tell you with one-hundred-percent certainty that He has our best interest at heart. If it suits His purposes that your face heal up right now, in Jesus name, I command it to heal."

Beryl's lips tightened and he closed his eyes as Javier did the same, palm to his burned flesh. A few seconds later, Javier removed his hand and walked back to Simon. Beryl touched his cheek.

"Something's happening," he whispered and Canaan leaned in to look at the rippled mass. "I feel it healing—and, and… there's no opposition!"

"Um, Javier," Simon said quietly and inclined his head toward the hotel exit and the strangers heading out, "we should get moving."

Javier agreed and said an amen to God. To Canaan, he said, "Follow us to Simon's place. We'll get settled in and make a plan."

"Javier," Canaan said and in an uncharacteristic move, put out his hand. "Thanks. *Again.*"

Javier shook it with a tight grin and watched him physically pull Beryl to the passenger side of the car. Beryl didn't need a leash, but he was so enthralled by the sensation in his face that he did not refuse the assistance.

43

Tuscaloosa, AL
November 12th, 3 a.m.

"Tonight, you will welcome your brother Kite," Isaac announced from across the space. He and Boris lay on the bunker's queen-size bed with Rafael and Kilmeade on pallets twenty feet away. "I expect him to arrive by eight and he is bringing a huge surprise."

"Yes, Master," Kilmeade said automatically and Rafael echoed the sentiment, his mind racing.

"Did you guys thank Boris for finding you this terrific place to hole up?" Isaac asked accusing them of something unspoken.

Rafael had overheard Kilmeade complimenting Boris on the issue when they first settled in. As he remembered the event, Isaac said, "Good. Don't take him for granted. He's my second, which makes him your superior."

"Fantastic," Kilmeade said and again, Rafael echoed him, afraid to formulate his own answers. Thinking independently around Isaac had become a stressful enterprise.

"In fact," Isaac said, his small form visible in the dim light as he propped himself up on his elbows, "you two address him as Master Boris from this point on, understand?"

"It will be as you say," Kilmeade replied for them both for the third time. The Last didn't seem to mind. Rafael attempted to sort his thoughts and Kilmeade, lying close enough to touch, patted his arm.

"How are you holding up?" he asked, speaking quietly instead of using telepathy, which had become useless anyway.

"I am worried for Iago, Master," Rafael said. "He serves no purpose to our leader, no purpose for anyone but me."

"Stop fretting, Rafael, it is unbecoming a Rakum," Isaac piped up, interrupting. "All any of you have to do is follow me. I'm going to set everything right. We will be better, stronger, and happier than we ever were under that fool Ta'avah."

"I am glad," Rafael said and nodded in the dark as Kilmeade patted his arm once again.

"Elder Kilmeade," Isaac said and waited for a response.

"Yes, Master," the Elder responded and remained reclined, eyes closed.

Not near as comfortable, Rafael rose to see Isaac in the low light. Isaac lay on his back, knees bent, with one hand in the air making shadow puppets on the far wall.

"About your brother, will he convert?"

"Master," Kilmeade said and didn't continue for several long moments. The Last remained quiet and waited. Finally, Kilmeade said quietly, "Master, the spirit in Damien is in Roman, I'm sure of it. He will not convert."

"That sucks," Isaac said and the room fell silent. Their boy king lifted his other hand and by hooking his thumbs, caused a shadowy bird to fly across the ceiling.

"Master, I have a house in California," Kilmeade said after a while. "It's yours. Several areas are light-tight and it sits on eleven acres, entirely encircled with a security fence."

"But it's dilapidated," Isaac said no doubt seeing the crumbling edifice in the Elder's mind. "We would need to renovate."

"I have money, Master, a lot of it," Kilmeade said. "It, too, is yours."

Rafael lay back, unable to prevent Iago from coming to mind. As he stared at the shadow puppets barking at each other and getting into a brawl as Isaac's left and right hands tangled, he wondered how Iago and Jimmy were faring.

"I don't care if you call him, Rafael," Isaac said. "You think I'm a tyrant, unbalanced and dangerous, but I'm not. My commandment is simple—put me first and you shall have anything you desire..." His voice faded out and he began speaking low with Boris.

Rafael slipped out his cell phone and pressed Iago's number. His friend answered on the first ring.

"Rafa! Are you okay? Where are you?"

"I'm well," Rafael said quietly. "I'm with Master Isaac and Elder Kilmeade in a safe place until nightfall."

"Thank goodness," Iago said and he lowered his voice. "We got a hotel—"

"Don't tell us where it is," Rafael interrupted. "And don't speak. I just wanted to know you're safe and tell you that we're making plans. You will be with me soon."

"*Bueno*," he said. "Roman is asking if he can speak to Kilmeade."

Rafael looked sideways at the Elder who shook his head. "Not now. I will call you again tomorrow night," Rafael said and disconnected the call.

"Elder Kilmeade, can we force Roman to come back to us? I'm certain my blood would revert him to his natural state," Isaac said. "Before you answer, let me finish. If we threatened him or threatened his loved ones, do you think he'd come back?"

"Master," Kilmeade replied his voice calm, although Rafael detected an edge to it, "the answer is an absolute *no*. If put to the test, he will choose the same path as Damien—he will give his life for whomever you put in danger."

"Yeah," Isaac said and fell silent again.

"I respectfully ask you to not speak of him. You know he won't convert and I won't stand by and allow any harm to come to him."

"Then you are weak," Isaac said, his voice now with the same edge. "That makes me very disappointed."

Kilmeade said nothing and Rafael held his breath. Sure, The Last wanted Elder Kilmeade for his blood, but would he put up with insolence? Rafael exhaled and did his best to clear his mind.

5 a.m. Athens, GA, Simon's house

Javier checked his watch and yawned. Simon had already gone to bed upstairs in his own room and Javier stayed in the basement with the two Rakum to discuss their situation. Beryl's facial burn had healed completely and he rubbed the spot often.

"If he had left my face alone I wouldn't hate him," Beryl said taking a swig off his Budweiser.

"It's a cluster," Canaan said thoughtfully. "We used to have autonomy, no one was trying to drink me dry every night, no one was trying to subjugate the grunts. Is this our future? What if we somehow unseat Isaac, what then? Who's the next power-hungry dick that attempts to take the throne?"

"You," Beryl said and smiled, looking down. Canaan tossed him a sarcastic humph.

"Isaac's in Tuscaloosa so I propose we stay here a bit and figure out our next move. I could really use Roman's advice," Javier said. His phone buzzed with a call and he recognized the number. "It's Roman," he said with a wry smile.

"We have trouble, Javie," Roman said sounding weary and distressed. Javier wasn't at all at all accustomed to attributing those adjectives to his former Elder.

"Kilmeade?" Javier asked making a guess.

"He's being held against his will by that kid. My brother won't ask for help or even admit he's in trouble, but the one with him, a Rakum named Rafael, has made it plain that they need help getting away." Roman sighed and lowered his voice. "Javie—I can't lose Kilmeade again. I have to help him break free and I'm not even sure I can in this...as a *man*."

"None of us are *just a man*, you know that. Come to Athens," Javier asked. "It would separate you from Isaac and give us time to plan. Elder Canaan is in the same boat and I can't let him return to Isaac to be lobotomized."

"I agree. You'll see us sundown."

"Perfect," Javier said and gave him the address. When he had disconnected the call, he paused to think. Canaan and Beryl remained quiet and finally he nodded. "I'm sure you heard—get some rest and in a few hours, the sun will be down and we'll have him to help us plan our next move."

"Javier," Beryl said clearing his throat to get his attention, "we never really got along and the reasons are Rakum reasons, which don't apply anymore. I don't think of you as a brother now that you're mortal, does that make sense?"

Javier offered a slight shrug.

"What I want to say is that I see you as a tool to get away from Isaac."

"That's fair," Javier murmured.

"You have my allegiance until this is over. If we break free, I'll go away. Don't expect me to start singing gospel songs, but for now my every skill will be at your disposal."

"I appreciate that, Beryl," Javier said with sincerity. "And I appreciate your candor. Simon stays here, though."

Beryl grinned and lowered his eyes with a chuckle. "Look, he seeks me out subconsciously. Ask Canaan."

Canaan looked away, his grin to the side.

"Javier, I promise not to take any blood from him," Beryl said and jabbed Canaan. "Even if he begs me to."

Javier huffed. "He won't, he isn't a Cow anymore. I know you can sense that." Javier looked at Canaan for back-up.

Canaan shrugged. "Honestly, Javie, he gives off mixed signals. He does pine for Beryl and every now and then," Canaan said and shrugged again to finish, "I can read him."

"*Dammit.* You aren't helping," Javier mumbled angrily and got to his feet. "Just give him space—both of you. It's weird for him, all of this. He thought he was done with the Rakum forever. He's confused. Stay away from him and he'll figure it out."

"Okay, okay," Canaan said.

"Thank you."

"Hey, wait," Canaan said standing up. "Explain this stuff that's happening to you. I mean, the sun isn't a problem?"

Javier shook his head. "I feel nauseated in the sun, that's all."

"You still drink blood, though. You took blood from Simon." Beryl offered.

"I don't *drink blood,*" Javier stressed. "I lost myself, I didn't plan..." Javier struggled to answer the unwanted question, thankful again they didn't know about Chloe.

"Beryl, shut up. Daddy's talking." Canaan turned to Javier. "We won't mention it again. So what else is different?"

"I'm stronger, more alert than when I was human—and it feels even more intense than when I was a Rakum," Javier answered, not ready to share news of the more negative symptoms. "Oh, and visions. When I sleep, I have visions of other people—that didn't happen when I was a Rakum."

"Visions about people you know?"

Javier thought a moment. "Vision might not be the right word. It's more like I'm peeking in on someone else, usually a Rakum. For instance, the last time I slept—" Javier rolled his eyes counting the hours since his last nap. Then he remembered it had been the night he killed and revived Chloe. He grimaced and Canaan noticed.

"What was that?" he said.

"Yeah, you cringed," Beryl agreed and tapped Canaan's bicep with his knuckles. "He's not so subtle with his countenance."

"B's right, Javie. Maybe there's a reason, but I can read you pretty well without telepathy," Canaan said. "It could be part of whatever is going on inside you."

"The last time you slept, you had a vision about..." Beryl prompted.

Javier gave them a small smile, happy they *couldn't* read his mind. "Right before I woke up, I dreamed about you and Beryl."

"Was I sexy?" Canaan joked.

"No," Javier said shaking his head and suppressing a grin. "It felt like I was watching you."

"What were we doing?" Beryl asked.

"Nothing," Javier began.

"Exciting," Canaan deadpanned.

Javier chuckled. "It was morning and you were in the dark, looked like a bathroom, could be that hotel we just left, actually. Did ya'll stay there yesterday? In the bathroom?"

Beryl looked at Canaan who grinned.

"Spying on us in the bathroom? Pervert," he laughed.

"I'm serious," Javier said. "I saw the two of you settle into a bathtub and sit side-by-side." Javier read incredulity in Beryl's face. "I heard you say Stuart had a room in that hotel and that you would call on him at sundown."

"Anything else?" Canaan asked. Javier shook his head. "Real boring talent, Javie! Maybe today, you can have a vision about paint drying. That would be swell!"

Beryl made a very small chuckle and Canaan turned to look at him fully. "Did the Grim Reaper just laugh?"

"No." But the corner of Beryl's mouth had turned up. "It sounds like he projected in his sleep," Beryl said nonchalantly. "Meryl and I did it a lot."

"Huh..." Canaan nodded. "Very few Rakum mastered that skill. Father Damien could do it and he was your blood father."

"Yeah," Javier returned thoughtfully.

"Or you could be getting that from Isaac, his blood, I mean, since he is a Father," Canaan said and then he reached over to grab Javier's elbow. "You know I wasn't trying to hurt you that night in Michael Stone's basement, right? I couldn't have known—"

Javier held up his hand. "Of course, I know."

"Good. We were all sorta snookered by that baby face. What a showman. He looked so sweet, didn't he?" Canaan said with a woeful headshake.

"I called him out, though," Javier said recalling the night in question. Isaac had fabricated his background and Javier told the entire group that the boy was lying.

"You also said Father Damien warned you about Isaac a century ago. Was there more to it?"

"What?" Beryl asked. "I didn't hear about that."

"I met Father Damien when I was twenty and he gave me a prophecy.

He told me that Isaac would be the last Rakum and he would try to take over. He also indicated he'd be very violent and would eventually try to kill me."

"*Shit*," Beryl whispered. "That's gruesome foreknowledge for a youth."

Canaan threw his arm around Beryl. "Unlike you, Javier was tough."

Javier shrugged both shoulders. "I honestly didn't think about it again until Isaac showed up."

Canaan's cell phone rang and he checked the caller ID. "Isaac," he said and pocketed the phone. "I wonder what he thinks is happening. I have to answer it eventually."

"Tomorrow, when Roman's here and we have a plan," Javier said. When Canaan nodded, he headed for the basement stairs. "I'll see you at sundown."

"Be strong," Canaan said, offering the common *au revoir* among the Rakum. Javier gave him an ironic grin and left them alone.

44

Knoxville, AL, almost to Tuscaloosa
November 12th, 2 a.m.

Eric slowed to exit the interstate at Knoxville, Alabama, twenty miles west of Tuscaloosa, where Pawsa told him to go.

Why do they have the same name as Knoxville, Tennessee? Why do so many cities and towns have the same name? Aren't there enough words in the English language to make each city name unique?

As was his habit, Eric pondered stupid stuff all the way to the Marathon and pulled up behind the pre-fab building they used for a store. Clicking the key fob to lock Jake's truck, he jogged to the restrooms on the side and chose one of five available stalls.

"I met a little girl in Knoxville, a town we all know well," he sang as he urinated in privacy. The old bluegrass folk song suited the night's adventures and he grinned, happier than he had been his entire life.

When he reached the next verse, he was finished and he stood over the toilet, thinking about Luella's eyes as her time was up. *"She fell down on her bended knee, for mercy she did cry,"* he mumbled barely keeping the tune. *"Oh, Willy, dear, don't kill me here, I'm unprepared to die..."*

Eric stared at the tile and chuckled at the lyric. Then his stomach churned within him.

"She never spoke another word," he said quietly. *"I only beat her more..."* A wave of nausea swam past and was gone again. *"Until the ground around me within her blood did flow..."* he said finishing the verse and putting his hand to his mouth. He was about to hurl.

"GO DOWN! GO DOWN! You Knoxville girl, with the dark and roving eyes," a boisterous male voice sang in the next stall. *"GO DOWN, GO DOWN, you Knoxville girl, you can never be my bride!"*

Eric leaned over the toilet and vomited. Bile, blood, and a liquefied Jack's hamburger plopped into the water splashing his tennis shoes. The smell of it brought on new heaves, although nothing remained but air.

229

"You okay in there, son?" the voice asked.

Eric ignored the Good Samaritan, spitting hunched over and unwilling to straighten up.

"Too much to drink, eh?" the mystery man asked. "Don't drive 'til you feel better," he said and Eric heard water running at the sink. The man resumed singing in a decent tenor, *"They carried me down to Knoxville and put me in a cell. My friends all tried to get me out, but none could go my bail..."*

The water went quiet and the hand fan started up. Over the roar, the gregarious fellow traveler finished the lyric with gusto.

"I'm here to waste my life away down in this dirty old jail, because I murdered that Knoxville girl, the girl I lovvvveed sooooo welllllll!"

Eric heaved one last time and stood upright. Catching his breath, a rap landed on the closed stall door.

"Good luck, son!" the voice said and walked away.

Eric flushed the toilet twice and unhooked the latch. The singing man hadn't completely exited the bathroom, but stood in the open door, facing the parking lot. He wore a State Trooper's uniform accented at the hip by the butt of a large caliber semi-automatic handgun. The blood rushed from Eric's face and he backed into the stall, locking the door.

"Uh, yup. Yup," the Trooper was saying in response to a static-y voice on his shoulder mic. "Maroon Titan, yup," he said and stepped out, allowing the heavy door to swing closed on its hydraulic lever.

Jake's truck was a maroon Titan.

Eric gasped and shoved his fist in his mouth. *WhatdoIdo? WhatdoIdo? WhatdoIdo?* Eric repeated in his mind staring at the flimsy stall latch.

"Run!" a voice hollered at him, but Eric didn't understand. Run where? The single exit had a fatso cop standing just on the other side.

RUN

RUN

RUN! the voices shouted, dozens, hundreds, maybe thousands of voices, all shouting for him to make a run for it. None of those voices sounded like Pawsa.

"Great Pawsa, my master, what do I do?" Eric whispered, a tear welling in his eye. He didn't want to go to jail, he didn't want to see his momma's face when the jury found him guilty of murder. After an eternity that only took five seconds, Pawsa responded and Eric did as he commanded.

▼ ▼

Elohim's minions were at it again, foiling a mighty spirit's well-laid plans. Ta'avah helped the Eric flesh slam his head into the door of the stall, adding his unnatural strength to the kid's puny musculature. He got eight mighty raps in before collapsing with a brain-bleed and skull fracture. It took a precious three minutes for the State Trooper to realize what was happening and break the door in. It was another eleven minutes before EMS arrived and started triage. Ta'avah sat quietly, keeping the heart going, but the brain was gone.

He bit his thumb at Elohim's messengers all around, shining bright white, aiding the disgusting authorities, individuals who didn't have the self-respect to handle an emergency call on their own—each man and woman who called upon their God to send help, to aid, to enable. Ta'avah cursed and kept the heart pumping.

"I don't need the brain. You haven't stopped me," he said to the air. The Eric flesh was loaded into the ambulance and he went along, comfortable and snug in the body so freely given to him, by word and deed. This one was alive and he legally possessed it.

"I only have to heal it up and I'm on my way," he said to no one, then recognized a few of Rah-keel's minions snickering. *Oh, they won't be laughing when I reach Isaac.* He'd make them bow. He will be more powerful and more amazing than even the One Elohim sent.

Ta'avah clammed up, again not ready to disturb the Lion. But it was true. He rode to the hospital and studied the fractured skull.

Piece of cake.

45

Tuscaloosa, AL
November 12th, 6 p.m.

It was 6 p.m. and they would soon be heading up. Even though the bunker was below ground and thirty feet from the main house's back door, Rafael caught the aroma of steaks cooking on an outdoor grill, presumably by their Cow host. His phone vibrated with a new call and he crossed to the furthest corner of the bunker's main room. The others would hear him, but a semblance of privacy was enough.

"Are you well?" Rafael asked when Santiago said hello.

"We're fine. *¿Y tú?* Are you heading out?"

"I am well," Rafael said. He put his hand on the wall and stared at his fingers. "It's good to hear your voice."

"Are we going to be together soon?" Iago asked.

Rafael sighed and heard the others moving around behind him. "Don't ask me again. As soon as possible, I will call you to join us." Iago was silent a few ticks before he apologized. Rafa disconnected the call and faced the others.

Boris was standing, stretching long arms to the ceiling. Isaac sat on the side of the bed facing Kilmeade who stood with his back to Rafael. It appeared they were engaged in a telepathic conversation. As he waited to see if he should join Boris near the exit or stay and greet Elder Kilmeade, the Elder approached Isaac in a respectful stance.

"It's not good, Master," Kilmeade said once he reached the bed and sat down so close their legs touched.

"Good? What matters what *you* think is good or not good?" The Last replied, his voice low. "Am I about to get another lesson from the wise old Elder?"

"I could withhold teachings that would make you stronger," Kilmeade replied, his voice gentle, "but it will take effort. I am a natural instructor. My inclination is to improve the lives of every Rakum I meet."

"How could *you* know something that would make me stronger?" Isaac asked with more animation in his tone. "I mean, what could you teach me that the greatest among our kind didn't already?"

Kilmeade laid his palm on Isaac's thigh. "*They* are gone. You are here and very alive. But," Kilmeade said squeezing his leg playfully, "if you stop learning, you will perish."

Isaac scrunched his face. "That sounds like a euphemism."

Kilmeade chuckled and shook his head. "If you read an instruction manual on flying a helicopter, can you then get in the seat and fly away?"

Isaac appeared to think hard about his answer and then shrugged one shoulder. "Probably not."

Kilmeade nodded with an approving smile. "Knowing and doing are two separate things."

"You're saying I need experience, not just knowledge," Isaac said, eyes on Kilmeade's hand.

"Yes, knowledge alone does not instill wisdom, *experience* does. That's why I say, as long as you live, you must keep learning."

"Okay, I'll buy that," Isaac said. He placed his hand atop Kilmeade's and spread out his fingers seeing Kilmeade's hand was much bigger. "You know something that will make me stronger and it's directly related to why you're resisting my request."

"Precisely," Kilmeade said. He rotated his hand out from under Isaac's and wrapped his fingers around the smaller ones. "What you need to learn—that I can teach you—is self-control. If you can control your urges, you can control everything around you."

"That's stupid," Isaac said and pulled his hand to his mouth, Kilmeade's on top. "Anyway, I'm aware that *you* have been chastised many, *many* times for lack of self-control."

Kilmeade chortled and shook his head. "If I may, Master, I was chastised for *rebellion*. I knew what I was doing and I chose to do it. There is a difference."

"I still think it's an excuse. When I draw off your blood, you're weakened and I am empowered. *That's* why you're putting on this charade, Professor Kilmeade." He opened his mouth against Kilmeade's skin and rested his sharp teeth on the surface.

"You're right," Kilmeade conceded rolling his eyes. "My Master, all of fifty years alive to my three hundred and eighty years, go ahead, do whatever you want," he said, his inflection not as sarcastic as his words.

Rafa didn't breathe and Boris stood stock-still near the door, watching. Isaac milked the silence and looked around Kilmeade to meet

Rafa's eye, all the while, his teeth pressed to the back of the Elder's hand. Rafa's mind was blank and he forced it to remain so. Another few seconds passed and both corners of Isaac's mouth turned up as he pressed sharp fangs deep into the proffered hand. Rafael exhaled and heard Boris do the same. Kilmeade expressed nothing, but used his free hand to gently stroke Isaac's blond hair.

"Whatever I have is yours, Master," Kilmeade whispered, his eyes on Isaac and his hand in the wavy strands that fell across the boy's forehead. Rafael took a step toward them and stopped short—Kilmeade was smiling to himself and Rafa recognized its hidden meaning. *"His inexperience and immaturity will be his undoing."* Rafa hoped he was right.

Boris turned then to the bunker exit, four steps up a short staircase, and pulled open the door. Their humble Cow Maury stood in the opening, an oven mitt on one hand.

"Masters, I've made you something to eat," he said and Boris stepped out of the bunker grabbing the man off the ground in a playful embrace. Rafa waited to see if he should follow him out and Isaac's rumbling voice tromped across his mind even as he continued to pull blood out of Elder Kilmeade.

"Go ahead, Rafael. Your Master is in good hands."

Rafael strode past them, eyes forward, and maintained a blank mind to join Boris topside for dinner.

"My vision for our people is a good one," Isaac said lying back on the bunker's only bed, arms up behind his head.

After he enjoyed another healthy dose of Kilmeade's blood, his attitude seemed much improved. Kilmeade agreed without speaking. He sat on the mattress, feet on the ground beside Isaac, awaiting permission to leave the bunker.

"This Cow will give me his entire inheritance," Isaac continued. "I have your property and your money and Boris has regular income from an annuity a Cow left him decades ago."

"This is good news," Kilmeade said.

"I'm working on a plan to access the wealth of the Fathers. That's billions of dollars."

"Fantastic," Kilmeade said softly.

"You're good with money," Isaac mumbled. "You will get more for us, all we need. I'll be a billionaire, the Donald Trump of the Rakum."

Kilmeade nodded in agreement.

Isaac had more to add. "We'll enlarge this compound, above ground *and* below; we'll renovate your California property, too. Then we'll have *two* headquarters, east and west. Much better than that lame set-up in Nevada. I will call our brethren home and I will empower them as Ta'avah did." Isaac paused and sat up. "No! We will be stronger than before!" Isaac's voice grew louder and a distinct rumble emanated from each word. "*I* am stronger than that idiotic brother of mine. I AM ZAHDONE! Powerful and Mighty, so wondrous and beautiful, none can compare! I will give every Rakum that bends the knee more power than Ta'avah ever could have imagined!"

Kilmeade's eyes grew wide, recognizing the transfiguration from flesh to spirit happening before him. He looked down and prepared to fall to his knees should the moment dictate. But Isaac relaxed, his breathing returned to normal, and he slumped back onto the pillow, smiling.

"I'm very awesome," he whispered.

"Definitely, Master," Kilmeade responded with sincerity.

Several minutes elapsed in silence until Isaac gently booted Kilmeade's back with his toe. "So, what do you think, Elder Kilmeade?"

"It is a sound plan, Master," he said.

"But?" Isaac said and sat up. "But what?"

Kilmeade's mouth went to the side. He wasn't even aware he had disagreed mentally, but he must have. "When I can articulate my reservations, I will share them with you," he replied with respect. The Last was powerful enough to imbue the Rakum with all they lost and more, but something would hold him back and Kilmeade honestly sought the words to express his misgivings.

"You can stop straining your brain, Kilmeade," Isaac said and swung his legs off the bed to stand.

Kilmeade noticed he had dropped the Elder title.

"Look at me." Isaac positioned himself to stand in front of Kilmeade, still sitting on the edge of the bed. "I have literally *millions* of advisors, all unseen, all of them created before the earth was formed, and all infinitely wiser and more knowledgeable than you. *Millions!* So hear me, I will only say this once."

Isaac paused and Kilmeade's eyes widened to assure him he was listening.

"I do not need, nor do I desire your advice or instruction any longer," he said, his voice rumbling again with Zahdone's vocal influence. "What I want from you is your blood, joyfully sacrificed, and your allegiance to whatever I desire to pursue."

"Of course."

Isaac smiled. "I will have you and Canaan at my left and right because of your strength and status among our people. You may be the last of Ta'avah's Elders, but over time, I will make *new* Elders."

Kilmeade sensed he was supposed to make a remark. "I didn't think of that, Master. Wonderful," he said and Isaac grinned.

"That's right. You *didn't* think of that, Professor. Have you considered this: *I* am a Father, so I am fertile. *I* will re-populate our race. Me. Zahdone. What do you say to that?"

"We will be stronger and better than ever, Master," Kilmeade said with meaning.

"Correct. I am perfect and unblemished. I have no human tendencies, no familial attachments, no weakness for mortals, or any duty to anyone, but myself. I won't tolerate subversion. I can subjugate you and Canaan for your blood, but I won't unless you force me to. Am I clear?"

"Crystal clear, Master," Kilmeade said and fell to his knees at Isaac's feet. They were too close for him to put his face to the floor, but he bent down so that his forehead pressed against Isaac's knees.

"Excellent," Isaac said. "And Elder Kilmeade, look at me..." Isaac waited until Kilmeade raised his face. "That Rabbit of Rafael's will be collected. Explain it to your pet. He is lacking and I fear he may be culled. He is unmatched in his attributes—I don't want to lose him."

Culled. Holding his emotions on the matter in check, Kilmeade nodded. "Of course, Master, your will is my will," he responded.

"I knew that you, of all Rakum, would understand; either I am master or I'm not—there's no in between." Isaac turned away. "Let's get some dinner. It smells awesome." He trotted up the stairs and left the bunker.

Kilmeade remained on his knees and stared at the far wall. His mind yearned to contemplate, compute, and ponder, but to exercise free thought would be a disobedience to Master Isaac. Unbidden, Kilmeade remembered how Isaac couldn't read Father Damien, Roman, or David; their faith in their God blocked him.

"Master Isaac is a better Father than any we have ever had," Kilmeade said in his mind, clearly and succinctly for the Last to overhear. *"Every Rakum alive today will bow the knee gladly when they meet our new leader."*

Isaac liked those words, and Kilmeade sensed his approval. He only wished he meant them.

46

Athens, GA
November 12th, 7 pm

"Roman and David will be here in about two hours," Javier said to Canaan as he descended the steps to the basement floor. Below, lounging on a long chaise, Beryl looked his way and then returned his focus to his phone. Canaan was busy removing aluminum foil from the small eye-level window they had covered before they went to sleep. Javier lowered his chin at Beryl who didn't look up. "Shouldn't he be doing that?"

Canaan swiveled his head to consider the positions of both men and grinned to the side. "That pup is a miserable servant. Trust me; I'm better off doing shit myself than depending on him."

Beryl flipped a quick bird without looking up. Javier huffed, but the Elder returned to his work, completely unfazed. "Okay..." Javier said shaking his head.

"Guap is bringing us two Cows," Canaan said without turning.

"Wait, that's not a good idea," Javier began, but Canaan held up his hand.

"*Shhh,* Mommy. Nobody gets hurt and the Rakum get a gut-full." Canaan crossed to the leather-lined full bar at the opposite end of the room and poured himself a glass of brandy.

Javier watched him, his mind racing for an objection. The Elder was right; the Cows wanted the attention and the Rakum had no reason to obey God. Finally, he said, "Stuart shouldn't—"

Canaan made a *tsk-tsk* noise and sauntered toward Javier, drink refilled and in his hand. "I told them to keep Stu out of it. They won't let him near this place."

Javier exhaled with a new thought. "Guap and Polly don't know what we're doing and if they choose Isaac's side, they're Rakum. They could be dangerous to the mortals in this fight."

Canaan smiled real wide and grabbed Javier's shoulder, swinging him inches, to and fro. "I thought of that, too. You can warn them. Tell them as little or as much as you want to. If they look like they're going to choose wrong, I will incapacitate them until we're done."

Javier's lips parted and he didn't say anything else. He'd seen it himself with Roman—an Elder could put a Rakum's lights out with a thought.

"I'm heading up," Beryl said and Javier watched him. When his foot touched the first stair, he looked backwards. "And don't worry about Simon—I stand by my promise."

"I know you do, pup," Canaan said with a threat. To Javier he said, "Let's trust him to be alone with Simon a couple minutes. I have something to ask you."

"Fine." Javier nodded.

"And Beryl," Canaan said rubbing his middle, "order your master some pizza." Beryl nodded and trotted upstairs.

When the door was closed, Javier shook his head. "God help Simon. Beryl is not done chasing him."

"He's not going to break his vow."

Javier buzzed his lips. "I know, I know, he's terrified of you."

"Yes. I am terrifying." Canaan winked and leaned his upper body on the bar. "Now that Mr. Grim is gone, I have to ask you—"

"No," Javier said. Canaan didn't need to complete his sentence; Javier read it all over his face. Since the moment he came down tonight, Canaan had one thing on his mind—*a taste.*

"Don't even say it," Javier reiterated since Canaan's mouth sat ajar.

"Daaaaamn," he said laughing and lowered his head onto folded arms. "That's harsh." He chuckled into the bar, the muffled sound softening Javier's stern expression.

Javier circled around to the serving side and poured himself a brandy. The first swig burned as it should, but each one that followed went down smoother than the previous. Canaan had grown quiet and Javier refreshed the Elder's glass.

"Javie," Canaan said head still down, voice muffled, "you have no idea how much I wish you never left us." He turned his face to Javier, but still leaned on his arms hunched over the bar. "Think of the fun we could have had together the next few hundred years. *Rakum* fun."

Touched and surprised, Javier joked, "I love you, too, sweetheart."

Canaan winked and chuckled. "Remember when Roman brought you to New York?" Canaan stood upright and spun around to lean on the cushioned edge of the bar. "What a peculiar pup you were," he continued and shook his head.

A slow grin reached Javier's face at the memory. Much of his past became fuzzy when he transformed into a mortal, but he recalled the meeting clearly. "Yes, I remember. You were something to behold."

"Was?" Canaan chuckled. "I guess you need glasses. I'm better than ever," he said and puffed out his chest to pound it like a gorilla.

Javier rubbed his eyes and pretended he couldn't see.

"Dork," Canaan said and leaned back again. "Anyway, I was making a point. You were peculiar. Remember what I said to you about your blood?"

Javier looked to the side, the memories flowing back like water.

"And..." Canaan nodded a few extra times. "I told you that because you drank mainly from Roman all that time, your blood would be special. When I tasted it, it *was* different from that of our brethren."

"What of it?" Javier asked suspicious of where he was going.

"I wonder if—"

Canaan's phone rang. After seeing the screen, he pocketed the phone. "Mighty King Isaac," he said and swigged his brandy. "Now back to my point."

"Let's drop it," Javier said and finished his drink. "We have a lot to do tonight. We'll rehash old times—"

"Listen," Canaan said in a serious tone, "this has to do with our upcoming showdown, if that's what it is."

"Oh?" Javier cleared his mind, recognizing Canaan wasn't simply trying to have another go at his blood. "Let's hear it."

"Is it possible that the Fathers were using you as an experiment?" Canaan held up his hand to Javier's instinctive objection. "Think about how they did Isaac—as far as I know, as far as the Elders were informed, you are the only Rakum that was raised on an Elder's blood."

Javier made a small noise and furrowed his brow. "Really? The only one? What about—"

"Previous generations?" Canaan interjected. "Elders are taught our history back to the Calling of the Ten. Trust me, you're it."

Javier nodded slowly. It was a curious coincidence that now, in the twenty-first century, the two experiments of the Fathers might be pitted against each other; one Father Damien's offspring and the other Abroghia's.

"I want to add my blood to this experiment—and no, I don't mean you have to drink it," Canaan added, predicting Javier's protest. "Look." Canaan went behind the bar and dug around in a drawer. When he found what he sought, he placed two corkscrews on the bar top. Miming turning it into his palm, he caught Javier's eye. "You and I swap blood. My Elder blood will be added to your system and…"

"You'll get the Anomaly's blood?" Javier asked, using air quotes at his new nickname. "Canaan…" he said, shaking his head.

Canaan smiled. "No, I mean, sure, that sounds cool, and probably it will increase my strength, but we are one hundred percent certain that an Elder's blood will increase yours."

"That's true," Javier said in a low voice.

Was it like taking medicine, as far as God was concerned? He wasn't drinking it. Was it a blood transfusion? Javier sought apropos Bible verses in his mind and came up lacking.

Canaan handed him a corkscrew and he took it. "We need to do it simultaneously because both of us will heal quickly."

Javier nodded.

"On the count of three," Canaan said and Javier held up his hand.

"Better lock the door."

"Can *you* lock the door, Anomaly?" Canaan asked, chin lowered.

Javier looked at the door and attempted to turn the bolt with telekinesis as he had when he was a Rakum. Nothing happened.

Canaan chuckled. "Your super-powers have a specific purpose, I think," he said, intimating it had something to do with God. With no obvious effort on Canaan's part, the deadbolt to the basement clunked and the Elder repositioned the tool. "On the count of three."

Javier put the point to his palm and on three, forced it into his flesh with a twist. He felt no pain and he and Canaan quickly clasped hands.

"Let me know if it feels weird," Canaan said, curious.

"You, too," Javier grinned, light of heart for the first time in a while. "I have a Father's blood in me. You might be knocked unconscious. That would make my night."

Five, seven, ten seconds passed and Javier sighed at the sensation of his skin knitting together. Neither released hands for a full minute and when they did, Javier watched Canaan's face. The clock on the bar shelf ticked; upstairs, Simon was overheard talking about a photograph from his past; a truck drove by on the road a quarter mile away.

Canaan smiled. "I didn't feel anything."

Javier returned the grin. "Neither did I."

"Well, that was anti-climactic," he said then and laughed, licking his healed palm. "Ooooh, salty."

"Keep in mind, when I took from The Last, I didn't change immediately," Javier said and accepted a towel to wipe his own palm.

"Okay, then. Report if anything happens and so will I," Canaan said. He set down his glass. "Let's head up and stop Simon from accepting a marriage proposal from Beryl."

Javier looked at the basement door. "Beryl's in his head."

"Yeah." Canaan reached the steps. "But he didn't take his blood," he said with a laugh and yanked open the door.

"Thank God for small favors," Javier said and followed him out.

Sleep didn't come easily for Simon when Javier, Canaan, and Beryl left him alone to get some rest. Just before, Javier spent thirty minutes convincing him that although Beryl would be with them in the house, he had been neutered by Canaan and posed no threat. It wasn't easy, but by the time he fell asleep around 6 a.m., he had convinced himself to at least not be terrified in the guy's presence. At 4 p.m., he woke, showered, and headed downstairs.

Simon entered the kitchen in the dark and yanked open the fridge. Sitting on the top shelf, taped to his Aunt June's apple pie was a note from his uncle Avi saying they had shoved off while he slept. Glad with the news, he crumpled the note and pulled a water from the door. The whispering noise of socks on tile behind him caused him to spin around with a quick gasp.

"Don't freak out," a soft voice said near the doorway as the recessed lighting was switched on. "I wasn't sneaking up on you. Honest."

It was Beryl and he didn't meet Simon's eye for more than a moment. He moved to the table, making a wide berth. Simon re-opened the fridge and told himself the danger was only in his head.

"No, it's cool. I'm fine," he said sounding strong and he grinned at his spookiness. All Rakum were quiet, he knew that. No need to flip out... "Want something to drink?" he asked him gesturing to the beverage door.

Beryl looked away with one corner of his mouth curving upward.

Simon added in a rush, "I mean Coke, water, milk... coffee?"

"Water," Beryl said and looked at him sideways. "And order us some pizza. You hungry?"

"God, yes," Simon said and rubbed his gut.

"Get enough for ten. Your buddies are coming," Beryl said.

"My buddies?" Simon asked. He couldn't mean Stuart.

"Humans. I should have said Javier's buddies. Roman. David Miller, whoever else," Beryl replied and looked away, the half-smile returning.

Simon furrowed his brow. The Rakum was being coy, which was a refreshing change.

"Got it," he said and retrieved his cell from his jeans pocket. After ordering six assorted large pies, he handed the bottle of water to Beryl with an extended arm.

"Don't be afraid of me. I apologize for being a jerk last night. I was surprised to see you, I should have been more…*nice*, is that the right word?" Beryl asked as he opened his drink. "Suffice to say, I realize that in your perspective, I'm a monster."

"Naw," Simon said and backed up to lean against the counter. He watched Beryl sip his water. What would be running through his mind? What did a Rakum think these days with the Fathers gone and their lives in the crapper? How arrogant and carefree they were—Meryl and Beryl— that night Beth Rider showed up on the stage in the Great Hall and changed everything. But now? Simon felt sorry for him, for all of them. And Beryl? He looked exactly the same, glowing with power and glory, with his burn healed, even more beautiful than Simon remembered. Was he evil? Hadn't Meryl been the problem? *What exactly happened to Meryl?*

Beryl leaned forward over folded arms and looked at Simon sideways. "I can hear your thoughts," he said and then looked back out the window into the dark yard.

"No, you can't," Simon said on the defensive.

"You think I'm beautiful."

"Shut up."

Beryl offered an apologetic shrug. "To answer the question I didn't just hear in your mind, Meryl is dead. Canaan hurt him, but Ta'avah killed him. The end."

"Huh," he responded conflicted on his news. Simon still experienced extreme embarrassment when he recalled how easily Meryl seduced him.

"Simon," Beryl said and readjusted, chin resting in his cupped hand with his elbow on the table surface. "Sit with me."

"I'm okay right here." Why was he so anxious? With Javier and Canaan both close by, why should he be wary? Beryl smiled then and offered a tiny chuckle. Maybe he really *could* read Simon's thoughts. Resigned for the moment, Simon pulled out the chair across from Beryl and dropped into it. "What the hell. You the only one up?" he asked.

"Big meeting downstairs. I was in the way," Beryl said and flashed Simon a genuine grin. When Simon blushed, Beryl winked. "See, I'm not so bad. Not a hundred-percent awful."

"No," Simon agreed and watched the Rakum's bright eyes. Did they just twinkle? Simon swigged his water and looked away. "We would be friends if you didn't attack me. I don't like it," he said softly.

"I dig," Beryl agreed. He waited for Simon to look his way before opening both hands to hold them apart wide. "You are a prize-worthy Cow. You deserve better treatment."

Simon stung at the Cow label. He discarded the status when he accepted the Messiah, although the last few days, now that the Rakum were back in his airspace, he definitely felt the pull in their direction again. Shouldn't he be praying it away? What would Beth Rider do?

"Resistance is futile, little Simon," Beryl said imitating a movie robot. "I could lull you right now," he said in his normal voice, smiling and showing white teeth.

Simon pointed at Beryl's face. "That's the Beryl I know. Right there," he said. "Now you sound like a monster."

Beryl laughed two short bursts and leaned back in his seat. "Oh, you are funny," he said, eyes to the vaulted ceiling. After a few seconds, he abruptly lowered his head to capture Simon's eye. "I want to be friends, but," he said and offered a winning smile, "I don't know how. You could teach me how to be a friend and I won't ever force you to do anything again. I promise."

"Oh, a promise," Simon said emphatically.

"It's real. I made a vow to Elder Canaan and he can fry my brain," Beryl said, this time very serious. Then his eyes lit up with inspiration. "Want to see a trick? Did Javier ever let you look into his mind?"

"Look into his mind?" Simon asked. "I don't think so."

"Not all Rakum can do it, so maybe he couldn't, but Meryl and I were *really* good at it. Put your hand flat, like this," he said and set his left palm on the table.

With his right hand casually supporting his chin, Beryl appeared trustworthy. *After all, it was Meryl who mistreated me. Beryl just followed his lead.*

"And we were following orders," Beryl said, his voice soft, his eyes bright and sincere. "Think of what you loved about the Rakum—how *non*-human we are. We had masters and there was no questioning them. It was a wonderful system. Do you see what I'm saying? Meryl and I adored you, but we had orders."

"I know, I know," Simon conceded and flattened his left hand on the surface.

Beryl covered his fingers with his own. "Okay, I want to show you a good one," he said and closed his eyes. After a moment, he opened them again, grinning. "Look."

Simon didn't know what he meant until in his own mind, he saw a fit young man, medium height with curly blond hair walking a small dog on a leash. It was night in a big city judging by the residential architecture and the canine urinated on a small decorative tree by the curb. Simon viewed the man from the front as if they were approaching one another. He closed his eyes and more details popped up behind his lids.

The man wore blue jeans, a T-shirt, and a reddish-orange leather jacket, suspiciously like the one Michael Jackson made famous in the eighties. Then the man looked Simon in the face and waved, his eyes growing huge.

"Master!" he said and jogged up until they were a few feet apart. "I saw Meryl going to Howard's loft last night and he told me you might stop by."

Simon opened his eyes and the vision dissolved. Beryl was still boring him with his gaze and he grinned as Simon worked out what had just happened.

"That was a memory—one of *your* memories?" Simon asked incredulous.

"Sure was." Beryl moved his right hand to cover his left atop Simon's fingers. "That was Danny Johnson, Queens, New York, 10:45 p.m., September 13th, 1984. You favor him a lot, don't you think?"

Simon had no reply, still marveling at how clearly he had just viewed a memory that was not his own.

"That's how vivid *all* our memories are, Simon. Rakum forget *nothing*. That's why you can believe me when I said I never stopped thinking about you. I remember every detail about the night I met you, what you were wearing, your cologne, your every word."

"So you remember my terror? How you left me for dead?" Simon asked frowning.

"Yes, I remember everything," Beryl said without expression. "So, did Javier ever show you that trick?"

Simon shook his head. Javier may not have had that particular skill, but he did show Simon many other things in their two years together. He had been a very caring and attentive master.

Beryl gave his fingers a soft squeeze. "He's not a Rakum anymore, Simon, and I am," he said. "Here, I can show you another trick. It's even better. Wanna see it?"

Simon considered their hands stacked on the tabletop. No internal alarms sounded in his spirit so Simon said okay and sunk into Beryl's shining gaze.

"Good. Relax your mind. Think of a huge white wall with nothing on it. Listen, do you hear a sound like water? Like radio static?"

Simon closed his eyes. "Yeah, I think I do."

"Good. Now wait for me. I'm coming over," Beryl said in a whisper. In his mind's eye, Beryl appeared next to him against the white wall and held out his left hand.

"It's better if we join hands," Beryl said and Simon heard his voice in his head and not his ears. They clasped hands and at first, they walked along the white expanse. Within ten strides, they were on a sidewalk at night on a quiet suburban road.

"What is this? It's not a memory," Simon said with his mouth inside the vision, but again heard nothing with his ears.

"We're in another place now. It's my place, see—it's nighttime. I only see the world at night. If we practiced this a lot, you could take me into the daylight and show me your places. I could see the world the way you see it. I would like that a lot."

"This is very cool," Simon said with meaning as he looked around the dark neighborhood. The lots stretched more than an acre each, with comfortable ranch-style houses peppered throughout. "Have you done this before? Maybe with Danny? Did he show you the daytime world this way?"

In his vision, Beryl looked at him briefly and then ahead as they walked. "No. He wasn't special. Okay, this is what I wanted to show you, over here," Beryl said and pulled him off the walk and into a grassy field between the developed lots.

Simon noted the resistance the taller grass caused and he looked down to his sneakers; they were wet with dew. Within another few seconds, his toes were damp in his socks. He looked to Beryl to ask him about it, but they had reached a post-and-rail fence where the Rakum stopped.

"See that?" Beryl asked pointing down. In the bright moonlight, Simon caught sight of a dark metal box at his feet half-buried in the crabgrass. "Pick it up and look inside," Beryl said standing by and releasing his hand.

Still puzzling over how his shoes could be dampened in Beryl's mindtrip, Simon lifted the rusty can and popped off the lid. Inside sat a photograph and he lifted it to the light of the moon.

"What is this?" he said aloud, squinting to make out the face in the print. Simon looked once and then looked closer. "I recognize this," he said and turned the print to Beryl. "I had this in my room." Simon pulled the photo to his face and nodded with certainty. "This is me at our senior year baseball camp. It was in a frame on my dresser. How did you get it?

Why do you have it? How am I holding a three-dimensional object if this isn't a real place?"

With an odd whoosh of air and a slight twinge of nausea, the field, the moon, and the photograph dissolved away and he sat at the kitchen table across from Beryl. His hands were free and Beryl's hands were resting on the smooth surface. Simon stared at him, mouth ajar. When Beryl flashed him a smug grin, he said, "Well?"

Beryl leaned back in his seat and laughed with joy. "My innerspace is a real place and you just went there with me. Look at your shoes—they're dry. We traveled in another dimension—actually went there, while your earth body stayed here. Your mind fills in the details." Beryl laughed again and rubbed his face with both hands. "That's a kick. I have *never* done that with a Cow before. That was fun." Beryl exhaled, his eyes flashing with excitement. "See, Simon, I knew you were special. You're different from the others," Beryl said sincerely. "Come away with me when this is over. I will take care of you. You will be happy."

"I'm not a Cow," Simon said under his breath and processed all he had seen. Yes, it was amazing and fun and interesting to "travel" to another place without leaving his seat, but what of the other question? Why would Beryl have his photograph in a can in some field?

"After Last Assembly, Meryl and I came looking for you," Beryl said still smiling. "We found your house and waited, but you didn't come back. Eventually, we were called to help Elder Rufus, but I took that photo from your room and put it on my lot for safekeeping. It's in Mississippi. Before Last Assembly, we were going to build there."

"Do you have photos of lots of people you miss?" Simon asked.

With a wry grin, Beryl shook his head. "No, Simon, just you. I wish Meryl could see you like this—older, wiser, stronger, just *more* than you were before. You were everything a Rakum needed then." Beryl showed Simon both palms. "Now you're even *better.*"

He lowered his eyes. The twins had been truly horrifying at Last Assembly. Even if Beryl never attacked him again, the past didn't simply disappear.

"Simon," Beryl said, his voice soft as satin. "I know I seem like a miserable jerk, but I'm a Rakum, not a man. I don't think like you do. That is why I asked you to come away with me. You can teach me how to make you happy. Teach me to be more like Javier and less like Elder Dawn."

"But I'm not a Cow anymore," he huffed. "I'm different now. I don't want to do what a Cow does for a Rakum."

Beryl's grin faded and he rubbed his eyes, this time with one hand.

"Well, that won't work for me," he muttered, then sent him a wicked grin. "You're too delicious to think like that."

"Stop saying that," Simon hissed, looking down.

"If you consented, Canaan would mark you for me," Beryl added wistfully. "You'd stop aging, you'd stay healthy, we could do a lot of really fun things for centuries."

Simon closed his eyes. The *old* Simon would have jumped at such an offer, but now? All he felt was dread. It was time for Javier to come in and save him. He did not want to spend even one more moment with Beryl, but getting his mouth to say no and his body to walk away proved impossible.

"Billions of people on this planet and I only want you."

"Stop," Simon whispered.

"Javier and Canaan are buddy-buddy, you know," Beryl said and paused. Simon refused to look up and meet his eye. Undaunted, he continued. "Javier knows I'm here messing with you and he just keeps on talking to Canaan. I can hear them down there. Just blah, blah, blah. And it's not about you. They never talk about you."

"Javier's coming, don't worry," Simon mumbled.

"Oh, sure, *eventually*. He always comes *eventually*."

The room fell silent and Simon took a few slow breaths. *I need to get away from here...* He could leave in the morning, go back to Boston. Take back his letter, tell his agent he didn't mean it, erase the past week from his memory with booze and—

"Simon!" Beryl said his name in a harsh whisper and he looked up. "I want you with me."

"No," Simon said, and he hoped, resolutely.

"*Why?*" Beryl asked back to his more gentle, but plainly exasperated tone. "Why would a man, even if he's not a Cow, why would he refuse my offer?"

Simon replied quietly. "Because the Spirit of God in me resists the spirit that compels you. That makes us like oil and water."

"Prove it," Beryl said. "Give me your hand."

"Why?"

"I know a Cow test. If you pass, I'll stop courting you, I promise," Beryl said and wiggled his outstretched fingers. "What harm will it do? Come on."

Simon put forward his hand, jerkily at first, and then determinedly, as Beryl closed his fingers. While he moved Simon's hand toward his face, he held Simon's gaze with his bright eyes. Simon's heartrate increased as the top of his hand made contact with Beryl's lips.

"Don't," he whispered, but Beryl only pressed his lips against the skin of his hand closed-mouth, lingering, unmoving, his eyes locked with Simon's. In his peripheral vision, Canaan and Javier walked into the kitchen in slow motion. Simon narrowed his eyes, but held Beryl's gaze. There were hands on his shoulders from behind and a voice rumbling as if underwater calling his name, but he watched Beryl. Canaan's shape appeared beside Beryl where he sat and Simon saw the Elder strike him hard across the jaw. Beryl's head snapped sideways, but he held Simon's eye. Then Beryl tossed him a victory smile and winked.

"You're a Cow," Beryl sent telepathically and everything went black.

47

Tuscaloosa, AL, Maury's house
November 12th, 8:30 p.m.

The Cow Maury remembered his place well considering how long ago his master stopped dropping by. Rafael sat alone in the media room in one of eight cushioned theater chairs, complete with drink holders and a fold-down food tray. An old Laurel and Hardy comedy played with the sound muted and Maury tip-toed in to collect Rafael's empty plate, eyes down. Rafael sensed the Cow wanted very much to look at him, but didn't dare.

"Maury," Rafael said, his voice soft. "Sit with me."

The man's heart raced and he smelled of cigarette smoke and marijuana. He didn't take good care with his health, but Rafael was no diagnostician. He pat the seat beside him and the Cow tentatively sat on its edge.

"Tell me about your master," Rafael said and when Maury didn't meet his eye, he added, "My name is Rafael. Look upon me. I prefer it."

Maury allowed a fraction of a smile. "You have a beautiful name, Master," he said. He tilted his head enough to see Rafa's face and he blushed bright red. "My master was called David. I met him while taking night classes at the university."

Rafael grinned, imagining a Rakum grunt in college. "How did you meet?" Rafael asked and Maury's lips parted. Rafael reached out and covered the Cow's pudgy left hand with his right. "If you're willing, you can *show* me."

Rafael raised his eyebrows until Maury settled in the chair. Being in close proximity to The Last was akin to being plugged into a powerful battery and every talent that waned after Last Assembly was slowly but surely coming back online. Rafael smiled warmly to Maury as he gently stroked the back of his shaking hand.

"Show me David," Rafael sent telepathically and Maury's eyes grew round. His smile widened as he recalled his master and Rafael saw David

Walker through Maury's eyes. Maury at seventeen, taking advanced classes with college-age and older night students, meets David in the library. David had four other Cows and gathered them often to pal around. The young Rakum was attentive and friendly, and Maury worshipped him.

Rafa's eyes widened and he looked at Maury's face. "Show me that one," Rafael said softly. "Some sort of violence—what was that?" Rafael had seen a flash of a dark and menacing figure approaching Maury and the memory was immediately quashed.

"Oh," Maury said and nodded. Rafael watched in Maury's memory.

David Walker, with all of his Cows, watching television in a comfortable room. The oldest one rises to answer the door and Maury only fully looks over when a dangerous duo dressed in hoodies and holding large knives bursts in, shoving the older Cow to the floor with their dramatic entry. Rafael can see what Maury saw—that the older Cow had been mortally wounded by the first thug's weapon. Rafael watched with pride as David Walker incapacitated the first hoodlum, then the second, and offered sympathy when Maury became frightened enough to release his bladder where he stood. The memory faded to black and Rafael met Maury's eye again.

"Thank you, Maury," Rafael said in a near whisper as he broke the contact. "I wish I had known him." Absently, Rafael found himself wishing he *had* met the guy before Last Assembly; meeting him as a human held zero appeal.

"He saved all our lives that day,"[i] Maury said quietly. "Well, except for Professor Oppum. He died from that stab wound. I passed out so I missed the rest." Rafael sent him a sympathetic nod. Maury's tiny smile fell. "He's truly gone, then?"

Rafael didn't know what he was permitted to divulge. "Master Isaac said he is dead. You should listen to him," Rafa said and Maury's eyes watered.

Rafael nodded then to Elder Kilmeade who had entered without a sound. Maury spun in his seat, startled with a grunt, and stood.

"Master! Forgive me! What can I do for you?" he burbled and Kilmeade waved for him to leave. "Yes," he said and backed away. "Thank you, Master Rafael," he said as he exited the room.

"Making Cow friends, Rafa? Really?" Elder Kilmeade asked.

The light from the screen obscured the detail of his face leaving Rafael guessing at his meaning. Kilmeade dropped his weight into the seat Maury had been occupying.

"I never cared much for them," Kilmeade admitted, relaxing

backward as the soft seat enveloped him. "Even as a youngster. Stab, slurp, *sayonara*. That's the only way to deal with those."

Rafael didn't know how he should respond. He had the opposite opinion of Cows; he had always loved the adoration in their eyes and the tender way they massaged his ego.

"Rafa, my pet," Kilmeade sighed and leaned back, closing his eyes, "I have word from Little Lord Isaac."

Rafael didn't smirk at the humorous title, but he wanted to.

"It is extremely unpleasant so brace yourself."

Rafa's mind immediately went to Iago.

Kilmeade rolled his head to the side and opened his eyes, his face a mask of woe. One name cascaded from his mind to Rafa's—*Yes, Santiago*—and Rafael swallowed. Kilmeade shook his head a few centimeters and said, "You are not a human, Rafael. You are a Rakum, proud and noble."

Rafael held his breath.

"Your obsession with Santiago ends tonight."

With jaws clenched painfully tight, Rafael nodded. Kilmeade's eyes reflected concern for Rafael and frustration with their leader. The Last couldn't see his face, so Rafael hoped their true feelings went no further than their eyes.

"He will be safe as long as you please your master," Kilmeade added. "But he will be shared."

Rafael made a noise in his throat desperately controlling his thoughts. He was capable of owning them, he simply hadn't needed to for decades.

"You pegged it, my pet. Our undisciplined years are behind us. Guard your thoughts, be a Rakum, and you will excel and find fulfillment."

"But not peace or joy," Rafael said in his mind, repeating snippets of the Rabbit's speech from the day she ruined their lives. Their God offered them an eternity of peace if they would only bend the knee and give up their own deity.

Kilmeade's eyes flashed and he tightened his jaw.

"No, I loathe all of that human idiocy," Rafael said aloud. "We need Master Isaac to fix everything she and her kind have ruined."

"Precisely. We are god of this world," Kilmeade said, "and they are our playthings. Do you understand?"

Rafael nodded, still reading a sub-context in the Elder's eyes. Kilmeade had learned to say one thing and transmit another; it was a good trick. Rafael would need to master it, too, if they were going to have any freedom of thought around their new leader. Kilmeade nodded then, encouraging him to try another.

"The mortals that follow the Rabbit's God are weak and stupid," Rafael said, suppressing a grin since he truly felt no animosity toward the humans; in fact, he liked a lot about them. "They're easy prey, too. If Master Isaac will allow it, perhaps we can go out tonight and kill a few for kicks."

"Let's ask him," Kilmeade replied. Then, his face fell serious and he lowered his voice. "Now, my pet, call Iago. Tell him that he and Jimmy need to come here now. Maury will meet them in the day and keep them comfortable until we arise."

Rafa's heart grew too big for his ribcage as he resisted the white-hot anger aroused by Kilmeade's command. Still, having no options, he fished out his cell. Iago picked up before the first ring ended.

"Master! Is it time to come?" Iago asked, excited and full of hope.

"Yes, you and Jimmy, come now." Rafael called out the address.

"Yes, Master! I'll rent a car, no problem. I can be in Tuscaloosa in..." Iago's voice faded and came back strong. "Six hours! You might still be up!"

"If we aren't available, the Cow here is named Maury. Trust him and do as he says," Rafael said, his voice tight. He disconnected the call and frowned at an unsummoned image of Boris taking Iago's blood. *He sure as hell better be gentle.*

Still looking into Rafa's eyes, the Elder sent another single visual transmission—*patience*—and reached out his hand, palm down.

Rafael unbuttoned the cuff of his shirt and rolled up his sleeve, prepared and willing to do what he could to keep the Elder strong; Isaac would be taking sustenance from Kilmeade daily until Elder Canaan returned. Kilmeade positioned himself to sink his curious fangs into Rafa's inner arm. Rafael stared off at nothing.

"There's a Rabbit headed this way," he mumbled as his stomach rumbled loudly in the cavernous theater room.

"Elder Canaan's woman, she will arrive shortly with Kite," Kilmeade sent silently, still feasting. Rafa's hunger burned deep inside him at her aroma and Isaac would probably not let him near her.

"This is a wonderful, wonderful life," Rafael said aloud, trying not to sound as sarcastic as he felt. The Elder nursed on his arm and Rafael pushed Iago and the new Rabbit as far from his mind as possible.

▼ ▼

"Kilmeade! Bring your pet in here and see what I have!" The Last screamed, his peculiar demon-influenced voice reverberating off the walls of the Cow's home.

Kilmeade grinned with humor as he detached from Rafa's arm with a wet smack. "Game on, Rafa!" he said smiling and dashed to the door.

The Last held court in the Cow's great room and with Rafael just behind him, Kilmeade zoomed in and came to a stop at the wide threshold. Minutes ago, Kilmeade heard two new heartbeats added to the grounds, Kite and Canaan's mate, now a Rabbit.

Kilmeade had waited to be summoned before ending his blood meal. Now, as he awaited instructions, Kilmeade noted how Isaac had rearranged the room to suit him. The furniture had been shimmied into a semi-circle around one over-sized Queen Anne chair where he perched, legs crossed under him, grinning ear-to-ear.

"Here, Elder Kilmeade!" he said and pointed to the empty spot on his left. Boris stood on his right, watching everything his master did with gigantic eyes. Kilmeade had to hand it to the guy—he was all in.

The Rabbit and the Cow were nowhere in sight, although Kilmeade heard their hearts and low talking several rooms away. That left the Rakum addition. Kilmeade scoped out the room, hearing Kite's heartbeat, but not seeing him. He got in position and gestured for Rafael to remain where he was until otherwise directed.

"Elder Kilmeade! How rude of you to not greet our newest arrival!" Isaac said still shouting, but now in his normal adolescent voice.

Kilmeade recognized the humor in their leader's tone and he grinned, looking around the room. It was to be hide-and-seek and he aimed to please their little lord.

"Yes, you got it. Find him. An Elder should have no problem seeing what's not there," Isaac said softer now, watching Kilmeade with shining eyes. The new game truly tickled The Last and Kilmeade decided to put on a real show.

"Kite?" Kilmeade whispered and sunk into a comical tip-toeing posture. Isaac burst out laughing, pointing like a kid at the circus. "I hear you, Kitey, Kitey, Kitey," Kilmeade said making a kissing noise. "Here, boy!" Isaac guffawed and Boris's laugh boomed around the room.

To his right, the heartbeat was louder, and still, no Rakum. Kilmeade smelled him as he moved toward the sound—an odor of travel, gasoline, convenience store snacks, sweat, and then incidental vestiges of Canaan's marked Rabbit. Kite was standing only inches from him and he could not see him with his eyes. Kilmeade lowered his lids and concentrated. It took several seconds, but the young Rakum's form materialized in his mind holding a huge wooden staff. *The Staff of Abroghia!* And he was using it to make himself invisible! Kilmeade's eyes flew open and he turned back to

Isaac.

"Kite! Reveal yourself!" Isaac said and a young black Rakum walked out of the shadows to approach the throne. He knelt at Isaac's feet, holding the staff angled toward his master. Isaac nodded to Boris who stepped up and took it off his hands. When Kite had backed away and found a place to stand, Isaac looked to Kilmeade. "Very good, Elder Kilmeade! You and I are the only two that saw him there. I'm super impressed."

Kilmeade's mouth sat ajar as he processed what possessing the High Father's staff might mean for their little master. On top of his thoughts, Isaac grinned and gestured to Boris who stepped before Isaac's chair and faced Kilmeade. Once their eyes locked, Kilmeade sensed a single flicker of doubt in the big Rakum before he hardened his gaze and moved the staff inches his way. Kilmeade's knees gave out and he hit the carpet hard.

"AWESOME, BORIS!" Isaac shouted with glee. "Do Rafael! Do Rafael!"

Kilmeade jerked his eyes to the doorway in time to see Rafael tumble to the ground in the same manner.

"Boris! Now you're awesome, too!" Isaac yelled and leapt up to stand beside his giant. "Now do Kite," Isaac said with a little less enthusiasm, yet his eyes still shone with excitement. Again, the Rakum that Boris focused his will upon dribbled to the floor.

Isaac grasped Boris's bicep with both hands and held him tightly. "You and I, Boris, we're a team. Now I want you to put their lights out— but be careful. Don't fry them," Isaac said with a grin, shooting a tiny glance to Kilmeade at the last.

Kilmeade watched the former grunt assume his mantle and will Rafael unconscious, then Kite. He rotated his shoulders to where Kilmeade lay prostrate on the carpet and gave him a smile.

"Good night, Elder Kilmeade," he said in his deep voice and he winked. "No hard feelings, Master."

Purposing not to resist in the least, Kilmeade's world went black.

48

The pizza boxes sat ravaged by the famished Rakum, but three pies remained untouched in case Roman and his carload arrived hungry. Canaan and Beryl, and Guap and Polly took four giggling middle-aged women down to the basement, promising to have them out and away within an hour's time. Javier sat in the kitchen with Simon, hoping to convince him he was not a Cow.

"It's not possible, Simon," Javier said, his right hand firmly grasping Simon's forearm. "If you've given your life to Messiah Yeshua, then you won't pine for the Rakum. It's a fact—you're not a Cow any longer."

Simon nodded his head, but he didn't mean it. "Beryl said—"

"Beryl is a devil, Simon," Javier said and regretted his choice of words. "Simon, what you feel for him, what you might feel for me, or what you think or wish I am, is plain old lust. It's lust. It's nothing supernatural or paranormal. You told me yourself, you don't feel like a Cow. You don't want to serve a Rakum Master, you aren't compelled to give your blood—in fact, you're afraid to do it. Why? I heard what he offered you. What's keeping you from running into his arms and saying, 'take me away!'" Javier's voice had grown loud and his cheeks were hot. He wanted to remain calm, but Simon's ridiculous lack of faith tested his patience. Maybe Roman could help the man out, but Javier was just about done trying.

"I'm confused," Simon said and covered his face with his hands. "God isn't helping me. He refuses to make these feelings go away."

"Have you *asked* Him to?" Javier asked controlling his tone, but barely. "Put forth some effort, bow down, confess that you're lusting after this ungodly thing and ask God to take it away."

A rap on the front door followed by a melodious bell interrupted

Simon's reply. Javier accidentally growled, revealing the depth of his frustration, and he rose for the front of the house. Simon followed behind him, blowing his nose.

When the door opened, Roman didn't expect the rush of emotion that coursed through him when he met Javier's gaze. All of Javier's current troubles were Roman's fault. The man was his son in every way that mattered and even as a Rakum Elder, he had sensed their bond was stronger than a Rakum's should be. In hindsight, Roman realized God had been setting them up from the beginning for such a time as this.

Roman stuck out his hand and when Javier grabbed it, he cupped his elbow with his other hand and yanked him into a shoulder bump. "Javie, thank God you're okay."

"I would say the same about you," Javier responded, his voice tense. "Come in. You remember Simon Miller." Javier gestured to the man behind him.

"Simon," Roman said giving his hand a quick shake. He was happy the former Cow found the Lord, but their personalities had clashed from the beginning. Roman moved aside and ushered in David who shook hands politely with them both. David was still cross with Javier for whatever he was perceived to have done with Chloe in David's absence.

"All healed up, Javier? Amazing. By the way, thanks for calling to let us know," David said already exiting the foyer. Roman gave Javier a small head shake and he left it alone.

"Where's the rest?" Javier peered around to the stoop and Roman closed the door.

"We dropped Santiago and Jimmy off at a hotel," Roman said and stepped from the foyer into the great room. Javier motioned and each man found a seat.

"That's probably best," Javier agreed, "if one of them is a Rabbit."

"I debated on leaving him alone, unprotected, but…" Roman said, and gestured to David, "…we decided their chances were better in a place with no Rakum presence."

"That we're aware of," David mumbled.

Roman waved his hands in surrender. "What could we do? We prayed for their safety."

"It's a wise move," Javier said. "There are three Rakum grunts in the basement that care an awful lot about Rabbits."

"Three?" Roman and David asked together.

"Beryl, plus two others. Guap and Polly," Javier explained. "They don't know what's going on, but Canaan is fond of them. I'm supposed to talk to them when they come upstairs."

"I know them," Roman said and looked at David, who shook his head. Roman rubbed his eyes. "How is Beryl behaving? I assume since he's here, he's not the same monster he was a week ago." Roman glanced at Simon, but he still stared at the ceiling, no reaction, nothing to add.

Javier squeezed his eyes closed and grumbled. "Canaan has him under his thumb." Javier looked at Roman and sighed. "Trust me, if Canaan wasn't here, Beryl would be a problem."

"Thank God for Canaan, then," Roman said and turned aside to yawn into his hand.

Javier looked at his watch. "I'll call them upstairs. They've been down there over an hour." Roman raised his eyebrows and Javier added, "Entertaining."

Roman slow-blinked and then turned to gauge the faces around him. David sat forward over his knees, his mind far away. He wanted to ask Javier about Chloe, he said as much in the truck, but now he was silent. Simon was leaning back into the sofa watching the ceiling fan. Javier was looking dead at Simon, frowning.

"Before you call them up, can we speak privately?" Roman asked Javier.

"Absolutely," Javier agreed, coming around to the business at hand and not whatever Simon had him upset over. "Ya'll give us a minute," he said apologetically to Simon and David.

Simon shrugged without looking his way and David stood up. Neither moved quickly enough for Roman's tastes.

"Go into the kitchen. We'll be there shortly," he ordered and they did as he asked. To Javier, he gave a small smile. *"Javie,"* was all that came out in an exhale of relief.

Javier rose and sat close to him on the over-stuffed leather couch. "It's almost too much, Roman," he said shaking his head. "I don't know where to start."

"Let's start with what we don't want to say in front of the others," Roman said. "We got word that Damien is dead. Santiago heard it from his master."

Javier frowned. He had tried to prepare his heart for those words, but he failed.

Roman commiserated with a pat on his knee. "Damien insisted on staying behind." Roman removed his glasses and cleaned them with his handkerchief, choosing his words carefully. "He shared the Truth with Kilmeade and Rafael before Isaac finished him off. Now I want to help my brother get away. The question is does God want me to?"

"I say yes. I've been asked by Canaan and Beryl to help them break free of Isaac," Javier said in a low voice. "Scripture says if someone asks you to walk a mile, go with him two. Canaan isn't one of us, but he's asking for help and we owe him."

Roman sent Javier a slow nod. In addition to the Elder's help in Jackson, Roman had grown to like the self-loving mook. "Then that settles it. We will help them break free from Isaac."

Javier agreed and then asked Roman to put out his hand. "It's time. I need to show you what's happening in my body since I drank from The Last."

When Roman put out his hand palm down, Javier took his fingers in his own and closed his eyes. Puzzled, Roman opened his mouth to ask a question, but Javier stopped him.

"Wait for it," Javier whispered.

Roman smirked, but lost the expression when a stream of unpleasant and alarming sensations flooded his mind and body. He startled and Javier held his fingers just tight enough that he didn't slip free.

"Help me, Roman," Javier whispered again, his voice plaintive. *"Sort it out."*

"Javier," Roman mumbled. *Sort it out,* he'd said. Roman closed his eyes and did his best to ignore the bile that threatened to rise as the sensations crawled across his system. *Sort it out.*

Roman put a methodology to the request and considered his feet, shins, knees, thighs—they tingled with electricity, begging to run and jump and exert themselves. His pelvis and torso, vibrated with the urge to be fulfilled—gut, groin, equally starving for satisfaction. His chest and shoulders battling a heart bursting from his ribcage, yearning for revenge, battle, victory, and more. And his throat and mouth longing to be filled and overflowing with blood—"

Javier jerked his hand off Roman's and stood up, turning away. Roman gasped, stood, and caught him before he took a step.

"What is that? Is that what you're experiencing?" Roman asked, flabbergasted at the torturous range of stimuli the man shared.

"Every second," Javier whispered and closed his eyes, forcibly calming himself. *"I don't lust for blood. That sensation is a lie,"* he said still whispering

as if afraid to hear the words.

Roman commiserated with a sad nod.

"I have to confess," Javier stated. "As a brother in Christ—apologizing to God isn't cutting it. I want to say it aloud and you're the only one I think I can do it with."

"Of course," Roman said leaning in, his hand still on his arm. "Go ahead."

"I've done some horrible things since I left the hospital. I was so confused—" Javier lowered his voice and looked down. "*I attacked Simon, I was brutal. Like an animal and I have never been like that before. Never.*" Javier cut his eyes toward the kitchen. When he turned back his face was the picture of dread.

"Okay, Javie, it's okay. He's fine now and he forgives you," Roman said believing his words.

"It gets worse," Javier continued. "When I reached my house and Chloe was there..." Javier swallowed and blinked slowly, buying time. "I was gentle, but still not in control. I attacked her, too, and *she actually died.*" When Roman's eyes widened, Javier grabbed his arm gently. "I revived her, she's okay, and she doesn't know. Nobody knows, but the two of us."

"Wait," Roman interjected, now more curious than ever how different Javier was than the Rakum. "You revived her how? Like you used to, in the old days?"

"No, no—that way doesn't work, I tried," he replied and worked to formulate his answer. "Once I realized I couldn't *will* her back, like I used to as a Rakum, I did chest compressions. When that failed, I gave her mouth-to-mouth. That is when she came back." Javier's eyes grew wide. "I am certain it was *my breath* that did it."

Roman did not react, but his mind raced. The creature he was turning into seemed like a Rakum trying to be an angel. Javier had inside him the influence of the devil from Isaac and the power of God in his spirit, and they wrestled for control as he transformed. By the time they faced off with Isaac, Javier better have made his choice firm in his heart or he could go either way.

"I know it's hard to accept," Javier continued, misreading his silence. "Understand, *neither time* did I lust for blood and I learned something important. It's not *blood* this mutation wants."

"What does it want, Javie?"

"How do I say it?" Javier looked around the room, frustration building. "It wants to *consume*. Gobble up. It is a void, a black hole, and it wants to eat everything. It is my thorn and if God has made me into a mutant Rakum-Human thing to fight for His purposes, this monster is the one I'll be resisting every moment."

Roman remained as he was, standing beside Javier, processing all the man had shared. "Have you tested your strength? Last night, dealing with Canaan and Beryl—how did you fare?"

"I was able to deflect Beryl when he was too handsy with Simon, but Canaan hasn't given me any resistance. I don't think he will. He senses everything that's going on inside me. Also, believe it or not, he's become a friend."

Roman mused, "There's hope for the old guy yet."

"I hope so," Javier said softly.

"Can he read you?"

Javier shook his head. "No. Both of us can initiate conversation, but he reads nothing of my private thoughts."

"I know you're glad of that."

"Sure, but he and Beryl *can* read Simon off and on."

"Okay," Roman said, still thoughtful. "So Simon's waffling."

"I'm afraid so. I tried to counsel him, but I'm sincerely hoping you will give it a shot." Javier sucked his teeth and exhaled. "I'm out of advice."

Roman patted his shoulder. "I will. For the time being, let's keep your monster to ourselves. David and Simon don't need to know the extent of your, well, *affliction*."

"I agree."

"Let's get Canaan up here and proceed with whatever God shows us."

"Deal." Javier jerked his head to the right and then returned his gaze to Roman. "Canaan is headed up; he heard our entire conversation."

"He listened," Roman said with a sardonic grin. "There's a difference."

"Yeah, that's Canaan for you," Javier said wryly, then nodded with approval at his next understanding from the Elder. "He indicates Beryl's still in the dark, along with the other two. He won't share any of what we discussed." Then Javier smiled. "He just said he was glad I haven't crushed him with my 'mutant super-powers'."

Roman sighed, "It's good he can keep a sense of humor."

Javier chuckled. "I could use some laughs. Anyway, go get some pizza if you're hungry. You might not want to see Canaan's Cows when they come up."

Roman agreed as Canaan entered the great room. He smiled wide at Roman and approached in big strides. He lay a heavy hand on Roman's shoulder and shook him roughly.

"Roman, you old dog! You look well," he said and released him. "Let me clean up my dinner mess and we'll talk."

Canaan laughed at his own joke and sent Javier a wink before heading back the way he'd come. Roman watched as four women shuffled down the hall away from them, presumably to a side exit, and he didn't wait for more.

"I'll see you in the kitchen," he said to Javier, but the man had already left. He'd had enough of Cows, too.

49

"OH, DAMN, we got some long faces up in here!" Polly shouted as he entered the room. Guap was right behind him rubbing his middle.

"Let's get in on this," Guap said smiling. "Rakum, Cows, and Apostates all working together for peace and harmony! Smells like nirvana!"

"You left out the Anominoie!" Polly laughed.

Javier watched them in silence, letting them get it out of their system. Canaan walked in from the kitchen with a Budweiser and both Rakum dropped the goofy act to pay him respect. When Canaan lighted onto the long embroidered sofa, Polly and Guap planted on either side of him and remained mostly quiet. Javier dragged a dining chair from the adjacent room and watched Roman, Beryl, and Simon pull up various seats as well. When everyone was seated facing the center, Javier cleared his throat.

"Roman and Canaan asked me to start this thing," he said, taking a moment to absorb each man's gaze. "Time is short so I will begin with you." Javier looked at Guap, knowing Polly would feel included. "What do you think is happening here?"

Guap looked briefly at Polly on the other side of Canaan. They were communicating silently and Javier didn't mind. The two *did* seem harmless and they gave him a general positive vibe. Finally, Guap spoke, his voice even.

"We get that my brothers aren't happy with the new management," he said tipping his chin to Canaan and Beryl. "We also get that because of something beyond our eyes—"

"But having to do with the Rabbit at Last Assembly—" Polly seamlessly interjected.

"Master Isaac hasn't been able to reach Elder Canaan or Beryl since they came in contact with you. He hasn't contacted us since we arrived. I agree with Elder Canaan; something about you blocks him."

"He called us telepathically last night after you left," Polly said, again sounding as if he picked up where Guap left off.

Javier looked at Canaan who nodded.

"Yep, they told me already," Canaan confirmed. "Isaac read that Beryl and I left with you. He thinks we're headed back."

Javier's eyes widened. "They lied to him? How—"

"Not *precisely*, Anomaly," Guap said.

"Let's drop the anomaly crap. Call me Javier."

"Heh, not precisely, *Hah*-veir," Guap continued. "Polly and I sent him the truth—Javier, Elder Canaan, Beryl and Simon all left together."

"And he left us alone," Polly added.

Javier cut his eyes to Roman. "Can they do that?"

Roman shrugged and looked at Canaan for corroboration. "It's possible. I mean, it's Elder level skill, but maybe they have more brains than you thought."

"Roman, if you only knew," Canaan chuckled. "Guess who these two are?"

Nonplused, Roman shook his head. "I remember them."

"You didn't know they were the bankers for the Ten. That's their secret," Canaan said beaming with pride over his knowledge. "When they told me, I was floored."

"Oh," Roman said thoughtfully and nodded.

Canaan continued, "Javie, Guap and Polly controlled and executed the entirety of the Rakum financial enterprise for the past fifty years. They're silly, but brilliant."

"Oh, yeah," Polly said and giggled.

"I'm a freakin' genius," Guap agreed hand above his head as if measuring his height. "And The Last?" he said holding his hand at chest level, palm down. "Normal brain."

Javier asked Canaan, "So it's possible to think one thing, send it to Isaac, and believe something else?"

"Roman said it—It's traditional thought management. Elders learn it as a matter of course."

Javier nodded. Before his transformation to mortal, he had not been in line for Elder training. The Elders were specifically bred from royal human bloodlines and raised to be stronger, smarter, and much more clever than any Rakum grunt. For Guap and Polly to approach those levels in such short years, Javier was impressed.

"Okay, that is helpful," Javier said changing his tone with the two strangers, happy to learn their clown act was affectation. "Knowing all that, Guap, Polly, answer me now: do you want to be part of Isaac's plan or help us subvert it?"

Guap leaned over his knees. "We don't exactly know what either of you have planned, but we know that Isaac is stronger than all the Fathers put together—Elder Canaan and Beryl felt it, too."

"You were Rakum once," Polly said to Javier, Roman and David. "Think of how scared you were of High Father Abroghia and multiply that times infinity," Polly added, receiving agreeing nods from the other Rakum.

"So when you ask us who we choose, we choose ourselves," Guap said. "Which group will preserve Guap and Polly, brains and body intact?"

Canaan laughed and leaned back, dragging both Rakum with him, a fist in the backs of each man's shirt. "My sweet, sweet little pups," he said, grabbing them into half-hugs now with his burly arms. "Javier brings a power much stronger than little Isaac ever imagined. Tell them, Javie. Tell them about *your* Father."

Absently, Javier glanced at Simon who sat forward over his knees listening and nodding and awaiting a plan. Beryl sat beside him and that's when Javier noticed: Beryl was watching Simon.

"Javier," Canaan said grabbing his attention. "The game is being played over in this arena," he said and swayed the two Rakum under his wing back and forth.

Javier nodded a few times and looked at Roman.

"Guap, Polly, this entire world was breathed into existence by the one True God. This unfathomable power created the Rakum's maker, Ta'avah, who you knew as Abroghia. Did you read Beth Rider's book?"

Both Rakum shook their heads.

"But you heard her speak at Last Assembly." Guap and Polly nodded. "So you recall every word she said," Roman stated.

"I heard the first part," Guap said. "I heard, 'in the beginning, God created the heaven and earth.'"

"'The earth was without form and void and darkness was over the face of the deep,'" Polly added.

"'And the Spirit of God hovered over the face of the waters,'" David finished from across the semi-circle.

"I pretty much zoned out the rest," Guap admitted.

Polly shrugged. "There's no denying the God she spoke of is real, I mean, He literally melted the brains of anyone who refused to attend that speech."

"Melted," Guap repeated and raised his hand to flutter his fingers down like water. "But He let me zone out and live. Good Guy."

"Me, too," Polly agreed.

"Thousands of Rakum listened and lived and did *not* accept Him as their God," Roman said. "I was the last of our circle to believe, so I watched those around me choosing sides. I asked you what you heard so I can pick it up there."

"With all due respect, Mr. Roman," Polly said and Javier discerned he still saw Roman as an Elder on some level. "I don't want to be human."

"He knows that," Canaan piped in, effectively preventing Guap or Beryl from repeating the same sentiment. "We don't have to be human to defeat Isaac. Go on, Roman."

"Canaan is right. God calls the shots and He has brought us together to do something about this abomination Isaac Akaron—"

"Ouch!" Polly blurted and laughed into his hand.

Roman continued, ignoring the interruption. "I'm not going to try to convert you into anything." Roman paused waiting for Guap and Polly to nod. Canaan released their necks and they leaned over their knees.

"Okay, sir, then proceed," Polly said with a straight face. He removed the knit cap he'd been wearing and rubbed his head. "And, sir," he said taking a moment to glance at his compadre on the other side of Canaan, "we're with Elder Canaan."

"Yeah, and he's with Javier—so proceed with that in mind. We are in," Guap said with finality.

Javier hid his joy at their decision and watched Roman prepare the story.

"Over the course of time, God created spirits that we call angels and demons. They were *all* designed to serve God, but the ones that rebelled are what we refer to as demons. They were cast to earth until the time of the end," Roman began.

"Um," Polly said and Roman held up his hand.

"For now, determine to believe everything I'm saying, no matter how foolish it sounds," Roman said, including Beryl and Canaan. "And don't ask questions."

"When you have a question," Javier offered, "stop yourself and ask, who transformed all those Rakum into mortals when they believed?"

"One tiny, winy question, please? Then I shall hush like a good pup." Polly said, making sad eyes. Javier and Roman gave him some rope so he continued. "Can you tell me why they needed to be mortal to follow Him?

Why can't a Rakum do the same thing?"

"Because in a nutshell, God is holy and only holy can co-exist with holy. A person only becomes holy—blameless before God—by accepting Jesus' sacrifice on the Cross. His death erases all sin. When you believe, your sin is washed away and His Spirit comes to dwell within you, forcing demonic spirits out. The Rakum automatically reverts to his natural state..." Roman paused to absorb each man's gaze and finished with, "...*human*. You were born human."

"Bummer," Polly grinned.

"That's a huge nutshell," Guap said softly.

"For some really big nuts," Polly added with a weak snicker.

"When this is over, we can explain it a lot better," Javier said with a kind wink.

"Thanks for trying," Guap said. "I'm going to nod my head. This is me nodding my head..."

"Me, too. You guys are nuts," Polly said with a thumbs up. "Crazy is fun. I like that about you."

Javier chuckled and looked for his previous train of thought. "Oh, okay, yes. God is real, He's right here in the room with us." Javier paused. Roman nodded and before he begin could again, Javier added using Polly's words against him, "Imagine how big you think Isaac's power is and multiply that by infinity."

The room fell silent and Roman picked up the thread.

"The spirits that rebelled number in the millions and Ta'avah-Abroghia was one of those. He created the Rakum race in his own image. Polly, Guap, you speak Hebrew. Even his name represents the Rakum race. *Lust*. Think about it."

Guap looked over at Polly and shrugged one shoulder. "Clever."

"I lusted tonight already," Polly whispered. "It was awesome."

Roman clucked his tongue. "The point is a *spirit* propelled Abroghia. The Spirit in Javier, myself, David, and Simon is the very Creator of the universe. Can you imagine a clay pot coming to life and destroying the potter?" The Rakum shook their heads. "No more can these fallen spirits raise a hand against God or His purposes."

"So all of that explains why we trust God to work this out for us," Javier said.

"What's the plan?" Polly asked, innocently enough.

Javier chuckled and looked at Roman in case he wanted to answer. He didn't. Javier laughed again. "We don't have a plan yet. The way faith works is you decide to trust and then you wait in His service."

"Ohhhh..." Guap leaned back and hummed the *Jeopardy* theme.

"I like this plan," Polly said. "It doesn't take a lot of planning."

"Very funny." Javier hardened his gaze at their mockery. "Since you're in with us, the next thing we do is have Canaan call Isaac on the phone. What Isaac says and what Canaan does will probably reveal our next step."

"Simon, David, Javier," Roman said rising to his feet, "come here."

Javier was close and he took Roman's outstretched hand. Simon had to step over Beryl's feet and he took his other hand. When they had made a circle, Roman prayed for the Rakum to hear.

"Father, have Your way with us, show us what we are to do next, and protect us from the enemy—"

"Pray for Marcy," Canaan threw in.

"And Father, keep Marcy safe from harm. Into Your hands, amen," Roman finished. Javier, David, and Simon agreed and they dropped the contact.

"Okay, Canaan," Roman said, and took an audible breath. "Call him."

Canaan nodded and pulled out his phone.

50

Tuscaloosa, AL, Maury's house
November 12th, 10 p.m.

W hen the three Rakum regained consciousness, Isaac divvied out chores to all but Boris. Kite was told to tap the Rabbit and then secure her in one of the bedrooms. Then he was to accompany Maury to a late-night appointment with his attorney. Isaac wanted cash— a lot of it, and Maury didn't keep much on hand. The lawyer would provide and sign whatever banking instruments were necessary and Maury aimed to please.

Kilmeade was to pinpoint Elder Canaan's location and if he was successful, Isaac would permit the two of them to have a night to themselves.

"Elder Canaan is mixed up with the Apostates and it's blocking my communication," Isaac told him after Kite left the room. Boris stood by silently, holding the staff in the same manner of the High Father in days of old. "Canaan and Beryl have custody of Javier and Simon and are bringing them to me. Find him. I don't like being blind."

Kilmeade had said he would and Isaac left him alone. Sitting quietly in the great room, Kilmeade concentrated on Canaan. The past seven years, Kilmeade struggled to read even fellow Rakum or open-minded mortals in his direct vicinity, but *before* Last Assembly, an Elder could contact any of the other ninety-nine with a mere thought. Thankfully, The Last's presence had been boosting Kilmeade's muted abilities and tonight, he had no doubt he would succeed. It took longer than expected, but he found him. Standing in a well-appointed room with many others, phone in hand, the Elder was preparing to call Isaac.

"Elder Canaan, how strong you look! Oh, how I have missed you!" Kilmeade said to him telepathically. Canaan turned his head upward in the natural and grinned.

"Are you spying on me, Brother Kilmeade?" Canaan said aloud with a smile, probably alerting the others to the contact.

Through a typical cross-dimensional haze, Kilmeade saw Javier and Roman standing nearby. Roman looked to the ceiling, frowning.

"Canaan, do tell Roman how I wish he could see me!" Kilmeade sent grinning, too.

"How's our Master?" Canaan asked aloud for those with him and held out the cell phone. "We're about to call him."

"He thinks you're headed here, but he sent me to make sure," Kilmeade responded.

Beryl walked up to Canaan then and looked around, unable to see or hear Kilmeade. The two Rakum Kilmeade didn't know sat on the couch behind Canaan, also looking up, but not seeing.

"Beryl looks good," Kilmeade sent with a chuckle. Canaan laughed and popped the pretty grunt on the head.

"Come here, doll-face," he said and grabbed Beryl close. "Pack your bags, Kilmeade. We're breaking you out of there."

"Don't bother," Kilmeade sent forcefully. *"Master Isaac is going to right everything that's wrong with our people. He is the great Zahdone, powerful and mighty, none can compare!"*

"Zahdone?" Canaan said and looked at Roman.

"I will tell him you're coming." Kilmeade started to withdraw certain the Elder heard his subtle hints.

"Wait—Marcy?" he asked this time silently and his smiling eyes became round with worry.

"Master Isaac is taking care of her," Kilmeade returned. *"Come home, Canaan."*

Kilmeade turned and Isaac waltzed back into the great room.

"Canaan has a phone in his hand to call you right now," Kilmeade said remaining seated. He held out his hands to see if Isaac would take them. When he did, he pulled him close and gave him a debonair smile. "He's in Georgia, Master, and I have his exact address."

"You are a very clever Rakum, Elder Kilmeade," Isaac said and he lifted Kilmeade's hands to kiss them. "Take your pet on the town. Get him some innocent blood—" Isaac's eyes flashed as he added, "I heard what he said. Tell him that if he doesn't kill an innocent tonight, I'll have Boris brain him with that staff."

Isaac's eyes remained friendly, but Kilmeade had no doubt he meant what he said. "Your will is my will, Master."

"Good. Bye, bye," Isaac said and dropped his hands. "My *favorite* Elder is about to call me and explain where he's been the past two days."

Kilmeade rose from the chair in a bow and backed away, hoping to be out of the room when the call came through. He made it to the kitchen where Rafael awaited him and got his pet to the garage before Isaac's phone rang. Rafael started the car and they left the house without a hitch.

Kilmeade grinned. "I bought us a little vacay," he told Rafael as they cleared the security gate. "But we must kill an innocent tonight. Choose your hunting ground."

"Shopping mall," Rafael said and Kilmeade plucked his pet's phone from the console to surf the internet for the locations. Rafa's stomach rumbled and Kilmeade said not a word.

"CANAAN!" Isaac said when he answered the ring. "EXPLAIN YOURSELF!"

"MASTER ISAAC!" Canaan said in the same excited tone.

Isaac's face fell. "Did you just mock me?"

"I didn't mean to hurt your feelings, Master," Canaan said. "You know I like you."

Isaac sat silent. What did Canaan mean by that? Why couldn't he be read? Isaac's face heated as his frustration grew.

"WHY ARE YOU STILL IN ATHENS!" he shouted unable to control his anger.

"Chill, Master, chill," Canaan said his friendly voice soft. "Beautiful, perfect boy, I got a little distracted along the way."

"Keep your empty compliments, Canaan," Isaac said in a whisper and pictured the woman tied to a chair with Maury's neckties. "I've decided. Your Rabbit will die."

"Whoa, whoa, whoa, Master," Canaan said, his voice still as calm as before. "If her light goes out, what's to keep me around? If her light goes out, I could stay forever in my Isaac-free bubble and keep my delicious blood all to myself."

Isaac closed his eyes and paced his breathing. What should he do? He looked inside, but Zahdone's answer was to kill them all. Where would that leave him?

"Get in here!" he called to Boris.

Boris lumbered in and leaned the staff against the decorative fireplace. "Master?" he said, his eyes filled with concern.

"Bring that Rabbit in here," Isaac said and returned to the phone. "Canaan, go on. Why did you call me if you're not coming back?"

"It's like this, Master. Me and Beryl and Guap and Polly don't want to be with you anymore," Canaan said sounding as if they discussed the weather.

Isaac shook his head. Why wasn't he afraid? What was going on over there in Athens that gave him such foolhardy courage?

"It's not about what you want, Canaan," Isaac said, carefully choosing his words as he awaited the Rabbit. "I am Master, I am god, and your needs do not concern me."

Canaan chuckled on his end. *"That's* why we don't want to be with you. No matter what plan you have for our people, none of it is about us. That's no life. You can keep it."

"What do you mean?" Isaac said, still trying to read the Elder's thoughts and coming up empty. "Are you going apostate?"

Canaan laughed again, louder. "Yeah, right," he said. "Isaac, remember when we met? Think about it. Try to recall how you felt about me in the beginning."

"This is stupid," Isaac said, but his mind went back. He had just formulated his plans to replace Rufus and the Rabbit's posse had been heading the same way. There he met Canaan—hadn't he been the perfect Rakum specimen? Isaac hadn't seen *any* Elders before him, ever, and Canaan had taken his breath away. Isaac didn't plan to, but he called up Canaan's every word, his posture, the way he controlled and dominated the mortals around him. Even the Rabbit, who frightened all of his brethren at The Cave years ago afforded Canaan respect and distance. Isaac exhaled, unhappy at his conclusion, yet he spoke it aloud for Canaan. "You were glorious."

"I am still glorious!" Canaan said with joy. "And nobody is forced to love me. Do you think I *can't* subjugate any Rakum or mortal I choose?"

He paused, but Isaac did not respond. The Elder was teaching him something and Zahdone made it difficult to learn.

"You could be like that," Canaan continued. "You could have the world at your feet. But you're only a child and children are selfish. A Rakum can have everything he wants and more, IF he has self-control."

"I HAVE EVERYTHING I WANT!" Isaac shouted.

"Um, little buddy," Canaan said in a low voice, "if you did, I'd be there with you and your sharp little teeth would be in my arm."

Boris strode in at a fast clip, dragging Marcy Haddle by the upper arm. She had barely kept up with him and had to be righted to her feet as he reached Isaac.

Pushing the phone in her face, Isaac handed it off. "Speak some sense into him before I turn you inside out."

"Canaan!" the Rabbit said into the phone, tears on her cheeks.

"Hey, baby," the Elder said, Isaac hearing every word from the mouthpiece. "I'm with Roman and Javier and they have a plan to get us out from under Isaac."

"Do it, babe," Marcy said and she met Isaac's angry gaze. "Do what you gotta do. It doesn't matter what they do to me—stop this little turd. He has no army—he has Boris and Kite, that's it. We're at 432 Charlie Court—"

Isaac yanked the phone from her hand. What was wrong with these people? To Canaan, he said, "So that's how it is, huh? You don't care if we hurt your woman?"

Isaac nodded to Boris who spun the Rabbit around roughly and smacked her hard across the face. She yelped once and fell silent.

"Master Isaac," Canaan said, his tone only slightly elevated, "Are you feeling crazy yet? You sound crazy."

Isaac growled with fury and handed the phone to Boris. "Keep that line open and show this Rabbit you're a better husband than Canaan ever was. Show her over, and over, and over, until she understands. Got it?"

Boris nodded and as he filled his fist with the Rabbit's frizzy hair, he grinned and said into the phone, "I always had a hard spot for redheads."

Isaac wished he could laugh, but he was too furious. He stormed out of the room instead and screamed.

▼▼

Javier grasped Canaan's bicep and swiped the cell phone from his hand. As he disconnected the call, he caught Canaan's molten gaze.

"She'll be okay, Canaan, she's *strong*," Javier said, his urgent tone fueled by the growing threat in the Elder's eyes. Canaan wasn't assuaged. His every muscle tensed and Roman instinctively stepped in front of Simon should he start swinging.

"Canaan!" Javier shouted, but the Elder had come unhinged.

"Take him downstairs," Roman said quietly, his posture reminiscent of his Elder behavior of long ago.

Javier pulled Canaan by the arm toward the basement door as he hurled curses in a series of staccato shouts. Javier's newfound physical strength came in handy as they reached the cellar entrance and Canaan attempted to bolt away.

"RELEASE ME!" he roared and yanked Javier off his feet when he refused to let go.

"GET. IN. HERE!" Javier said and successfully jerked the Elder through and slammed closed the door.

"Javier, stop it!" Canaan growled and wrestled all the way to the polished cement floor. Shaking violently, he wiggled out of Javier's grip and spun to face him in a crouch. "Don't do that again! Keep your hands off me, I'm warning you!" he shouted.

"Get a hold of yourself," Javier said in an elevated voice, no longer shouting. "You did great up there. You were perfect."

"OH? And now Marcy is expendable?" Canaan snarled, still facing Javier wrestler-style. "I do my dance, the token Rakum Elder, and my beloved takes my punishment?" He shook his head slowly back and forth. "I don't think so." Canaan's shoulders dropped a fraction. *"Boris has my princess..."* he whispered, the pain in his face more than Javier could bear.

"Canaan, please," Javier persuaded, not knowing what else to say. The Elder had executed the phone call flawlessly, befuddling Isaac more than they could have hoped and Kilmeade's input had been essential. Javier stepped up to Canaan and gently cupped his thick neck. "We now have what we need. You heard him. Kilmeade gave us its name—*Zahdone*. We have its name," Javier stressed and Canaan dropped his chin.

"What? What?" he muttered, not truly trying to comprehend.

"Zahdone, the demon of pride and arrogance. Now we know what has possessed The Last," Javier said close to his ear, caressing the back of his head through his sweaty curls. "It's not Ta'avah. *Now we have its name.*"

Canaan exhaled slowly and peeked at Javier, head still down. "Why do you keep saying that?"

"We're dealing with demons; we use their names against them... *I can command him by name,*" Javier whispered. "It gives us a huge advantage."

Canaan blinked. "Does Zahdone know your spirit by name?"

"Oh, sure," Javier said with a victorious grin, "but he would never say it—my Spirit's *very* name expels demons from this earth." Javier gave Canaan's neck a squeeze. "You have done great."

"Javier, no, I've hurt my Marcy," Canaan said, broke free and turned away. "She needs me and I am more useless than ever."

Javier followed him and re-established tender contact with the back of his neck. "Canaan, I have a confession."

"What," he mumbled.

"I could translate there, right now," Javier whispered. Canaan rotated his face, careful not to dislodge Javier's hand. "I feel the surge from our blood swap. I'm positive I could go there right now..."

"But," Canaan said, discerning there was more.

"But I'm not *supposed* to," Javier whispered. "It's not time."

"What the hell are you talking about?" Canaan asked in the same octave. "The time is to stop Boris from ravaging my wife." Shaking off the hand on his neck, Canaan took Javier's shoulders in his fists.

"I can go, but the consequences are steep," Javier said, his voice saddened by the anguish in Canaan's face. "If I go now, I can stop Boris, but not Isaac. I could even get her out of there. But I will miss my shot to defeat Isaac. Forever."

"You can't know that!" Canaan replied growing louder with each word.

Javier nodded. "I can and I do." Javier held the underside of his wrist into view. "The blood of the Fathers comes with visions and prophecy. I can save Marcy, but I won't be able to disable Isaac."

The truth of his words took several long seconds to sink into Canaan's understanding. A Father's vision was always accurate; there had never been an argument to that fact. It was useless to try to explain how Javier *really* knew—by listening to God.

"Damn it all to hell," he whispered and closed his eyes. Suddenly, Canaan snapped to attention. "Stop Boris telepathically!" Canaan shook Javier's shoulders. "The Fathers had us all on a mental leash and you carry Isaac's blood! You can do what they did. Try!"

"Yes, but..."

"Javier, a Father can contact any Rakum he focuses on. You can do it. Picture Boris's face. Call him. Make him stop!"

Javier gave it some thought. He remembered Boris's face, but he didn't recall his distinct smell. As a Rakum grunt, his telepathy was lacking, but when it worked, it worked by his target's aroma.

"Dammit, Javier!" Canaan said and shook him again. "Hurry!"

"Okay, okay," Javier said sharply and escaped Canaan's grip. He looked to the low ceiling and called up Boris's face. What he thought would take several seconds, happened instantly—six-foot-six Boris and a screaming Marcy Haddle tangled against the wall of a brightly-lit great room.

"BORIS, RELEASE HER!" Javier roared in his mind and the Rakum grunt responded instantaneously by pushing away from his victim. Her blouse was ripped and her blood dripped from his slack mouth.

"What? What?" he repeated, spinning in half-circles, looking wild-eyed around him. By the wall, Marcy Haddle dropped to her knees, rolled several feet away and jogged out of view.

"BORIS, SLEEP!" Javier commanded and the huge Rakum fell to the hardwood floor with a thundering thud. "He's down," Javier hissed to Canaan and sought to follow Marcy by the aroma of Canaan's mark.

She had bolted to a side exit with no opposition. Javier took a precursory impression of the entire house and didn't sense the other occupants. Back on task, Javier witnessed her run into the night and take off down the driveway.

Still watching her in the hazy transmission, he whispered to Canaan, "Call the Tuscaloosa PD and send them to..." he followed Marcy as she left the grounds of her new prison and dodged a passing car to run down an adjacent street. Javier forced his inner-eye to read the signage. "Send them to the corner of Petunia and Berry Lane," he said to Canaan who had already dialed 911 and given them the address of the house.

"Marcy, Marcy, it's Javier," he said, not knowing if a mortal could hear him, or even knowing how any of it worked with his new abilities. The woman ran on. Javier grabbed Canaan's wrist as he spoke to the emergency phone operator. The Elder had given the information and was hanging up.

"Canaan, speak to Marcy," he whispered, hoping to use a tactile boost to the Elder's advantage.

Canaan needed no additional encouragement. *"Cee! Cee, baby..."* he sent silently. *"The police are coming."*

"Canaan? Oh, God!" she said and went to her knees at the dusty curb. Javier watched her through the filmy transmission as she covered her mouth with both hands. "Thank God, thank God!" she said.

"Cee, use the police—ruin Isaac's day place," Canaan said.

Javier heard police sirens and when Marcy waved the cruiser toward her, he brought his mind back to Simon's basement.

"Oh, God," he said and collapsed onto the chaise. "My head! Canaan," he muttered. "My head!"

Javier pressed his palms into his temples and massaged heavily. The pain induced by the previous exercise was worse than any migraine contracted as a mortal.

"Canaan!" he shouted and didn't see the Elder approach and cover his hands with his own. The pounding lessened with every beat of his heart until it disappeared completely. Javier exhaled with relief and opened his eyes to see Canaan bent over him, hands still upon his, a cautious grin on his face.

"It lives?" Canaan said and withdrew his hands. "I owe you. That woman has endured enough because of me. Thank you."

Javier clambered to his feet and dusted off his slacks. "You don't owe me anything," Javier said and ran his fingers through his hair. "I liked that part at the end—use the authorities to send Isaac and his Rakum into a panic." With that, Javier caught Canaan's eye and inhaled sharply. "I gave Boris an incredible jolt. He won't come-to for hours."

"Dammit," Canaan muttered and turned away.

Javier sighed. "I didn't think."

"There wasn't *time* to think," Canaan said, his back to Javier. "You did what you needed to do." Canaan cursed and shook his head. "That idiot was only obeying orders. Maybe I'm getting soft, but there's just not enough of us left to let him die."

"Isaac might get him out of there before the cops..." Javier began and then stopped. "No, I didn't sense him around."

Canaan turned. "Kilmeade!" he said. He put out his hand to Javier. "Your blood is working on me, too. I know I could reach Kilmeade with a boost..."

Javier stepped up and took Canaan's fingers in his. Canaan closed his eyes and Javier did, too.

"Kilmeade!" the Elder shouted. Happening in an instant, Kilmeade appeared vividly as he sat in a black SUV watching crowds of people mill outside the car. Canaan said his name again and Kilmeade looked up.

"Can't get enough of me, I see," he said and smiled, his cautious manner belying he already intuited something was wrong.

"There's been some excitement. Boris is incapacitated in the house and the police are headed there now. Can you get him to safety?" Canaan said in a rush. "We had to save Marcy from him just now, but dammit— do we have to lose another brother to Isaac's foolishness?"

Javier read similar concern for the wayward Boris in Kilmeade's eyes as he heard the tale. Javier marveled at the spectacle: the Rakum's last two Elders revealing an extraordinary and selfless allegiance to their kind. Boris had just attacked Marcy and was barely prevented from raping her, and here Canaan was trying to save his life. And there was Kilmeade, no doubt mistreated by the inferior Rakum and just as determined to see him to safety and not burned up in a hospital room at sunrise.

"*Truly a wonder,*" Javier found himself saying to God in his heart. "*These two can't be too far from You to be saved, right?*"

Next to Kilmeade, behind the wheel, Rafael did not hear or see any of what transpired; he remained quiet and watched Kilmeade's profile.

"Head toward the house, but be careful," Kilmeade said to his companion. "The human authority has been sent there."

Kilmeade returned his attention to Javier and Canaan. "I'll get him to safety," he said and winked, not hiding his weariness. "I'll have to wing it. Don't watch," he said to Javier. "In the thick of the fight, I'll put a Rakum's life over a mortal's without a thought."

"Do what you have to, but Boris doesn't need to die," Canaan said.

"I agree," Kilmeade said and disconnected the contact.

Javier was silent and Canaan flopped down on the basement chaise.

"What now? It's more than four hours to Tuscaloosa by car and you're the only one that can translate there," Canaan said, his mind far away. "And less than seven hours till sun-up. Isaac will need a light-tight place."

"I will go alone, Canaan," Javier said quietly.

"The hell?" Canaan said and sat up.

"I'm serious," Javier nodded. "I have a few very strong advantages." He held up his pointer finger. "The Spirit of God is in me to cast out Zahdone," he said and held up his second and third fingers. "The same God gave me physical strength to defeat him in the flesh, and three, I can fight in the sun." Javier grinned. "I only need to locate him and from listening to Beryl earlier, I believe there's a way we can get his exact location."

Canaan frowned. "But alone? All of us, against Isaac, tomorrow. We'd have all night. Leave here at sundown, get there before eleven and have eight hours to fix everything."

"He will go underground by then," Javier said. "He will hole up and get the advantage." Javier shook his head. "No, it needs to be now while he's off-balance. You can help me find him. All the Rakum can help me. Let's go upstairs."

Javier didn't wait for more discussion. He hurried up the steps and Canaan shuffled behind him, grumbling.

51

"**M**arcy is safe," Canaan said, "and Javier has a plan. Take it away, superman."

Javier didn't expect Canaan to apologize to the others for his earlier behavior and he didn't. The Elder dropped onto the couch and gestured to Polly and Guap to join him.

"Thank you, Canaan," he said with gentle sarcasm. In as few words as possible, he told the crowd what had transpired in the basement. When he reached the end, where he told them he would go alone, tonight, the one he expected to object did so immediately.

"Absolutely not!" Roman said and rose to walk to where Javier sat. Javier stood and prepared to be lectured. "Why would you go by yourself, risking yourself when we *need* you in order to finish this? If he kills you, we're sunk. God has raised you up in this condition to defeat Isaac. We agreed on that already!"

Javier nodded, holding his tongue. Roman saw right through him.

"YOU'RE NOT GOING BY YOURSELF," he shouted and looked at Canaan. "I can't believe you're going along with this!"

Canaan shrugged and conceded with a grin. "He's the anomaly," he said and elbowed Polly and Guap who chuckled.

"You said you're going to cast out Isaac's demon by name, is that what you said?" David asked, concern filling his face and leaning forward on his chair. Javier nodded, ready to get the show rolling, but David had more to say. "In the Bible, demons fled every time Jesus commanded them, but that wasn't always the case with His disciples. What if it doesn't come out? You'll be all alone."

Javier sent David a sympathetic grin. "I have to do what I feel God wants me to do. I gotta trust Him all the way." Javier looked at Roman for confirmation. "If I doubt Him at any time, we're lost. Roman, help me out." Javier watched Roman's face. He was angry that Javier insisted on going alone, but he also was the only one that knew the extent of the torture he suffered under the monster inside.

"No matter, to me it seems foolhardy," David frowned and leaned back again. "You have one, two, three, four Rakum that could go with you. Isaac only has one now—Kite, right?"

"It's the death wish," Beryl said leaning his body toward Simon who sat beside him. "Javier wants to be a martyr."

"Is that right, Javier?" Simon asked in a soft voice. "Do you expect to die? Are you planning to give your life for us? Is that what God has in mind?"

"Hey, ya'll stop it," Javier said finally. "I do *not* have a death wish, I do *not* think I'm going to die, and I'm *not* taking any of you with me. End of discussion. This is what we're going to do." Javier crossed to the center of the room. To Roman, he lowered his chin and said, "Trust me. I need you to trust me. I know what I'm doing."

Roman shook his head. "It's not right."

"Elder Canaan," Javier said, giving the man his title in front of the group, "I need you on my right." The Elder stood and got into position. He then gestured to Polly, Guap and Beryl who stood and joined the rough circle around Javier. Then he looked at Roman. "You, David and Simon pray for us, okay? Pray we are successful."

Roman nodded and David asked, "What are you about to do?"

"The five of us are going to locate Isaac," Javier said and turned back to the Rakum. "It will take all of us, because he's a Father and a demon; he knows how to hide and how to block us. The thing he doesn't have is what I do—the power of God right here inside me."

"Go for it, Javie," Canaan said. "Let's do it."

"Let's connect," Javier said and placed a hand on Canaan's shoulder on his right and Beryl's on his left. Each Rakum followed suit and Javier said aloud, "Beryl, how did you and Meryl do that projection thing? What's the method?"

Beryl raised his eyebrows, thought a moment and said, "You need a starting point. You said you incapacitated Boris in a room—you could start there."

Javier nodded. "Okay, then what?"

"Imagine yourself standing there, and if it works, you will feel like you're actually there. You can start looking for him telepathically, like you would any of us in this room."

"Easy-peasy," Canaan said and squeezed Javier's shoulder. "Guap and

Polly, Javier will use you as a battery. Beryl, walk with him. I'll lend my power and be on hand if I can help."

The Rakum all agreed and Javier sent up a prayer for help. He looked at Roman one last time and his old friend and former Elder sent him a nod. Javier nodded back. Four Rakum and an Anomaly closed their eyes and began their search.

Picturing the place he'd dropped Boris to the ground, he waited to see what would happen. In the space of a minute, he could walk in the room Boris had occupied. His body was in Athens, but his mind did an amazing job of filling in three-dimensional details.

He became aware of Beryl beside him when the Rakum said to the air, "Where is Isaac?" To Javier, he said, "Keep hold of my hand."

And Javier did.

▼▼

The entire neighborhood flashed red, white, and blue, as several police cruisers, two unmarked cars, and an ambulance unloaded police and EMS responders to Maury's house. Kilmeade had Rafael park two lots away so watching from more than a hundred yards they would arouse no suspicion.

"I'll say one thing for this new life," Kilmeade said to Rafael with a smirk, "it's not boring."

Rafael agreed with a tired grin. His stomach rumbled and he chuckled. "I forgot to eat." He leaned back in the driver's seat and rubbed his middle.

"One of those unluckies will help you there," Kilmeade said, watching three attendants wrestle the gurney as they approached the waiting van. "Boris is huge. Look at them struggle," he said with a laugh.

"I'm glad Javier's on our side," Rafael said, not completely joking. "He called you telepathically. He called and put Boris out like an Father. Something pretty bizarre is going on inside that guy."

Kilmeade said nothing, not interested in digging into Javier's abilities or where they came from. Their God was real, He had spoken to both of them through Damien, He said He *loved* them. What did that mean? And why did it mean anything? What bothered Kilmeade the most was that once he heard that Javier's God loved him and considered him *a son,* he wanted that more than anything in the world.

It was insane. Rakum don't experience familial ties. Rakum don't have *sons* or *fathers* to love. Rakum didn't *love* at all. Kilmeade halted his thoughts, afraid he'd swap sides and be human by sunup.

Rafael's phone rang and he put it to his ear. Kilmeade heard Iago on the other end giving an update of their location. They were safe, tucked away in a hotel awaiting Roman's next move. Kilmeade had taken a risk, but as soon as they pulled away from Isaac's tonight, he had instructed Rafa to call Iago back and tell him to stay with Roman. When his pet hung up, he gave Kilmeade a relieved nod. Two less souls to worry over for a little while.

The ambulance pulled away from the house and Kilmeade watched them pass, headed to the hospital. They had a single escort and he counted only one officer inside. He tipped his chin to Rafa, who pulled in after to casually tail them down the main drag.

"In two miles they'll turn onto Prospect Street," Kilmeade said. "That's where we'll stop them."

Rafael nodded, his expression grim. Kilmeade didn't fault him; neither of them enjoyed wasting human lives, but priorities sometimes dictated it. Kilmeade needn't explain the plan; they had both overcome mortals before. Rafael offered to take out the cop and leave the medical crew to Kilmeade.

"No, let me have the cop," Kilmeade replied. He could take a bullet more easily than Rafa, although it wouldn't come to that. Overcoming a single police officer would take little effort.

Rafa's heartrate increased with the excitement of the hunt as he followed their mark onto Prospect. The street had a single residence that sat dark and quiet. Rafael revved the Lexus' engine and sped around the cop to ram the ambulance hard. The van traveled forward a few yards and then gave in to his pressure and rolled into the culvert, glass and plastic shattering on the cement.

Rafael was out of the driver's seat and in the shadows before Kilmeade opened his door. Kilmeade grinned. They had spent several evenings together, but this would be the first time he saw the pup in action.

Not wholly distracted from his own duties, Kilmeade dropped into the dark shadow of their SUV and watched the police officer call for backup on his shoulder mic, his sidearm out and ready. The man didn't yet see Rafael or Kilmeade and crept toward the ambulance, shouting instructions in an authoritative voice.

Kilmeade wasted no more time. He rushed the cop from behind and disarmed him with a vicious blow to the wrist. Bones shattered as the pistol clattered harmlessly to the asphalt. Kilmeade pulled the man into the ditch with a hand over his mouth.

"Shhh, shhh," Kilmeade whispered in his ear. He didn't *have* to kill him. It wasn't mandatory. Kilmeade smiled with the fun of the hunt, holding the man tightly against his chest. So rarely did the Rakum tussle with humans this way. Before Last Assembly, they had Cows for blood and were proud to remain under the radar of the mortal authority; for centuries they'd mastered hiding in plain sight. The cop struggled, kicked, and fought, but he was no closer to being free.

Kilmeade took two more steps into the dark culvert and watched Rafael snap the neck of a female attendant who was screaming with blind terror. The driver lay in the ditch and his pulse did not thump in Kilmeade's ear.

"Look at my pup," Kilmeade whispered to the policeman. "He can be deadly."

The cop grew still, watching Rafael stab the last remaining EMS responder's neck. Rafael fixed his mouth to the wound and the police officer resumed his panicked thrashing. Monitoring his output, Kilmeade sent a jolt of electricity through the man until he was still. He lowered him onto the ground, the man's strong heart pumping happily along. *One will live, at least,* he thought and grinned.

Within seconds, Kilmeade had Boris free of the gurney straps and carried him to the backseat of the SUV. When the Rakum was folded neatly inside, he turned to call Rafa. His pet was already behind the wheel starting the engine.

Kilmeade smiled. "I sure wish I'd had you with me decades ago," he said.

With a grin, Rafael wiped his chin. "I'm feeling much better now."

"I bet," Kilmeade said and braced himself as Rafael sped away from the accident scene. "Take this road four miles and when you see the hospital, pull into the doctor's parking lot. There's a manhole cover there," Kilmeade said, flipping internet pages on Rafa's iPhone.

"Oh, fun," Rafael said, his grin falling.

"All part of the adventure," Kilmeade replied and turned to see Boris, still unconscious across the backseat. "I'll have to revive him to get him underground."

"He'll be pissed," Rafael said, mostly to himself.

"But alive." Kilmeade shimmied around to reach him from the front seat. As Rafael piloted the car to their destination, Kilmeade reached for Boris's sweater and used it to pull him upright. His heart sounded good, but he had no R.E.M. He was truly out, comatose. Kilmeade made a noise of surprise and Rafael glanced back.

"Can you do it?" he asked.

"I can do anything I set my mind to," Kilmeade said with a smile.

"Don't forget, I'm very powerful."

Rafael grinned. "Yes, Master, you are. The finest Elder I've ever met."

"Good answer." Kilmeade winked. "Now, Boris. Come back to the light," he said with a chuckle.

Placing his palms on either side of the big man's bald head, he concentrated on bringing him back. It was to be a combination cure, rejuvenation and healing both, as Javier had inadvertently fried the Rakum's synapses.

Three minutes into the work at hand, Rafael had reached the hospital and slowed to pick his way to the physician's lot. Kilmeade released Boris's head and shoved his body between the front seats with a grunt to pile into the back on top of him. Now straddling his lap with Boris's head lolled back, Kilmeade bit down hard on his own wrist, ripping open a wide laceration. Once he had pinched the huge Rakum's lips apart, he forced his blood into Boris's mouth.

Immediately, the brute sputtered to life, spitting and shaking his head. He made an attempt to be free, but stopped all movement when he saw who held him down.

"Master!"

Kilmeade gave him a curt nod. No matter what Isaac was to the grunt, without the boy wonder around, Boris recognized an Elder's superiority.

"Elder Kilmeade, I didn't mean—what happened? Where am I? What's going on?"

Astride his lap, Kilmeade put his left hand on Boris's shoulder and rubbed his head with the right. "You were unconscious, arrested by police, and being carted away in an ambulance. Rafael and I rescued you."

Rafael parked the car and turned in his seat. He nodded to Boris and watched Kilmeade for instructions.

"There's a manhole fifteen yards to that tree line. According to the internet..." Kilmeade paused and crossed his fingers in Boris's face. "...the access goes down thirty feet and the tunnel travels five miles. We'll have to hunch over, but we can walk. We'll remain there until sundown."

Boris nodded. "Thank you, Master," he said. Kilmeade patted his head and crawled off him.

"Thank Elder Canaan," he replied as Rafael opened the door for them to climb out. "When you see him, thank Elder Canaan."

Boris said he would and followed Kilmeade and Rafael to the sewer access. It would be a stinky, wet, and unpleasant day down there, but beggars never could be choosers.

Isaac could not believe his eyes.

Again? he marveled as a police cruiser pulled away from his new Day place, leaving another behind, idling and empty. Well-hidden in the neighbor's chin-high manicured shrubbery, he watched the front of the Cow's house. When he turned the Rabbit over to Boris an hour ago, he'd been beside himself with rage. He had walked up the driveway, and before he knew it, he had gone more than a mile. The fresh air had done him good, but to return to see the best safehouse ever created ruined by the invasion of human authorities?

How did this happen? Isaac asked the air and got no answer. He searched for Boris and nothing. He called for Kite.

"Yes, Master," the grunt replied instantly.

"Police are raiding Maury's house!" he shouted in his mind. Kite did not respond, so Isaac yelled at him again. *"How did this happen? Why weren't you there? What is taking you so long?"*

"Master, I..." Kite fumbled for an answer. "The attorney just finished. I was—"

"WORTHLESS!" Isaac interjected, sending his thoughts accompanied by a punishing electric jolt. *"IMBECILE! You are more than WORTHLESS!"*

Isaac shimmied backwards the way he had come and when free of the prickly branches, he turned and strode quickly away from the direction of the house. The moon was full and the clear suburban sky revealed every star. Supernatural sight was unnecessary and Isaac found himself wishing for a raincloud to obscure his escape. He looked to the cloudless sky. Could Zahdone control the weather? Isaac thought he might be able to, but he needed to get to safety. He needed to hide. There would be time later to discover all of his amazingness, but for now—he needed help.

"Come get me! I need you to pick me up!" he shouted at Kite. He got no response and this time it wasn't that the Rakum was too stupid to think of an answer. He was out cold. "GET UP! GET UP!" Isaac shouted at first silently, but then aloud in the moonlit pasture. Kite was down for the count. Isaac cursed Zahdone and immediately took it back.

"I can't curse myself!" he sputtered angrily. Jumping up and down with his fists clenched, he yelled sharply for Kilmeade in his mind. *"Kilmeade! Come pick me up!"*

No response. The Elder didn't hear him. Isaac tried again—the line was dead.

The air grew still and the hairs rose on the back of Isaac's neck. Spinning two full circles, he took in his surroundings, squinting, trying to simultaneously view both dimensions. Shortly, he caught a glimpse of Javier d'Millier impossibly present in two places at once. In perfect detail, Isaac saw the former Rakum standing in the room where he last saw Boris as well as in another room Isaac had never seen before.

How is he doing that? Isaac's heart sounded in his ears. *Isn't he mortal?* And d'Millier was seeking Zahdone, calling his name between the worlds. Isaac severed their connection tossing up a block as the Fathers taught him years ago. No matter what Javier had become, he would not be able to see Isaac again telepathically.

Spooked and alone, Isaac took off running for the next tree line, the estates in Maury's neighborhood three and four acres each. "What is going on? Zahdone, what is happening?"

Nothing.

Of course, nothing. *I am Zahdone. I have to ask myself!*

Isaac reached cover and hunkered down in the shadows. No one chased him, but it was only a few hours until sunup. Priority number one—find shelter. Oh, where was Boris?

Calm, calm, calm... Isaac hugged himself caressing his own arms. Elder Kilmeade had tried to teach him to control his urges, control his temper. Elder Canaan had tried last week and tonight to teach him how to lead and be admired for leadership well done. Why couldn't he learn?

Calming his mind, he sought to see as Zahdone sees. In less than a moment, the air around him filled with wispy spirits, black, gray, some an orangey brown. These shapeless entities moved with sentience, yet did not look at him or acknowledge his presence. Zahdone's minions, he realized. "What happened at my house?" he asked them and as a unit, the multitude agitated into action.

"Javier d'Millier," an untold number of ethereal voices chanted. *"Empowered by Elohim. Rakum Boris. Disabled. Female—gone."*

Isaac's bottom lip poked out and he hugged himself tighter. "Damn that Javier. Damn Elohim," he mumbled.

White light filtered through the dancing wisps at his spoken word and Isaac shielded his eyes. A dozen shining beings—Elohim's angels—looked down on him, arms folded, scowls on their horrid faces. Isaac rose to his feet and bit his thumb at them. Turning calmly, he walked to the curb and shoved his hands in his pockets. The idiotic white beings followed him, wordlessly judging his every movement. He fingered some cardstock in his pocket and fished it out.

Stu Loudon,

The Turnip Trucks,

Lexington, Kentucky.

With a phone number! Isaac punched the number on his cell and by the time the Cow picked up on his end, the nutty white-light spirits were gone. Isaac's face filled with a grin at the sound of Stu's voice.

"Allo? You got Stuart," he said, the Aussie accent amplified by the tinny connection.

"Hey, Stu, it's Isaac," Isaac said and paused to discover, if anything, what the Cow knew about him and his role among the Rakum.

"Isaac?" the Aussie said, but his mind was working it out. *"Isaac, The Last?"* he whispered after a second and Isaac imagined him hunkered over, guarding the mouthpiece with his hand.

"In the flesh," Isaac said cheerfully.

"Oh. My. God," Stuart said, punctuating each syllable.

"Yes, I will be your god," Isaac said with a forced laugh. "Hey, you wanna help me out?"

"Master Isaac! Anything!" Stuart cooed, the tide of his emotions rolling into his voice. "Whatever I have is yours!"

Isaac giggled for Stu to hear and he fiddled with the phone until he was able to snap a photo of his face. When he had it, he attached it to Stu's phone number and hit the arrow.

"I just sent you a photo. Tell me when you get it."

"Ohmygod, yes, Master, *ohmygod,"* Stuart whispered. Then, "Master Isaac! You are so beautiful! OHMYGOD!" Stuart said and Isaac laughed.

"You want to meet me?" he asked.

"Please! More than anything in the world. Please. Please!" the Cow cried into the phone.

"Okay, I am coming there right now. If you want me to come directly to you, I need you to stare at my photo and say my name, over and over." Isaac paused to let his instructions sink in. The Cow had an open mind and an open spirit, he was eager to please and was no trouble to locate geographically. If he wanted to translate to Stuart's town, he'd just go. But Isaac needed a driver. He waited for Stuart to speak.

"Anything you say, Master, is my command!" he finally said. "Your name—just say, *Isaac?*"

"Say, Isaac-Zahdone, Isaac-Zahdone, Isaac-Zahdone," Isaac replied. "Chant it, let me hear you."

"Yes, Master!" Stu said excitedly. *"Isaac-Zahdone, Isaac-Zahdone, Isaac-Zahdone."*

"Good, Stuart," Isaac said quietly into the mouthpiece, "stare at my face, chant my name, and wish in your heart that I was there with you..." Isaac grinned at the last part—it would make the Cow feel special, but of course, it was nonsense. He only needed the concentration; the photo and the mantra helped the target focus.

"Isaac-Zahdone, Isaac-Zahdone, Isaac-Zahdone," the Cow gatherer repeated in a lilting voice, made all the more sweet with his foreign inflections.

Isaac listened to his adoring voice even longer than necessary before he allowed the lightness in his middle to pull him to the man's side. Father Damien had told him how it was done, and finally, Isaac-Zahdone had the life experience *and* necessity to make it happen. He didn't intend to, but he blinked, and at the re-opening of his eyes, he stood before Stu Loudon in Tuscaloosa, Alabama.

"Oh, god!" Stuart startled at Isaac's sudden presence and then fell to his knees. "Oh, Master! Kill me now! I can't handle your... your..."

Isaac grinned. "You're funny, Stuart," he told the man and put out his fingers to pull him to his feet. The Cow instead covered them with sloppy kisses. Isaac laughed. "No, dummy, get up, and look upon your master."

Stuart Loudon clambered to his feet, maintaining a humble stance by stooping is six-foot frame. His eyes darted to and away from Isaac's, and Isaac reached out to hold both of his hands in his own.

"Stuart, you may look upon me," Isaac said, chin tilted up. He fluttered his long blond eyelashes and the Cow dared an extended glance. "Another Cow saw me and didn't know I was a Rakum," Isaac said when the man would look at him more than three seconds. "How 'bout you? What do you see?"

"You look like an angel, Master," Stuart said in a soft voice. "I would know you as a Rakum, as the leader of the Rakum, as god of all who love your people."

"Wow," Isaac said, truly impressed. He dropped the Cow's hands and Stuart whipped off his coat and unbuttoned his sleeve. Isaac's shook his head. "No, I don't take blood from mortals, Stuart. I'm above that."

Stuart's face fell, but he nodded. "Oh, of course, you wouldn't, no, you are above in all ways..."

"Exactly," Isaac said nodding. "But I can do this for you," he said and reached up to Stuart's face. He stood a head taller, but with the Cow hunched over, Isaac easily fit both palms to his cheeks. His skin on Stuart's face gave the man immense pleasure and he closed his eyes. To seal their bond, he sent the willing Cow a mental visual. It would translate into whatever Stuart wanted most, but would never get. Isaac suppressed a grin when the Cow imagined himself naked with Isaac holding his face.

That was Cows for you.

Isaac let the man fantasize several minutes, the entire episode meaningless to him personally—a Rakum didn't reach sexual maturity until age one hundred, and he was many, many years from reaching that milestone.

Not too far away, Javier d'Millier and a crowd of apostates plotted against him. Javier had even been able to mentally affect his favorite, Boris. Isaac exhaled at the thought of harm coming to the only Rakum he actually liked. He let the Cow Stuart dream and he made plans.

52

Athens, GA
November 12th, 11 p.m.

Sitting in the passenger seat of Stuart's pickup truck, Isaac watched the house. If Stuart hadn't told him which one it was, he never would have found it. Every Rakum on the premises was invisible to him. Invisible to his Rakum senses and invisible to Zahdone's minions. Infuriated as much as frustrated, Isaac did his best not to take it out on Stuart. The more time he spent with the Cow, the more he wanted to end him.

"You want me to smoke 'em out?" the Aussie asked, aware by Isaac's complaints that there existed a barrier. "I have some petrol in the bed of the truck."

Isaac liked the idea of destroying the Cow's lovely property, but such excitement would bring firefighters. "No, idiot," Isaac hissed and turned his face to Stuart's. "I want that Javier to come out. By himself."

Isaac pondered. How could he get him out? He had no allies. As soon as he finished petting Stuart, he scoured the immediate area for Rakum presence. None of the Brethren resided there or were traveling through. He looked back at the Aussie—the eager Cow was all he had.

"Okay," Isaac said and looked at the dark sky. "I'll go in there."

"Master! There's eight of them!" Stuart reached for Isaac's forearm, but remembered the rules and withdrew his hand before making contact. "Four of them are Rakum, I told you." The Aussie's eyes filled with concern and Isaac exited the truck in a huff.

"There could be a hundred in there, idiot!" he said in a harsh whisper, walking across the neighbor's yard toward his goal. Stuart followed behind him at a lope. "I am the great Zahdone! I do what I want!"

When he reached the stoop, he stood before the grand double doors. A fake pine wreath hung on each, and a brass knocker marked with a big "M" gleamed with polish. He needed to hear his minions, they screeched and howled at him from their dimension. Before he touched the knocker, he closed his eyes to see them. If he only had more time to figure out his amazingness, he wouldn't be so pensive.

"Don't go in there—wait for them to come out," a myriad of the voices suggested in unison.

Isaac snarled at them to be quiet, but they persisted, even more agitated than before.

"You have no power in there, Elohim! Elohim! LOOK! SEE!"

Remembering how frantic Zahdone's minions became around the white-light beings, Isaac looked for them in the spirit. He might have gasped for Stuart began asking if he could be of help; the entire house glowed bright white with the light beings lined up shoulder to shoulder around the home's brick walls.

"What in the world?" Isaac said aloud and opened his eyes. When he did, he was looking into Elder Canaan's face.

"Master Isaac!" Canaan said and yanked him into the house with a fist full of his shirt. "Look, everybody! We have a special guest!"

Unable to prevent it, Isaac was tugged through a gigantic foyer and into a large room with vaulted ceilings where seven others stood chatting. He recognized them all, but because of the muted state of his abilities in the angel-protected house, he couldn't read a soul in the room. The only happy note was the horror on the faces of those frightened by his unexpected appearance. Maybe he could fake it... Isaac shook off Canaan's hand.

"Don't touch me!" he shouted and shuffled away. "This ends NOW!" Isaac made his expression as fierce as possible, but the element of surprise had worn off; one by one, each face regarded him with curiosity instead of fear.

I have a pocketknife... One of the mortals in the room would be the weak link. Isaac picked him out and awaited his chance. It was going to get ugly, but he would get out.

"He's in over his head, Rah-keel," Ta'avah said smiling. A hundred spirits traveled with Rah-keel and Zara when he called them this most recent time. They witnessed Isaac traveling *their* way—via the intra-dimensional highway known as the *Mobius continuum*. If he hadn't entered their plane, they never would have been aware of his movements. Now Ta'avah knew where to go to apprehend the vessel he wanted most.

"You will be rewarded for this, my brothers," he told the wispy shapes he saw in his mind. You start choosing your vessels and when I am inside the boy, I will make sure you sit at my right and left."

The spirits faded away, arguing over which Rakum to inhabit. Ta'avah inside Eric piloted the stolen Kia toward Athens, Georgia. He had meticulously repaired the Eric flesh's skull, but the young man remained comatose. His parents were being called to decide on whether or not to pull the plug, and as soon as the medical staff left the body alone long enough, Ta'avah expertly animated him and exited the hospital.

Now that he was less than twenty minutes from the address of Javier d'Millier's Cow, he so much wanted to brag to Elohim. Brag on how once again, His plot to ruin a mighty prince's plan had failed. But he didn't. Ta'avah-Eric drove on, adhering to all traffic laws, watching for police, and planning a glorious future.

▼▼

The initial shock of seeing Isaac mere moments before he translated to confront him ended in short order. Javier was the first to speak when Canaan yanked the kid into the room.

"Isaac Akaron," he said and took a single step out of the circle the group had formed before The Last's arrival. "You were not invited, nor are you welcome." Javier had a flash in his mind—a vision of a thousand brilliant beings standing guard around the estate like an Army of God. He softened his gaze, his apprehension gone. "And you have no power here."

Isaac looked at the faces surrounding him and Javier sensed that slowly, every man in the room picked up on the kid's reduced power.

"Elder Canaan," Isaac said then, dropped his shoulders, and clambered to the Elder's side. He grasped the Rakum's muscular arm and hugged it close. "Something's happened to me. Please, don't let them hurt me."

Canaan chortled, but didn't shake him off. "Fool me once, pretty boy," the Elder said and sent Javier a wink. "Here's your opponent. A baby Rakum scared to death."

"I don't get it," David piped up from the back of the room. "What's going on?"

"It's the Anomaly and his voodoo," Polly said with a cautious grin.

"Oh, the *voodoo* that *you* do, Javier!" Guap added with boisterous gusto.

"Elder Canaan," Isaac whispered to Canaan. *"I need to leave. Please, help me get out of here."*

Javier heard every word, as would the Rakum in the room, but he couldn't let that happen. The experiment Ta'avah began so long ago had come to an end.

"You have to face the music now, little buddy," Canaan gently told him. "You're a Rakum. Don't be so pitiful. Take your punishment. Enjoy it. If you'd been discipled properly, you'd know how to do that. Damn shame you never graduated First Ritual."

Roman moved within reach of Javier and spoke in his ear. "Javie, if this Rakum has had no Ritual Training, all of his power is spiritual and I think his spirit is paralyzed."

"I think you're right," Javier responded, holding Isaac's gaze. The boy's huge blue eyes were larger than ever, shining with anxiety. What did he think they were going to do to him? *What am I going to do? Behead him?* Javier turned sideways to Roman.

"He is possessed by Zahdone. What happens when his spirit is cast out?" It never was Javier's concern if Isaac lived, only that he be stopped. Tonight, after all he had seen and heard about the kid, he realized the only sure way to stop him was to end him completely.

"Lay hands on him and assess it," Roman said, still whispering. *"You might hear from God what to do. Listen, speak to his spirit. Find out if there's a soul in there to be saved."*

Javier nodded. As mortals, Simon and David would not have been able to hear Roman whispering, but all of the others had no auditory limitations. Javier mentally gathered various telepathic concerns and questions from the lot and finally he looked at Canaan.

"Well? What do you think?" he sent telepathically, careful to block everyone else from snooping.

"I can hold him still for you," Canaan sent back. *"He's literally shaking, and it's not an act. I think he forgot about that great and mighty Zahdone shit."*

Javier almost grinned, but didn't. He approached Canaan and wrapped his left hand around Isaac's right bicep. A spark jumped between them and Javier didn't let go. Inside, he asked God to guide and help him. Aloud, he said, "Zahdone, prince of the air, I command you in the name of Jesus Christ, Yeshua HaMoshiach[16], to show me when you entered this Rakum. Show me now!"

Javier did not look into Isaac's face, although he noted the boy's eyes had widened. He expected the demonic spirit to comply and it did—within the space of a few seconds, images streamed to him and he focused his

---

[16] (Hebrew) HaMoshiach means "the Messiah." *Yeshua HaMoshiach* translates to Jesus Christ.

attention.

A breeder dying on a table. A baby born dead. High Father Abroghia watching on, but not seeing a black amorphous shape surrounding and then melting into the center of the lifeless newborn. When the new Rakum opened his mouth to take his first breath, Javier broke the contact and returned to Roman a few steps away.

He met Roman's eye and shook his head. *"The baby was born dead,"* he said as quietly as possible.

"What does that mean?" Beryl asked and inched closer, leaving Simon's side for the first time that evening. Polly and Guap also stepped close to hear Javier speak to Roman. Javier glanced at Canaan who still held the boy firmly by one arm. How much should he say aloud? Zahdone didn't need to know his strategy, did he?

Javier opened his mouth to give them an oblique overview when Isaac collapsed onto the hardwood floor. In the millisecond Canaan dropped contact with him to reposition and yank him up, Isaac lunged out of reach and faced the group, his back against the wall.

"The next one who touches me will die," he hissed.

Javier stood furthest away from him now that he ran off, but also against the far wall, David was a mere six feet on the kid's left. From that distance, if Isaac thought to use even his normal Rakum power, he could easily kill any of the humans present. David had his eye on Javier and seemed to be asking what to do. Javier received a flash in his mind of David dead on the glossy hardwood floor and he crossed toward Isaac to draw his attention.

"Isaac, let's you and me take this downstairs," Javier said, now in the center of the room, halfway to the youngest Rakum. Isaac's eyes flicked over to David and he grinned wickedly.

"You think I'm gonna—" he leapt toward David and stood before him, looking into his face. Before the man could flinch, Isaac shoved his chest with both hands and David slammed into the drywall behind him.

"No!" Javier jumped forward and he and Canaan reached David at the same time, each on either side, lowering him carefully to the ground. Behind them, Isaac giggled and resumed his posture against the wall, now a good twenty feet away from where they knelt with the injured man.

"Two broken ribs, punctured lung," Canaan sent telepathically and Javier sensed the barrier he sent up against any other Rakum hearing their conversation.

"Heal him," Javier sent back and stood to face Isaac. "Isaac, come on, I dare you. Come to the basement with me. Are you scared to face me

alone?" Javier said, trying a little juvenile play on the juvenile.

Isaac shook his head. "Javier, your face," he said and laughed into his hand. "It's too wonderful to see that face when I—" Isaac shot off to his right and grabbed Roman around the waist, pinning his arms at his sides. Isaac did not squeeze him any harder than to hold him still and he waited for Javier to speak.

Javier stepped forward, his eye on Roman and his mouth a straight line.

"Finish him quick, Javie," Roman managed in gasps.

Javier's heart jammed into his throat, it would only take Isaac the slightest effort to break his best friend in two and he was unprepared to lose Roman tonight. With an anguished cry, he gained on Isaac at the speed of thought and wrapped his arms around the Rakum's head. Isaac released Roman in surprise and clutched at the muscular arms that now immobilized him and blocked his vision.

Electricity buzzed in Javier's inner ear and he realized Isaac was attempting to send a jolt to his spine. The sensation did not last long; by sheer will, Javier successfully put the danger out. Isaac screamed in fury.

"ZAHDONE! I cast you out in Jesus' name!" Javier shouted in Isaac's ear against his cheek. Isaac's response was to point at Beryl who stood in a protective stance in front of Simon.

"Help me!" he said, and when Beryl only squared his shoulders as if preparing to receive a jolt himself, Isaac screeched like a caged animal. "Beryl! Polly! Guap! Canaan!" he shouted, and as he did, each man hit the floor, holding their heads, writhing in pain.

Javier trained his eyes on Guap who was nearest him. The Rakum's pained expression told him everything he needed to know—Isaac was going to kill all of them with the only trick he knew.

"Father!" Javier prayed in his heart. *"What do I do? What do I do?"* Javier's mind raced as he held firm to Isaac's head. The Rakum kicked and yanked him around, but Javier had fifty pounds on him and because of the anomaly, matched his strength tit for tat.

Like a Rakum.

Javier turned his mind to everything he learned about the powers of the Fathers. He wished Roman could help him remember. He wriggled to his left and caught Roman's eye catching his breath across the room.

"The strength of the Fathers!" he sent with his eyes, his will, his mind, and mouthing the words, hoping his closest friend would interpret at least one of his transmissions.

Roman lowered his chin and focused hard on Javier's gaze. He was going to try to *think* the answer to him. Javier waited—if he listened, he should be able to hear Roman's transmitted thought as well as he had heard Simon earlier. When a few moments elapsed, Javier nodded. *"Go ahead..."*

"Whatever you will, it shall be done."

Whatever you will, it shall be done. Javier repeated the phrase to himself. It didn't make sense in human terms, but by the third repetition, he recalled why it made sense to a Rakum.

"And be quick—Isaac knows this, too."

Javier closed his eyes and willed every attack on the men present to cease immediately. He envisioned a shield of light that fell from the ceiling and enveloped each man, effectively blocking them off from Isaac's efforts. A quick glance found Canaan getting to his feet. One by one, the Rakum were rising and shaking their heads, all but Canaan horribly spooked. Javier shot a tiny peek at David and found him unconscious, but healed by Canaan's earlier efforts.

Isaac went limp in his arms, swiveled and slipped away.

"Aren't you clever," he snarled as he turned to face Javier. "I want you to hold that shield on every man here while I fry your brain." Isaac surged forward and grabbed Javier's head. He was several inches shorter, but had locked one arm around Javier's neck and pulled him downward, while the other hand braced against Javier's chin. "And when you're dead," Isaac breathed, his lips at Javier's ear, "I'm still going to kill them all. Your friends will die. You will die, and it will be all your fault."

Javier resisted his strength and the boy was not able to turn his head even a fraction. A few seconds into the new move, Isaac took note that Javier was as strong as he was so he held on tight and tried a new tactic.

"Okay, superman," he whispered. "You're as strong as me, but you're all spread out and I'm not."

Javier squeezed his eyes closed and pictured the shields on each man—they were all intact. When he opened his eyes, Isaac rolled his face so it pressed into Javier's cheek.

"All. Spread. Out," he whispered, accenting each word.

Javier's spine grew hot.

"He's going to fry me!" he said to God, as well as to Canaan. *"I feel him, he's doing it!"*

Javier concentrated on keeping all of the men in the room protected and found himself powerless to resist the white-hot spear that had begun its work drilling a hole in his spine. When he opened his mouth to again, pray against the demon, he had no voice. He opened his eyes to make sure all of his friends were still okay and he had lost his vision. He grew quiet and listened to his own heart—was it still beating?

"Father, I'm sorry—I tried. I really did," Javier prayed, realizing he was about to leave his flesh forever.

"Don't be so melodramatic."

Canaan's voice.

"I'm here, buddy, I'll break those chains. I can see what you did—I see the shields in your mind. Drop the one on me—trust me."

Javier wasn't sure if he was alive or dead, but he made an effort to release the protection on Canaan alone. Immediately, the pain in his spine melted away and he opened his eyes in Isaac's grasp. His vision clearing as slow as mud, he saw Canaan behind Isaac, both hands on the Rakum's blond head, not squeezing, but sending the very same punishment to the boy that he had been putting on Javier.

"You will pay for that, Elder Canaan," Isaac growled. At that, he released Javier and in a violent burst of energy, he leapt from between them and landed twenty feet away near the kitchen entrance. "CANAAN!" he shouted and Javier grabbed the Elder under the armpits as he slumped to the floor.

In what seemed to be only a second, Javier saw the group flock to Canaan's aid while Isaac ran directly at him. Isaac slammed into Javier, his arms embracing him like an old friend, and he looked deep into his eyes.

"It's time you spoke to Zahdone," he whispered telepathically and Javier blinked.

When he opened his eyes, he was no longer in Athens, Georgia.

53

J avier shook himself, blinked rapidly several times, and stomped his feet—nothing changed. He had transported. He stood alone in a dusty valley, the sky a literal blanket of stars, so bright and clear, he had a notion to reach out and touch them. But he didn't; he kept his hands at his sides and turned in a circle. He could see for miles, every pebble and slip of scrub-grass was illuminated with a thin fluorescent outline. At the farthest reaches of his sight, a mountain range encircled the place he stood, and as he scanned the ground from far away to right up to his feet, he noted the white-sand soil, the tiniest insects, the salty air.

I am in a dry lakebed, he thought and turned one more circle. *But where? And where is Isaac?*

"Javier d'Millier, I see now why you were chosen," a voice whispered, blowing across the sandy floor to reach Javier's ears with substance. *"I would have chosen you, too. You are rare and wonderful, indeed!"*

Javier crossed his arms and peered into the moonlit expanse. No other form was visible. He closed his eyes and waited for anything that might be seen only in his mind's eye. It didn't take long.

"So very clever!"

In his mind, a man stood near him, hands in jeans pockets, wearing a soft blue cotton pullover, standing casually, resting most of his weight on one foot. And he looked familiar.

"You'll see me now, little Javier," the voice said and Javier opened his eyes. "Hello."

Javier did not respond. The man standing with him in the dark flats was Isaac Akaron, aged to an adult. Same friendly eyes, same little-boy smile, but taller than Javier, and built like Canaan, strapping and muscular.

"I picked this face because I like it. I have millions more," the voice said and morphed into a hunched over elderly man Javier didn't recognize. He grinned a toothless smile and seamlessly shifted into another form, a tall Asian warrior-type, with long black hair flowing past his shoulders.

Javier sighed, less impressed with shape-shifting than he was interested in why he no longer stood in Simon's living room. The entity before him chuckled and transformed back into adult Isaac.

"I am Zahdone and I brought you here."

Javier tilted his head and said, "Oh? Where is this?"

"Lake Tuz, my favorite place on earth."

"Turkey..." Javier nodded, happy he was still *on* earth.

"We have great plans for you," it said and smiled, Isaac's mouth making the entity seem sweet and believable. "I brought you here to show you great and wonderful things. Things that will prosper you, and—"

"And give me a hope and a future? Please, Zahdone," Javier said, derision evident in his tone. "Quoting Scripture. How original." Javier looked away and sighed. *How do I go back?*

"I was present when Yirmeyahu recorded those words."

Javier turned back and gave the demon a bored stare. Maybe it spied upon (or irritated) the Prophet Jeremiah, yet it mattered not to Javier. How could he get home? To the demon called Zahdone, he said, "You can take me on a hill and offer me the world, but I'm not making any deals with you."

"There are no hills here, but I *do* offer you the world."

"Really?" Javier shook his head. "I've read this part. I can't be tempted by your Matthew 4 wilderness scene."

Zahdone didn't miss a beat. "Oh, *Javie*," it said, now using Roman and Canaan's endearment for him. "I am not *Satan*." The thing in Isaac laughed, blue eyes flashing. "There is no Satan. That's such a funny story, we laugh about it, my brothers and I."

"Oh, I see," Javier said. "You're still trying to tempt me. I've been down this road and you have nothing I want." Javier shook his head. What else was it going to lie about? Next it would say there was no God.

"The One you call God is Elohim. He is real. All that other hogwash is not, sorry to say," the demon said with a sorrowful gaze. "And Elohim finds you very special. That makes you extremely interesting to us, too."

"I want to go back now," Javier said and looked around again. Could he will himself back? Was he at the mercy of this demon or would God enable him to return?

The demon stepped close and placed a gentle hand on his shoulder. Adult Isaac's eyes were kind and full of sympathy as the demon used its other hand to tenderly touch Javier's chest, fingers conforming to his pectoral muscle.

"You heart is strong," it said and allowed that hand to slide down Javier's sternum to rest at his diaphragm. "Feel this."

Javier looked at the hand against his body. Nothing special happened in his sight, but inside, the monster he had shown Roman came to life. It had been so quiet since his battle with Isaac began, he forgot it even existed. The joint aches, the questionable yearning for blood, and the urgent thirst for fleshly fulfillment rushed headlong to his awareness.

"No!" Javier said and stepped back.

The demon moved with him and its hands did not budge from contact at Javier's shoulder and middle.

"I am not a monster!"

"Of course, you're not," it said using Isaac's soft blue eyes to calm his frantic mind. "You are a perfect being and when you consented to my presence in your body, I sang praises to your name."

Javier blinked. "The hell I did."

Zahdone's hand on his shoulder massaged slowly and the demon waited to catch Javier's eye before continuing. "How else are we speaking like this? How else are you capable of super-human feats? It is I, you asked me in, I am here. And I have made you complete, just as I make Isaac complete. And you see how powerful that one is," the demon said, pride seeping from its bright gaze.

Javier wrapped his fingers around the demon's wrist at his middle. He couldn't remove the hand, but he kept it in his grip nonetheless. "I never invited you in. You are a liar."

The demon's forehead creased. "Me? Lying?" Isaac's huge blue eyes shimmered with innocence. "Open your eyes to what you've become, a beautiful amalgamation of Elohim and Zahdone—a marriage to create the perfect man. You are Tamim[17], perfect and complete!"

"I did NOT consent, you are LYING," Javier restated, easily dismissing the demon's *you are god* crap. Even though it was impossible that he ever invited a demon to enter him, he looked back and still saw no circumstance where there could even be a *misinterpretation* of such a thing. Unless... Javier paled. *Isaac's blood.* He voluntarily drank from The Last, no one coerced him. Zahdone noticed his change of expression and gave him a wide smile showing white teeth.

"TAMIM—the perfect man! Look at you! Billions of people on the planet, Javie, and you are the only one who is Tamim!"

"Stop saying that!" Javier growled and again attempted to dislodge the hand on his stomach. "Get off me."

---

[17] Hebrew for *perfect, whole, complete.*

"Wait! I misspoke! Out of ALL of flesh born to a woman since Creation, there has been NOT ONE marriage of Elohim and Zahdone inside a man, until now. —And here you are. *You ...are ...God in the flesh.*"

Javier laughed weakly. The words that fell from the demon's lips were lunacy. Of course, he wasn't God. But... *What is that?* A curious tingle arose in the skin under the demon's hand across his abdomen. It didn't tickle, *per se*, but Javier recognized the sensation; if allowed to grow it would bring with it tremendous pleasure, something he did not need to experience standing in a Turkish lakebed with a demon as old as the world.

"You will finish what Elohim and I started when Isaac Akaron was born. This has been planned from the beginning, that you, Tamim, the Complete One, will mentor Isaac The Last and bring him up to serve you. You shall never want for anything ever again, *and you will live forever.*" It whispered the final phrase, leaning in to touch foreheads with Javier.

"Release me," Javier said, his voice low and without inflection.

"Oh, let me pet you, Javie. You have missed so much these last several years, searching and searching..." The hand on his stomach moved slightly and fell still. "You were searching for me. I watched you. I waited. I coached Elohim on how to corral you to His side..."

"You're insane," Javier whispered, barely audible, his eyes closing in an autonomic response. The teasing tingle turned into an incredible peace that ran from the hand at his middle, down to his toes, and then it made a leisurely trip past his hips, up his spine, and ending between his ears, caressing every nerve. Javier gasped.

"This fulfills you, this is wonderful, you have needed this. There is no reason for you to go without. There is no reason to return to your old existence, Javie," the demon said, moving its hand a fraction of an inch toward his belly button. "Why would you?"

Javier's brained clouded and his body buzzed with pleasure. "You don't know me," he gasped. "I know who I am. I'm just... I know..."Another involuntary noise escaped him as a jolt of pleasure hit him again, lower and with urgency.

"You will *rule*, and not just the Rakum. You have Zahdone *and* Elohim with you—the Creator and His son, to empower you to rule the human race. You will fulfill the Prophecy of the End. You are GLORIOUS."

"Zahdone is a tiny, insignificant demon," Javier whispered, unable to speak any louder, the sensations numbing his tongue. *"I will cast you to the dry places, never to be heard from again."*

Zahdone scoffed. "You use the word as if it has meaning. 'Demon' is just a term a man makes with his mouth, as meaningless as the term, 'vampire,' or 'werewolf.' Demons are a bedtime story to keep human children in line and convince them to complete their chores." The demon shifted the hand from Javier's shoulder to cup the back of his neck. "You are Master now. Master Tamim, my god and king, take your portion."

The hand on Javier's middle withdrew and the demon brought its wrist to its mouth. Biting down with Isaac's pointed teeth, it opened an oozing wound and thrust it toward Javier's mouth.

"No." Javier turned to the side. "I'm not a Rakum. I am just a man."

"*You* are insane if you can't see that you are more than a man." Zahdone represented the wound. "Tell me you don't want this. You know the blood is the life. You've known since birth. All Rakum know this."

"I ...am not ....a Rakum..." Javier shook his head. He didn't want it, but the monster inside *did*. His stomach growled, churned and yearned. His mind showed him vision upon vision of his own sharp teeth buried deep in adult-Isaac's throat, grabbing on tightly and not letting go until the demon fell bloodless to the dry ground.

"*I want to go back,*" Javier prayed and closed his eyes to the pain in his gut. "*I repent, Father, I repent. I never should have consented to Isaac's blood. Please forgive me and wash me white as snow with the blood of Yeshua Hamoshiach, Jesus Christ, who died on the cross for my sins...*"

"Take your portion, little Javie," Zahdone said gently in adult-Isaac's dulcet voice. "Like you did as a proselyte, remember? Eight-year-old Javier drinking his master's blood for the first time... Elder Roman showed you how to step into your mantel. Step in again, Javier-Tamim, and you will rule..."

Javier remembered the power, the glory, and the pleasure that transferred that day. That eight-year-old inhuman proselyte knew who he was and where he was headed, and Roman mentored him until he grew into a powerful and wise Rakum, master of his world.

But he was not a Rakum any longer. He was a child of the one true God, and more than anything, he wanted to hand Jesus his burdens. Aloud he said, "No, I love Jesus..." In his heart, he had a request. "*I want You, Yeshua, and I can't remember how to get back. Please show me the way.*"

Then, he heard in his deepest, inward parts, "Jesus said to him, away from Me, Satan..." The sweet as honey voice applied balm to his scorched soul. Now remembering the Scripture and its context, Javier opened his eyes and pushed against the demon's robust chest.

"BE GONE, ZAHDONE!" he shouted, finally enjoying full use of his voice. "For it is written, worship the Lord your God and serve Him only! In Yeshua's name, LET ME GO AND BE GONE!"

In a flash of light, Javier was back in Simon's living room, young Isaac in his grasp, the both of them on the floor holding each other around the neck.

'NOOOooo!" Isaac yelped and slipped free. In a blur, found his feet and reached Simon. He fixed himself around the man, wrapping him up with both arms from behind, a pocketknife pressed into his throat.

"Take me out of here," Isaac said in Simon's ear. "Nice and easy. I have nothing to lose, so no tricks."

Javier watched his friend's face morph into a mask of terror. Beryl and Javier both stepped toward him and Isaac admonished them as one would a bad dog.

"Nu-unh! Back!" Isaac yelped and pressed the tip enough to pierce Simon's skin. Javier willed his shields back into place, aware that his stint to Zahdone-land had lowered them to nothing. Poor Simon was paying the price.

Javier looked at Canaan.

"What?" the big Rakum sent. *"You and I can get to him in an instant, but not before he slices Simon's throat."*

"Oh, God!" Simon cried out. "I'm bleeding! He's going to kill me! Javier, help!" he yelled, moving away from the group toward the kitchen. Behind him and latched on tight, Isaac held the knife in place, filling the room with the aroma of Simon's blood. Javier detected the aroma as whatever monster he had become, so he knew all the Rakum did, too.

To Canaan, Javier sent, *"There's no time. Both of us will rush him. If he punctures Simon's throat, heal him up. I will take care of Isaac myself."*

The Elder sent a miniscule nod and watched for his signal. Isaac had made it to the threshold and when he looked back to the door to the yard, Javier and Canaan reached him in a rush.

"NO!" Isaac shouted as they both grabbed hold of him.

Javier and Canaan attempted to pin his arms, but Isaac surprised them with his agility. In a fluid movement, the small pocketknife entered Simon's throat to the hilt and he dragged it outward, opening a horrid gash. Bright red oxygenated blood rushed from the severed jugular vein and painted all four of them as they struggled.

Simon gurgled and his eyes were wild. Javier called for help and Polly and Guap matched his efforts in subduing The Last as he screamed and was finally pried off.

"HEAL HIM UP, CANAAN!" Javier shouted with exertion as he,

Guap, and Polly wrestled Isaac toward the larger room. Javier called for Beryl, but he had run to Simon, applying pressure to his wound with both hands. Isaac met their efforts with equal muscle forcing Javier to concentrate on the fight at hand. He sent up a prayer for Simon and yanked The Last out of the kitchen.

"We only need to hold him down," Javier said, grunting with effort. Roman and David hovered nearby, staying out of reach of Isaac's flailing limbs. Despite his lack of spiritual might, Isaac had no loss of Rakum strength and in the end, it took all three of them to get him to the floor.

"Hold him there," Javier barked, gesturing to Polly who rested all of his weight on one knee planted in Isaac's back. Guap sat on the kid's legs, facing backwards, hands encircling his ankles. Isaac screamed to be released and Roman thrust a handkerchief in Javier's hand.

"We don't need the neighbors calling the police," he said, amazingly serene.

Javier shoved the cloth into Isaac's mouth and pressed his flushed cheek to the cool floor with both hands.

"David, Roman, okay, come over here," he said, composing himself. When they were in position, he had them kneel and join hands. "Now we're going to cast Zahdone out. I'll pray and you agree, okay?" Both men nodded.

Javier closed his eyes and asked God to help him find the words. Casting out demons was something followers of the Messiah did from ancient days, but now? It had become a joke to the world.

Using the Scripture as his guide, Javier commanded the demon by name to depart. The first thing Javier noticed was that his body ached—from head to toe, the sensations that sent him discomfort all day and all night had stepped up. A migraine worse than any he had ever experienced tinged his vision and a fire seemed to have erupted in every nerve. He called the demon out, and with every passing moment, his pain grew. Yet, the exorcism was working and Zahdone was on the run.

Ignoring his aches as best he could, Javier prayed with even more fervency. Isaac screeched around his gag and convulsed between them. At one point, when Javier relaxed his mind, he saw a raw spirit version of Zahdone, holding onto the young Rakum's body with a death grip, its featureless head screaming through an empty mouth.

"I see it!" he yelled. "Get out, Zahdone! We cast you out in the name of Yeshua!" Javier shouted. His vision cleared and as he continued to pray, he saw only the young Rakum, now weakening underneath them. Isaac's gaze fixed on an unseen point, unable to move since Javier held down his head. When another minute passed, the Rakum stopped resisting and was still. Polly and Guap did not get off him, but they each craned their faces around to see. Javier lifted his hands and did the same.

"No heartbeat," Guap mumbled and Polly nodded.

Roman reached forward to Isaac's neck, feeling for a pulse. The room had grown silent and each man watched for Roman's call.

Roman lowered his chin and shook his head. "Isaac is gone."

Javier exhaled and thanked God in his heart. He sat back on his haunches and thought to rise when Guap and Polly turned their faces simultaneously to the kitchen, inhaled sharply with lips parted, and nostrils flared. They didn't have to say it, Javier recognized the action.

There was a new Rabbit in the kitchen and Javier screamed Canaan's name.

54

Athens, GA
November 13th, Nearing 1 a.m.

Judging by the grisly scene on the kitchen floor, it was evident poor Simon had nearly bled out before he could be healed. Javier stood in the doorway to the kitchen, his shoulders drooping.

"Canaan? What were you thinking?" he asked, intuiting the answer. They wanted to save his life and he had lost too much blood. *Correction,* Javier thought miserably, Beryl probably begged Canaan to do it.

The Elder's eyes narrowed a fraction as he looked Javier over and then the odd glance was gone. Javier disregarded whatever it meant, too much going on to care, and watched him rise to his feet. Beryl remained on the cool tile with Simon's upper body across his lap, his eyes glazed still coming around.

"Isaac?" Canaan asked, but read the answer in Javier's face. At that moment, Guap entered with Isaac's body over one thick shoulder.

"Somewhere out there is Ta'avah and he will be looking for this Rakum's body," Javier said gravely. "He's a Father and probably not truly deceased. We have to dismember it. Polly will find us a good place."

Canaan nodded. Besides Simon, no one in the group would be squeamish about disposing of a corpse.

Simon, coming aware of his surroundings after the pain of being marked, brought his hands to his throat and sat up, pushing away from Beryl.

"Isaac tried to kill me!" Simon said, coughing as he struggled to his feet. Behind him, Canaan lifted him with strong hands and helped him balance. Beryl stood and shoved his hands in his slacks pockets, his face unreadable, although Javier guessed his stoicism reflected his self-control around the world's newest Rabbit.

Javier glimpsed Guap beside him, jonesing like an addict. Polly did the same dance behind them in the living room. Javier did not need to tell them to stay off Simon, but he pitied them, remembering well enough what it was like to be near a Rabbit and be unable to feast upon it.

"Take Isaac's body to the garage and put him in the trunk of one of those cars. The keys are kept on the green board by the door." Javier waited for Guap to nod and move away, walking backward, his eye on poor Simon.

Polly also watched Simon, a strange upturned grin on his handsome face, and followed Guap out backward.

"That one—" Polly said pointing at Simon, "is my new best friend. I love, you, man," he said then and blew Simon a kiss. He backed all the way out of the room and howled like a wolf when the door closed behind him. Guap joined in and their noise filled the house.

"Idiots," Canaan mumbled with a grin.

When they were gone, Beryl covered his nose with his hand and left for the garage in their wake. Simon watched everything with huge eyes.

"You killed Isaac?" he asked incredulous. "So it's over?"

Javier walked up to him and shooed Canaan, who whispered as he passed, "*We need to talk,*" and he thumped Javier's forehead. Javier nodded and waited for Roman and David to also leave the kitchen.

Javier pulled out a chair at the dinette for Simon to sit and he settled into a chair, never losing Javier's eye.

"Okay, you're freaking me out," he said in a low voice.

"Simon, Isaac is dead, but he stabbed you in the neck before we could stop him." Javier touched Simon's forearm. "You lost so much blood that you were dying, even after Canaan sewed you up."

Simon's free hand went to his throat and he massaged his neck. It was sticky with blood, but he found no wound.

"I was in the other room fighting Isaac and I didn't have any say in what they did to you."

"I was dying?"

Javier nodded. "Yes, and Canaan marked you, Simon. It saved your life," Javier said gently.

"What?" Simon shook his head. Javier had taught him about Rabbits when the man served him as a Cow. His current confusion stemmed solely from his now-proximity to the term. "What?" he asked again.

"You're a Rabbit," Javier said and gave him an encouraging nod. "We can all go about our business, but keep in mind, Guap, Polly, and Beryl will all be horribly tortured by your scent." Javier exhaled and looked around the room. "There's more to do—we're not finished."

Simon's brave face slipped and Javier watched his eyes grow glassy with tears. He refused to cry, holding back as much as possible. When Javier stood, he blurted, "I don't want to give blood to any of them. I am not a Cow!"

"I know," Javier said and patted his shoulder. "Stay near me or Canaan until we finish this. The Rakum will depart when we finish with Ta'avah." Javier shook his head. "I want us to pray again—Ta'avah is near and he wants Isaac's body."

"I'm a Rabbit," Simon said, not hearing Javier.

Javier clasped his shoulder. "Go change your clothes. I'll wait for you at the foot of the stairs."

Simon hung his head and turned away. Javier walked him to the grand staircase to the second level and watched him ascend. When he turned the corner out of sight, Canaan touched Javier's shoulder from behind and he jumped.

"Just what I thought," Canaan said with a low chortle. "You didn't hear me, did you?"

"What? No..." Javier said, instantly realizing the significance of such a thing. "So?"

Canaan grabbed his head and pulled him close, burying his nose in his wavy hair. Javier mumbled a complaint and waited.

"Mortal," Canaan said sadly. "You cast out your own demon, you idiot."

Javier considered his words. He flexed his arms across his chest and stretched with a grunt. His tongue found his teeth that had been elongated by ingesting blood from The Last—they were normal.

Canaan nodded. "I want my super-mutant-man back," he said with a frown.

What does this mean? Javier's mind went to Ta'avah. When they found him, he and Roman intended to cast him back to the spirit realm, too. Would his eviction result in all of the Rakum reverting to humans?

Canaan caught his eye and winked, unaware of Javier's inner turmoil. He needed to speak to Roman. In private. And the super-ears of all the Rakum need not tune in.

Roman jogged back into the house from the garage after instructing everyone to wait for them. He had even suggested they not open the garage until he, Javier, and Simon joined them, in case Ta'avah was in the yard. The angel guard Javier described earlier stood around the house itself;

there had been no vision of such beings protecting beyond that.

At the bottom stair, Javier turned to meet him, worry filling his face. "Canaan said you needed me. What's up?"

Javier gestured for him to follow him up the stairs. He put a finger to his lips and then pointed to the garage. Roman nodded and followed him. Whatever it was, he didn't want even the sharpest Rakum overhearing.

Javier rapped on a closed door and Simon opened it with a grimace. "I'm ready," he said, now wearing a white Polo and khakis.

"Simon, do you have a pen and sheet of paper?" Javier asked and pushed inside.

Roman shadowed him growing more curious. Whatever it was had Javier immensely agitated. Simon reached in a backpack on a stool next to the window and handed him a spiral notebook and pencil. Javier thanked him and pulled Roman to the small desk. He opened the notebook to a clean sheet, put the tip of the pencil to the paper, and looked at Simon.

"Please wait in the corner," Javier said. Simon didn't move immediately and Javier explained in a soft voice. "I want to keep you safe so I need you to stay in the room. But the Rakum can read you sometimes and this is something the Rakum shouldn't see. Okay? Please, just for a minute."

"Whatever," Simon grumbled and slumped to the corner. He leaned his back into the wall and looked at the ground.

"What?" Roman whispered.

Javier wrote in block caps to save time, ZAHDONE'S INFLUENCE HAS BEEN CAST OUT OF ME. I'M NORMAL AGAIN. TA'AVAH IS THE FATHER OF THE RAKUM. IF WE CAST TA'AVAH OUT, WILL ALL THE RAKUM BECOME HUMAN?

Roman read the note twice, the implications boggling him the more he thought about it. Of Abroghia's original 100,000 Rakum brotherhood, Only five to seven thousand remained, if that many, and they were scattered across the globe. What would they do if they awoke as humans with no explanation? Was it fair? Was it right? Roman had no easy answers. He removed the pencil from Javier's hand and wrote, I DON'T KNOW. MAYBE.

Javier took the pencil back. THEY DON'T WANT TO BE HUMAN.

Roman sighed and then shrugged. THAT PART IS NOT UP TO US OR THEM. WHAT DO YOU WANT TO DO? STOP?

Javier frowned. "Of course not," he hissed. "I had a vision while I was wrestling Isaac to the floor that Ta'avah is here, nearby, inside another body. I didn't see a face, but I got the sense he intended on possessing Isaac while he still lived. Now Isaac is dead—"

Roman interrupted with an urgent whisper. "We need to behead him; as a Father, the lack of a heartbeat may not be the end of him. He could be resurrected by the right demonic power."

Javier put the pencil to the paper again. SO WE WILL PRAY TO CAST OUT TA'AVAH IN SAME MANNER AS ZAHDONE, WITH NO RESERVATIONS. –GOOD?

Roman nodded and Javier yanked their note free and ripped it up. The Rakum element with them would never agree to help if they knew they might lose their self-supposed deity, so it had been wise for Javier to keep it between them.

"Um, guys," Simon mumbled from his corner. He was looking out the window into the front yard. "Stu and another guy are coming up to the door."

Javier met Roman's eye and they both turned to jog to the stairs.

"DON'T OPEN THAT DOOR!" Roman shouted with authority just before they reached the foyer. David's hand was on the latch and he startled to see the two of them gallop into the space. "Don't! Hands off!" Roman said and pressed his weight against the door. "Thank God. Thank God."

▼ ▼

"That sounds exciting," Canaan said to Beryl at the sound of Roman's shout.

He left the garage and walked toward the front door, sensing the rest of his brethren right behind. Since Isaac's elimination, the four of them seemed closer, tighter-knit. Beryl, Guap and Polly followed respectfully, even though it took all the control the three had to keep from leaping on Simon as soon as they saw him in the foyer. It wasn't supposed to be, but Canaan found their withdrawal pains funny. It was good to be an Elder. Canaan grinned and reached the foyer.

Simon had his back to them and didn't hear them approach. He placed his hands on the new Rabbit's shoulders and Simon startled with a curse. Canaan shook him playfully.

"Sneaky, sneaky," he said in Simon's ear and looked at Roman. "Who's that?"

Javier's face whipped around—he hadn't heard them either, which was a damn shame.

"Who's watching Isaac's body?" he asked with a gasp.

Canaan followed his line of sight to the Rakum behind him and shrugged. "Uh-oh," he said with exaggerated calm and gestured for Guap and Polly to return to the garage.

"Canaan! That's Ta'avah out there! He shouldn't be allowed near Isaac's body!" Javier barked and pushed past Roman to yank open the door. The stoop was empty.

▼ ▼

Ta'avah had pulled behind the dusty white pickup and switched off the car. The messengers of Elohim hadn't impaired him the entire way. Maybe all his worry over his bad luck of late was simple paranoia. It wasn't unheard of, considering all he had accomplished the past four millennia and all he stood to gain tonight. With the confidence of the ages, he exited the compact vehicle and strode up to the twitchy Cow leaning on the front of the truck.

"Hey, fella," he said in a decent southern accent. The man literally leapt in the air and spun around.

"GEEZUS, MATE!" he yelped and put a hand over his heart.

Ta'avah-Eric grinned. The guy must have been deep in thought because the Kia was no stealth machine. Ta'avah now had Rah-keel's and Zara's full participation on his mission, because Zahdone had royally screwed everything up. With all of their energies combined, Ta'avah knew everything about Stuart Loudon, his affection for the Rakum, and his newest venture gathering Cows for his masters.

"Sorry 'bout that." He put out his hand to the taller man. "Name's Ta'avah—you're Stuart."

"Yeahhh," he replied, initially seeking Ta'avah's motives. The Cow was extremely tuned-in and even though the Eric flesh was not a Rakum, in the space of a minute, Stuart Loudon discerned his new acquaintance was not human. "Ta'avah... I'm... ?" His face formed a million questions and Ta'avah, still holding his hand, pulled him close.

"I am the master of them all," he whispered in the Cow's ear, sensing Stu breaking out in gooseflesh at the sound. *"Even that tiny blond one you love the most."*

"Ohhhh..." Stuart crumbled to the ground, his senses overloaded.

Ta'avah hadn't even begun to show the Cow his awesome power, the Cow's mind doing the work for him. He flashed Stuart a genuine smile that caused even pimple-ravaged Eric's face to appear half-way handsome. Classic comeliness meant nothing to Stuart—he was already in love. By the time he was lifted carefully to his feet, he saw nothing but shining glory when he looked into the demon's borrowed face.

"Zahdone is gone. Cast to the dry places. The boy's flesh grows cold! They put him in the garage! HURRY-HURRY-HURRY," a thousand combined spirits reported to Ta'avah in his mind. Accustomed to attending both dimensions at once, he listened as they transmitted everything they had seen through the windows, and all the while, he wrapped one arm around Stuart and caused them both to walk toward the house. Stuart stood a head taller than Eric, but he instinctively hunched down, which Ta'avah liked.

When their toes touched the first step of the stoop, the idiotic messengers of Elohim parted enough for them to cross to the door. Ta'avah snarled at them with Eric's mouth, but they weren't looking at him. They were mesmerized with the Cow under his arm.

"Whatever," he mumbled silently, *"you are always looking the wrong way,"* he said, addressing Elohim, if He was listening, which He probably was. Whatever a feckless and brainless Cow meant to the Creator of the universe didn't interest Ta'avah in the least. The boy's flesh growing cold in the garage—that was his goal.

"Ring the doorbell once," he told Stuart. "When they open the door, run and hide. Try to distract them as long as you can."

"Yes, Master," Stuart said, his eyes huge and seeking approval.

"You're an excellent Cow." Ta'avah tipped his chin and allowed his fingers to brush Stuart's stubbly cheek. "When I have revived Isaac, I will come back for you." Ta'avah wanted badly to milk him, but his borrowed flesh wasn't a Rakum and Eric already demonstrated he couldn't digest blood. No matter, in minutes, he would reanimate Isaac and have everything he always wanted and more.

Ta'avah backed away and turned for the garage. By the time he reached the wide car-sized door, Stuart rang the bell. The garage door was down, but with focused thought and the compliance of a dozen minions, the door roared to life and began to roll slowly up its frame. Ta'avah stayed out of sight as the portal finished its circuit and only popped out when it stopped in the apparatus up top. Guap and Polly stood in the garage, both had been leaning on a black Mercedes and they gawked at the sight of him.

"Guap, Polly, is Isaac in that car?" They nodded, mouths ajar. "Good. Put him in the back seat and drive it out here immediately," he commanded. Outwardly, he appeared to be a nerdy college dropout, but untainted by the Rabbit's fool religion, the two Rakum in the garage recognized their master as soon as their eyes met. The bankers jumped into action. Polly slipped behind the wheel and Guap carefully extricated Isaac

311

from the trunk and placed him across the backseat. He then strolled out of the garage and met Ta'avah on his knees. He didn't speak, but Ta'avah understood why; he'd been caught helping the enemy and it was best to remain mum.

Polly backed the sedan and unlocked the doors for Ta'avah to enter.

"Come, Guap," he said to the Rakum on the cold grass. "I have use for you." Without question, Guap rolled onto his hands and stood, eyes down and chin to chest. Ta'avah folded himself into the back as Guap climbed into the passenger's front.

"Drive," he said to Polly with no need to stress urgency. The slender Rakum stomped on the gas and drove them away from the house at speed.

Ta'avah lifted Isaac's still form into his lap, face up, and cupped the back of his head with one hand. He put the other palm to the car's lining above him and called his spirit brethren to his side.

"It is time!" he shouted in the spirit and the car immediately filled with wispy entities, so many, if viewed in their own dimension, Polly and Guap were completely eclipsed.

"They're following us, Master," Polly said, his voice barely audible.

"Lose them!" he barked at his driver. He lifted one dirty sneaker and kicked the back of Guap's seat. "Do you have a cell phone?" he shouted louder than necessary. The spirits working on Isaac's flesh made a cacophony the junior Rakum couldn't hear.

"Yes, Master!" Guap answered as loudly as Ta'avah had.

"Find us a place to work—an abandoned warehouse, an abandoned factory, old mall—anything! I need space and I need quiet!"

"Yes, I will do it!" Guap yelled, his anxiety evident. Ta'avah sneered, not concerned with the Rakum's happiness.

In his lap, Isaac's body twitched.

55

Despite the terror of their current situation and maybe because of it, Javier grinned at the sight of Roman piloting their car down the dark neighborhood streets at breakneck speed after the Mercedes that held the dead Isaac. In their past lives, Roman and Javier both enjoyed auto racing, drag racing, and the occasional street race, and only their last few years together did they purchase race-worthy cars to play with. Roman shifted down as they turned a corner and he glimpsed Javier watching him.

"I know, I just ran a stop sign," he said, smiling with exhilaration. In the backseat, Simon moaned.

"I think I'm gonna be sick," he said and grabbed his belly.

"Go ahead if you have to, Simon," Javier said and braced himself as Roman took another corner. They were gaining on the other car and headed toward the industrial outskirts of town. "We can't stop now."

The car behind them flashed its lights and Javier lowered his window enough to wave once. Canaan drove Beryl and David in the Camry Guap and Polly had arrived in earlier that evening.

"Was that Stuart Loudon at the front door?" Roman asked and Javier nodded. Ten minutes ago, when they opened the door and found no one there, Canaan heard the garage door go up. As soon as they turned to run for the garage, Stuart had popped out of the bushes and lunged at Roman and Javier like a madman. Kicking, biting, and screaming, flipping around his arms, legs and sharp angles, the clunky Aussie did everything within his power to keep them from reaching the cars. Javier and Roman had covered their heads from his haphazard blows and slipped out of his clutches repeatedly before reaching the garage door. The only reason Canaan's car was behind them and not in front was because Beryl physically held Stuart down so he, Roman, and Simon could get into the nearest car and drive away.

"You could have warned me—he's insane," Roman added applying the brake.

Staring ahead, Javier sighed. "All Cows are crazy, remember?"

"Touché," Roman said with a curt nod.

"Hello," Simon said from the back. "I wasn't crazy." Javier and Roman both ignored him.

"They're turning into this lot..."

Javier looked out his window and Simon scooted from his seat in the middle to look out.

"This mall was flattened in a tornado two years ago," Simon offered from the back. "I looked into buying the land as an investment..."

Javier didn't respond, Simon's business ventures being of the least importance. To Roman he said, "I'm scared as hell."

Roman smiled. "Welcome back to the real world, Javie. You know you don't need super powers to defeat the enemy. The only power we need is faith. God will do the rest."

"You're right, you're right," Javier said with a sardonic smile.

"How did Isaac die?" Simon asked, staring out at the dark lot and crumbling buildings. Ta'avah's car had turned into the courtyard and Roman crawled their vehicle the same way. "I didn't think anyone would *die* from having demons cast out of them. I don't get it..."

"Simon," Roman answered for Javier, "Isaac was born dead so he had no soul to live on once that demon was cast out."

"Huh," Simon replied. Javier detected sympathy, which threatened to make him angry. He monitored his tone and elaborated.

"I saw his birth in a vision, clear as day. That baby was born dead. I watched the demon enter his body and bring him back to life."

"That's sad," Simon said mostly to himself.

Javier caught Roman's eye, who read his growing irritation. Roman slow-blinked, shaking his head a fraction. Javier took a deep breath.

"Roman, you and me and David will pray together when we cast out Ta'avah. Simon, it'll be better for you to wait in the car." Javier swiveled to see his face and he shrugged, still looking out into the dark night.

Roman halted the car and pointed ahead with a knuckle. "They stopped."

"Here we go," Javier said and opened his door.

▼ ▼

"The doors are locked, yes?" Ta'avah asserted and one of the goons up front hit the button. Sitting in the back seat of the luxury automobile, hidden by thickly-tinted windows, Ta'avah exhaled and relaxed his mind, working in tandem with the two superior spirits that could possibly bring a dead adolescent Rakum back to viability. In his arms, the body of his blood-son jerked and twitched as literally millions of invisible entities compelled by Rah-keel and Zara performed their magic. A Rakum was not human, and decades of consuming the purest of body fuel—Rakum blood—should have made each cell extremely resistant to assault.

Ta'avah clapped his hands together above the Rakum in his lap. *"He lives, I know it. Do they see? Rah-keel? Do they see?"*

"Wait," his spirit equal gasped, gathering impulses of information from his minions. *"YES, BROTHER! Cell-death has not been initiated. My children are bringing him back. Go in! Go in!"*

"I need him to awake—wake him," Ta'avah said in his mind and with his mouth. The two Rakum up front turned in their seat to watch, but he could not spare even a fragment of attention on them if he was about to transfer to his new vessel.

"I will remain inside," Rah-keel piped up. *"I will open his eyes—we will do it together."*

Ta'avah cursed, but watched for his chance. Sharing the vessel with Rah-keel was not ideal. He half-expected Zara to take his shot, too. When the body's eyes opened and focused on his borrowed face, Ta'avah smiled. Isaac was no longer there, but the empty vessel had a heartbeat, brainwave activity, and a longing for a spirit to give him purpose. Out of time and out of chances, Ta'avah funneled his essence into the open eyes of the resurrected Rakum. Only when he sensed his every atom slow and become immobile did he cease his efforts.

"I AM HERE!" Ta'avah shouted with Isaac's mouth. The Eric flesh had slumped into his lap and he put one palm to the greasy forehead and shoved him off. In his peripheral vision, Guap and Polly, looking over their shoulders from the front seat, watched him with huge eyes. Ta'avah took several deep breaths, enjoying even the minutiae of being truly Rakum again. He expanded his chest one more time, feeling his heart might burst with joy. "FINALLY! I HAVE WON!" he shouted.

The car shivered as if rubbed by an outside force. Uninterested in the cause, Ta'avah leapt forward between the two front seats and in a blur of movement, grabbed Guap with his hands and brought his throat to his mouth. Guap gurgled and didn't resist, simply braced himself on the dashboard and the ceiling. The car shimmied again, this time more violently.

"Master," Polly said maintaining calm for the moment. "Would you like me to see what that is?"

Ta'avah ignored him and pulled Guap's blood out as fast as it would come. The car was shoved again, this time with a man's form visible pressed against the driver's window.

"Master, they've blocked us in with their cars," Polly said low.

Guap's blood thinned and Ta'avah pulled back, not concerned in the least about the black-red liquid staining his chin and shirtfront. When he opened his hands, Guap slumped forward until his head rested on the shiny dash. His breathing was steady, but he would be unconscious a while. Ta'avah languidly blinked and swiveled to see Polly's face.

"None of that matters now, pup," Ta'avah said. "I will reprimand my wayward children. You stand by."

Ta'avah scooted back into the seat and caught movement from Eric on his left. The boy was coming around, which was impossible.

The blood-shot green eyes that opened and met Ta'avah's were not those of the comatose worshipper—it was Zara, prince of sickness and affliction taking intelligent possession of an available and consenting vessel. The comatose youngster would take a little longer to animate with a single spirit inside, but still, Zara displayed forward thinking, as usual.

"Smart move," Ta'avah told him and reached for the door handle on his right. When he pushed on the door, it opened only three inches before clicking into a car parked up against them. Ta'avah looked through the tint into the night. Roman had parked so close to him that he would not be able to exit on the right. Ta'avah scooted to Zara-Eric and reached over him. Pushing open his door, it also slammed into an unmovable barrier—the Camry the Elder had driven up in.

Ta'avah growled low in his throat and was screeching by the time he forced Isaac's small frame into the front seat and over Polly's lap. Canaan had leaned against the driver's door so he would shove out that way. Polly obediently flattened his arms at his sides to give Ta'avah access and the door unlatched.

"CANAAN, MOVE OFF THIS DOOR IMMEDIATELY!" he shouted loud enough to reverberate in the small space.

Canaan's back was to him, and he twisted halfway around to meet Ta'avah's eye. "Is that Father Abroghia in there? Or Ta'avah? Or the Tooth Fairy? You spirit-folk keep me on my toes," he said chuckling.

Ta'avah closed his eyes, gathered his concentration and prepared to send the insubordinate Elder into the next world.

▼▼

"Don't get hurt, Canaan!" Javier barked from the opposite side of the Mercedes. Canaan nodded and backed away from the car, palms up.

316

"I was just kidding around, Father," he said and the partially open door gently finished its arc. "No harm done, see?" Canaan went to his knees and clasped his hands together, the posture all chastised Rakum used for the Fathers before Last Assembly.

Javier motioned again for Simon to stay in the car and he stepped over to Roman's side. Both of them had begun to pray for everyone's safety as the very air around them crackled with spiritual energy even a mortal could discern. David jogged over to them from Canaan's car, his eyes never leaving the form of little Isaac facing off now against the prostrate Elder.

"Where did Beryl go?" Roman asked in a whisper and David shrugged his shoulders.

"I will deal with you later," Ta'avah said in Isaac's voice. Canaan lowered his eyes and Ta'avah touched his head, barely making contact with his hair. The Elder crumpled to the concrete. Ta'avah's head swiveled left and his gaze grabbed Javier's with purpose. "YOU come."

Javier shook his head and Roman grasped his upper arm.

"Remember, you are not fighting that demon. It's not you—it's God."

"I got it," Javier said and he and Roman both walked slowly to the front of their car where the asphalt leveled. To Ta'avah he pointed a finger. "You come *here*."

"Truly my soul silently waits for God. From Him comes my salvation..." Behind them, David began praising God in a few memorized Psalms. *"He only is my rock and my salvation. He is my defense. I shall NOT be greatly moved..."* Sometimes singing, David's voice became the background track that soothed Javier's frazzled nerves.

"I have won, Javier," Ta'avah said and strolled to where they stood. "You fought the good fight. It's time you came home to your true Father." Ta'avah took a step toward them and Roman commanded him to stay back. He did not advance, but put his hands on Isaac's little boy hips. "Really, Roman?" He smirked. "Stop this nonsense. I am taking you back to me. You, David, Javier, you will draw near me again and I will make you stronger and better than you were before." Ta'avah still did not move toward them, but his hands came out, palms up, offering them immortality if they'd only come. "You will know power and pleasure like never before."

Under his breath, Javier praised God and repented of his sins. He watched Ta'avah and heard him speaking to Roman, all the while he cleansed his soul before Almighty God, preparing for the battle ahead.

"Shut up, foul spirit," Roman shouted across the huge lot, bouncing off a crumbling nearby edifice and creating an impressive echo. One side of Javier's mouth turned up in a grin.

"Oh, God, You are my God, and early I will seek you," David called from his spot behind them. *"My soul thirsts for you, my flesh longs for you in a dry and thirsty land where there is no water..."*

Javier pointed then at Ta'avah. "That's where we send you, Ta'avah, Prince of Covetousness, Lust and Murder! We send you to the dry places, we cast you out in the name of Jesus Christ. Yeshua HaMoshiach commands you to be gone!"

Ta'avah laughed in huge guffaws and looked up to the starry sky. Polly stood by, his face a mask of confused loyalties. Javier didn't fault him—he had no reason to trust the people of God and he had admitted honestly that he would serve whatever master kept him alive. Javier *was* happy, though, that for the moment, Ta'avah wasn't using the Rakum to attack them physically.

"Be gone, Ta'avah!" Javier shouted again and he took a step forward. Javier called more commands to the demon and Roman was heard repeating his every word.

"I grow weary of this game," Ta'avah said frowning with Isaac's expressive face. It looked like he thought to advance, but he did not proceed. After another few seconds, he called to Polly. "Quiet them," he said and Polly nodded.

The athletic Rakum reached for Roman and shoved him down with ferocious strength, showing no sign of holding back. Roman prepared for the ground by balling up, but he still landed hard on his side and his head slapped the asphalt with enough force to jar his senses. Javier prayed for Roman in his heart and repeated his commands to the demon, advancing another step.

Behind him, David called his next verses out in boisterous song. *"But those who seek my life to destroy it shall go into the lower parts of the earth! They shall fall by the sword! They shall be a portion for jackals!"*

"Oh! That's you, Ta'avah! Be gone, in Jesus' name!" Javier yelled, grinning now because of the anger in the demon's face.

Ta'avah roared with fury and raised his arms up high. Javier ducked as a rotted tire rushed toward him, leaving the ground to aim for his head. So the demon was going to throw things? Javier prayed even louder and took another step forward.

▼▼

On the far side of the commotion, Beryl opened Simon's door and slid into the backseat, catlike and without a sound. Simon jumped only slightly, too wigged out and emotionally exhausted to truly startle.

"We have our Father back, little Simon," Beryl whispered, now watching along with Simon through the car's dusty windshield.

Simon turned halfway to see Beryl's face hoping to divine more of his feelings on the subject.

"He's about to subdue Javier and Roman," Beryl said and tenderly touched Simon's thigh in the close quarters. Simon looked at the hand and didn't speak. "I wanted to tell you that everything I promised you stands—even with Father Abroghia back, I will take care of you."

Simon rolled in his lips and watched as, because of the Rabbit mark, Beryl violently rubbed his nose before returning his attention to the battle a few yards away.

"You have good self-control," Simon mumbled, commiserating with a monster and feeling guilty for it.

"Nah, it makes me feel alive," Beryl said with a grin, rubbing his nose again and watching out the windshield.

Simon took a deep breath. He was a failure, pure and simple. In fact, ever since Javier returned to his life, he'd been falling back into his old ways. The Rakum were causing him to regress, it was *them*. How was he to resist? In his mind, a memory popped up from the days leading up to Last Assembly when he, Javier, and Roman were on the run. Simon had been reading the Old Testament in his copy of the Tanakh[18] and came across a verse about the Nephilim in the Book of Genesis. These were mighty men of God who mixed their seed with women of earth and had children with them. At the time, Simon imagined the Rakum *were* those mighty men created by the mixture, and as he studied in the commentary to the verse, he saw that the sages said the Hebrew term "*Nephilim*" meant, "to draw away." That the creatures' very name meant, "to draw someone away from God." Miserable with the realization that this is what had happened to him—*again*—Simon sighed and leaned backward into the seat.

"Oh, watch this—Javier's looking pretty wobbly," Beryl said and grinned, still without looking over.

"Beryl, God will use Javier and Roman to cast that devil out of Isaac," Simon mumbled. "Messiah Yeshua says all believers have the authority to command spirits, so eventually, Ta'avah is going to be cast out. He's just hanging on amazingly well for the moment."

Beryl looked his way, his eye sympathetic. "You really believe that? You can see with your eyes that Javier and Roman are about to be fried, but you keep on believing they will win. Blind loyalty is a good trait." He lifted his hand to stroke Simon's cheek. "Do you mind this? Is this

---

[18] The Jewish Scriptures comprised of three divisions: the Torah, the Prophets, and the Writings (these books comprise the Christian's Old Testament).

creepy?" he asked and his hand stopped moving.

"I don't care," Simon sighed and leaned forward over his knees. He covered his face. "Will this ever end?"

"You don't care about what?" Beryl asked and leaned over, too. He locked the door with his elbow and looked into Simon's face when he turned.

"Screw it," Simon whispered and lifted his right arm across his body toward Beryl. He had been wearing short sleeves, his thick winter jacket on the floorboard where he had kicked it earlier.

Beryl said nothing, but grasped his wrist with one hand and dug out his knife with the other. Simon squeezed his eyes shut and waited for the sting in his inner elbow. It was quick and Beryl's warm mouth was there instantly. After several hard pulls and an embarrassing groan of delight, Beryl sat up and pressed his thumb firmly against the healing puncture wound.

"*Shiiiiiiit...*" Beryl moaned, his eyes squeezed tight and his head against the back of the soft leather seat. "*Shit. Shit. Shit...*" he whispered and Simon closed his eyes, a deep frown on his face.

Finally, Beryl's breathing evened and he chuckled audibly. Simon did not open his eyes until Beryl released his arm.

"Simon, *Judas Priest!*" he said, his voice raspy. "Go with me. Right now. I can get us far away from here."

Simon thought to reply, but Beryl held up his hand.

"We won't be on the run," he said, head tilted in sincerity. "I will serve Father Abroghia, but we can get away from this fight and let the fanatics sort it out."

Simon shook his head slowly, a sadness filling his face.

"What is that?" Beryl's eyebrows went up. "Your expression. Is that pity? What?"

Simon looked deep into Beryl's eyes and *did* pity him. Finally, Simon sighed. "Tonight, Ta'avah will be cast out."

Beryl gently took Simon's shoulder in one hand. "Ta'avah will win."

"Where is your scar?"

Beryl's free hand went to his face. "Your God broke Isaac's curse on it. You remember."

"And?" Simon said, waiting for the Rakum to do the math. If God overpowered Isaac and they had all learned that the demon in Isaac was Ta'avah's equal, then that means? He watched Beryl's eyes for understanding.

"Are you concerned that your God is stronger than Ta'avah?"

"The God of Israel *created* Ta'avah. How can a thing that is made best its maker?"

"It's only Javier."

"And only Javier healed your face, then?"

Stubbornly, Beryl shook his head. "You can't *know* any of this. It's *hope*, pure and simple."

Simon sadly shook his head. "Beryl..." Simon covered the hand on his shoulder with his own. "I don't believe. I *know*."

"You know what?"

"I *know* the God of Israel and I believe in His Son. The Power that breathed the universe into existence is inside me. He's inside Javier and Roman and David, and they have Ta'avah on the run. Look and see. Ta'avah can't get near them—he's throwing things!"

Beryl left his hand beneath Simon's and looked at the fracas playing out a few yards from the car.

"Ta'avah *will* be cast out, and all of you..." He paused and Beryl looked back at him. "...will be mortal when he's gone."

"That's ridiculous," Beryl said too loudly and he jerked his hand to himself. His mind seemed to be racing and his left hand went to the door handle behind him. "There's no way—Roman said he wasn't going to convert anyone, Javier wouldn't..." Beryl opened the door partway.

"*They* won't be converting anyone. You'll just be human—your spirit father is going to the dry places. It's a place he can never reach you again." Simon reached for Beryl's closest arm and grabbed it firmly. "At Last Assembly, he left voluntarily. Think about it," he said, glad again that he forced himself to finish reading Beth Rider's Rabbit book. The insight into the spirit realm made tonight much easier.

"None of that matters—it doesn't make sense," Beryl said, arguing more with himself. He had already told Simon he read the book, too. He knew that High Father Abroghia's spirit left without being cast out, left to return at an opportune time. Which he did when he found the wounded Meryl and assumed his body.

"Ta'avah hasn't been cast anywhere—but when they succeed, he won't be back. That means your spirit-father will be gone, erased. How can you remain Rakum when the Rakum spirit is gone forever?"

Beryl backed out of the car, his eyes wide. Holding Simon's gaze a moment longer, he bolted away heading for the fray. Simon wanted to care what he did next, but he couldn't. He slumped back, held his healed arm close and sighed.

56

"**P**olly! Grab Roman!" Beryl yelled as he swooped behind Javier and yanked him backwards hard enough that the man slammed into the concrete. Beryl rolled Javier onto his front with his foot and stepped on his lower back to hold him in place.

Polly had been close by, ready for another command from their resurrected master. Without hesitation, he surged forward, caught an already weak Roman in a headlock, and held him in place.

"Because?" he sent telepathically.

"If they succeed, it could make us mortal! It's a trick!" Beryl increased the pressure of his foot in Javier's back and bent down to speak. "How dare you!" he yelled. Javier tried repeatedly to rise, but as expected, he was as weak as a baby without his earlier mutant powers. "I'm sorry, Javier, I can't let you continue."

"Wait! Wait!" Roman gasped in Polly's grip, his larynx compressed by a cement-like forearm. "Javier—it's not you. Remember—it's not you..." he gasped and fell unconscious from lack of oxygen. Polly lowered him to the ground, his eyes asking Beryl if that was enough.

Beryl collapsed on top of Javier, straddling him, a knee on each side. Javier was praying and his voice seemed much too calm for his current circumstance. In his peripheral vision, Ta'avah in Isaac's body went down to one knee and clutched his head.

"In the name of Jesus Christ, Yeshua HaMoschiach, I cast you out, Ta'avah, to the dry places," Javier said in a clear voice.

Beryl leaned over to grasp his chin in one hand. He had snapped many human necks. It was so easy.

"Ta'avah Rakha! And every other unclean spirit, I command you leave this vessel now!" Javier's voice boomed across the dark abandoned lot.

Ta'avah-Isaac screeched and Beryl winced at the noise. He placed his other hand to the base of Javier's skull as the man shouted his prayers into the broken asphalt. It was okay; he never liked Javier much anyway.

"I cast you out and you may never return to earth. NEVER, in Jesus' name, amen. LET IT BE SO!"

Javier finished and Beryl applied pressure to the man's neck by rotating his hands. Javier resisted and struggled to rise. After one attempt, he got his palms under him to the gravel and shoved upward. Beryl tumbled to the side and landed hard on his leg. Puzzled he had been dislodged, Beryl leapt to his feet and grabbed Javier again around the middle pinning his arms to his sides.

"Beryl, quit!" Javier barked and shuffled his feet until they faced Ta'avah-Isaac. "Your master is gone! Look for yourself! It's over!"

Javier's voice echoed across the lot with power, more than Beryl thought was normal. His eyes fell on the recumbent body of Isaac Akaron, peacefully on his back, arms and legs out from his body. Javier had ceased struggling, also watching the corpse of what had been vessel to two very powerful entities in the space of a few hours.

"Let go, Beryl," Javier said, softer now. "It's over. I need to check on everybody."

Beryl unlocked his arms and stepped away from Javier who jogged to where Roman lay unconscious. Beryl approached Isaac's body and knelt next to it. The eyes were half open and his lips apart, yet he looked merely asleep. Beryl put his hands to the boy's cheeks and then leaned over his mouth. Out of the corner of his eye, he noticed Elder Canaan coming around.

"What happened? My head is killing me," he mumbled to no one, and Beryl looked up to meet his eye. "B? You okay?"

Beryl returned his gaze to the corpse and his shoulders drooped.

"Well, is he *dead*-dead or *mostly* dead?" Canaan asked and scooted over without fully standing. He reached Isaac's side and also lay his palms on the body in several key places. "Dead, dead, the dick is dead," he joked, but Beryl wasn't laughing.

"Elder Canaan..."

It was Polly. He walked toward them with halting steps, every other footfall, looking behind him at Roman and Javier.

Canaan got to his feet and strode to meet Polly before he reached the body. "What, buddy? You look lost."

Beryl watched Canaan drape an arm around the Rakum and then stop dead.

"What tha...?" he whispered and took back his arm. His eyes found

Beryl's and he gestured for him to come over. Thinking on Simon's warning, Beryl shook his head. "Get over here!" Canaan growled low in his throat.

"Master, I don't feel right," Polly said in a low voice and tried to take hold of Canaan's forearm. He pulled out of reach.

"Nuh-uh," the Elder said and waited for Beryl. "Come here, B. I'm not asking you again."

Beryl recognized affection in his demeanor. Their past hadn't endeared them to each other, but the last seven days truly had made up for a lifetime of animosity. He wanted the Elder to comfort him if the unthinkable had happened.

Had it happened? What would it feel like?

He put one foot in front of the other and did not meet Polly's eyes. The Rakum banker looked terrified and Beryl was frightened enough on his own.

Canaan regarded Polly with another glance as Beryl came within arm's length. When he could reach him, he filled one fist with Beryl's shirt and yanked him close. The pup did not resist and once up against Canaan's chest, he remained there, facing forward, barely breathing.

"Shit," he whispered. After a moment, stronger and angrier expletives passed his lips and he did not release Beryl. Instead, he opened his hand and wrapped one arm around the pup's back, held him tight, and cursed at the dark sky in a booming voice. A frigid November wind swept through the lot, dipping the thermostat several degrees. It barely registered, Canaan's mind racing with the most unpleasant revelation.

"What's going on?" Guap asked emerging shakily from the Mercedes. Polly turned to watch him approach and then they stood side-by-side and stared at Canaan awaiting an explanation.

"You guys are transforming," Canaan whispered and met Polly and Guap's eyes. Beryl shook his head, his face in Canaan's chest. Canaan made no effort to make him shake it off. This was no small thing and Rakum stoicism would no longer be expected of his soon-to-be-former brethren.

Polly looked at his arms one by one, looked around the lot, and then to his partner. Guap mimicked his movements and they spoke to each other in low tones. Canaan heard every word, but said nothing.

"What's different?" Guap whispered. "What happened to cause this? Is this for real?"

Is this permanent, Canaan figured he was really asking. In a millisecond of concern, Canaan thought of his own condition. He did a self-check and everything seemed to be in order. He looked at the car nearest him and with telekinesis, caused the headlamps to flood the area with halogen light. He exhaled and looked for Javier.

"Javie! Something's happened over here." Canaan's expression must have been grim, for Javier jogged over.

"Thank God, you're okay," Javier said when he reached them. "When Ta'avah knocked you out, I had no way to know if he killed you. Thank God…"

"You cast out the demon?" Canaan asked, and without thinking, his free hand stroked Beryl's head still against his chest. That's when Javier noticed something was odd about the Rakum's behavior.

"What?" he said and looked to Polly or Guap to fill him in. "Are you okay? Is everyone okay?"

"They're transforming," Canaan said quietly. "Is this because you cast out Ta'avah?" Canaan was much too afraid to ask why he hadn't changed.

Javier looked at all three Rakum, shaking his head. Then he looked back to Roman who was sitting up on the asphalt leaning on his hands.

Canaan discerned from his position that the man suffered a few contusions, a bruised trachea, and a sprained ankle. *I'm still me,* he thought and tenderly removed Beryl from his chest.

"I'm going to help Roman," he said to all three men. "None of you goes anywhere, right?" he asked, in actuality *telling,* and the Rakum nodded. "Javier, comfort them," he said and walked briskly away.

When he reached Roman, Javier had the four of them in a circle, each man's hands to the shoulders of the man beside him. Javier wasn't praying, but he was encouraging them and giving them tips on what to expect. After all, he'd transformed, albeit voluntarily, over a period of hours seven years ago.

"Canaan," Roman said when their eyes met.

Canaan knelt down and placed his palm over Roman's ankle. It took only moments and he moved on to the obvious injuries to the man's face and throat. "Remove your shirt," he said and waited while the sweater and t-shirt were pulled over his head. Canaan stole a glance at Beryl and then returned to healing all of Roman's injuries.

"Canaan," Roman said again, stronger now, "they're becoming human?" Canaan nodded. "And you're not?" Roman asked and Canaan shook his head. Roman shivered and pulled his clothes back on. "Thank you, now go see if Javier's hurt."

Canaan stood, helped Roman to his feet, and turned back for the group. David and Simon entered the area cautiously regarding every participant and then eyeing the body on the ground. Canaan pulled the back of Javier's flannel shirt out of his jeans and lifted it up. He had no obvious wounds except very light abrasions and he left him be.

"Elder Canaan," Beryl said then, leaving the circle to stand by his side. He didn't say anything more and Canaan gave him a friendly grin.

"Watch and see, Beryl," Canaan said and shook his shoulder like days of old. "Something amazing will come of this. Trust me."

"Canaan, hey," Roman called, trotting briskly to their position as if he'd never been injured. "What about Kilmeade? How's my brother?"

"Oh, shit," Canaan murmured. Hoping the transfusion of Javier's special blood had matured enough to boost his telepathy, Canaan sent his inner eye to find out.

▼▼

Tuscaloosa, AL, Storm Drain
November 13th, 2 a.m.

Dozing, but not truly asleep, Kilmeade sat on his haunches in the smelly sewer drain. Boris on his left and Rafael on his right, both matched his posture as they did their best to avoid the walls and the floor of their hiding place. Using purely his Rakum sense of time, he discerned it was nearing 2 a.m. and not a single human soul had entered the sewage system so far to search for them.

He inhaled to initiate a huge yawn when simultaneously, an odd aroma hit his nostrils. On his right, Rafael turned to him and tried to read his eyes. Kilmeade sent him a telepathic greeting and Rafael didn't hear it. Kilmeade then put his finger to his lips and when Rafael understood, without making a sound that might disturb Boris, he came close and pressed his face into his pet's hair.

Rafael mouthed, *"What?"* and Kilmeade showed him the shush gesture again. Picking up Rafa's left wrist, Kilmeade brought it to his lips and nicked the smallest abrasion to the top of his hand. With an experimental movement, he tasted the tiny red swath that welled at the injury and sadness crushed his heart.

Rafael read his face and began to grow aware of whatever had happened, feeling different in his body. Kilmeade again hushed him and hooked his thumb at Boris. Kilmeade did not know the huge Rakum well enough to predict his behavior and wanted to think of a way to ease the news.

Rafael rose from his crouching stance and stood, bent over in the low ceiling pipe. His eyes grew more and more frantic every second and Kilmeade rose as well and put both hands to his shoulders. *"Wait, shhhh,"* he mouthed, trying to think of a plan.

He didn't come up with one fast enough.

"WHAT IS THIS?" Boris yelled, lifting his bulk from a stooping stance. "ELDER KILMEADE, SOMETHING'S WRONG WITH ME!" he shouted, his eyes wild and he swept his head to and fro.

"Boris," Kilmeade said softly and reached for his forearm. "Boris, shh, I'm here. Shh shhh."

"Something is dreadfully wrong!" Boris said, still yelling, only slightly turning down the volume.

"I feel it, too," Rafael said, his voice also nearing panic mode. "I'm losing my eyesight, am I going blind?"

"Rafa, Boris," Kilmeade said meeting their eyes one by one, "somehow, both of you are transforming into mortals. Both of you smell... you both smell like a combination of Rakum and mortal."

"No I am NOT!" Boris yelped and turned away. He began to shuffle back the way they'd come in. "I'm getting out of here!"

Kilmeade gained on the big man and grasped his wrist in his fingers.

"I AM LEAVING!" he shouted and yanked at his captive wrist. When nothing happened, he turned his angry eyes on Kilmeade. "LET. ME. GO!"

"Boris, get a hold of yourself," Kilmeade said in a terse tone. Boris yanked his arm again. "Boris, sleep." Kilmeade caught his head as his body collapsed beneath him. He eased the huge man to the damp pipe floor and called Rafael over.

"We will remain here until sundown. Then, and only then, will we investigate what is happening. Understand?" He watched Rafael's eyes and disturbed but still obedient, the man nodded. "Good. Sit. Relax," he instructed and hunkered down himself once Rafael had.

"You are not affected?" Rafael inquired in a somber voice.

Kilmeade shook his head.

"I guess next I'll hear God knocking..."

Rafael had whispered his remark rhetorically and Kilmeade tried to read his expression. Rafael looked his way, using his cell phone's home screen illumination to better see.

"Have you heard any knocking?" he asked, eyes begging for good news. Kilmeade held his tongue. He nodded. "I understand."

Kilmeade thought about his next remark, worded it several ways in his mind before sharing it with Rafael. He had to be careful not to trigger any transformation for himself, and since he wasn't sure how it worked, he would be extra cautious. Still... his pet needed comforting...

"Ask the God of the mortals to allow you to hear Him," Kilmeade said in a halting voice, resisting the urge to fear the unknown and controlling his every thought. "You heard Him speak through Father Damien at the house. He will catch you."

Kilmeade clammed up and after a thoughtful moment, Rafael nodded, leaned against the filthy wall behind him and slowly slid to sit in an inch of smelly slime.

"Brother, are you well?"

Kilmeade lowered his head at the welcome sound of Canaan's telepathic voice, overjoyed and overcome to hear he wasn't alone.

"Brother, are you still there?"

Kilmeade replied, eyes closed, *"I am extremely happy to hear your voice in my head."*

Canaan chuckled on his end. *"The boys are living a nightmare right now."*

"I sense you have been tussling with Isaac?"

"Javier, Roman, and David have destroyed him once and for all. The spirit of Ta'avah was cast out of him and we think that's why our brethren are transforming..."

"But you and I?"

Canaan didn't reply and Kilmeade hadn't truly meant to ask.

"Roman is well and sends you his greetings..."

Kilmeade exhaled, not even aware he'd been holding his breath for such news. Then he added without forethought, *"Canaan, join me here. Do not trust the humans with your life."*

Canaan assured him he would arrive before sunup. Kilmeade took comfort knowing that and reached out to squeeze Rafa's shoulder. Oh, how he missed his pet already.

EPILOGUE

Maury slogged through his front door without turning on the lights. The police had questioned him for hours and didn't believe a word of his fabricated story. They wanted to know who kidnapped Marcy Haddle (thankfully, she pointed no blame his way). And who was Boris? Why was he unconscious in Maury's house? Why was he grabbed from the ambulance, and who killed the attendants and incapacitated the police officer escort? Maury's only defense was his iron-clad alibi; he had been in Virgil Cohen's office from 9:30 until the police called his cell at eleven. It had been scary for a good thirty minutes when the police put Maury in a holding cell until they could get his lawyer on the phone.

Should Maury be worried about Kite? His attorney said the man passed out soon after Maury left. The police sergeant finally did tell him which hospital they took the Rakum to, so Maury called them up and told the nurse the man suffered from a severe case of XP. Maybe they'd keep him out of the sun. Maury didn't really care. Now, why was that? Something was different, but he couldn't put his finger on it.

Currently, it was two in the morning and the house was dark. Where were the masters? Maury touched his belly. For the first time since he met his first Rakum, he experienced no urgency at the thought of them not returning. No sadness that they weren't there and no joy at the thought they might return. What was going on?

Maybe he needed a joint. Maury called out for Master Isaac, then tried Master Rafa, and the quiet house echoed his voice. Little Travis trotted to his side and asked to be petted. Maury stopped off in the tiny security closet behind the kitchen to check the bunker cameras. It was empty. Not a soul—man, Rabbit, or Rakum—remained in the house.

Maury shrugged and tromped toward the back, stopping at the study to reset a blinking digital clock, again without turning on any lamps. He fiddled with the gadget until it read correct and when he turned to pass the fireplace, he kicked something large and heavy.

329

Maury shined his cell phone on it and discovered a huge staff. Testing its weight, he lifted carefully with both hands, tilted it horizontal, and toted it toward his finished basement. He had fifteen-hundred square feet of collectibles down there from all his favorite movie franchises. He had *Star Wars, Lord of the Rings, Game of Thrones, Star Trek, Outlander,* and even a little horror stuff to boot. He had swords, bows, guns, light sabers, and all manner of costumes and accessories purchased off eBay and Craig's List. His insurance appraised the value at over a million-five.

The overhead LEDs powered up automatically and a whoosh of wind met his face as he opened the climate-controlled cellar. A few careful steps to the ground level and he looked for a place to put his new toy. The staff was nearly as tall as the room, so he leaned it against the wall between his Gimli Axe and his authentic MP40 submachine gun from his favorite *Highlander* episode. Once it was balanced, Maury took a longing look around his delightful assortment and smiled. The Rakum's staff looked cool there. *Very* cool.

All the way up the stairs, he wondered why he wasn't in love with them anymore. It didn't make sense. The door swooshed open, he went back into the house, and the light clicked off behind him. At least he had a cool thing to remember them by.

Canaan attended the unpleasant work of decapitating Isaac's body and he didn't mind taking over Javier's leadership role to assign tasks to all those standing on the tarmac in the aftermath. Roman, Javier, Simon and David took Simon's two cars back to his garage. Guap and Polly went to Simon's, picked up the Kia the stranger arrived in, and brought it to the abandoned lot. By careful subterfuge, only Canaan knew the young human Ta'avah arrived in was alive. When he checked the boy and found him to be comatose and brain dead, he stopped his heart.

Better safe than sorry, with all the spirit shit going on, he told himself as he tucked the dead kid behind the wheel of the Kia. When Isaac's pieces were tucked in the Kia's small trunk, Guap and Polly ran Canaan back to Simon's.

At Simon's house, Canaan leaned against the foyer's back wall and listened as Javier spoke with Stuart Loudon, filling him in on the end of the Rakum he used to adore. It was surreal and incredibly sad to see the Aussie had also transformed. He had no desire for the Rakum and damn it all to hell, Canaan hated that the look in Stuart's eyes had become cold and distant.

"The Cows are gone the way of the Dodo, Brother," he sent Kilmeade telepathically. His counterpart across town answered back in short order.

"Never cared for Cows, really..."

Canaan chuckled quietly and tipped his chin watching Javier say goodbye to the Aussie and close the front door. His swarthy mini-me turned to Canaan then and sighed.

"Stuart Loudon is going to stay in town and keep an eye on Simon after everyone clears out." Javier rolled his eyes resignedly. "I hope Simon goes back to his baseball career. Stuart is practically homeless. He'll siphon his livelihood off Simon if he can."

"You humans with your tiny little problems," Canaan said with a grin.

"Touché. How about you?" Javier asked, true concern in his face. "Are you staying here tonight?"

"No," Canaan replied flatly and shook his head. He then crossed his arms and pumped his biceps in rapid succession. Javier broke a grin. "I have a date with a man much more interesting than you."

"Oh, he's definitely more interesting than I am." Javier nodded. "Canaan, Listen," he said and stepped close. "David, Roman, and I are going back to Tuscaloosa in the morning. We plan to make ourselves available full-time to any of the Rakum who need help assimilating and Stuart has given me access to his website to help the Cows, too. Will you keep in touch?"

Canaan took a deep breath and looked to the side. He didn't know what he and Kilmeade would do, but he had no intention of dropping out. Javier misinterpreted his silence and placed a warm palm on his tattooed forearm where his sleeves had been scrolled upwards.

"You make the rules and we will follow them, but don't disappear."

Canaan chuckled. "At least you still love me." Taking the back of Javier's neck, he yanked him close into a brief one-armed embrace. When he pushed him away again, Roman entered from the living room and nodded to them both.

"Did you reach Marcy?" he asked Canaan.

"I did," he replied and didn't say more. Over the phone, Marcy delivered the familiar lines and sentiments, but their relationship had been damaged. Canaan couldn't tell which way it would go, so he hoped his silence told his friends the subject was closed.

"Inquire about the Bushman girl," Kilmeade sent over and Canaan had a sense their continuous telepathic connection gave the other Elder comfort. The tiny female came to mind and he shook his head.

"How is the girl, Chloe?" he asked Javier who gave him a blank look. "What? Her toothy blood drinkers are all gone. She'll need counseling." He chortled at himself, but neither Roman nor Javier joined in. "You can laugh. That was funny," he said without dropping his grin.

"She's home. She's fine."

Javier said no more and Roman cleared his throat. "Are you going to Kilmeade?" Canaan nodded and Roman exhaled with relief. "Good. You will watch out for each other. He won't carry a cell phone so I may send you messages for him now and then."

Canaan shrugged and he sensed Kilmeade liked the idea of having an Elder for his new personal secretary.

"Tell Kilmeade that Santiago and Jimmy arrived a short while ago. Santiago said he's no longer a Rabbit—he performed a test already. He's normal again."

"So all the Rabbits..." Javier trailed off.

Canaan's mind galloped, showing nothing on his face. Simon, Marcy, Beth Rider and her daughter, all of them would return to normal. Javier's God had truly performed a number of amazing feats, which left the obvious question: why leave two Elders in their Rakum state? With sincere effort and deliberate purpose, Canaan did *not* ask that question aloud nor in his mind.

"Lastly, Canaan, tell my brother that they will stay here until Rafael or Kilmeade contacts them. Simon agreed." This time Roman shrugged. "It's a new world for them, too, being Cows one minute and just... *poof.*"

Canaan shook his head. "It's a cluster."

Roman agreed with a frown and turned back the way he'd come. Canaan sensed he was giving Javier some good-bye room.

Javier watched him go and Canaan heard low voices from across the house as Simon and David discussed the night's events. After a long moment, Javier rubbed his palms together.

"I'm not a religious guy. Did you know that?"

332

"Hah!" Canaan laughed one short burst and stopped when he saw Javier was serious. "I mean, why do you say that?"

Javier smiled. "I was called to battle for the Lord this past week, but before Elder Rufus put a contract out on us, I was just a man running a translation business from home. I watched DVDs, shopped for groceries, argued with David about leaving his socks on the living room floor. You know—normal stuff. I didn't go to church and I didn't witness for God."

"Okay..." Canaan waited for the punchline. Javier chuckled.

"I just needed to preface what I am about to say now." He shifted his weight and crossed his arms, now matching Canaan's posture. "God gave me a message for you—I'm serious."

Canaan squeezed his eyes closed with a comical grimace. "I'm ready," he squeaked.

Javier grinned. "I'm supposed to tell you that God is going with you and Kilmeade." Javier shrugged, eyebrows high at Canaan's expression. "I have to tell you that you've been a wasteland your whole life, but God has made you into a place worth saving and He won't allow you to go to eternity without Him."

"Is that a bible quote?" Canaan asked as the blood drained from his face. Beth Rider's six-year-old daughter said the very same thing to him in private before they went to Jackson to stop Rufus. It made no sense then and he had ignored it, but now...

"I looked it up—I kept hearing it loop in my mind as we left the lot tonight. It's a combination of verses from the prophets talking about Israel." Javier took a deep breath. "I think God plans on using you two for something else and then bringing you close to Him."

"Oh, no," Canaan shook his head. "Lalalalalala, I don't hear you." He wanted to appear unaffected, but Javier had ruined his mood. He was ready to get going. It was 3 a.m. and time to enter the sewer.

"Okay, you need to go, I get it," Javier said chuckling and squeezed his arm with affection. "Beryl, Guap and Polly will speak with you outside," Javier said in a sad voice.

Canaan gave him a long look and said, "I'll contact you in a few days. We'll be leaving town when the sun goes down. First to Nashville, for Marcy, and then I don't know."

Roman popped back in, his arm outstretched for Canaan, in his hand a sealed manila envelope. "Please give this to Kilmeade."

He said he would and forced it into a fold and into his jeans pocket.

Canaan walked past Javier into the frigid night and purposed to not look back. He would miss Javier, maybe Roman, too. Such un-Rakum-like behavior caused him to wonder if he'd been weakened by the recent events, but...

Hell, I'm my own boss now. I'll do what I please.

"Hurry up," Kilmeade sent and Canaan forced a grin for the guys at the Caddy. Beryl, Guap, and Polly leaned casually upon its wide hood and stood to attention when he reached them.

"Guys," he said with a nod and without singling out Beryl. "I have my phone—you can call me if you need me. Javier and Roman will help you, too." All three nodded, but he read the apprehension in their eyes. "Do I have your word that you will come to me or them if you wig out?"

"Hey," Polly said, his voice subdued, "I'm still the sexiest beast alive."

"Besides El Guapo," Guap added in the same put-on tone.

"Plus, given time, you'll be wanting to tap old Polly, Elder Canaan," Polly winked. "Oh, yeah, I'll be delicious, I just know it."

Guap punched his arm with fake joviality.

Canaan nodded his head and squeezed each man's shoulder. "Where will you go?"

Guap answered first. "Javier said this could take hours or weeks, so we decided to stay with Simon until we transform completely. After that? We'll travel."

"We still manage the wealth of the Fathers so there is plenty to do," Polly finished, receiving a nod of agreement from Guap.

"B? You staying with them?"

Beryl nodded and didn't meet Canaan's eye more than a second. Canaan worried for him, but needed to get underground. This night couldn't end soon enough.

"Guap, Polly," he said, "watch over Beryl for me."

"Of course," Guap replied sending Beryl a wink. "He's much better looking than this pile of dog shit I'm saddled with."

"The pile of dog shit promises the same," Polly added sounding almost like himself.

"Okay, go away," he said to the two bankers and they headed back to the house. Canaan blocked Beryl's exit and stepped close, tilting his chin and considering the man's sad face. "You don't look good."

"Thanks," he mumbled.

Canaan took his upper arm in one big hand. "I will take your sorry ass into the sewer with me tonight if I have to..."

"Fine."

Without a word, Canaan walked around his car tugging Beryl along and placed him in the passenger side.

"Okay," he said and got behind the wheel. "But no complaining— you hear me?" Canaan then said in a high voice, "*It stinks down here. I'm cold. I'm hungry. My socks are wet. I want my mommy, blah blah blah.*"

The tiniest grin touched Beryl's face before he looked out the window.

Canaan reached the end of Simon's drive when his cell chimed. With a huff, he flicked the phone into Beryl's lap. "What is it?"

Beryl read the screen to himself and Canaan jabbed his arm. "Out loud, dummy!"

Beryl winced. "Ow, dammit!"

"Geez," Canaan chuckled. "I can see you became a human *girl.*"

"It hurts now!" Beryl growled back. He returned his gaze to the phone. "Javier sent a screenshot of a dictionary definition. It's for the word *anomaly.* Something that deviates from what is standard, normal, or expected."

"What tha—" Canaan began, but the phone chimed with an additional text message. Beryl read it off.

"Javier says that's you now."

"What a jerk," he mumbled and grinned. Beryl dropped the phone in the console and looked out the window. Canaan piloted the car away from Simon's house and switched on the radio.

"*On my way, honey,*" he sent Kilmeade with a laugh.

"Behold, I stand at the door and knock...."

What in the world? Kilmeade turned the single sheet of paper over a few times. All that was written was a bible verse in his brother's hand.

"Behold, I stand at the door and knock. If any man hear My voice and open the door, I will come in to him, and I will sup with him, and he with Me."

"*You don't like Roman's farewell?*" Canaan asked telepathically, hunkering down beside Kilmeade in the low clearance drain.

"*It's a Bible verse about Jesus knocking on my heart, I think,*" Kilmeade sent back with a grin. *"Father Damien told us that he opened the door when Jesus knocked and that's how he became mortal."*

"Oh, damn," Canaan replied and grew thoughtful.

Kilmeade shoved the paper back into the envelope and handed it to Rafa. Boris snored, still peacefully incapacitated, and Beryl sat on his haunches on Canaan's other side showing no interest in anything they were doing.

"It's the knocking again," Rafael whispered once he read the letter in the glow of his cell phone. Kilmeade offered a near invisible nod. "Wait, look." Rafael flipped the envelope upside down over his hand and a flash of silver tumbled into his palm. "It's your babies," Rafael said and handed over the lockbox key.

Kilmeade took the tiny key and unfolded a note tied to its fob. Roman had written, "Do the right thing." Kilmeade puffed a small laugh and shook his head.

"Your babies?" Canaan whispered, creasing his brow.

"That's what he said." Kilmeade returned the key to Rafael for safekeeping and balanced his weight over his haunches. He'd most likely tump into the sewage in his sleep, but for now he was dry. And when the sun went down, he would lead them all up top and figure out the rest.

END BOOK THREE

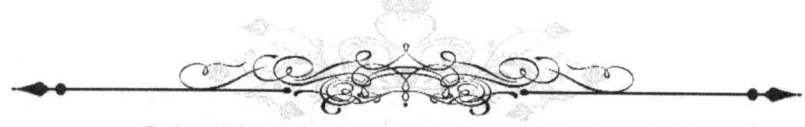

DON'T MISS ELLEN'S NEXT BOOK!
Follow Ellen C Maze on Amazon.com to get new release updates and improved recommendations. To find, pull up this or any title by Ellen C Maze and click the hyper-linked author-name. It will take you to the
"Click to Follow Author" page.

Turn the Page for the
Sneak Peek into Book Four
ANOMALY, Beyond the Rabbit

THE RABBIT SAGA INCLUDES 6 NOVELS.

The first 3 involve the Rakum becoming aware of a Creator and the last 3 bring every last one to choose sides. Books 1-4 Now Available.

Books 5 & 6, expected in 2019. Check back with the author at www.ellencmaze.com *or the series publisher, LittleRoniPublishers.com.*

Email the author or publisher for updates on all new releases.
Author Ellen C Maze: ellenmaze@aol.com
Little Roni Publishers: submissionsLRP@gmail.com

Sneak Peek into Book Four
ANOMALY, Beyond the Rabbit

This is from Chapter Four; earlier chapters reveal the period immediately following Kilmeade and the others exiting the sewer. The Elders set up temporary housing near Roman, David, and Javier as they figure out the next move.

He had to come out eventually. At sundown, like a stalker, Chloe parked herself a block away to see if the Elders returned to visit Javier. She watched Canaan enter and wasn't leaving until she asked him about Kilmeade. To pass the time, she studied for her Psych quiz with one eye on Javier's front door.

The day she met Kilmeade, the Rakum cornered her in Javier's hallway and mesmerized her with no effort. He wasn't like those depicted in Beth Rider's book, nor the monsters that abducted and terrorized her in November. Just then, Canaan exited at a brisk walk and did not look at Chloe when she popped out and trotted his way.

"Canaan! Wait!" she called, and didn't he grin? Still, he walked on. Unlike the slender athleticism she noticed in Kilmeade, Canaan was beefy with muscle and a dramatic tattoo snaked out of his collar and left sleeve. His curly blond hair fluttered in the cold wind and he didn't acknowledge her even when she reached his side. "I need to see Kilmeade," she said, breathing hard. "Since you guys live together you can get him to call me."

The Elder climbed into the truck and closed the door. Only after he switched on the vehicle and lowered the window, did he turn. Grinning, he met her eye and Chloe looked away, unnerved by his ice-blue gaze. Catching on, Canaan did not speak until she braved to look up.

"Did you just call us *you guys?*" he asked with a toothy grin. "Together, we're 746 years old. How old are you again? Twelve?"

"I'm twenty," she replied gauging his seriousness.

"Like I said, *twelve,*" he huffed. "Here's some advice; you'll catch more flies with a little sucking up."

Ignoring his false indignation, Chloe asked, "How can I reach him?"

The man shook his head, still faking offense. "Can't hear you."

Chloe furrowed her brow in frustration. "Please, um, Master Canaan? The Amazing Canaan?" Chloe's eyes widened as she thought of more grandiose titles. "Your Highness? Oh-Mighty-Handsome-One?"

"Any of those will bend an Elder's ear." He grinned, propped his chin on his palm and gave her an adoring gaze. "Now, what did it want?"

"Your Wonderfulness, will you please tell Elder Kilmeade I want to speak to him?" Chloe said with exaggerated respect. It was a game for this one and she didn't mind playing.

"Like to, but honey, Kilmeade doesn't like humans."

"He likes *me,*" she said defiantly and Canaan's grin widened.

"Ooh, it is *sassy!*" Canaan chuckled. "Look, tiny, I gotta look after my brother. Do you know what you're asking? Rakum Elders don't make *friends.*" His gaze remained playful, but Chloe's mind went blank. Canaan held up three fingers. "Blood, sex, violence," he said, his opposite hand manually lowering a digit with each word. "That is the limit of our interest and not always in that order."

"I just wanted to talk to him..." Chloe sighed, growing perturbed. Kilmeade had come on strong when they met; it never occurred to her their interaction may have been meaningless.

"What a lip. Look at it," the Elder teased regarding her with a tight grin. "Don't pout, tiny. Kilmeade has spoken of you." Canaan checked his mirrors. "I'll tell you how to reach him, but you've been warned; he doesn't want to bake cookies, gossip, and paint toenails. *Comprende?*"

Chloe nodded slowly. "Okay."

Canaan fluttered his eyebrows. "Do this..." He put a finger to his temple. "Picture his face, look for his thread, and grab it." Chloe's mouth must have dropped, because he added, "That's all there is to it. *Easy.*" Without another word, he abruptly drove away.

Chloe watched him go, her mind racing. *Can I really speak to Kilmeade telepathically?* She walked to her car, planning what she would say in case she attempted and he answered.

When she was home again, Chloe had the house to herself. As teaching physicians at the University, her parents had gone on a medical missions trip. In the three months since she was kidnapped by a devil and rescued by God, she'd attended class and kept up a happy face. Her parents didn't know she'd been abducted; how could she tell them when those involved were of supernatural ilk? Her mother already thought she was a wild child, so Chloe depended on her coping skills and advice from Roman to keep her mind and spirit strong. The now-human Elder helped her understand her infatuation with Javier when he was under the influence of Isaac's blood. He also helped her and David remain friends after their awkward break-up, telling them all that God probably orchestrated her puppy loves with David and Javier as part of His plan to bring the Rakum race to a complete end.

Complete, except for two Elders...

Chloe switched on the lamp beside the sofa and furrowed her brow.

Did God play matchmaker to bring about His purposes? Roman had tried to give her examples from the Bible, but Chloe had been distracted thinking about Kilmeade. *And Canaan thinks I can contact him telepathically...*

Chloe collapsed in a pile on the sofa and pondered the possibility. When in the horrible Rufus's clutches, he spoke in her mind. It terrified her knowing that one who wanted to kill her could communicate with her so intimately. Then when Javier showed up as the Anomaly, he heard her thoughts. So why not this Elder?

Chloe dimmed the lamp to the lowest wattage and closed her eyes. Only for the tiniest second did her conscience whisper to her to think twice. Blocking her inner voice, she brought up Elder Kilmeade's face from the other night. He hadn't given her much attention, but the first time they met, he'd been brazenly flirtatious.

"Elder Kilmeade," she thought, not realizing until the words flowed that she might be beginning their conversation. *"Please come see me..."*

Chloe experienced a peculiar lightness in her middle. Had it to do with telepathy? She hadn't felt it before, so she experimented more.

"I have questions only you can answer," she thought, picturing his face and the way his gray eyes twinkled when he shot her each daring compliment upon their first meeting. The floaty feeling resumed and she exhaled; if she could only fall quiet enough, even to the extent of holding her breath, she might hear a reply. She counted to ten not breathing and definitely heard a soft chuckle in the very back of her ear. Without opening her eyes, she sat up.

"Did I do it? Did I reach you?"

"Breathe, Miss Bushman, breeeeeeeathe..." the voice teased.

Kilmeade! She grinned. *"Why won't you come see me?"* she sent as goose pimples covered her arms.

"You live at 220 Poplar?" the voice asked.

"Yes," Chloe said aloud and opened her eyes. The connection remained, and she sensed a tether to the voice on the other end. Then with an almost audible pop, the string snapped, and she was alone. Suddenly anxious, Chloe got to her feet. Was he really coming over? A full-blooded Rakum Elder at her house while she was all alone? Chloe looked at her watch, checked the locks and the alarm on the doors, and hoped she'd done the right thing.

Nearly four hours later, Chloe lounged on the leather recliner in her dad's den; the voice never came by. She flicked off the television and the room slumped into the brownish glow of an amber desk lamp. Chloe grumbled about the late hour, stretched her arms to the ceiling, and turned for the hallway.

"How scandalous!" Elder Kilmeade said from the doorway. "Inviting me over when you're all alone..."

"Oh, god!" Chloe hissed with her hand over her heart.

Leaning casually against the threshold, Kilmeade grinned. "You rang?"

"Oh, god," Chloe said again softer. "You... You just came in?"

He shrugged. "You invited me. I'm here. What do you want?"

Chloe paused, thrown off by his sudden appearance. "But that was..." She glanced at the wall clock. "...three-and-a-half hours ago."

"I am not a dog. I go where I want, when I want." He held her gaze, his chin lowered. "Come close," he said and held out his hand.

Chloe's throat tightened and she hugged herself. She was still dressed, thank God, although her sweater was tattered and her sweatpants too loose. When the voice hadn't shown within an hour, she'd dressed down for no one's eyes but her own.

"You look delightful. Is that cashmere?" Kilmeade asked, hand still waiting for her to reach out. "Give us a feel."

Chloe unwrapped her arms and looked at her front. It *was* cashmere, but it wasn't likely the Elder wanted to touch it; he wanted her closer. While she wrestled with what to do, he closed the distance between them. Inserting his fingers underneath to caress the soft weave, the back of his hand brushed her skin. Chloe gasped and stood frozen in place.

"I knew it," he said inches away. He waited for her to look into his face and he smiled on her. "Would you like to tell me why I'm here?"

"I... I wanted..." Chloe began and stopped.

"I'm not very patient," Kilmeade said and moved his hand from her sweater to touch her face. He ran his fingers down her cheek and then over her lips. "Your mind is bloated with conflict. Shall I choose?"

"I wanted..."

"You want...?" Kilmeade sent her a tiny smile. "Tick-tock."

Chloe swallowed and sought the right words.

Kilmeade's thumb brushed her bottom lip when she hadn't replied. "Allow me to help. You want to let your blood. Right now."

"Oh, no, I..." Chloe stuttered. Part of her indeed wondered what it would be like if he took her blood as Javier had in November. But hadn't she just wanted to talk?

"I no longer prefer human blood, Miss Bushman. Haven't for decades," Kilmeade said absently, his eyes trained to her neck. He pushed her long brown curls aside. "But a female that consents? I would make an exception."

"*Umm,*" Chloe moaned wishing he wouldn't rush her.

"Do you?" Kilmeade's two fingers touched her chin and he turned her face to his. "Consent? I have to hear it."

She found her voice. "I don't think I'm supposed to..." The Elder rolled his eyes and began to pull away. "No! I mean, yes! I mean, it's okay," Chloe said in a rush, clutching his thick biceps through his burgundy sweater. "Yes."

Kilmeade drew her close in an instant and pushed elongated teeth through her skin. One arm embraced her gently, but the one at the back of her throat pressed their contact together too firmly and she reflexively struggled to be free.

"*Be still,*" she heard in her mind as she began to panic. Then it was over. The punctures stung only a moment before the sensation of his tongue pressing against the wound melted the discomfort away. Then he backed completely and leaned against the threshold across the room.

Chloe dropped to the sofa, and with her mind numb, she watched him savor the aftereffects. When the clock noisily rang the quarter hour, Kilmeade met her eye and smiled.

"That was a treat," he said with quiet reverence. He seemed to be waiting for her to speak or move, but she did neither. When she still hadn't reacted, Kilmeade stood off the doorframe and thrust his hands into his slacks pockets. "Three, two, one. Bye," he said out of patience.

She wanted him to stay. She wanted him to leave. And she wanted him to do it again. All of this was moot, for the Elder turned on his heel, waved his fingers from behind, and disappeared down the hall. Chloe didn't hear him exit the front door, but she hadn't heard him earlier, either. She turned the dimmer to full-light and relaxed into the couch.

Rufus took her blood when she was terrified, Javier when she was unaware, and Kilmeade took it by consent where she recalled 100% of the experience. And she was, well, *fine.* Tired, sleepy, but no worse for wear. Chloe allowed the moment-by-moment recollection to return and pondered it until she fell asleep where she sat.

End of Sneak Peek

Look for *Anomaly* on Amazon.com or LittleRoniPublishers.com. Email ellenmaze@aol.com to join the mailing list for on all new releases in this series.

An Ozzie Lends a Hand...

For *Rabbit Redemption*, Australian author and poet Stu Loudon graciously lends his name and dialog assistance to fill out our Cow character of the same name (but not the same personality, honest).

The real Mr. Loudon is an extremely prolific and popular slam poet in his region and he also writes thrilling and thought-provoking fiction. Please look for his work on Amazon.com and other fine booksellers under the pen name, Stu Loudon.

Darkness Visible by Stu Loudon
(with a bonus section showcasing American author, Roxanne Evans)

A son seeking revenge for his father's rejection...
A hero of the people has his true motives brought to light...
A killer facing the consequences of his actions...
This is DARKNESS VISIBLE.

Stu Loudon brings you an anthology of dark speculative fiction, examining the dark, the light, and the shadows between. Included is a preview of Stu Loudon's WHAT LIES BENEATH series; two stories featuring the characters from his soon-to-be-published novel, PONTIUS.

[i] You will find the entire story of how David overcame the would-be killers and in the process, took the Dying Buzz, and experienced the euphoria forbidden his people, in *Rabbit: Chasing Beth Rider (Book One)*, LOOSE RABBITS Bonus section.

Little Roni Publishers
Byhalia, MS
www.littleronipublishers.com

www.ingramcontent.com/pod-product-compliance
Lightning Source LLC
Chambersburg PA
CBHW050733230626
47052CB00002BA/8